MW00795310

HURRICANE IN PARADISE

PARADISE SERIES

BOOK 10

DEBORAH BROWN

This book is a work of fiction. Names, characters, places and incidents are either the product of the author's imagination or used fictitiously. Any resemblance to actual persons, living or dead, or to actual events or locales is entirely coincidental. The author has represented and warranted full ownership and/or legal right to publish all materials in this book.

HURRICANE IN PARADISE

ISBN-13: 978-0-9984404-0-8

Cover: Natasha Brown

PRINTED IN THE UNITED STATES OF AMERICA

HURRICANE IN PARADISE

Chapter One

A gust of wind blew the front door open, sending it bouncing off the wall. Creole stumbled into the entry, his black hair whipping around his face. A crack of thunder boomed behind him, announcing the fury of the rapidly approaching storm. "Madison Westin," he barked, sounding like an angry dog. "What in the hell are you still doing at home?"

Dropping a small bag at the bottom of the stairs, I watched as my boyfriend veered left, going into the kitchen, dripping wet from the sheets of rain slamming the house in all of Mother Nature's ferocity. The wind's howling sounded like someone screaming at times.

Luc Baptiste was his birth name, Creole the undercover moniker he used in his employment as a Miami detective, but only a handful of people actually knew that little fact. He stood over six feet, his muscles accentuated by his soaked t-shirt. At the moment, he had a two-day scruff of beard and his eyes were an irate blue; when they turned a deep cobalt, I knew he was more than mildly annoyed.

Another bolt of lightning flashed through the garden window. I counted under my breath and listened until thunder rocked in the distance, the eye of the storm getting closer. It was just beginning to make its presence known.

"You need an umbrella." I watched as he shook the water off like a wet animal. "The news said the hurricane won't make landfall until tonight."

He scowled, looming over me, his brows pulled together. "You promised you'd be going with Fab and Didier to Miami." He tugged on a tendril of red hair that had escaped my hair clip.

When I first moved to the Florida Keys, living by myself got old—fast. So, when Fabiana Merceau showed up one day with her suitcases, she caught me off guard, but I was happy to have her move in and had never been sorry that she became a permanent fixture. Not long after, Fab met her supermodel boyfriend, Didier, and decided, without a word to the man, to go to the hotel where he was staying, pack up his belongings, and unpack everything into the closet upstairs. Didier was a quick fit as a friend and family member. And nice to look at over morning coffee, or any other time. It made life easier that we had erratic schedules and were rarely all in the house at the same time.

"I didn't make any promises." I tried not to flinch at the weaselly tone in my voice. "No one asked my opinion, or I would've told all of you that I didn't want to go anywhere." I tossed him a towel from a stack that was going into the Hummer if I got scared enough to change my mind and leave. "The news always over-dramatizes the weather reports. Its only forecast to make landfall as a category two. If it turns out to be a 'rain event,' they'll still close the roads and take their time in reopening them, leaving us hanging out for several days since there's no way to sneak back home with only one road in and out of the Keys." I tried not to roll my eyes when, upon hearing the word "sneak," his dark scowl returned.

"You've lived here long enough to know the back side of the storm can bring the most damage."

I ignored his lecturing tone. I didn't think now was the time to tell Creole that I wasn't aware there was a difference. I'd ridden out a few hurricanes, often in the dark, the electricity not able to handle the onslaught, and when the sun came out again, the only damage left in their wake were piles of leaves and tree branches. I'd thankfully never experienced one of the more destructive ones.

Tarpon Cove sat at the top of the Florida Keys. The last damaging hurricane to roll through happened before my arrival. The old timers liked to say, "It's been a damn long time since we had a direct hit."

Lightning skated across the sky in non-stop

action, the wind shrieked, and the lights flickered.

"Let's go." He reached for my wrist and pulled me into his arms, lifting me slightly, just enough to draw me against his chest.

My fingers curled into his thick, dark hair, and I traced a line over his lips and ran my hand over his jaw, feeling the scratch of rough stubble. He tilted his head and kissed me, then gave a low growl and deepened the kiss.

"What about the cats?" I took a moment to appreciate the muscled chest resting under my fingertips. "Fab texted an address on Ocean Boulevard, which makes it a good bet that it's a five-star hotel. Good luck sneaking Jazz and Snow in. I don't know what kind of traveler Snow is, but Jazz will meow loudly enough to make his presence known. I'm not leaving them behind. I don't understand people who do that."

Snow, my long-haired white cat, had been pregnant when I first rescued her from life with fifty other unrelated felines. Thankfully, she'd only had two kittens—a boy and a girl. Neither looked remotely related. They had both been adopted by my friend and employee, Mac, who was eager to become a new cat mom. My only condition was that they be spayed or neutered; all three went to the vet on a discount plan.

Jazz, my hundred-year-old, long-haired black cat, had adjusted quickly to getting a trophy girlfriend in his old age. A few sniffs, a handful of hisses, and they were sleeping together.

"One of Didier's designer friends offered up his beach-front digs." Creole made a face, which usually made me laugh; instead, I returned a half-hearted smile.

Creole shook his head; he'd made up his mind that we were leaving, and he was not letting me talk him out of it. He crossed the kitchen and retrieved the cat carrier sitting on the floor by the island. He scooped up Snow and stuck her in first, followed by Jazz. Since they had both been rudely woken from sleep, it took him less than a minute, neither meowed, even when the door banged closed.

Our eyes flew to the garden window over the kitchen sink, where the pelting rain had picked up speed, sounding like gravel was being thrown at the glass. The winds ramped up to a yowl that steadily grew in intensity.

"We should stay." I avoided eye contact, knowing he'd veto the idea, but I had to suggest it.

"We are not going to be one of those couples that makes the news because we had to be plucked off the roof. How would I explain being so stupid to my boss? Remember him? Chief Harder? And in the next breath, I'd have to justify the squandering of county funds on my rescue."

"Take off your clothes." I stared up into his deep-blue eyes and winked. "I'll toss them in the dryer. Unless you want to drive to Miami in wet clothes?"

He peeled off his shirt, followed by his jeans. I openly stared while he undressed. "I know what you're up to." He shook his finger at me. "It's not going to work. I've got a change of clothes upstairs." He turned out of the kitchen and took the stairs two at a time.

The wind continued to grow, the storm beating the sides of the two-story Key West-style house that I had inherited from my Aunt Elizabeth. A sizzle of lightning strikes followed by an ear-splitting crash had me running to the French doors that led to the pool area. Flicking on the outside lights, I peeked out, and immediately noticed that the palm that had stood in the far corner since before my aunt bought the house now lay on its side, a row of flower pots crushed under its weight where it had landed perilously close to the pool.

"That could have been worse," I muttered to myself. I didn't like leaving the house to fend for itself any better than leaving the cats to do the same. I crossed my fingers, certain I had nothing to worry about; the house had withstood many pounding storms, never sustaining more than minor damage.

"Ready?" Creole called from the bottom stairstep, my suitcase in one hand.

"Am I following you?"

"Nice try." He laughed. "You and the cats are

riding in my truck; that way, I can keep an eye on you."

Happy not to be driving in the pouring rain, I gave in and crossed the room, picking up the small tote lying on the floor next to the banister.

Chapter Two

A week later, when all the power had been restored, Fab and I were headed back to Tarpon Cove in separate vehicles. Annoyed when Fab made a snotty comment about the cats riding in her Porsche 911, Creole had offered up his testosterone truck. At any other time, it would have been funny that it took several tries to hike myself up into the cab. After much fiddling with the seat and having to sit up straight for my feet to reach the pedals, I was relieved that at least it started with no problem. After a few miles of jumping and jerking down the road, my driving smoothed out. I said a silent thank you that I hadn't run into anyone that knew me, so at least my driving skills wouldn't be used against me as a source of amusement.

The first thing I noticed, when merging onto the Overseas Highway, the main road that ran through the Keys to the southernmost point of the U.S.—Key West, were the piles of tree limbs that were stacked on the side of the road. I groaned when I spotted a couple of refrigerators, thinking a new one was in my future. I'd wait until it was hauled out of the house to even open the door—there was nothing like the smell of rotten food that had been sitting for days. The overturned outhouse I saw was only funny if no one had been in it as it was swept over on its side.

Turning the corner onto my street, I spotted my refrigerator, secured with rope, already sitting at the curb and was surprised to see that there were four cars parked in front of my house, two sticking out of the driveway. I drove by slowly. Not recognizing a single one, I made a U-turn and parked at the neighbor's across the street. They'd offered their driveway up as additional parking when they weren't in town, which was often since it was a summer second home. All the houses on the block had withstood the storm. My potted flowers had taken the biggest hit.

Fab's hot rod careened around the corner and screeched to a halt behind Creole's truck.

If only I had gotten out sooner, she wouldn't have seen me sliding to the ground. The hot French woman would have been able to jump and land gracefully on her feet.

"Party?" Fab's blue eyes snapped as she inventoried the cars. "And you didn't invite me?" She started across the street, reaching for the Beretta she kept in the back of her black designer skinny pants. "Did you notice no one else on the block has company?"

I grabbed a hunk of her almost-long brown

hair, and she stopped suddenly. "What's our plan?" I retraced my steps and reached back inside the truck, retrieving my Glock from my tote bag on the floor.

"I wish you'd stop doing that," Fab grouched, pointing to my gun.

Fab had harped over and over about not leaving home without a firearm on my person, which I rarely did. But who could have known I'd need one to get into my own house? I left the truck's engine running, the air conditioner on for the cats, and locked the door. Thank goodness Creole's truck had a combination lock and I knew the code.

I ignored her comment. "Wouldn't it be better to call the sheriff now, instead of after we shoot someone?"

Fab snorted in response and grabbed my hand. "We're going in through the back."

We crept down the widely known "secret path" that ran down the side of the house. Everyone in the family and a handful of friends knew of its existence, but a stranger would have to get lucky and stumble upon it.

Between the loud music and water splashing, it sounded like a pool party was in full swing. "I'd like to start by shooting out the speakers." Fab smiled evilly. "But since they're probably yours, I'll refrain."

"Put your gun away, and we'll walk in like we live here, like whoever it is did. Don't look at me like that. When it comes to self-defense, all bets are off."

Fab peered around the corner, turning back to me. "We can take them," she said with confidence.

I followed her into the pool area. Three men lounged around the pool, two women in chaises; they had tossed the pillows to the ground. Even with a quick glance, I was certain that I hadn't met a one of them. I crossed to the outside kitchen area and flipped a switch, turning off the music.

After moving in, I'd turned the underused patio area into an outside entertainment area, doing away with the dining room in exchange for a larger living space. My family ate more meals out here than inside at the kitchen island, which was impossible anyway if everyone showed up with their significant others.

At the sudden silence, all eyes turned in our direction. "Lowlifes" came to mind. A bushy-haired man stumbled out of the house, beer in hand, wearing one of Fab's silk robes. I knew Fab recognized her lingerie from the growl that rumbled out of her.

Apparently more upset than I'd thought, Fab pulled her gun and pointed it at the man. "Start by explaining what the hell you're doing here."

His hands shot into the air, and the beer can hit the ground, beer spilling out over the concrete. "Woah, sister, this here is my crew, and we live here."

"The hell you do," I snapped, making note that when he got angry, his eyes turned a beady black. "I don't know what kind of scam you're running, but you're not the owner, I am." I cut off his response. "You have one opportunity to get out and do it now."

"Or what?" he sneered. "Your bimbo friend is going to shoot me? Oh, I know." He jumped up and down in excitement. "Call the cops? Go ahead. And when all is said and done, I'll be staying and you'll be going. In addition, there will be the matter of the monetary consideration for scaring me and my friends, because I'll be suing you."

I glanced over my shoulder. All the other men had stupid smiles on their faces, and the women had slipped off the deck chairs into the pool, making use of the inflatable toys. All eyes were on the confrontation. They didn't seem to mind that the pool was dirty, filled with debris from the storm. The trashcan was overflowing; when they finished a beer, they tossed the can at it and let it lay where it landed.

Fab's bullet skimmed to the left of his leg, chipping a paver, and he side-jumped in an uncoordinated dance move. "Get out." She waved the gun at him. "Next bullet blows your manhood to bits."

The wincing gasp from his friends was audible in the enclosed area.

"Want me to call the law?" one man asked as he reached out, picking his phone up off one of my beach towels.

Bossman nodded. I cut to the side around him to block the French doors, making sure no one could go back inside. His accomplice fidgeted with his phone.

He probably didn't pay the bill. In disgust, I fished my phone out of my pocket, dialing 911 and reporting the intruders to the operator.

Looking inside my house, I gasped, my knees going weak at the condition of my living room and kitchen. The floor was covered in clothes, shoes, and beer cans, with pillows thrown about. From the doorway, I could see the kitchen sink piled high with dishes, the cupboard doors standing open, and my trashcan lying on the floor, where it had been dragged out of the closet and tipped over.

"When all is said and done, I'll own this house," Bossman said, smug smile firmly in place.

* * *

The doorbell rang, and I kicked personal belongings out of the way to get to the front door. I realized I hadn't heard any sirens in the distance and took that to mean someone familiar with the address had been sent to answer the call.

Kevin Cory leaned his six-foot frame against the doorway, arms folded, smirk firmly in place. "Who died?"

How this sheriff's deputy always drew the short straw was a mystery to me. Those around me had to constantly remind me that he was "almost" family, as my brother dated his sister. We had recently come to an unspoken truce, but it remained to be seen how long it would last.

My arm swept out in a flourish. "No one—yet."

Kevin walked straight into the living room, pausing to check out every inch of the room. "Man, what a pigsty."

"Arrest this man for breaking and entering." I pointed at Bossman, who had followed me in from the patio. "And his friends, who are squatting and making use of my pool."

"This is my house," Bossman said adamantly.

"Shut up and sit down," Kevin ordered. "Let's see some identification."

The man reached down and grubbed through a pile of clothes, pulling out a pair of cut-off shorts, extracting a square metal cigarette box, and finally producing a license.

Kevin plucked it from his fingers. "Carbine Wills. Ebro?" He raised his eyebrows. "So you were one of a population of what—ten? They must have been sad to see you go." He turned the driver's license over several times. "What's your story? I already know hers." He turned slightly, looking at me and putting a finger to his lips.

"I rented the place, and she barged in, threatening to shoot." Carbine cast me a gloating sneer.

"Show me the paperwork," Kevin demanded. "If all you've got is excuses, you're going down to the station."

Fab's bad luck, Kevin was facing the patio doors when she stepped over the threshold. He watched as she reholstered her gun in a swift movement.

"Did you shoot anyone?" Kevin asked her. "Come in, join the party."

Fab pasted a phony smile on her face. "If I do that, the five out here will take off." She inclined her head towards the patio. "Once they hit the beach, you know the chances of catching them are nil."

Kevin groaned, crossed to the double doors, and disappeared outside. I heard him shout, "Everyone out of the pool. Sit at the table." After a moment of silence, he bellowed, "Now!"

I wanted to sit down but continued to stand, my germ phobia kicking into high gear. My fists clenched at the complete disregard for the furnishings. The sides of my mouth turned up at the thought of how good it would feel to beat the stuffing out of Carbine like he'd done to a couple of my couch cushions.

Carbine, on hands and knees, pulled a beat-up

briefcase from under the daybed. He fiddled with the combination and threw up the lid.

I could have picked the lock faster than that. I leaned over in hopes of catching a glimpse of the contents, but Carbine glared and turned it sideways, retrieved the paperwork, and slammed the lid shut.

Kevin came back through the doors and told Fab, "I'll guard the door." He made a shooing motion.

Carbine got up off the floor, crossed over to Kevin, and held out the paperwork. Kevin jerked it out of his hand.

Fab didn't like being relieved of her post. Kevin and Carbine would both be dead if looks could kill. Not to be deterred, she marched to the kitchen island and slipped onto a stool. From her vantage point, she had the same view as Kevin.

No one said a word as Kevin perused the paperwork. Finally, his eyes boring into mine, he inclined his head toward the front door. "Let's take this outside."

Not expecting this reaction, I felt my stomach clench into a tight knot. I shot Fab a confused look and headed to the door.

Kevin closed the door behind us and motioned for me to follow him to his car. "This isn't personal."

That's not what I expected to hear. I didn't say anything, staring up at him and hoping I wasn't about to be arrested.

"He has a signed and notarized lease, the latter being a little unusual. I do know the notary, and she wouldn't knowingly lend her name to anything illegal. I imagine she was brought in because this is a power of attorney signing. Do you know a Donte Prince? He negotiated the lease, supposedly on your behalf. You're going to have to take this to civil court." He waved the lease. "A judge will have to decide."

I shook my head. "Never heard of the Prince character or Carbine. I evacuated for the hurricane and came back to find 'legal' squatters, and there's nothing you can do, even though you know it's my house?"

"I'll run his license and see if I get a hit on anything." He slid behind the wheel of his car.

I pulled my phone out and hit speed dial. "Turn around," I said to Fab when she answered. I could see her through the garden window, and I waved as she did as I asked. "Not good news." I related everything Kevin had told me. "I know from owning rental units that if Carbine's savvy enough—and it appears he is—he can prolong his living situation for months."

"What about our personal belongings?" Fab snapped.

I watched Fab, clearly frustrated, scoop up her hair, wrapping it into a ponytail. Stray hair hung out here and there, but a little mess made her hotter. I was happy not to see my reflection in the glass; it was off-the-charts humid, and my hair felt like it weighed ten pounds.

"I thought of that. Since it's too late to shoot the lot of them and call it self-defense, we're not leaving until Spoon sends over a guard to prevent theft."

My sixtyish mother had a younger boyfriend named Jimmy Spoon, who was well-respected as a major badass. He'd be my first call, and my lawyer the second.

I turned at the sound of my name, meeting Kevin in the middle of the driveway. I left the phone line open so Fab could listen in.

"Clean," he said.

"Hats off to Carbine; this scam of his was perfectly executed. And he has your blessing." My few minutes of self-pity had evaporated, and now I was heating up into full-blown anger. "Now what?"

"Actually, you and Fab have a right to be here. I'll inform Carbine that he's not getting rid of you so easily and to play nice."

"Great," I said heatedly. "He won't be congratulating himself for long. He'll be out faster than he thinks."

"Take a breath." Kevin reached out, and I stepped back. "Sorry, I forgot you don't do touchy-feely. I know you're irritated that I can't kick his ass to the curb." He sighed. "This is where I feel compelled to remind you that you also have to play nice and can't kill him or have any of your friends do it. Mysteriously going missing wouldn't be a good idea either."

"You're no fun." I half-smiled. I didn't tell him I'd rejected the idea of murder already, and I also didn't need to remind him I didn't have to get my hands dirty. Between Fab and me, we had a handful of acquaintances that could persuade the mangy group to relocate with no blood shed…well, maybe a tiny bit. The problem with the lot of them was that they had impulse control issues, and when a foot or an arm showed up somewhere, the cops would be back banging on the door. "Can you make them move their cars so they're not blocking the driveway so I can at least get my SUV out? It is illegal to park halfway in the street."

I didn't want Carbine thinking he had free use of the Hummer and wanted it removed from any temptation to break in and hotwire it for a joyride. I'd gotten an amazing deal from Fab's client, Brick, who owned a car lot. I didn't look for him to be so accommodating a second time.

"That's something I can do." Kevin headed back into the house.

"You need to get out here," I told Fab, who was still listening in. "We've got choices; we can live here like one big communal family or relocate until the law kicks their butts down the street." I disconnected the call.

I almost threw my phone when Spoon's number went to voicemail. I remembered that I had one of his employees, Billy Keith, in my address book, and he was my next call. It saved time to call him myself when I would've requested him anyway. What exactly he did for Spoon was unclear. But if there was a problem and Fab or I needed help, he was always the first to arrive.

Billy answered immediately. "You okay? You never call direct."

"I need you to get your skinny ass to my house ASAP. I've got big trouble, and you have the mean-stink skills that are required."

His growly laugh rolled through the phone line. "On my way." The line went dead.

Chapter Three

The last thing Kevin said before blowing around the corner was "get rid of them legally."

Fab and I agreed, not long after that, that we wouldn't be cohabitating with Carbine and packed up what we could stuff inside the suitcases stored in the garage. What I couldn't take, I shoved inside my walk-in closet and locked the door. It surprised me that the jewelry and cash I'd left behind hadn't been touched. It also appeared that no one had spent time in my bedroom, but I wasn't sure how long that would last.

Fab hoisted herself up and peered through the back truck window at the cats. "They're still sleeping. At least they don't have their faces pasted to the window, howling."

I laughed. "I called Susie. I wish I'd taped the call. She has a snooty, condescending tone that rivals yours." I mimicked the woman: "Mr. Campion is the best criminal attorney in the state—he doesn't do real estate."

Susie was my lawyer's assistant, but her title should have been "bulldog," as she single-handedly weeded out those clients that didn't enhance his pristine image. I had long ago found myself at the top of that list.

"Now what?"

I retrieved my ringing phone from my pocket. "Hold that thought." I accepted the call and hit the speaker button.

"This is Susie. Mr. Campion wants you to fax over any paperwork that you have ASAP. He's referring you to another lawyer and asking that your case be expedited." One would never know from the tone of her voice that we'd just finished a contentious phone call.

I mouthed "paperwork" at Fab and grimaced, wondering what our chances were of not getting caught if we sneaked back in to steal it from under Carbine's nose.

Fab reached under her shirt and handed me a stack of papers with a big smile.

I stumbled on my first words, staring in awe at the lease I now held in my hand. "I'd like to take you to lunch, apologize for any past misunderstandings," I practically stuttered to the woman on the other end of the phone.

There was an overly long pause, and I checked the screen to see if Susie had hung up. "It's part of my job, Miss Westin. If that's all, my other line is ringing."

I started to thank her again and realized she'd hung up.

Fab laughed. "There's something missing. She

tells you to take a hike and then resolves the situation in…minutes?"

"I failed to mention that I ended the first conversation with, 'Next time a busload of Cruz's relatives come to town looking for a fistfight and waterfront dinner reservations, The Cottages will be booked.' And for once, I disconnected first."

The Cottages was a beachfront property I owned, and in exchange for legal advice from my attorney, Cruz Campion, my property manager, Mac, made sure his family had a good time. At the time of our handshake agreement, he'd failed to mention he had hundreds of relatives.

Billy's truck came careening around the corner. Fab flagged him into the driveway next to Creole's truck.

Billy slid out. With his tall, thin physique, he managed to blend in and not attract attention, but those he'd had previous run-ins with crossed the street when they saw him coming. He'd recently hooked up with Mac, and judging from the consistently silly look on her face, he made her a happy woman. She was dying to share details, and it frustrated her that I didn't ask.

"William." Fab waved.

He glowered back at her. He'd made his preference for "Billy" known to her, but she ignored it.

I explained the problem and said that it was important to get them out quickly, and even more important that they didn't steal anything during their stay or on the way out. I also told him that Carbine was clearly the leader and had no fear of the cops showing up. He'd just gone toe-to-toe with Kevin and, after their talk, stood in the doorway and made a brooming motion.

"I could scare the holy you-know-what out of him—make it clear that he'd better leave now or keep one eye peeled over his shoulder." Billy glared at my house.

"He might run, but only as far as the sheriff's office. He's overly confidant in this scam, which makes me think he's pulled it off before." I had an increasingly worse sinking feeling in my gut about the fact that I had no idea when I would be able to return to my house. "I'm thinking we're in for a long wait unless I pay him off. Something tells me cash would get his attention, but I imagine his demands would be outrageous. I'd like to know how and why they choose my house. Who goes house hunting during a hurricane?"

"Squatters are becoming a big problem," Billy said. "Vacation homes are prime targets. Most of the squatters have weak stories, though some come up with hokey paperwork, but Carbine has taken it to a new level. Generally, they go quietly."

"Triple pay if they don't steal *anything*," I said.

"Last time you offered that, the bossman grumbled and said, 'she pays too much.'"

"This time, the bills come to us," Fab said. "Spoon's only participation is his okay for you to work for us."

I hooked my arm in Billy's, pressing the house key in his hand. "Come in and I'll show you around so the cover story I just made up sounds legit." I opened the door and escorted him inside.

"Thought I got rid of you." Carbine assessed Billy with amusement.

"This is my boyfriend, and you'll be seeing a lot of him." I made the introductions and headed upstairs. "That's Fab's bedroom," I whispered, pointing to the first door on the right. Pulling my key out, I unlocked my bedroom door, at the end of the hall on the opposite side, and handed the key to Billy. "Make yourself at home. Bed is damn comfortable. I locked my valuables in the closet. Just keep Carbine out of the bedrooms."

Billy sized up the room, then stuck his head in the bathroom. "You know I'm a crappy roommate. Like things my own way."

"I'm counting on you being a royal pain. Just make sure the cops don't get called. With my luck, Kevin will show up, and he knows you don't live here. He'd probably make you leave."

"There will be no cop-calling while I'm here. I'll go downstairs and pay a welcome visit to let them know not to do anything stupid. I got a friend that can be Fab's boyfriend, and we can do guard duty in shifts."

"Before I forget, thank you. With you here, I

don't need to worry about the house being stripped."

* * *

I snapped my fingers to garner Fab's attention and pointed to Creole's truck, reciting the four-number code. "Parallel park that monster."

We'd already transferred the cats to the back of my SUV, along with the suitcases. The trunk of her Porsche wouldn't even hold her shoes.

"You afraid you'll jump the curb and leave tire burns in the neighbor's grass?" Fab responded to my scowl by laughing.

"Go ahead and laugh. You'll need a favor eventually, and I'll make you feel *really* bad." I shouted the last word.

My phone rang, and Fab quirked her brow. I looked down and held up the screen so she could see Spoon's face.

"You can handle that one on your own." Fab hopped in the truck and gunned the engine several seconds later.

Show off!

I barely got "Hi" out before Spoon cut me off and relayed his conversation with Kevin in a bristly tone, making it clear he didn't care for the deputy's insinuations. But Spoon and I both knew that if I'd called him first, the squatters would be gone already.

"I'm putting you on speaker so Madeline can

listen in," Spoon said. "Your mother got the same lecture that I did."

"Snotty brat," Mother humphed. "Kevin always seems to forget we're not a family of killers."

Fab had her parking skills down and raced back up the driveway in a few minutes. She didn't appear happy that she hadn't waited until after the phone call; missing any part of a conversation irritated her.

After relating everything I knew and answering Spoon's questions, I had a big one of my own. "Can Fab and Didier stay on your boat? Then she won't rush back to Miami. I'm afraid she'll enjoy it too much and not want to come back." I made a face at her.

"Where are you going?" Mother asked.

"I'm going to Creole's."

"No, you're not," Mother said adamantly. "No one knows where he lives. We wouldn't be able to visit you until this was over. The two of you can come to my house."

My eyebrows rose into my hairline, and I shook my head. "That's sweet of you, but also awkward."

Fab giggled, making an inappropriate scissor action with her fingers. One step ahead of me, she moved aside before I could smack her.

"The boat sleeps eight. It will be close quarters, but you're not going to be there long," Spoon said.

"That's a nice offer, but I have the cats to worry about," I reminded him.

Spoon woofed out a laugh. "First off, they're cats and will acclimate. And they're geriatric, so I highly doubt they'd ever entertain a swim or the long jump from the bow to the deck."

I lowered my head and took a deep breath.

"Good, that's settled," Mother said.

We said a group good-bye.

"Thanks." Fab motioned for me to get into my SUV to finish our conversation. "I know you called Spoon so I wouldn't do anything drastic if you weren't around to keep an eagle eye on me. Not that I'm not still thinking about it. But it's a better plan than the one I concocted. I had two, really."

I closed my eyes, taking a breath. "I'm afraid to ask."

"Plan A was to follow you to Creole's. That had me a little worried since you drive so slow, I figured you see me."

"You promised," I hissed.

Creole's beach hideaway was off-limits to everyone but me. He guarded his privacy. I understood that; he didn't want anyone he'd ever arrested showing up.

"I didn't do it," Fab pointed out in exasperation. "Once the subject of where to stay came up, I was determined that we weren't splitting up. So this works out perfectly. Even at home, it's mostly just the three of us. Creole sneaks in and out at odd hours. He can do that on the boat."

"Your backup plan?"

"Tie you up and drag you back to Miami. I had second thoughts on that one—what if I got pulled over? I'd need you to make up a story for me, and I wasn't sure you'd come through after I treated you so shabbily." Fab smiled slyly.

Fab and I jumped out of the SUV. For once, there would be no argument about who was driving, as we both needed to get our cars to the boat.

Billy joined us. "I've got this worked out. I'll keep you updated if anything happens."

"If you have any problems," I said to Billy, "call, and I'll send her." I motioned to Fab.

Fab jerked on my arm, escorting me back to the SUV. "Warning: I'm following, so no detours."

"Yes, ma'am." I saluted.

Chapter Four

Two days later, while sitting out on the deck of the boat, Fab announced to Didier and me that she and I had an early morning meeting with Brick. After she promised to stop at our favorite coffee place on the way, I didn't ask any questions and just agreed.

Brick Famosa was Fab's oldest client, and she stayed loyal to the man despite the fact that he often misled her on cases, which on more than one occasion had resulted in an exchange of gunfire.

To my surprise, living in the close quarters of the boat had been easy so far. The cats had acclimated quickly to the smaller space; Jazz and Snow had sniffed around and, fulfilling Spoon's prediction, had shown no interest in what was on the other side of the railings. They spent a lot of time on their backs in the sun. Creole had stayed both nights, but this morning, he'd had to leave while it was still dark outside.

Didier hugged Fab. "Remember, it's okay to say no to the bastard."

Tucked away at Creole's, I would have missed mornings with the hot, shirtless Frenchman. His blue eyes flashed in my direction, letting me know I was also being reminded to be careful.

"You're lucky Mother didn't show up again this morning or you'd be explaining why she couldn't tag along," I teased Fab. Mother had stopped by the last two mornings on the pretense of bringing coffee, when what she wanted was updates and to ogle Didier. "Or would you out Spoon, telling Mother he asked, or rather demanded, that we not involve her in any of our *schemes,* which he politely changed to *jobs,* without telling her he was the one to suggest it?"

"I hope I'm smart enough not to tread that slope." Fab grimaced. "But a girl can get desperate."

"I'd swoop in and save you. You can be assured that Spoon would heap the blame on both of us."

Didier laughed. "Another thing Creole and I agree on: you two are better off working together than going off on your own." He stared at Fab until she squirmed.

"I agree," she conceded and scooted closer to him.

Jazz wound his way through my legs, meowing, he wanted a lift up to the island. He smelled food and even though he'd never eat a muffin, he wanted to sniff one and decide for himself. Snow was only interested in her morning tuna; any other food tidbits didn't interest her.

"The new lawyer called, a Ms. Hayley," I updated Fab. "She got us an emergency hearing before a judge at the end of the week. The woman is impressive. She put an investigator on the case and on the man, Donte Prince, who signed the lease. Turns out his business address is a PO Box. The notary was questioned and, for a few bucks, supplied the address she'd copied off his driver's license into her official book, which turned out to be an empty lot."

Fab perked up. "With that information, can Ms. Hayley get the house back?"

"She thinks our best bet is that Carbine isn't stupid enough to show up in court and risk leaving in handcuffs."

"I hate this waiting," Fab grouched.

"Me too." Didier's eyes flashed. "It seems the laws are more accommodating for the criminal, while you're left to hire a lawyer to get back what Carbine essentially stole."

"Here's the best part. She cooed over and extolled Cruz's virtues." I grimaced. "Before you ask, I ignored her, not bothering to mention she was wasting her time, and got off the phone. I've met his wife—another gorgeous couple—totally in love." I smiled at Fab.

"Didier's it for me." She spoke directly to him. "I never imagined I'd be so lucky."

* * *

We left Didier sitting in a lounge chair, busy on his laptop and awaiting a business call. He'd confided that he and my brother, Brad, were looking for another property. The current project was almost finished, and they already had a buyer. In a couple of days, they'd be setting up a meeting with their investors, who consisted of family members and significant others.

Fab blew into the driveway of Famosa Motors, illegally parking the SUV in front of the roll-up doors. It was too early for the slick salesmen to be waiting to pounce on a possible buyer. The owner, Fab's biggest client, Brick Famosa, liked to hold these meetings early in the morning.

Fab jerked my hand back from playing with the night bell, shooting me one of Mother's "behave" looks. We came to a halt in front of the reception desk. In place of the usual irritating bosomy blonde sat a woman with spiky, fluorescently red hair. No one would ask if the color was natural.

"Good morning, ladies." The woman stood. "Ms. Merceau and Ms. Westin, I presume. Mr. Famosa is expecting you." She waved to the stairs.

I craned my neck upward, guessing the Amazon to be every bit of six feet tall. She didn't have the signature double D's of the previous receptionist, which I'd always thought were a job requirement, but was still curvy without the aforementioned assets. Men would still find her hot; the ones she didn't scare off, anyway. She exuded a "kick your ass without breaking a sweat" aura.

Fab recovered from her surprise before I did. "Where's, uh… Bitsy." She glanced over at me.

"Mitsy, the poor dear, had a sickness in the family, and she's taken time off." She extended her hand to Fab. "I'm Everly Lynch."

I bit back a laugh; good story, and I didn't believe a word. Good riddance to Bitsy, whatever the reason.

Fab ignored her hand. "Don't screw us, and we'll get along fine."

"You'll be pleased at my level of professionalism." Her smile was perfect, a dentist's dream.

"Were you promoted from the…uh… Gentleman's Club?" I almost said strip joint. We were making a lousy first impression, but based on previous experience, we had every right to be leery until we knew her better.

Brick owned a variety of businesses; pawn shops, bail bonds, if there was cold cash to be made, he was in, and it didn't bother him that most people found them seedy and turned up their noses.

Everly laughed, her eyes narrowed. "I got this job by good old nepotism."

"Good luck," I said and found I meant it.

Fab eyed her up and down, as though sizing up an adversary.

Just then, Brick pounded on the window of his second-floor office, putting an end to our girl-bonding gone awry. He had a one-hundred-eighty-degree view of the lot and the busy boulevard running through the upscale commercial district.

Fab pulled me toward the stairs. We walked up sedately instead of making it a race, jumping and laughing all the way.

"Everly's very different, looks-wise, from Bitsy," I whispered. "The male clients won't be disappointed. She's so striking—it's hard to take your eyes off her. Nothing bimbo about that woman."

"Did you see her shoes? Lime-green stilettos."

Everly had paired the eye-catching shoes with a sedate black suit. She reeked sexiness without having it on display. There was also an impression of scariness that gave one pause.

I wanted to laugh at Fab's sigh. "Just the shoes will have the male customers thinking dirty thoughts." She pushed me through the door of Brick's office first and followed.

"Thanks for coming so early." He slid the coveted snack bowl across his desk to within arm's reach of us both, then settled his massive frame into a custom chair. Not an ounce of fat on this dark-haired, dark-eyed Cuban. He waved us into chairs in front of his desk and handed us each a bottled water.

"This case must stink if you're buttering us up

with sweets, which you usually only share after threats from us to leave." I noticed he'd added an amateur boxing trophy to his collection of plaques awarded for good deeds.

"I'm setting a new tone for these meetings. You do your part and lose the snarkiness." Brick opened a folder and withdrew a sheet of paper, shoving it across the desk. "Here's the pertinent information."

"This is a name and address." Fab frowned. "Puny, in terms of full disclosure. You know the rules our boyfriends set for us working for you. I'm not ignoring them and risking losing Didier."

I half-expected Fab would add a foot stamp, and it disappointed me when she didn't. I kept a straight face, knowing that Creole had explained those rules in detail to Brick and then blacked his eye.

"You'll need this too." He handed over another sheet.

I intercepted it. "Tomorrow." I read the note at the top of the page. "Nothing like the last minute."

The big man ignored me, as he was wont to do.

"Look, this is a freebie, a friend of the 'family.'" Brick must have noticed the flash of anger on Fab's face. "I'm paying you," he reassured her. "Letty Gill is an old, boozy drunk who lives in the middle Keys. She's racked up several drunken misdemeanor charges and needs an escort to court. Her brother is afraid if Letty doesn't show up, she'll get a long jail sentence and it will kill her."

"How old is old?" I asked.

"Well, her brother's nearly seventy, and he's her younger brother, so she has to be north of that. She's never had a felony charge or anything violent." Brick's cell phone rang. He looked down and scowled, sending it to voicemail. "She's just a dumb drunk. The last charge was for driving drunk; her car broke down out on the highway, and she decided to dance home in the middle of traffic."

"Any reason Letty or anyone else would want to shoot at us?" Fab asked.

"No, she's harmless, by all reports. A minimalist dresser, according to the 'drunk and naked in public' charge. You get the idea."

"I'm surprised that didn't garner a felony sex charge, making it mandatory for her to register as a sex offender," I said.

Brick stood and grabbed a clothing bag from the coat rack. "There's a dress in here for her court appearance. So we're good." Brick laid the bag across the corner of his desk and sat back down, his polite way of saying "meeting over."

Neither of us took the hint. "Where's Bitsy?" I asked.

"Sick family member," he grunted. "I think Everly is going to work out great, don't you?"

"I think she could kick your ass if you're not

careful." I stood and flicked my finger through the bowl. "Cookies?"

He shot me a disgusted look and pointed to his office door. "In our new get-along spirit, stay off the banister. You fall, and my insurance premiums will go up."

I picked up the garment bag and followed Fab.

Fab ignored Brick's instructions, flinging her jean-clad leg over the banister and riding to the bottom. She was always dressed for fun; in my skirt, my butt would show all the way down.

Everly was outside, in deep conversation with a salesman I didn't recognize. Fab paused and watched the two for a moment, then steered us in a different direction so that we wouldn't cross paths.

She slid into the driver's seat and nodded toward the new receptionist, saying, "What do you make of Spike?"

"I think *Everly* is permanent and that Bitsy, despite many opportunities, wasn't capable of learning from past mistakes. Brick maintained a pretty controlled demeanor when we started asking questions. The whole sick-family story was BS. But I'm happy her departure had nothing to do with either of us. Everly is no slick, big-boobed blonde; there's more to her than atrocious hair color."

"We should order a background check on Spike. Something feels off."

"Feelings! I must be rubbing off on you." I grinned.

Fab ignored me. "You're in charge of planning this next job."

"Why me?"

"Letty's old, a drunk, and female; she could be Miss January's twin. You already have the hands-on experience and skill with alcoholics—male and female. You'll get her to court in one sober piece, and if it makes you feel better, I'll supervise and then take credit."

Miss January was a long-time tenant at The Cottages, a rental property that I owned in Tarpon Cove. I'd helped her out, but I'd never been responsible for getting her dressed and to court. I'd say a prayer that Letty was sober when we showed up. If not, we'd have to call her in sick; showing up drunk in front of a judge would guarantee her incarceration.

My phone beeped. I read the message and groaned. "New tenant. He's cute."

Chapter Five

Fab slowed as she drove past The Cottages, where the long-term renters and vacation guests were partying together in the driveway. She hooked a U-turn and parked in the driveway of the yellow house across the street. Now that my property manager, Mac, and an ex-tenant, Shirl, had bought the duplex, we had carte blanche to park in the driveway or sit on the front porch, with its view of my property. It made it easier for Mac to keep an eagle eye on the comings and goings over there from her living room window when she wasn't in the office.

"No." I poked Fab's arm. "Back in, so we can see better." She ignored me and killed the engine.

Ten individual units made up The Cottages, built around a U-shaped driveway, each one brightly painted in a different color. The partygoers were getting their drunk on early, ignoring the two separate areas to drink and dance—the large pool area on one side and the barbeque pit in the opposite corner.

"You first." Fab pointed to the passenger door.

We both got out and crossed the street. Mac,

who'd seen our arrival, strutted over to meet us as we stepped into the driveway. I was happy that it was a subdued group and that their noise wasn't echoing out into the road, thereby ensuring a sheriff's department call.

Macklin Lane stood in front of me in a white gauze tent dress that she'd cinched at the waist with a piece of rope, pulling it up to the tops of her black biker boots.

"What's going on?" I asked in exasperation.

"The newest tenant, Rocks Johnson, is a wine distributor, and he's hosting a tasting to get to know everyone. He even brought food." Mac pointed to a table under the basketball hoop.

At the end of the driveway stood Liam; corn chip in hand, he waved. Even though he was a teenager, he'd become the most reliable source of information on comings and goings in the neighborhood.

Mother and I had already unofficially adopted Liam, whose mother, Julie, was dating my brother. They were the first two I rented to after I took over management of The Cottages. They were planning to move when Brad and Didier finished renovating the apartment building they were working on. I wondered if that project would be sped up now that they had a buyer.

"I was so impressed when Rocks showed up in a suit, business card in hand, the whole works." Mac blushed when she saw Fab's and my looks of disbelief.

"Did you at least run a check on him?" I asked.

"You're always telling me that I have a good BS detector," Mac reminded me. "I have a good feeling about this one."

I groaned inwardly. I had a feeling also, and it wasn't good.

Fab poked me in the back. We both knew that Mac not answering meant she'd let Rocks move in when all she knew was what he told her. We'd learned from past experience that the bigger the pat on the back a renter gave himself, the bigger the problem they turned out to be.

A tall, well-built man approached in a pair of flowery board shorts, a suit coat unbuttoned to show off his bare, tanned muscular chest, and a striped tie. He bowed and ran his hands through his light-brown hair.

"Rocks Johnson." He stuck out his hand and eyed Fab like a delicious morsel. "I hear you're the owner."

Fab ignored his extended hand. "Tell me about yourself. Start with whether Rocks is an alias."

He laughed in a smug, arrogant way. "I changed it after my wine line started selling. Great marketing idea, don't you think?"

"I didn't know they had vineyards in Florida. What's the name of your wine?" Fab flashed an arrogant look of her own.

"There are a few," I said.

Rocks gave me a quick glance and dismissed me, turning back to Fab. I made a face at Mac. He put his arm around Fab, and she knocked it off. Not deterred, he extended his elbow, which she also ignored. "Let me pour you a glass of our bestseller."

"Hey, Auntie." Liam showed up at my side and whispered, "I don't think it's real wine. Tastes like…" He stuck out his tongue.

"Where are Joseph and Miss January?" I asked.

Both were tenants who I'd inherited with the property. The doctors had served each of them up a death sentence a long time ago, sending them home to put their affairs in order. In response, they'd toasted that proclamation with liquor and a cigarette.

"I found Miss January standing on the corner, weaving around in a circle. I ditched my bicycle in the bushes and helped her home." Liam checked out her porch. "Didn't want her to fall, so I helped her to her cottage. I'm sure she passed out two seconds after she lay down on the couch." He scanned the driveway. "Joseph gulped a bottle of that *wine.* Not long after, he puked in the bushes and went inside, clutching his gut."

"He better not have killed my flowers," I grouched.

Liam leaned in and kissed my cheek. "It smells over there."

Just great.

Liam's phone beeped and a minute later, he waved and headed to the beach. I moved within a foot of the table, as I wanted to have a good vantage point to watch Rocks charm Fab. He poured her a glass of wine. True to form, Fab took a sniff. First, she scowled, then held the glass up and eyed the contents, finally taking a drink. Seconds later, she blew it all over Rocks' chest.

Rocks jumped back but not quickly enough, the liquid spraying his bare chest. It made me wonder if others had spit out his wine. Good thing he had on a black suit jacket—no stains, or none that would show anyway.

"What the hell is this?" Fab screeched out in a snit, checking the front of her top. "Don't tell me this is wine because if it is, it's terrible."

Rocks wiped down his chest with his hand and then ran it over the butt of his swim trunks.

None of the partygoers said a word. All eyes had been trained on Fab from the moment she lifted her glass, and when she yelled, no one said anything; a few even looked away. One older couple, fear on their faces, propelled themselves from their chairs and snuck around the back of the nearest cottage, circling back to their own. Their door slammed behind them.

Fab picked the bottle up off the table. "This has a screw cap," she said in disdain.

I pinched Mac's arm. "If there is any trouble,

I'm holding you responsible. And *you* will be the one to send him packing."

The sound of a driver revving his engine turned my attention to the street. A strange pickup truck moving too fast squealed into the driveway and right up under the basketball court, sending the food table flipping against the fence. An unidentified man jumped up from the bed of the truck, gun in hand, and shot the wine bottles displayed on another table to bits, sending glass flying in all directions. Everyone dove for cover.

Fab and I hit the ground, rolling over with our handguns out. The man still standing had no interest in anyone but Rocks. He turned towards the man and took a point-blank shot. The gun only clicked, empty. "You steal from me, and you will pay," the man yelled. "You won't be so lucky next time. I promise you, you'll be meeting your maker." He banged on the back window, and the driver ground the gears and, in a cloud of smoke, lurched backwards out of the driveway.

"What in the..." I jumped to my feet from where I'd crouched, reholstered my Glock, and stalked over to Rocks, who had lost his footing when the gunman had him in his sights. Fab had pushed him out of the way at the same time the man pulled the trigger. He lay sprawled on the ground, and I gave him a swift kick in the butt. "What the hell just happened?"

Fab had crawled behind a tree; unhurt, she stood and brushed dirt off her jeans.

The handful of vacation guests that remained peeked through their fingers from where they'd dropped to the ground and covered their heads.

Rocks attempted to grab my ankle. I stepped back and whipped my gun out again. "Get off this property—now," I ground out in rising anger. "I don't know what kind of felonious scam you're involved in, but you're not doing it here."

The color drained from his face. Now unsightly and pasty, he appeared unsettled by his brush with death and about to lose the contents of his stomach, but he still managed to smirk. "I've a signed lease. It's none of your business anyway. Baby Girl owns the property." He reached out to Fab, not realizing she'd retreated from his side and was now standing a foot away, cell phone in hand, capturing the scene on video. "I'm going to get a restraining order against you."

I flipped him my middle finger. *Baby Girl.* Rocks sputtered in outrage. Fab and Mac laughed.

At the sound of sirens rounding the corner, I reholstered my gun once again.

Kevin pulled up into the driveway and chose another space to park in, as his assigned spot was littered with shards of glass. He had become a Cottages tenant when my brother snuck him in after his last place erupted in flames. His neighbor had been cooking drugs and apparently got the recipe wrong. I'd wanted him out since day one, but it hadn't happened yet. I suspected that if he were given the choice between our frigid relationship and moving, I'd draw the short straw.

Kevin slammed the door of his car and looked around. "It's been a while since gunshots were reported on this property. Anyone die?"

"Don't ask me what happened. A man I've never seen before sped into the driveway, shot up the wine bottles, then turned his gun on Rocks Johnson over there." I pointed to the man, who had slithered in the direction of his cottage and now had his hand on the doorknob. Too slow; he'd missed his opportunity to hide inside.

"Rocks," Kevin shouted. "Have a seat. I have a few questions for you." He turned back to me. "Let's hear your side."

"It seems the shooter had a grudge with your new neighbor. He looked disappointed to leave Rocks standing, but he was out of bullets and hadn't brought backup. So his truck flew back out of the driveway. That's all I know."

The driveway was now clear of everyone; with Kevin's back turned, they'd all taken cover inside their cottages. Even Mac had beelined for the office. Only Fab, never one to be left out of anything, had remained. One couple was bold enough to raise their blinds. I'd bet if Kevin turned in their direction, they'd hide in the bathroom or the closet.

"He's a snake oil salesman." Kevin glared in Rock's direction. "I thought you weren't renting to trouble anymore."

"I've been busy trying to get my house back from professional squatters," I reminded him. "Mac can apparently be charmed by a pretty face. And now he has a lease."

Kevin grunted. "Pretty, huh? Don't see it myself."

"Why are you being so nice?" I asked.

"Because Julie told me it wouldn't kill me, and so far, it hasn't." Kevin chuckled, amusing himself.

Fab stood behind Kevin. Waving her arms, she pointed in the direction of the pool and moved off to one side. Rocks had changed course, apparently figuring the beach was his best escape route.

"You better hustle, or Rocks is going to get away again."

Kevin looked over his shoulder. "Johnson, stop and turn your ass around," he thundered. "I'm not going to tell you a third time. Where did the rest of them go? They all snuck off!" he said to me in disgust.

"That couple." I pointed to cottage two. "Knock nicely. They're old, and if they keel over from a heart attack, don't be blaming me."

"I wouldn't think of it." Kevin stomped off.

I was happy not to be Rocks. Kevin's frustration was at an all-time high, and he was about to show the man just how much.

Fab waited until Kevin turned his back, then crossed the driveway to stand next to me. Mac, who'd appeared out of nowhere, trailed behind her. The three of us stared at one another. I pinched my arm to make sure I hadn't spaced out and had a ghastly daydream.

"My forthcoming observation is a freebie; you won't be receiving a bill." Fab's lips quirked. "Time to get rid of Rocks—now. Whatever unfinished business he and the shooter have, the guy in the truck will be back, and you might not be so lucky next time. Someone could end up dead."

"You." I frowned at Mac. "Turn on the southern charm and bounce his ass to the street. I'd enjoy getting the job done myself, but I'm sure he's telling on me for brandishing my weapon, so the usual warnings from Kevin will be forthcoming. If I were Rocks, I'd pack and leave today, but he doesn't look that smart."

"When can we go home?" Fab whined, tugging on my top.

I smacked her hand away. "You can leave me here, and I'll walk."

"You're ridiculous." Fab pouted.

"I've got to text Billy." Mac giggled. "I agreed to keep him in the loop when trouble went down. I may sic Billy on Rocks. He has a way of getting people to do what he wants faster than I can."

"That's because he scares the hell out of people." I closed my eyes and exhaled a deep breath. "How are things with the new boyfriend?"

Facing Mac, Fab snapped. "He better treat you right, or he'll have two women with guns tracking him. He won't like it if he opens his eyes one night and we're staring back."

Mac got a dreamy smile on her face. "Billy treats me good; he's always a gentleman. And way better in the sack than my husband ever was. He's inventive." She winked. "I keep thinking it will stop being fun, and then he surprises me with something new."

"I'm happy for you." I turned to Fab, hoping she'd take the hint and say something nice and be sincere about it.

"Yeah, me too," she grunted.

Mac smiled back at Fab in a way that conveyed *I've got such a girl crush on you and I don't care how rude you are.*

Kevin came around the corner. Rocks ran inside his cottage and banged the door shut.

"You got anything to add?" Kevin asked Fab.

She shook her head and made a face in response.

Kevin glanced around, briefly checking the windows of each cottage. "Rocks doesn't know anything. Never seen the man before. Says he's a friend of yours." He squinted at Fab. "Something about you being the owner and trying to make him the fall guy."

"How does that explain the man pointing his gun at Rocks and not the new owner here?" I gave him a devilish smile.

Kevin paused for a long moment. "You're not very funny."

"You know none of that is true," I said, biting back a laugh. "You live here. You know the regulars, and that the tourists never bring trouble; they only come looking for a ring-side seat."

"The Cruz family—now there's a weird bunch." Kevin rolled his eyes. "The last busload corralled me and wanted to go on a ride-along. They stated a preference for a night that we'd see action."

"You can do that?" Mac jumped up and down with excitement, already adding that to her bucket list of amusements.

"I'll tell you what I told them: 'I'll arrest you for jaywalking, and you can get an intimate look at the booking process.' I did tell them that they would probably be released with a ticket to appear. The time for them to worry was if one of them was issued a prison jumpsuit."

Kevin was clearly amused at most likely scaring the heck out of Cruz's family. For a brief second, I thought it would be funny to see the look on my esteemed attorney's face when he was told that his latest batch of visiting relatives had been locked up.

Kevin turned to leave and paused. "Where can I get ahold of you?" he asked me.

"My mother's." I'd had that lie rehearsed in advance. "You have my number and Mother's; you can call either one."

"Same warning as before; Rocks disappears, and you will be the chief suspect." He waved and walked back to his car.

"What's up with him?" Fab asked in a suspicion-laced voice.

"A get-along lecture from his sister. For now, he's being nice, and we will act in kind." I shook my finger at her. "But beware, in case he has a swift turnaround and goes back to being a total pain." I said to Mac, "Convince Rocks that there are more beautiful beaches elsewhere, and he should go seek one out."

"What about the mess?" Fab nodded to the far end of the lot.

"You two can go; I got it covered." Mac surveyed the driveway. "I'll get Crum to put on a skirt, give him the key to the shed, and he'll be happy to play with the shop vac."

Crum, a retired college professor, was a tenant who'd come with an impeccable resume and references. Meeting him in person…eccentric was kind; downright weird was more apt.

Fab nudged me. "Where's Liam?"

"He got a text before the bullets started flying

and headed off to the beach to meet up with a friend. Depending how far away he was, he might have heard the shots. I texted him and told him I'd call when it was okay to come back."

Chapter Six

"Gunshots. No one died. Dinner?" I said out loud as I texted Creole. "He's not going to be happy to find out after the fact, but there was no advance warning." I blew out a loud, frustrated sigh, adding in a few more sound effects. "I need to go to Jake's. If you have other dinner plans, you can drop yourself off at the boat."

"I'll call Didier from Jake's."

My cell phone rang, Creole's picture popping up. "That was fast."

"You okay?" His words were clipped. "Why, after so many requests, am I the last to know that there's been a shooting?"

"I'm fine. And for your information, you are the first to know, except for Kevin, and he got the call." My voice went up with every word until I ended in a shout. I hung up on him and threw my phone behind me, wincing when it hit the window. "I need a drink."

"We've got that emergency hearing in two days." Sitting at the signal, waiting for the green light, Fab revved the engine, and the sports car in the next lane did the same. "We either get the house back legally or I've got a posse in mind to scare the hell out of that motley group. The second option being my first choice, but I get that you have to go the legal route."

I rolled down the window, and when she shot forward, I waved to the guy she'd left behind; he hadn't made it past the crosswalk.

Fab yanked on the back of my shirt. "Get your head back in here; you know I hate that."

"The Gulf air in my face…smell it—salty and clean."

Fab careened into the parking lot of Jake's. Once a half-owner, I'd bought the rest from the previous owner, who had loan sharks nipping at his heels. I'd inherited the rest of the block from an old-timer who didn't want to see it sold and replaced with condos; the bar was, so far, my only moneymaker. The old gas station, circa 1940, was now an antique garden store selling assorted junk, as suggested by its name, Junker's. Fab's lighthouse sat at the far end, her idea of office space. She'd gotten it free—why take cash for a job when you could get an old building? It was now a tourist attraction; people stopped constantly to have their picture taken. The sign on Twinkie Princesses, a freshly painted roach coach parked parallel to the street inside the parking lot, offered, "We fry anything," if only it were ever open. The two women paid their rent on time, and so I overlooked the fact that it might be a cover for something more nefarious than deep-fried Oreos.

Fab parked by the back door; getting out, she pulled her phone from her pocket. "Your boyfriend is on my phone," she growled. She stuck her head back inside the SUV and looked into the back. "Your phone is in pieces."

I shrugged and headed inside, waving to Cook and heading to the bar. "Margarita, rocks, salt," I ordered from Phil the bartender as I slid onto a stool. "Follow it up with a pitcher."

The tall, willowy blonde smirked at me. She didn't have to ask; she knew it had been a bad few days. It wouldn't surprise me if she knew all about today's shooting already; her sources were impeccable and for sale, except in my case. We'd arranged a trade. I dreaded the day she passed the bar exam and hung up her lawyerly shingle, and although I'd be happy for her, I'd miss seeing her behind the bar.

"I'll have a martini, three olives," Fab ordered.

Looking around the bar, I asked, "When does the next shift show up?" I glanced at my mother-of-pearl watch, forgetting that I'd never set the time. "We need a meeting."

"Hey, doll," a man yelled at Phil from the other end of the bar, pounding his fist on the bar top. "Refill."

Phil dipped my glass in salt, filling it with the green margarita mixture. I barely refrained from licking my lips. She slid it across the bar. Fab's followed, and when Phil tossed in the olives, a little gin splashed up. Phil's lips quirked.

I downed half the glass, thinking I should at least order chips before I got completely sloshed. But I couldn't drink another if I wanted to get home. *Oh yeah, I didn't have a home.*

Phil walked to the other end of the bar, drink in hand for the obnoxious customer. I watched as the two exchanged words, which I couldn't hear over the conversations around me. She set the glass down, and the man grabbed her wrist, pulling her with such force that she slammed up against the edge of the bar top.

Fab leaped up on a barstool, gun in hand, and stepped up on the bar. "Get your hands off her," she boomed.

The man loosened his hold, and Phil stepped back.

It surprised me that she didn't bring out the Mossberg shotgun for a little show; she wasn't afraid to get in anyone's face. I caught Fab's attention and motioned to the door with my thumb.

"Out. Don't make me tell you again." Fab must have been practicing her mean-girl stare; it was more intense than usual.

Whatever he was about to say, he bit back the words when two burly regulars stood, arms crossed. The man got the message and headed for the door.

"Don't come back!" Fab yelled at his back.

I toasted Fab and Phil with a smile and a wink.

Fab reholstered her gun and leaped off the bar, landing gracefully. The bar erupted into applause.

"Drinks on the house." Phil refilled my glass.

"They already are." Fab sniffed. "Didier is calling—again. I've got to answer before he cuts off the sex."

Phil and I laughed at her.

"It's not funny. Sometimes I try to distract him; it used to work, and then he caught on. He can be a stubborn man." Fab wiggled her way to the deck, a few men turning to watch her go.

"Don't tell them where we're at," I yelled. "Let's have some music." I crossed to the jukebox, reached behind it and flipped the switch, then danced my way back to my seat.

"Bad day, Boss?" Phil smiled sympathetically.

"Bad week." I refilled my glass. "Got a pen?" I passed her a cocktail napkin. "Check out Rocks Johnson. He claims to be the maker of Rocks Wine, which tastes like swill in a bottle. He's a new Cottages tenant." I told her about the shooting. "Anything I can blackmail him with—outstanding warrant, whatever—I want him gone. Now."

Phil belly-laughed. "Rocks Wine is a five-dollar bottle of flavored gut buster, alcohol content about eighteen percent. It's not even wine; the liquor board made them take that off the label. College kids drink it, and most just get sick, probably from the sugar high. It has the distinction of being voted one of the five worst so-called wines ever."

I downed my glass, slamming it down on the bar a little hard. The stem broke. "Oops." I picked up the pieces, handing them to Phil. "I need another glass."

Phil set a clean, salted one down. I reached for the pitcher, but Phil batted my hand away, refilling the glass.

I cocked my head to look at the pitcher. *One drink left*. I sighed. "I'll be needing a refill."

Just then, Fab, who had perfected the art of appearing out of nowhere, slid onto the stool next to me.

"How's the boyfriend?" I asked Phil. I'd never gotten any details about how she and Miami's Chief of Police had hooked up. When I asked Creole, he responded, "My boss's love life is none of my business."

She seemed surprised by the question. "We're friends," she said firmly.

"So you haven't…uh…" Fab trailed off, embarrassed.

"Since you hooked up with the chief, we haven't gotten detail one about how it happened, and now you're saying…what…no sex?" I raised an eyebrow.

"Slow down, sister, you've had enough to drink." Fab reached for my glass and pushed it out of my reach.

"You know I do the occasional job for Creole.

The chief wanted to meet me. We're friends—with occasional benefits. End of story." Phil scowled at me.

"You need to improve your story-telling skills. Talk to Mother; she'll give you pointers." I giggled. "This is totally none of my business, but how is the chief in…well, you know." My cheeks burned.

"You're right; it's none of your business." Phil poured the last few sips of margarita from the pitcher into my glass and pushed it back in front of me.

"You're no fun." I stretched out my arms, laying my head down. "You go." I squinted at Fab out of the corner of my eye. "I'm staying here and getting drunk."

"Time to go home. Didier and Creole are cooking." Fab stood up and took a couple of steps toward the kitchen. Realizing I wasn't behind her, she stopped and turned, a frown on her face.

"I'm going to live here."

Phil laughed. "Have you forgotten there's no place to sleep? A booth would be damned uncomfortable."

"You've got two choices." Fab shook her finger, coming back to stand in front of me. "You get off that stool, and we'll get our butts back to the SUV." She ignored my pouty lip. "Or I'll drag your ass out of here, and you'll be the hot gossip for at least a week. And in the retelling, we'll have brawled and I knocked you out cold." She smiled smugly.

* * *

"You okay?" Fab looked me over intently as I wobbled down the dock.

"Too much to drink," I moaned pitifully. "On an empty stomach. I think I'm going to be sick."

"I'll hold your hair back. But if you get anything on me, you're dead. Understand?"

"You're the best friend…" I started to cry.

"Oh, for pity's sake, stop that. Don't look now, but Creole just jumped off the back of the boat and is headed this way."

I turned, stumbled but managed to stay on my feet, and headed in the opposite direction.

Fab wrapped her arm around my shoulders, forcing me to stop in my tracks. "Oh no, you don't." She turned me around. "Besides, whatever you say while drunk, plead amnesia in the morning." She jerked me to a stop, hands on my shoulders.

"Stop with the sudden moves," I whined and got a shake in response.

"I made you a promise. I've never gone back on one yet, have I? We are going to get the house back." She squinted past me, as though the answer was just beyond my shoulder. "Pretend to be sober. Don't say anything, and maybe they won't notice."

I giggled. "They already know."

I felt my feet leaving the ground, and in one swift move, I was settled in Creole's arms. "Put your arms around my neck," he ordered.

I ignored him. "I'm drunk." I leaned back as far as I could in his arms, letting my arms trail behind me, and laughed. "I like it when you carry me."

Chapter Seven

My eyes opened slowly, and I fought waking up, wanting to drift back to sleep. Finally, I peered out from under the blanket, first trying to figure out where I was, then feeling the slight side-to-side motion and wondering what I was doing on Spoon's boat. Then it came back to me in glorious color. After Creole put me on the couch, we kissed, and I laid my head on his shoulder and fell asleep, or some would say passed out. The upside was, I didn't get sick.

Creole sat down on the bed next to me, brushing the hair out of my face. "Happy I didn't have to wake you up." He handed me two aspirin and a bottled water.

I eyed the steaming mug of coffee on the nightstand and pointed. "Sorry about last night."

"None of that." He helped me to a sitting position, handing me the coffee. "It's been a hellish few days, and I haven't been here for you. I've got time off coming, and I'm going to whisk you away." He stood and took his t-shirt off, tossing it on the end of the bed. "Suck that down," he ordered with a smile. "We both have places to be."

I groaned.

"I checked out the old woman on this new job of yours, and for once, Brick was telling the truth. Just a harmless old drunk. If she gets any wise-ass ideas, shoot her in the butt; that will stop her."

I half-laughed over the rim of my mug. "I might get away with that if it were a crusty old man, but not a woman, drunk or not."

Creole pulled my phone out the pocket of his shorts. "I slaved for a good minute or two, putting this back together." He put it in my purse. "No stories needed about yesterday's excitement; Kevin called everyone and spread the word."

I gulped down the last of my coffee, checking to make sure I got every last drop. "What was the purpose of Kevin making all those calls? To stir up trouble? He's worse than a neighborhood gossip."

"Spoon hung up on him when he started to lecture. Didier told him, 'I've heard this already.' Kevin apparently wasn't listening; he continued, barely taking a breath, and Didier ended the call mid-sentence. I think there's more to that story because Didier was angry when he hung up." Creole tossed back the blanket. "Shower time."

* * *

"Princess is awake?" Fab said.

Turning in the direction of her voice, I saw Fab sitting at the table, laptop in front of her.

"Just the two of us?"

"The guys just left. They both had appointments and took off with the usual admonishments to call if…you know." She stood and stepped into the galley, washing out her mug. "Good thing you woke up when you did. I was about ready to insist Creole roll you out on the floor. We've got to get the old woman to court."

I looked down at my rumpled skirt and grimaced. I hated living out of suitcases, and small ones at that. "You'll need to walk her into court." I wanted to make myself comfortable on the couch and go back to sleep. "Don't let me drink tonight; we have to be in court tomorrow ourselves. 'Hung over' never makes a good impression on a judge."

* * *

Fab rocketed down the Overseas and would've missed our exit if I hadn't waved and pointed wildly. It appeared to be out in the middle of nowhere, but I knew there was a small shopping area down a nearby side road that catered to locals.

The directions and landmarks Brick gave us, such as the dolphin mailbox that leaned precariously right, got us to the address without driving around. Fab pulled up in front of the chain that ran across the driveway. The two-story house, raised three feet off the ground, sat towards the back of the lot, and there were two outbuildings, barely noticeable from the street.

The structures had suffered surprisingly little hurricane damage in the recent storm. This wasn't a regular housing tract; everyone had acreage. Letty Gill's was a weedy field that had been recently shaved into a neat stubble. A large pile of tree limbs was stacked near the road.

I scooted forward on my seat. "I don't think Letty lives here anymore." The front door had a sheet of plywood nailed over it. A 2x4 was nailed across the middle of each window, giving it an old-fashioned, rugged jailhouse appearance. A single scraggly flower vine grew up the far side of the house. "This was easy. Don't forget to bill for travel time."

"We're going to get out and check out the entire house."

"Don't you mean me?" I pointed to her feet. "You're going to tromp around the dirt and weeds in your fancy sandals?" I waved my hand, cutting her off. "Why did you take your change of clothing out of the back? And why should I get dirt on my flip-flops?"

"Someone needs to throw all those ugly rubber things away."

"If it's you, I'll mutilate your stilettos and leave them in a pile in the middle of your bed."

We engaged in a glare-off. "You're in luck; I, at least, still keep a change in the back."

"I took it out and forgot to put it back in. And now my tote is sitting on the bench in the entryway of the house we're not living in," Fab huffed.

I climbed out of the SUV, went around to the back, and grabbed my small bag, unzipping it and pulling out my back-up uniform. "I don't want to go home covered in bug bites."

I quickly exchanged my skirt for sweats and shoved my feet into tennis shoes. I eyed her black linen ankle-length pants and silk capped-sleeve blouse. "Nice outfit—hope it doesn't get all dirty when you accompany me on the tour around the property that you insist on."

"Honestly, I didn't think about a change of clothing. Brick made no mention of the rural setting. It will take you two minutes, but don't go where I can't see you."

"Yes, Mother." I gave her a quick salute, holding onto my phone, and started up the drive, stopping at the bottom of the porch steps to snap pictures. No sign that the porch had been used in a long time. There was a large, old dairy box sitting on the top step, which was empty. As far as I knew, the milkman was a thing of the past.

The steps didn't appear to have any dry rot when I stomped on them, holding onto the handrail and listening for any signs of them giving way. I raced up and gave the plywood over the door a good stiff kick. I couldn't hear a single sound from inside. I kicked again. I peeked through the spaces between the boards over the window. There were no curtains, but only a little natural light reached the inside. It was like looking into a dark hole, the few pieces of furniture that dotted the room barely visible.

Fab honked the horn and waved out the window to go around the side.

I turned back and smiled, wondering how long it would take her to trade her heels for my flip-flops. Starting on the right side, all the first-floor windows were either boarded up or covered by curtains and too high to peer into without a ladder, due to the whole place being three feet off the ground. On the second floor, they were all uncovered. The back door had an odd square box that fit over the knob of the steel security door. I beat on the screen a few times, which garnered no response. The house had a creepy, sad vibe. The woman had neglected it, and it showed. I peeked around the far side and spotted a sawed-off tree trunk. I wandered over and checked it thoroughly for insects, since an impressive mound of red ants was not far away, then sat down, wondering how long it would take for Fab to get annoyed and come looking for me.

My phone rang, Fab's picture popping up. *That was quick.*

Before I could say anything, Fab blurted,

"Brick wants us to check out the inside. When I told him the place was boarded up, he told me to figure it out."

"Did you bring a power saw or a crowbar?" I asked in exasperation. "Don't you worry about your manicure; I'll figure something out."

"No. Come back to the car. The hell with this job. It's clear that no one lives here, and Brick can accept that or not." She disconnected.

Checking out the first story, I saw that two windows were open—one cracked and the other open at least a foot. A tree branch brushed the side of the house between the two windows. The end of the limb was skinny and would never hold a person's weight, but it got more substantial as it ran back to the tree. Fab could climb that in a snap and get in the window for a look around. I'd followed my brother up a tree or two as a kid. Maybe—I looked up again—I could do it.

I jumped up and ran back to the SUV. Fab stood by the passenger door, arms crossed. "Where have you been?"

I ignored her question and flung open the back door. I unzipped my bag and extracted a pair of half-finger gloves I had borrowed from Fab and not returned. "Be right back," I called over my shoulder and ran around to the back of the house.

I stood in front of the old oak tree, following the lines of the branches. *Before I dismiss this as a bad idea, I should try.* I put one foot in a V that was about a foot from the bottom and swung myself onto the lowest branch of the tree. I climbed about halfway up the tree, my feet scrabbling against the smooth trunk to get a hold, reaching as high as I could and pulling myself up higher, my feet finding branches to use as footholds. I positioned myself against the trunk of the tree, wishing I could reach the next branch, which was just out of reach. Without it, I was unwilling to go any higher. With nothing to hang onto, I accepted that I didn't stand a chance of reaching any of the windows.

"Get down from there right now," Fab screeched as she hurried around the corner of the house. "Even I can't get up there."

I heard the shock in her voice and said, "Yes, ma'am. It didn't look that hard standing on the ground."

"Get the hell down. Now!" she yelled. "You're going to owe me a new pair of shoes."

Re-examining the termite-ridden shed next to the fence, I stared at the large round lock; now that lock-picker extraordinaire had deigned to make an appearance, hopefully she'd have it off in seconds. "Make yourself useful and pick that lock." I pointed.

"Why?" Her eyes filled with suspicion.

"A ladder would be helpful. Stand back." I went back down the tree the same way I'd gone up and, two feet from the bottom, turned and jumped to the ground.

I knew she didn't have a lock pick on her, so I took mine from my back pocket and handed it to her.

"This is really old," Fab said in awe before popping the lock open. "Stand back." Stepping back, she threw the door open.

I peered inside to see if anything was about to crawl or walk out. The small space reeked of mold, the corner of the roof damaged, exposing it to the sky. I spotted a wooden ladder with round rungs that had to be a hundred years old in the corner and dragged it out through the dirt, which turned out to be more work than I'd imagined and left me breathless.

Tilting it against the side of the house took a little work, as did making sure it fit under the window. "If this wobbles even a little, you better hold on. Push your butt against the bottom steps." I climbed slowly up the first couple of steps; it didn't feel like a rickety mess, but it looked like one, and I had my doubts about how this would work out. Finally, I made it to the first-floor window. "Kitchen," I yelled down.

Leaning forward, I reached across, giving the bottom of the window frame a shove. It barely moved. The wooden rung under my foot gave way, and I slipped. One foot hit the next rung down and the other one went through the opening, my leg straddling it at an odd angle. Pushing upward, I grabbed the windowsill as the ladder wobbled, followed by a cracking noise.

"You're going to kill yourself, and I'll be the one in trouble." The worry in Fab's voice came through loud and clear.

"Hang onto the damn ladder." I shoved my fingers under the bottom of the open window and worked it back and forth. It went up, but not enough to climb in, unless I went in head first. Then what? Hit my head while rolling off the sink, most likely.

"Boost your right leg up," Fab said.

I hooked my arms over the sill, sticking my head inside. It took zero seconds for the odor to assail my nostrils. I gagged and, at the same time, spotted several dead cockroaches on the counter, toes up. I held my breath, forcing myself not to make any sudden movements, and slowly backed out of the window, leaning to one side to suck in a breath of fresh air. "Someone's dead," I yelled.

"If you barf, it better not be in my hair," Fab grouched.

"Your sympathy overwhelms me. Don't let go of the damn ladder." I backed down the rungs, testing each one before putting my full weight on the old wood.

Trying to negotiate the missing rung, I lost my balance and hit the ground with a hard thump. Fab kept the ladder from toppling over on top of me.

It could have been worse. At least I didn't land on

my head. I rested my head on my knees. Eventually, I got up slowly, and the only real pain came from where I'd landed on my backside.

"You're lucky." Fab checked me over, putting her hand on my forehead.

I pushed her hand away. "I don't have a headache; my butt hurts."

"When you update Creole, just remember the part where I said this was a bad idea and then saved your life."

"I don't remember those exact words. Ms. Gill won't be in court today—she's dead. Trust me—unfortunately, once you smell death, you never forget." I rubbed my backside.

"That's so un-ladylike." Fab enunciated her words slowly.

"I'm going to tell Mother you were mean to me," I whined.

"Did you see a dead body? What if it isn't Ms. Gill?"

"I can ID the dead cockroaches." I sighed with relief that I hadn't put my hand on one. "If you're suggesting breaking in, I don't want to hear it." I covered my ears. "I don't want any part of it." Jumping to my feet, I dragged the ladder back to the shed, putting it back in its place. Picking up a branch, I snapped off the end and shoved it in the jam to keep the door closed, since the lock seemed to have disappeared.

I limped over and picked up the broken rungs.

"I'm out of this case," I informed Fab. "Whatever you decide to do, do it after you take me back to the boat."

"Brick's not going to like this." Her eyes narrowed.

"Too damn bad. Ms. Gill is either dead or not home, and either way, she won't be making her court hearing today. Your best bet is to call local law enforcement for a welfare check. And that bit of advice pays back the last freebie you gave me. So that makes us even." I left her glaring at me and started back to the SUV.

I got into the passenger seat and sat down with a groan. Fab was busy talking on her phone; it wouldn't be a stretch to assume that it was with Brick. That cop brother of his could get someone down here to bash the door in and have a look around.

Fab slid into the driver's seat. "Brick hung up on me. Told me he didn't want to hear excuses; just find out what the hell is going on. Wants me to go in."

"No," I yelled.

Any additional conversation was cut off by the arrival of a turquoise 1960 Cadillac that frankly looked its age. The windows rolled down, a jowly, grey-haired man sat behind the wheel. He laid on the horn and parked on the SUV's back bumper.

"Since I'm the calm one—" I poked Fab's shoulder. "—I'll do the talking. You shoot him if he gets any weird ideas. I'll visit you in lockup as often as they let me."

Fab snorted and slid out, slamming the door.

The man stuck out his stubby hand. "Carter Gill," he introduced himself, checking Fab over and clicking his teeth. "Get the door open?" He looked me up and down too. "You're not bad. Brick sure knows how to put out." He whistled, and two pit bulls jumped out the driver's side window and came running, sitting by his side. "Don't worry about them; they're good boys."

"Friend of Brick's?" I struggled not to roll my eyes. "How can we help you?"

"I'm so worried about my sister, Letty. I'd have checked on her myself but I couldn't get in the house." He didn't bother to sound sincere. He wanted something.

"Why didn't you call the police?" I asked.

"Brick assured me you two could handle this. Door unlocked?" He started around the back of the house, the dogs following him.

Fab shook her head before I could answer. When he was a few feet away, she said, "Let him find out for himself."

"I thought this was billed as a family friend; I do remember freebie being mentioned. Does that bastard ever tell the truth?"

Fab shrugged.

"Unfortunately, with my low-life experience, I can tell that man is up to something. Wonder how disappointed he'll be when he finds out

Letty's dead?" I asked.

"It could be someone else, and Letty is on the run." Fab grinned.

All I wanted was a shower and a margarita. Seemed liked a good idea until my stomach twinged as a reminder that two drunken evenings in a row was two too many. All this drama was turning me into a drunk. I took my phone out of my pocket and called Creole. I flashed her my phone screen so she'd know why I wasn't putting the call on speaker phone.

"Hey, babe," he answered in that commanding voice that sent tingles through me.

"Just wanted to tell you I love you."

Fab made a gagging noise.

"Were you hurt?" he demanded.

"I'm fine. Didn't want you to forget, that's all. Remember the old woman Fab and I are taking to court today? Well..." I relayed the events of the morning, omitting the whole ladder episode. And Brick's reaction and brother dearest.

"Hey, bitches," Gill bellowed. "The door's not unlocked, and I can't see any sign you even tried. You're not scamming me; I won't pay." His face reddened to the color of a ripe tomato. The dogs hung back, no longer at his side. "Is she at least dead? I'll need her will and other documents."

"Whoever that is better not be talking to you two," Creole bristled. "Get the hell out of there," he said as Gill approached, yelling obscenities.

I signaled to Fab, and we jumped back in the

SUV. Fab gunned the engine as Gill reached the front of the SUV, thinking to block us from leaving.

"Don't hit the dogs," I said.

Fab drew her gun and pointed it between Gill's eyes. He covered his face and slowly stepped out of the way. Fab left a pair of tire marks in her wake, jumped the curb, and took off down the street.

"Fab was her usual impressive self," I told Creole. "In another minute, we'll be halfway home."

"Text me the address. I'll take care of this. You two go back to the boat, and hopefully, by the time you get there, I'll have answers for you." He hung up.

"It's handled." I put my phone on the console. "Ignore Brick until Creole calls back. We both know this isn't our fault; let's hope Brick agrees. You might want to mention that if we don't get extra pay, we'll sic the boyfriends on him."

* * *

It took a couple of hours for Creole to call back. Fab and I were back on the boat by then, and she was annoying me, wearing a hole in the carpet, pacing back and forth. Brick had called her twice since she sent him a text that we were waiting for a call from the sheriff's department. He didn't want law enforcement involved, but he backed off when she informed him that Creole had called while Gill was ranting at us, hearing every crazy word out of the man's mouth.

Creole finally called back. "Sad news. Your Ms. Gill is dead. Called in a favor because I'm nowhere near the area, and she was found in her bed, television on, no signs of foul play. Pretty good way to go. Oh yeah." He half-laughed. "The brother thought he was going to loot the house in front of the cops, and they threw him off the property and told him not to come back without court authority or risk arrest." He sent a kiss through the phone.

I relayed the news to Fab.

Fab called Brick, who had already heard from Carter Gill. He yelled from the start of the call. Fab held her phone away from her ear, shaking her head. Finally, she turned off the phone and threw it on the table.

Chapter Eight

"Isn't it just a little weird that Carbine didn't show up for court today?" Fab asked as we took the stairs down three floors to the exit of the Miami-Dade courthouse, bypassing the elevator, not wanting to ride with a hoard of people.

"I'm just happy he lost and I get my house back."

Fab and I had arrived early, cooling our heels outside the assigned courtroom. We watched every time the elevators doors opened, expecting Carbine to appear. When he didn't show up on time, the judge moved the case to last on the docket. Neither Fab nor I had any patience for sitting; we paced the hallway and waited for our lawyer to call us inside. To say Ms. Hayley wasn't happy about the delay was an understatement. "Damn Campion, he owes me big for this."

The judge called Ms. Hayley to the bench and fired questions at her, which she answered competently. His clerk handed him a file that he flipped through before dismissing the case.

I had to hand it to Ms. Hayley and her investigator; they'd unearthed a lot of dirt on

Carbine's business activities, and the man had been involved in a laundry list of illegal schemes. He was a nightmare for landlords, as he had a reputation for being a professional non-paying renter. According to court documents, he frequently pushed evictions to a court date, like today, then pulled a no-show and disappeared before the sheriff showed up with the eviction notice.

"Case dismissed," the judge said, followed by the bang of his gavel. I released a huge sigh of relief. Even Fab appeared less tense.

Fab waited in the hall while I thanked the lawyer. In the parking lot, Fab and I argued about where the SUV was parked until she hit the car alarm, and it turned out that we were closer than we'd thought.

"I wish Carbine was headed to jail." I kicked off my heels as Fab used a back exit to get to the street.

Since the whole area was crawling with law enforcement, Fab backed off the gas and drove within the speed limit. I didn't mention that her driving no longer made sick. Why spur her to new dramatics?

Why Carbine had picked my house, I'd never know. The man had certainly moved in with his ducks all in a row. He'd thought, with his phony paperwork, that he'd be able to stay for several months; he wasn't counting on someone with legal connections. I'd like to have seen his face when the process server arrived with the Order to Appear notice in hand.

"I heard the lawyer tell you that Carbine and his crew had a day or two before the sheriff would post the notice and we'd be rid of them." Fab rolled down her window and gave two of Miami's finest a thumbs up. "Let's go by the house and check it out."

The girl had all the luck; she didn't hit a single red light all the way to the Interstate.

"Billy called earlier." I gave her the update: "This morning while we were in court, the lot of them packed up their cars and hit the road. He kept an eagle eye out, making sure that there weren't any attempts to carry off anything that didn't belong to them."

"I drove by early yesterday morning to see if Billy was slacking." Fab smirked.

Just great. I shook my head.

"I took him coffee." She looked proud of her ruse. "I needed to find out how he planned to contain four men by himself. I met his friend, who wasn't impressive. On my way out, Billy whispered, 'Looks can be deceiving; I'm a good example of that.'"

"Fabiana." I sighed. "You've been here long enough to know that the so-called normal ones are the ones you need to keep your eye on, far more than those you know are nuts."

"Billy told me that when he first got there, he wasted no time in sitting them all down, introducing himself, and making it clear he had no tolerance for thieves, which he emphasized by pulling his gun. Thanked them for their time and went into the kitchen for a beer, lingering to judge the reaction. Not five minutes later, two of them left and never came back."

"I'll be happy to go home and find them all gone." I crossed my fingers.

"That same night, he scared off another squatter, who'd failed to attend the meeting. When he ran into him on the side path while doing his nightly rounds, he shoved his gun in the man's face, demanding, 'Where's the redhead? She owes me money.' The man stuttered something about not knowing any redheads. Billy's final threat was, 'If I find out you're lying, I'll be back.' The man turned around and ran to the street, and Billy heard the engine of his car start." Fab looked disappointed that she'd missed the action.

"Billy told me that, after Kevin threatened to have any cars hanging out into the street towed, all of them disappeared except one," I said. "An old Ford Falcon he thought belonged to Carbine, but which was registered to an old man in the panhandle."

"The boat's nice, but I'm ready to go back home."

* * *

We parked in one of the beach parking lots, two blocks from the house. "We'll start by casually walking by the front of the house, then double back around and cut through the path into the pool area." Turning the corner, Fab poked me. "Those are police cars parked in your driveway."

"Does it take two deputies to post a notice?" I pulled my phone out of my pocket and called Billy. The call went to voicemail. Putting my hands on Fab's shoulders, I turned her around. "We don't need to get caught lurking around."

Fab grabbed my hand and steered me onto a shortcut to the sand. We blended into a crowd that had gathered there. A coroner's van had pulled into the parking lot, and the attendants were in the process of unloading a gurney. I knew without asking that Fab would follow them. I grabbed the back of her shirt and twisted it into a knot, holding tight. "Oh no you don't. Someone is dead, and we don't need to get in the middle of the drama. We get in enough trouble without following it."

For once, Fab didn't disagree, and we raced back to the SUV.

As soon as the doors closed, my phone rang. "It's Mother." I answered, putting the call on speaker.

"Where are you?" Mother asked, sounding a bit frantic, before I could utter a greeting. "Are you in Tarpon?"

"We're close by. You okay?"

"Come straight to the boat," she ordered. "Do not stop anywhere. I know you can hear me, Fab; no speeding."

Fab and I exchanged "what's up?" looks.

"We were going to stop and get some food. Do you want anything?"

"I'll take care of the food." Mother hung up.

Fab pulled out onto the highway, cutting across the median to the lanes going to the other side of the Cove.

"Madeline must be in trouble." Fab knew every shortcut in town and took the one down to the docks. "Maybe she's being held at gunpoint for something we did. But we've been angels lately."

I laughed and stared out the window. *Angels, indeed!*

Minutes later, Fab flew into the parking lot at the marina. "We need to get our guns out of the back," she reminded me.

Courthouses take a dim view of people who try to get through security with firearms. Creole had put a locked box in the back of the SUV that held our guns for those special occasions. It fit inside the spare tire compartment.

"Do we run down the dock, guns raised, ready to shoot at the slightest movement?" I scoped out the parking lot. Another quiet day, not a lot of cars. We'd parked in the front row, a couple of spaces from the walkway.

Fab handed me my holstered gun, and I

attached it to my waistband, positioning it in the small of my back. We both changed our shoes.

"I'm going to carry mine behind my purse."

Mother almost ran up the dock, meeting up with us just inside the gate. "Hurry up, before someone sees you."

"Are we going to need our guns?"

"You thought I was in trouble; that's sweet." Mother smiled.

"What the hell is going on?" I asked.

"Madison Elizabeth." Mother turned, hands on her hips.

If I weren't a grown adult, I'd be worried I was about to be grounded.

"You're in for a lecture now," Fab whispered.

"It's Fab's fault." I pointed a finger at my friend. "She's a bad influence."

"You could give me a warning when the bus is coming so I can jump out of the way." Fab yanked on the end of my hair.

"There would be zero fun in that."

Spoon stood at the bottom of the steps up to his boat, holding his hand out to Mother. He nodded to Fab and I and grinned.

"You must be in on whatever is going on, Big Guy. If we worried for nothing, I'll ask my friend here to shoot you. Lucky you; she rarely does anything I ask," I said.

"I haven't shot anyone in a while; I wouldn't want to get rusty."

"You two are not funny." He scowled.

Fab and I laughed at him as we climbed aboard.

"Where's the food?" I looked at the table for some familiar packaging.

"Creole's on his way, and he's picking it up," Mother said.

"Stinkin' hamburgers," Fab yelled. "That's all he ever gets."

Mother pinned Fab with a glare. "I'm sure that by the time he gets here, you'll have calmed down."

I put my arm around Fab and led her to the back bench. "Cheer up. You know Didier probably left something slimy and green in the refrigerator." I looked over her shoulder. "I see something that's going to make you happy," I said and pointed behind her.

Creole and Didier were walking up the deck, Roscoe's bags in their hands. "The best burgers in the Keys." Fab's prophecy had come true; it would be burgers and fries for our late lunch.

Fab jumped up from the bench and awaited Didier at the top of the stairs.

Creole passed out individual bags while Mother distributed drinks and glared once again at Fab, setting an iced tea on the table in front of her.

I had a bad feeling when no one uttered a word about why Fab and I had been summoned and the guys had showed up.

"The chief gave me a long weekend." Creole kissed my cheek.

Fab dropped her hamburger bag on the table, shooting Creole a glare. "Why don't we go get some real food?" she said to Didier.

Didier picked up the bag and dumped out the contents on the table, handing her a burger. "We're staying."

Fab leaned back in her chair and shot me a sly wink.

I bowed my head to hide the big smile on my face. If I had any guts, I'd say, "Let's go."

Creole looked at Mother. "So, you didn't—"

She cut him off, shaking her head. "The cops are looking for you, honey. They want to question you regarding the murder of Carbine Wills."

"So that's why he didn't show up to court." Fab completely took apart her hamburger, separating out each item.

"In my house?" I dropped mine on the table, no longer hungry.

"You got lucky there." Creole put his arm around my shoulders, giving me a quick hug. "Wills was found on the beach behind your house, rolled in a fishing net and tucked behind one of the boulders."

"That's why I wanted you to come here," Mother said. "Kevin came to my house looking for you. I told him I didn't speak to you every day and I didn't know where you were."

"Little weasel," Spoon growled. "Wouldn't tell us what he wanted. So I called a friend right in front of him and found out. Prick got in a little-girl huff and left."

"Mother, where's your outrage when your boyfriend uses the 'P word?' I only said hell."

Despite her glare, she laughed. Turning to Spoon, she shook her finger and said softly, "Really, honey."

He responded with an overly long kiss, the twinkle in his brown eyes a little unsettling.

Okay! It's official. Those two have a sex life. I laughed at myself; that had been evident for a long time, even before they were "official."

"I have an announcement." I stood and found myself off-kilter a bit, with Creole's hand under my skirt. He must have anticipated me moving forward, as he trapped my leg with his. "I didn't murder anyone, not on purpose, accident, or just because it was a nice day."

"We know that." Mother clucked. "You do need a lawyer to be with you during questioning, though, and Cruz is in court this afternoon."

"How would you know that?" Fab asked.

"Fabiana, that's none of your business," Didier whispered, just loud enough for everyone to hear.

She glared and slid away from him, then turned back to Mother. "Well?"

"I called and talked to that nice assistant of his, Susie. She said she'd take care of it. Told me not to worry; you were a pro at getting out of trouble."

"Did Susie happen to mention that she loathes me and only takes my calls because she has to?" I shot back.

Mother stood, holding out her arms. She hugged me, whispering, "She wouldn't dare." I hugged her even tighter. "Susie called back and said Cruz will be calling you later. That's why I thought it was a good idea to hide you, and Spoon thought, since you're already here, that the boat is the best place. He thinks Kevin won't look here."

I sat back down. "Is that how you got the weekend off?" I asked Creole. "Mother called your boss and offered to fax over a written excuse of some sort?"

"I'm sure she would have." He winked at Mother. "If I hadn't answered my phone."

"Why doesn't Kevin want to speak to me or Fab?" Didier asked. "He may think I'm too pretty to shoot anyone, but Fab..." He laughed at her disgruntled look. "She's even cuter when she tries to look shocked and innocent at the same time." He leaned over and brushed her lips with his.

"What about Creole?" I asked. "He could get in trouble for not turning me in."

"Kevin hasn't gotten a warrant, so he must not have anything that points directly to you. As Didier said, there are at least two more people on this boat with motive," Creole pointed out.

"What about Carbine's lowlife friends?" Fab demanded.

"How are we going to find them? Either of you recognize any of them?" Spoon asked Fab and me. "Whether or not one of them killed Carbine, or knows who did, they'll have hightailed it out of town and be long gone by now."

"Billy!" Fab jumped up. "He probably has pictures of everyone who stopped by the house."

"Even if Carbine was murdered in the living room, I didn't do it, and I have an alibi for every second of my time since we left the property," I griped. "If he was murdered inside, hopefully it wasn't on any of the furniture; the area rugs are easier to replace."

Fab raised an eyebrow, as if to say, *That's not very sensitive.*

Creole picked up my ringing phone and checked the screen. "Ms. Westin's office," he answered.

No one said a word.

"She's busy," he said cheerfully. "Pencil, pen, yeah…somewhere." He grabbed up a boating magazine, making a rustling noise. "Go." He stuck his index finger in the air, writing whatever the person was relaying. "Madison will be there. If not, I'll call you back. Okay, doll?" He held the phone away, looking at the screen. "Susie hung up on me."

"She does that a lot," I said.

"What did she say?" Mother demanded.

"Madison is to meet with Cruz at his office at five regarding her legal issues," Creole said in a snooty woman's voice.

Everyone laughed.

Chapter Nine

"Nice ride." Creole hit the steering wheel of the Hummer as we headed down Highway One from Cruz's office. "I think it's the first time I've driven Fab's SUV."

"I think most people not only think it's her car but that I also don't know how to drive," I said. "Thank you for coming with me to lawyer extraordinaire's office."

"Cruz has a ginormous ego, but he earned it." Creole and Cruz had met when Creole testified in a couple of his cases. They weren't friends but had mutual respect. "He's got a near-perfect record in court, and he's not a lawyer who built his name on getting the guilty off. I liked that during your discussion he was making a list of other possible suspects. It'll annoy the heck out of him to have to come down to the Cove and mingle with the common people for tomorrow morning's meeting at the sheriff's department."

"One thing I've always liked about him: he'll do what's in his client's best interests and not just what's expedient."

"How many of his relatives have you

entertained?" Creole asked.

"A lot. When he first pitched the idea, I had no idea they would show up by the busload. They're an exacting bunch. If one group gets a shooting, which happened a couple of times in the early days, the next group wants more excitement. Can I tell you a secret?"

"We have secrets?" Creole glared at me.

"I'm not sure whether this is illegal, but if it is, you might get in trouble and then I'd have to post your bail. Just so you know, I'd bend my rule of no jail pickups in the middle of the night for you."

"Spill."

"Even though we've reinstated our old rule at The Cottages of not renting to felons, drug addicts, and general law-breakers, sometimes one of them slips under the radar. Mac wanted to hire drunks to come fight, and when I said no, she came up with using the tenants as a sideshow. She's thinking about having a 'welcome' pool party and inviting the regulars and a few of the odder people from the neighborhood."

Creole shook his head and laughed but went silent when he spotted the red flashing lights behind him. On reflex, he checked the speedometer. "What the hell?" He pulled onto the side of the road. "Wonder what this is about?" He powered down the window.

I flipped up the visor and watched as two

uniformed officers got out of their car, one coming to the driver's side and one to the passenger side. A banging on my window made me jump. Creole opened the window from his side.

Kevin rested his forehead on the top of the frame. "Out," he commanded me.

Creole grabbed my arm. "What's this about?" he demanded.

"This doesn't concern you, and if you try to interfere, you'll be arrested." Kevin watched my every move. "Don't make me tell you a second time, as I could make a case for resisting arrest."

I leaned over and kissed Creole's cheek, then whispered, "Call Cruz." I opened the door and slid out. "What a piece you are," I said in disgust. "I was sitting across from Cruz when he made arrangements for me to show up at your office in the morning."

"I guess I didn't get the memo. Hands behind your back," he ordered.

"I'm under arrest?"

"Yes and listen up for your rights, although you probably have them memorized." He flashed a smarmy smile.

He cuffed me and shoved me into the back of his squad car. Trying to get in the backseat with one's hands restrained takes concentration to avoid falling.

After a few words with Creole, the other officer made his way back to the car and climbed into the passenger seat as Kevin slid behind the wheel. I thought of a snotty remark but held back.

We'd found out from Cruz that Carbine had been shot at point-blank range after first being used for target practice. Next to him was a Beretta that was registered to me. The cops surmised that Carbine was lured down to the beach and killed after not being cooperative in a painful interrogation; either that, or he didn't have the answers. The killer got as far as wrapping his body in a fishing net, but must have gotten interrupted by something and walked off without a single witness. They hadn't been able to locate any of the people who'd taken up residence in my house along with him. Back at my house, the place had been ransacked, and it was reported that they'd lived like pigs during their short stay.

My questions were many. Why would I leave my gun behind at the scene? The Beretta had been in the junk drawer, and I'd forgotten to retrieve it. The fishing net sounded like a lot of work. Why toss my own house?

Kevin pulled up to the back door of the station. He led me up the steps, past a large room that held several desks, most not occupied, and into a room with a holding cell. It wasn't five-star accommodations, only a mattress, toilet, and sink.

"I'd like to call my lawyer," I told him with a

smirk. "And until he gets here, I'm not saying jack."

"You don't want to cooperate, that's fine; you can sit in here all night." Kevin pointed to the phone on a nearby desk.

I knew Cruz would be long gone for the day and left a message with his answering service.

"How can you give your word to my lawyer and not keep it?" I asked as soon as I hung up. "Instead of being a bastard, why not say, 'we need to talk to her tonight'? You must be salivating at the thought of arresting me, and it doesn't matter to you if I'm guilty or not. For the record, I'm not guilty."

"That's what all criminals say." His face red with anger, Kevin ushered me into the cell, slammed the door, and stomped away.

So much for a truce.

I sat on the edge of the mattress, thinking about Creole, and knew he was furious, and also that he would do his best to make sure I didn't stay here long.

It was cold in this place; they must hire people with polar bear skin. I wanted to wrap the thin blanket around my legs but shuddered at the question of who'd used it before me and whether it had been washed.

What a terrible week. I squeezed my eyes shut to hold off the tears; I would indulge later, I promised myself. I crossed the fingers on both hands that I wouldn't get moved to a big-girl cell that came with a change of location, clothing, and shoes.

Chapter Ten

Sitting with my back against the cement wall, I nodded off several times. This time, my eyes flew open when my legs, which I'd curled underneath myself, cramped, and the other occasion, my head had dipped from one side to the other. With only a postage-stamp-sized window to give me a clue, I wondered what time it was and what was happening on the outside.

The outer door opened, and a deputy appeared in front of the cell, keys in hand, and unlocked it, motioning me out. "Turn around, hands behind your back." He twirled a pair of cuffs. He didn't inquire about my accommodations, a man of few words. I followed his example, certain I couldn't find anything nice to say and that appearing unstable wouldn't help my case. He guided me by the elbow to a corner office; peering through the large window, I saw Sheriff Tatum, whom I recognized from his re-election posters, on one side of the desk, Cruz and Kevin on the other, the only open chair between the two.

I could see the outside through the window on

the opposite side of the office. It was daylight, so that meant I'd spent the night, and since there'd been no room service, I assumed it was early morning.

"You okay?" Cruz's eyes lit on me, checking me over from head to toe. His expression was angry and frustrated. He worked to keep it from erupting. "I'd have been here last night, but these two went home after bringing you in and they needed to be present for this." He stood and pushed back the chair. "Do you think you can take the cuffs off?" He directed the question at the sheriff.

Kevin jumped up and, without any eye contact, removed them.

The sheriff started off with a vague apology about the "mix up" of my being arrested instead of waiting for the meeting that had been scheduled. I didn't understand how my spending a night in jail could be written off as "oops."

Kevin nodded in agreement. "I apologize for any inconvenience, but you can understand that unpleasant tasks are part of my job."

"That's such drivel," Cruz barked. "Pull a stunt like this again, and I'll be filing a complaint with internal affairs."

Kevin glared at the angry attorney and immediately looked away.

"Let's speed this along. I have another appointment." The sheriff flipped on a recorder, noting who was in the room and why we were here.

"Do you have a time of death?" Cruz asked. "My client has an alibi for the last two days, corroborated by eyewitnesses." He produced a file, which he set in front of him.

Sheriff Tatum barely glanced at a report before answering. "Between one and three in the morning two days ago. Body was discovered yesterday morning."

"My client was on the boat of Mr. James Spoon, along with four other people, and all will vouch for her presence there. There is also videotape of the entire marina area."

The sheriff raised his bushy eyebrows and snorted at the mention of Spoon's name.

"The people that you refer to are most probably her friends and relatives," Kevin interjected. "None of them are exactly pillars of the community, and they wouldn't think twice about lying. Not to mention that her almost-stepfather, Spoon, has a criminal record. Do you have someone remotely credible?"

"That was years ago, and you know it," I snapped at Kevin. "By your standards, no one can turn their life around. That means you'll always be an—"

Cruz clamped his hand on my shoulder with just enough force to stop me from blurting out something inappropriate. I turned away and sent my lawyer a silent thank you. He leaned in and whispered, "I'm going to get you out of here. Don't give them a reason to keep you locked up."

The sheriff fired questions from a prepared list, making tick marks as he went down the page, most of which Cruz indicated I could answer. He did ask about the court case, and Cruz interjected, answering the questions and informing him that, although he hadn't been the attorney of record, Ms. Hayley was, and that they'd stayed in touch on every aspect of the case.

My stomach rumbled loudly, but no one offered me anything to drink, much less eat.

"Do you have enough evidence to charge her?" Cruz asked.

"We're not booking her. Thank you for your cooperation." The sheriff nodded. "Don't leave town. Do you have any questions?" He directed that to Kevin.

"If Madison has anything helpful to add, she should call us first," he responded.

You'll drop dead before that happens.

"If you need to speak to my client again, call my office, and I'll arrange to have her here." Cruz stood, held out his hand, and helped me to my feet. He grabbed his briefcase, putting his hand to the small of my back.

"Sorry for the misunderstanding," the sheriff said. "It won't happen again." He directed the words to Kevin.

I didn't acknowledge the other two, mainly

because I didn't know what to say. *It's been fun.* Except it wasn't. Cruz led me down the hallway and out the door. The fresh air felt good on my face. "Thank you," I murmured. "I appreciate you, even though you're a pain sometimes."

Cruz laughed. "You did really well—you didn't rush your answers and gave brief, direct responses. As of now, you're their prime suspect only because I think they don't have anyone else, and you have an alibi. I wouldn't get excited; they will be keeping their eyes on you."

I closed my eyes and pinched the bridge of my nose. "Anything else?"

"There is one thing." Hands on my shoulders, Cruz turned me around.

Creole was leaning back against the passenger door of the Hummer, arms crossed, looking so disreputable it sent tingles up my spine. Slightly worn jeans, t-shirt hugging his biceps, his hair a mess, stubble dotting his chin and cheeks, and dark sunglasses covering his emotions, which I was certain matched the scowl. Before I could run to him, Cruz grabbed my arm, stopping me from fleeing.

"It's well-established that you owe me, and this is a big one. My grandmother is coming for a two-week visit. Much to my chagrin, she insists on spending one of those weeks at The Cottages. Even though I promised her a better time."

I flashed a devilish smile. "How about a little wager? I bet she'll talk more about the week she spends at The Cottages than the week with you. I win—you owe me. You win—same thing."

He glared at me like a bug under a microscope. "Under no circumstances do you allow any felonious activities to take place while she's there. Understood? Then we've got a deal."

"How old is Grandma? And Grandpa?"

"She doesn't discuss her age, and Grandpa is in heaven, as I tell my kids."

"Sounds like my mother. I'll get them together for lunch and introduce your grandmother to cigars and poker." I laughed at his exasperated expression. "Where do you get all these relatives? They arrive by the busload, and granted, we do get return visitors, but most are newcomers."

"The Campion family is a large one. We have a family reunion every year, and I admit, at times it's difficult to remember all the names and where they fit on the family tree."

"We'll take good care of her."

"I'd outright forbid her, but she still has a way of making me feel like a naughty ten-year-old. I got in plenty of trouble as a kid, and she never ratted me out once." He smiled fondly. "I'd do anything for her, including fulfill this ridiculous wish of hers. She's heard about other family members' trips, and she demanded to experience it for herself. If anything happens to her, you'll feel the full force of my wrath."

"Look at our overall track record with your

family. No one has been shot, beaten-up, or arrested. There have been a few minor injuries, mostly conjured up by the men in your family so that they can look down Nurse Shirl's top at her enormous…while she soothes their piddly aches and pains."

Cruz humphed. "Your boyfriend is waiting. Good guy, by the way. I'd approve if my sister was dating him."

"Did I say thank you? While sitting in that cell last night, what got me through was knowing you wouldn't let me rot."

"I should use that in my advertising." He took his keys out of his pocket. "I'll have Susie send the dates of Grandmother's visit to Mac."

"Prepare yourself, counselor; you're going to lose this bet." I waved and could swear I heard a groan as I ran into Creole's outstretched arms. He lifted me off the ground and whirled me around, then slid his fingers into my hair to cradle the back of my head, pressed his lips to mine, and kissed me hard.

Cruz revved his silver Bugatti, honked, and waved as he left the parking lot.

"You two looked intense. More legalese?"

"Just a wager I plan on winning." I gave him the limited details of Grandma Campion's upcoming visit. "I may have to use you and Didier in a shameless fashion, have her to dinner and have you two serve the food shirtless." We both laughed. "Cruz doesn't seem worried that

Carbine's murder is going to involve any more incarceration, which has me feeling less jittery."

"We'd go on the run before I let that happen."

"Someplace warm all year round, I hope."

Chapter Eleven

Creole drove straight to his beach house, which was located south of Tarpon Cove off a road that appeared to go nowhere. His house sat at the end of a dead-end street, the nearest neighbor a half-mile away. An investor had originally bought the property, and when he got zero interest in a quick flip, he sold it to Creole for a great deal.

The front side of the house didn't have windows, but the back side was a long wall of pocket doors that slid into themselves and overlooked the Gulf. He'd renovated the interior himself, opening it up into one large space for the kitchen and living room, the bedroom behind a pair of bamboo screens. The bathroom was complete with a shower that could accommodate six and a clawfoot bathtub with a view of the water below.

My favorite spot was the back patio and the pool that overlooked the beach.

Our two days together went by fast. I accompanied him on his runs on the beach, riding a bike, the only way to keep up. The one time I walked, Creole took off running and picked me up on the way back, finding me sitting on the shore.

"Thank you for bringing me to your house. You always know what I need."

"I like the isolation—no traffic and no people. We can enjoy one another, and your shell collection can continue to grow."

At home, I used the shells for mulch. Since he had no potted plants and only a couple of trees, I worked on filling a large flower pot to take home with me.

On Monday morning, we sat at his kitchen island—which was half the size of mine, but we only needed room for two—and I poured him the last of the coffee. "You've got a meeting, and I get my house back today."

"You should double-check and make sure law enforcement has released the property."

"Too late." I picked up my phone and checked the screen. "No phone calls or messages, so that means there were no problems. Mother arranged for a cleaning crew to show up early. It's supposed to be a surprise—she's using Cook's wife's niece, daughter-in-law, cousin, or something; that's how I found out about it." I almost laughed at his expression, knowing he was trying to figure out what relation that would be. I didn't want to interrupt his thought process to tell him that my description might not be exact.

He rose from his stool, hands on his hips. "You made that up, didn't you?"

I laughed, caught his squint, and laughed some more. I knew I was in trouble and didn't care.

He stalked the two steps toward me; moving backward, I stumbled. He tried to catch me, and we ended up on the floor. He rolled underneath me, cushioning my fall, and managed to kick the stool out of the way, and in retaliation, he tickled me until my laughter turned to shouts of "No more, no more."

He scooped me into his arms and kissed me.

So much for his meeting.

His phone rang, and he walked me to the couch, retrieving it off the table. He glanced down. "It's Didier." He answered. "Slow down and tell me what happened."

I wished he'd hit the speaker button, but Fab and I had been forbidden to do that when either of our boyfriends called one of us.

"Fab's missing," Creole relayed to me.

"That's nonsense." I stood up, seeking my phone. "Is she in the Porsche?" I asked while calling her number. It rang several times and went to voicemail.

"Yes," he answered, telling Didier he was putting him on speakerphone.

"Fab left an hour ago," Didier's voice boomed through the phone. "I had a business call, and she went to get soufflés from the Bakery Café. The restaurant says she was never there; she didn't call, and she's not answering her phone."

"I know for certain Fab would never deliberately worry you." I kept to myself the thought that, even if one of her sleazy clients had called, she'd just have made up a story and roped me in for confirmation. "If it gives you peace of mind, we haven't pissed anyone off lately. Except maybe Carbine, but he's dead, so it's not him."

Creole rolled his eyes at me.

"I'm calling in a missing person's report."

"That'll just piss Fab off if she's not in trouble. Let's try to find her ourselves first," Creole said. "Who are you calling?" he asked me.

"Brick. He can activate the GPS on the Porsche, and then we'll know where her car is. He'll hop on it because he hates when a luxe auto goes missing." Brick didn't answer, which made me grind my teeth. I sent a text: "911. Fab." Then I paced around the room.

While Creole reassured Didier, it took less than a minute for my phone to ring.

"What?" Brick damn-near yelled.

"Fab's missing. Can you activate the GPS and tell me where the car is?" I took off Creole's shirt, tossing it over a chair, and cut across to the bedroom closet.

"I'll call you back," Brick snapped.

"I'd like to hang on." I pulled out a skirt and dressed, slipped into a pair of flat leather sandals, and moved around the room, shoving things in my tote.

"Hope he doesn't take all day," Creole grumbled, shoving his feet into a pair of tennis shoes. "We're headed in your direction," he told Didier.

Brick came back on the line as Creole and I were headed out the door. "It's in the Cove, parked on Main Street in the two-hundred block."

"Thanks, Brick. I'll call you as soon as we get there."

"You need anything else, I better be your first call. You know she's a friend."

My eyebrows shot up. *Probably his only one,* but I wasn't mean enough to mention that, not right now anyway. I hung up. "Didier, that's the same block where the Bakery Café is located."

"We'll meet you there," Creole told him and reassured him that we would find her and there would be a simple explanation. He hung up, opening the SUV door. "If you were missing, I'd be out of my mind. Didier's emotions are strung tight." He hugged and kissed my forehead before closing the door. "Let's hope this isn't some kind of *notice me* game."

"Fab doesn't play those games. She doesn't have to. Those two are wild about one another; she even tries to behave once in a while to make him happy. Now that's love." I stared out the window, for once wishing we were speeding. "I don't have a good feeling about this."

"Get over here." Creole stretched out his arm,

resting it on my shoulder and flicking the ends of my hair. "No worrying."

It was a straight shot down the Overseas, and I said a silent to prayer that the traffic was light all the way back to the Cove.

* * *

The café was just another couple of short blocks away now. I kept my eyes peeled out the window, looking for Fab's Porsche and the woman herself.

Creole stopped in the front of The Bakery Café, pulling in next to Fab's sports car. Didier was pacing back and forth in the road. Creole went to console his friend. I dug out my wallet and pulled out the emergency twenties, stuffing them in my pocket.

I walked up to the first person I saw in a uniform. "Were you working an hour or two ago?"

"No," she said, turned up her nose, and walked away.

"I was," said a busboy who'd overheard. "You leave something behind?"

I reached in my pocket and produced a twenty. "See the Porsche over there?" I pointed. "It belongs to my friend. You see which way she went?"

"Smokin' hot?" he asked. "She got arrested, don't know what for, hauled off in the back of a cop car. She called the male deputy a bitch."

I walked back to where Creole and Didier stood, both watching me approach. "Fab got arrested. My guess is it was Kevin again."

"For what?" Didier bellowed.

Several of the diners sitting at the outside tables turned their heads.

"Let's go find out. Follow us," Creole told Didier.

"Don't worry. I can get her a lawyer and bail," I said to reassure Didier.

Creole and I got back in the SUV. The police station was a five-minute ride. We parked next to Didier.

"What now? Didier goes in and finds out about bail? They won't tell him anything about why she was arrested," I said.

Creole opened his window, sticking his head out and waiting for Didier to lower his passenger window. "Interesting development. Get in." He motioned to the back seat. "There's more room." Didier started to argue, but Creole cut him off with a hand wave. I kneeled and started to climb over the seat, and Creole snagged the back of my skirt. "Where are you going?"

"Tell Didier to sit up front. You can keep him calm." I slid into the back seat, scooted up, and stuck my head between the seats.

Didier opened the back passenger door.

"Sit up front." I flicked my finger forward.

That caught him off guard and made him

smile as he got in.

"Cruz is here." Creole pointed over the steering wheel. "Unless there are Bugattis on every corner."

"I'm surprised, whenever he parks it somewhere, that it hasn't been stolen when he comes back." I peered over Creole's shoulder. "He has two small children; I wonder if he has a minivan for weekends."

Creole and Didier laughed at me.

"The chances of Cruz being here for someone other than Fab are nil." Creole smiled in the rearview mirror. "So just sit tight. We're going to pull over next to his car so he can't get away without all of us seeing him. Wait until I tell the chief that Cruz now represents Fab."

Chief Harder was his boss, and before meeting me, he'd had Fab on his radar as someone he'd like to see arrested. He'd felt the same way about me and had been slow to come around. He was now of the opinion that I wouldn't do anything illegal, but the jury was still out on Fab.

We didn't have long to wait, but then again, Fab had been here for more than an hour. Didier was the first to see them. He jumped out of the SUV and strode over to jerk Fab into his arms for a short hug before releasing her. Fab made the introductions between the two men.

Creole and I got out and leaned against the car. I waved to Cruz, who shook his head. Didier and he split away from Fab. I ran to her and threw my arms around her.

"How dare you worry us?" I whispered.

"I knew you'd find me," she said smugly. We walked over to Creole.

Creole hugged her, which surprised both of us. "Didier damned near went crazy."

"I wasn't allowed to make a call before we left the Bakery, or I'd have called or texted." Fab grinned at me. "I told Cruz that whatever deal he had with you covered me. He didn't quibble and came down here, though he grumbled about the drive."

"What happened?" Creole asked.

"Cruz called and told me to get to the sheriff's department. I was calling Didier to tell him when I ran into the deputy, almost knocking us both to the ground. Told me snottily to watch where I was going. I unleashed more than a few colorful words on him." She shook her head at her own bad behavior.

"You have to appear in court?"

"Thank goodness for Cruz. He was standing in the reception area when we walked in. I didn't get booked, and I don't know why. He had a discussion with the sheriff, and I couldn't hear a word. Next thing I know, when the questions about Carbine were over, I got to walk out the door. Cruz grouched, 'Don't ever do that again.' Didier's going to flip." She grimaced.

"What did they want to know about Carbine?" I asked.

I noticed Didier and Cruz were huddled in conversation by his car.

"What was I doing and when was I doing it?" Fab said.

"I take it you were your usual evasive self." Creole traded glares with her.

"Cruz coached me: 'short and truthful.'"

"Where are those two going?" Creole pointed to Didier and Cruz, who were headed back inside the police station.

Fab walked towards the cars. "Knowing Cruz, he doesn't want to make another trip down here. He grumbles about it every time. It will prevent Kevin from arresting him while he's out somewhere, like you. I'd feel damn guilty if he were. Didier could have been a society darling, but because of me, he's a suspect in a murder investigation."

"Didier had his pick of women before you came along. Was he in a relationship? No! He told me once he'd never been in love before you. Don't you think that if he'd never met you, a part of him would be lonely?" I flashed her a sad smile.

"That's why I like having you around—to make me feel better."

The three of us got in the SUV. Fab slid behind the steering wheel, Creole and I in the back.

Creole threw questions at Fab. When did we first discover the squatters? What did she see, no matter how minor? Her opinion of Carbine? Any ideas she hadn't shared about who might have murdered the man?

To my surprise, she gave direct answers. I laid my head in Creole's lap and closed my eyes, trying to remember whose shift it was at Jake's because I was hungry.

It was two hours before Didier and Cruz reappeared. "What the heck were they talking about in there?" I asked, looking at the clock.

Creole and Fab got out and met them in the parking lot. They didn't talk long. I climbed back in the front while Didier and Fab got into his car. Creole waved from the front of the SUV; he'd received a phone call, which didn't last long.

Creole slipped back behind the wheel. "Didier told me to tell you that you don't owe Cruz for him and Fab. He gave the lawyer his card and told him to bill him. Cruz looked disgruntled but didn't say anything."

"Cruz is probably annoyed that it will interfere with our agreement that Mac basically entertains his relatives. He does host a dinner in a nice restaurant for them, which it surprised me to learn he shows up at." I adjusted the side mirror, making sure Fab and Didier were behind us. "Are we headed back to the beach house?"

"Your mother and Spoon are at the boat. She *cooked* dinner." Creole chuckled.

Mother's cooking was a running joke in the family. It wasn't that she couldn't cook; she was a good one but chose not to, instead ordering take out. With those that weren't in the know, she passed it off as homemade.

Chapter Twelve

"I don't want either of you going anywhere alone." Didier crossed to the galley, shirtless, hair disheveled, to pour himself another cup of coffee. He engaged in a stare-down with Fab, who hadn't agreed to anything. She pointed to her empty mug, and Didier filled it for her.

"On the bright side, none of us were booked for murder," I said cheerfully.

Creole reached for me, and I slipped out of his grasp, putting a chair between us.

Fab said a few choice words to her boyfriend in French. At least, I assumed so, judging by her tone and body language. His response was swift and in an irritated tone.

"You two stop that." I stepped between them. "You know I can't eavesdrop when the only words I understand are naughty ones."

Creole ran his hand through his unruly hair. "Fab asked him to define 'alone,' and he responded 'you know damn well what I mean.' Satisfied?"

I turned on Didier. "You used a bad word?" I want to laugh at Didier's frustrated expression. His fault—he was the one always admonishing us over our language. He and Fab looked half-amused, so mission accomplished by not minding my own business.

"Good morning," Mother called out from the bottom of the steps.

I winked at Fab. Now that Mother had moved to Tarpon Cove, she was becoming a regular fixture in the morning. I'd bet Fab that Mother liked to start her day with extra eye candy, as both Creole and Didier tended to lounge around shirtless. The only time she didn't show was when Spoon didn't have an early morning appointment.

Creole stood, meeting her before she started up the steps, taking the pink bakery box and shopping bag from her hands and offering his other hand to help her on board.

"What's for breakfast?" Fab snooped through everything Mother had brought.

Didier scowled at her.

"You dissed the cats? There's no cat food." Fab looked at me, and we laughed.

Jazz and Snow didn't seem to be bothered by being uprooted from their home. There were plenty of places to sleep, the food stayed the same, and there were people around to pet them.

Mother shot Fab her signature "you better behave" look, which had little to no effect on her. "I have good news," Mother announced, clearly pleased with what she was about to say. "Your house is clean, top to bottom, and the stuff left behind on the floor has been put into boxes and moved into the garage, in case someone comes looking for their belongings."

"I suppose there's always the chance that Carbine will wake up at the coroner's office. But probably not, since he's been autopsied," I said.

"Madison." Mother whooshed out a loud sigh. "Where do you get these ideas?"

I pointed at Fab.

The guys laughed.

"That means we can move back in today," I said.

"I forgot," Fab said. "We've got a job at the funeral home today."

"What's the status on this person? Dead or not?" I asked.

"It's complicated," Fab answered.

"Am I wearing something in basic black, or are we local mourners, so I can just wear a bathing suit and cover up?" I asked.

Fab shook her head. "Don't embarrass me."

I reached out and kicked Didier's foot. "Come with us. Free sandwiches. Casual dress."

Didier crossed his arms over his chest. "I'm not going. Take your mother."

Last time Didier was at Tropical Slumber, he'd complained that the place gave him the major creeps. It was bad enough to attend the funeral of a loved one; he wasn't hanging out there.

"I can't today; Spoonie and I are going to lunch."

"I thought you were banned from calling him that?" I reminded her.

"Sometimes I forget." Mother sat back with a satisfied smile on her face.

* * *

"You never did explain *complicated,"* I said as Fab pulled into Tropical Slumber Funeral Home.

The old drive-through hot dog stand had been given several makeovers besides the obvious of being turned into a mortuary. It now had a house, a six-car garage, a separate one that held caskets, and a crematorium in the back. In Dickie and Raul's zest to be a single stop for all funeral needs, they'd recently added a pet graveyard under the patio area. The duo boasted that it had brought in business from all of south Florida once word got out.

"The 'deceased' woman is alive, but she has a good reason for pretending to be dead." Fab slid out from behind the wheel and went to say hello to Raul, who waited for her on the red carpet that ran from the parking lot to the front door.

"Thanks for the details," I grumbled and got out of the SUV, waving to Dickie.

Fab always left out all the drama in a retelling, just listing off the facts, and sometimes skipping a few of those if they showed her in a bad light.

Dickie and Raul couldn't be more different. Raul was of average height, with a body builder's physique; he handled the business affairs. Dickie was over six feet and painfully thin, his skin translucent; he was the artist.

I headed toward Dickie, knowing he would give me straight answers. "Do we get to shoot anyone?"

"You're here for our peace of mind and to prevent flying bullets. I take it you didn't get any details." He looked paler than usual, if that was possible.

I shook my head in response.

Dickie let out a long, frustrated sigh. "Sometimes, you can't say no to a friend, even though you know you should. I know the answer to my question, but I have to ask: can I trust your discretion?"

I knew from past experience that if word got out that you couldn't say no, it was an open invitation to be walked on. "Nice" was a character trait to be exploited. "Fab and I don't talk about our cases except when events warrant it; then, we confide in our boyfriends. I assure you, they're a tight-lipped pair."

"Bernie Stone at the coroner's office has a sister, Karen, who you will meet later. Her husband murdered her, or so he thinks. He left her for dead alongside the road and called a man he'd hired to dispose of the body. When the man arrived, she was still alive. The husband, thankfully, was a poor shot; thought he'd shot her in the chest, but missed and it entered her shoulder. She fainted, which saved her life."

Astro and Necco, their two Dobermans, careened around the corner, skidding to a stop in front of us. I held out my hand, and both dogs wanted to shake at the same time.

Raul and Fab joined us, their arms linked, and we walked into the reception area. I headed for my favorite red brocade, plastic slip-covered chair by the door. Its proximity to freedom put it at the top of my list for sitting. It certainly wasn't for its comfort; after a while, it made my butt hurt, which was when I invariably signaled Fab that it was time to go.

"Dickie was kind enough to fill me in on the details that seem to have slipped your mind." I glared at Fab, who stood on the opposite side of the room, the one closest to the viewing rooms.

My sexy, hot friend had a ghoulish streak; she'd be sticking her head in every room before we left. I'd never asked about her fascination with dead people; I didn't want to know.

"Karen offered to pay the man more not to finish the job. He assured her that he wasn't a murderer but still took the money. Or rather, her diamond wedding ring, as she didn't have any money on her. They shook on the deal just as her husband called, and she listened in on speakerphone. Karen said her husband called the man Carl before asking, 'Did you get rid of the body?'" Dickie sat down and pressed the back of his head against the wall. "Apparently, her husband, with the help of a coroner friend, has claimed the body of a homeless woman who'd drowned. Which is who we're holding the funeral for."

Raul pulled open a drawer in the round table that sat in the middle of the room, retrieved a bottle of aspirin, and shook out two, handing them to Dickie along with a bottle of water. Usually, the table held a fresh flower arrangement, as it did today, but there were times when they anticipated a big turnout and it held food.

Raul continued the story. "After assuring her husband that he'd dealt with her body, Carl drove Karen to her brother's house and dumped her about a block away."

"Good thing she had the ring to bargain with. There's a good chance she'll get it back. If he's stupid enough to show up at a pawn shop, he's busted. The cops will want him, and they'll send out a picture of the ring." I petted the dogs, who were now lying on my feet. They didn't fool me—they wanted a sandwich, and I was their best bet. I wanted one too, but we'd arrived too early for funeral food leftovers. "Fast forward—why hasn't the husband been arrested and is instead arranging to throw a sham funeral? I also want to know why you agree to these ridiculous requests, but I suppose it's none of my business, although I don't like being told that."

"Don't pay attention to him." Raul waved

offhandedly. "These unusual requests get us on the news, hence more customers, and it's not like they're freebies. They have to pay the regular rate—dead or not."

Dickie banged his head against the wall, wincing. "Karen was in denial until she saw the announcement of her funeral. Some rubbish about still loving him..." he said in disgust.

"She's not turning him in to the police, but instead attending her own funeral? What exactly does she get out of that?" I paused, thinking I should be more like Fab: not interested in pesky details. "What are we doing here?" I tried to cover my annoyance but failed.

"I don't want to get arrested." Dickie covered his face with his hands.

Fab, who was closest to him, moved to his side and patted him awkwardly on the shoulder.

"Karen wants to wait until the funeral is over and then confront him," Raul stated simply. "She wants to humiliate him in front of their friends and family, and then watch as he's led away in handcuffs."

"Where are the police?" I asked. "They aren't going to stand for this kind of game."

"Her lawyer wasn't keen on the idea either, but he's meeting with the Miami police department, as it happened in their jurisdiction. I'm hoping they show up soon and ruin the damn surprise," Dickie said.

"Why are we here?" I wanted to shoot Fab a

dirty look, but her back was turned, and after a minute of comforting Dickie, she headed into the only viewing room with a name tag.

"To make sure the husband doesn't get away and that no one gets hurt," Raul said, flushed with embarrassment.

"If the husband makes a run for it, Fab can chase him. She always lording it over me how much better shape she is in than I am; time for her to show off her skills. If he uses his car to get away, I'd prefer to shoot out the tires, but in this case, I'll give his license plate number to the cops."

A long black SUV drove slowly past the open door. Raul went and stuck his head out the door. "Karen just arrived." He continued to stare. "Mourners are arriving, gathering in small groups."

"Astro, Necco," Dickie called. A moment later, the dogs were on their feet and following him down the hall to their residence.

"Too bad you're not that well behaved," I said to Fab.

She shot me her mean-girl stare in return, and I laughed.

"No funeral, real or pretend, for me. I'm taking the outside," I told Fab.

"Once the funeral starts, Karen is coming inside to wait here in the reception area. I'll signal when she makes her grand entrance," Raul said.

I did my best not to cringe, a shudder shooting up my spine.

"Fab can stand at the back of the room. I'll wait out here, and when Karen shows up, I'll go outside."

"You didn't listen very well when we got the *stay together* lecture this morning." Fab didn't bother to hide her annoyance. "We both need to see what's going on to react accordingly. If deputies swarm this place, we go out the back."

* * *

While Fab was in last-minute conversation with Raul, I snuck out the front door and claimed the wood bench with a wrought iron backing just outside the door. Guaranteed sore butt. I suspected Dickie and Raul went for the ornate design for appearances, forsaking comfort.

Fab practically stormed out the door. She sliced her index finger across her neck, cutting off the tirade she knew I was about to launch. "Raul will text when the service is winding down, and I'll go back inside," she huffed. "Next time Dickie or Raul calls, you tell them no. If something goes wrong and one of them gets hurt, you know you'll feel guilty."

She had a point.

"This is a freebie!" I tried to mimic her, but it came out a bit screechy.

"Your attempts at imitation are pitiful. It's

hard to duplicate perfection. Just be yourself."

I looked both ways to make sure no one was nearby and made a loud, extended retching noise. "What's our plan?" It didn't take long to realize she didn't have one. I sighed and said, "Keep your eyes on Karen. There's a chance this whole scenario goes awry and someone really does die. Mister Karen isn't going to take her resurrection very well once the shock wears off. Five dollars says he runs. I would. And don't forget pictures or a video for Mother."

Fab pointed and groaned. "You're not going to like who just pulled up on a sheriff's department motorcycle."

I turned and caught sight of Kevin, dressed in his uniform, parking the bike in front of the hearse. "You thinks he's here to escort the mourners to the cemetery?"

"Must be something the husband ordered. Raul told me that the body isn't leaving here; it's illegal to knowingly bury the wrong body."

"You tell Raul to give Cruz a quick call before he and Dickie answer questions. I'm not sure whether Cruz will remember he represented Dickie once, but I'll certainly remind him. What they know and when they knew it is a bit murky and could get them into big trouble."

Fab continued to stare at Kevin. "If he doesn't have a clue about what's going on, I say we don't enlighten him. Once he recognizes the SUV, he won't be able to stop himself from finding out why we're here. Thanks to the luxury of tinted windows, he can't see in; if he thinks we're inside, my bet is he'll go over and peer in the windows."

"I'm going to cut him off, find out what he knows." I got off the bench, where I'd been partially concealed by a pillar, and cut diagonally across in Kevin's direction, stopping him from reaching the SUV.

I got within a foot before Kevin asked, "What are you two doing here?"

"We were invited. And you?" I said.

"None of your business." He turned and stomped back to his bike.

Fab now stood behind me. Her phone beeped. She pulled it out of her pocket and poked me, inclining her head toward the funeral home. We walked to the entrance together and got there in time to see a woman with black netting over her face open the door to the main room. Fab followed her.

"Pics," I whispered and got a head shake in return.

Showtime.

Instead of heading back outside to do the coveted outdoor duty, I couldn't resist a peek at the surprise, "Honey, I'm not dead" party. I tucked myself into a corner, a perfect spot for not missing out on the good stuff. Once of us should have been professional enough to ask the grieving husband's name.

The service was nearly over, which I appreciated. The guests were thanked for coming, and instead of heading for the exit, they swarmed around the grieving husband and steered him towards the door. Karen pushed away from the wall and blocked the aisle. Lifting her veil, she gushed, "Saunders, it's me."

He spotted her immediately, and his hands slapped the sides of his face in horror. Only a few of the guests were able to get a good look at her face. A few whispers later, and they were all staring, most doing double- and triple-takes. They appeared shocked, except for a teenager towards the back, who skirted the side wall, a big smile in place, and produced his phone.

"A ghost?" Saunders uttered as he fell to his knees.

"Surprise, devoted husband. I'm still alive."

"I'm so sorry for everything," he sobbed. "Please forgive me. I do love you and always have. I changed my mind, I swear I did, but it was too late."

"What the hell is going on here?" Kevin whispered.

Startled, I jumped a little, but composed myself quickly. "That's Saunders." I pointed to the man, who had crawled over to his wife and was jerking on the hem of her dress, and gave him the basic facts.

Kevin grunted and walked back outside.

None of the invited guests moved an inch,

caught up in the unfolding drama.

The sound of sirens caught Saunders' attention. Wrapping his arms around her leg, he begged, "Forgive me."

Karen gave him a blank stare, staying silent; she lifted her foot and kicked his arm away. He rolled onto his hands and knees, then jumped up and ran in my direction.

At that point, I didn't care if he got away; the deputies and a K-9 unit would have him in custody before the hour was up. But Fab's face clearly said, "Do something."

I stuck my leg out and sent Saunders tumbling to the ground, almost taking a spill along with him. Four deputies converged on the reception area. Spotting him sobbing on the floor, they surrounded him and took him into custody without any more drama.

The video-taking teenager flagged down one of the deputies, handing over his phone, and they stood side by side to watch the screen.

Fab stood between Raul and Dickie, doing all the talking to the cops. I caught snippets of the mourners' conversations; some were disgusted that Karen had waited to show herself, a few implying that she'd driven poor Saunders to do something uncharacteristic, as he was "such a nice man." Others withheld judgment but wanted to know more. The big speculation was about Saunders' motive.

I had a few questions I'd like answered, which

I knew would never happen. Now I was fixated on leaving. I waved to Raul and Dickie and walked back to the SUV.

I slid into the driver's seat, having to remind myself that it was okay to drive; after all, it was my car. Fab never saw it that way. I started the car and was tempted to rev the engine in a warning that I'd leave her behind if she didn't hustle.

"You know I hate your driving," she huffed, sliding into the passenger side.

"I know it makes you sick," I said, lacking sympathy. "Roll down the window before you barf. Or hold it; we're not going that far."

"The boys think you're a rock star for tripping Saunders. I told them not to get carried away."

"Why did Saunders want his wife dead?" I asked, cutting around the back past the crematorium and then speeding out of the driveway.

"Greed and jealousy. He thought his wife was going to leave him and take her money with her."

So now he's traded his life for a jail cell.

"Let's go home."

Chapter Thirteen

Our first night back in the house and Mother had planned a party, judging by the familiar cars parked in the street. Creole had reminded me more than once to double check with law enforcement to make sure the house was not still part of a murder investigation and that I had the legal right to move back in. It wasn't and I was happy to be home.

Fab and I had gone back to the boat for a second check to make sure we hadn't left anything behind. The boyfriends had loaded our bags in the back of the SUV earlier, and our last stop was Spoon's so Fab could retrieve her Porsche. If she'd left it in the marina parking lot overnight, it would have been gone in an hour. I tailed Fab to the light and pulled up alongside her. She powered down the passenger window, yelled, "Race you," and revved the engine. The light turned green, she shot forward, and I followed her exhaust trail.

By the time I arrived, Fab had parked in the driveway and was leaning against the back of her Porsche, arms crossed. Spoon and Liam came out the front door, laughing about something. If I had to bet, it was some outrageous thing Fab had said, like, "Get your asses out here and schlep the bags." However she got the help, I was happy not to be carrying them upstairs or leaving them on the floor to trip over.

Liam opened the door, and I slid out. "Brad's going to be late; he's meeting with a client. Heard about the guy on the beach. Told Kevin he was wasting his time, thinking you were a suspect. He pretty much blew me off."

"Wouldn't it be nice if life was so easy that we could take our problems and dump them in the Gulf?" I laughed. "What's happening inside? I live here and have no clue."

"Grandmother!" he announced, knowing no other explanation was needed. "It's a family get-together, and I told her not to invite Kevin and to stop feeling guilty. He probably wouldn't want to come anyway."

"I don't want you to get caught in the middle."

"Mom's not happy with him either. Hopefully, no more bodies will show up, and that will improve his mood." Liam looked down at my stomach. "Are you hungry?" He reached into the car and grabbed my purse, slipping the strap over my shoulder. He grabbed the last of the bags, and we went inside.

Mother hugged me just inside the door.

"Do I have time for a shower?" I asked.

"Dinner in an hour, and it's a seafood feast."

She saw me looking around the room. "Creole will be here soon."

I kissed her cheek and went upstairs. The house was so sparkly clean, you'd never know it had been inhabited by pigs. I thought about telling her to send everyone outside and not get anything dirty.

My hair felt like it had doubled in size from the off-the-charts humidity. I pulled it back in a twist, and it took two clips to get it to stay in place. I stepped under the waterfall showerhead, resting my head against the tiles and letting the cool water spray over my back. A long shower was one luxury I'd missed while staying on the boat.

The bathroom door opened.

"Who's there?" I demanded.

"A burglar," said a familiar voice.

"Would you go next door? I just came from a funeral." I choked out a dramatic sob.

"I'll make you feel better." The shower door opened, and Creole stepped in, wrapping his arms around me for a long kiss. "That *funeral* comes under the chief's jurisdiction since the almost-buried wrong body came from Miami. The husband has been booked on attempted murder, and more charges will be forthcoming. The chief takes a dim view of people being able to procure bodies for fake funerals. There's sure to be more arrests."

"Enough business talk." I handed him a bar of

soap. "Hopefully, everyone will eat and run."

"You will not voice that sentiment." He shook his finger at me.

* * *

Although the night air was exceedingly warm, Mother and I set the table out by the pool with my seashell dishes. The dinner, as it turned out, was also a business meeting to update the investors in the current real estate project, who were all family members, and bring them up to speed on the next project that Brad and Didier were eager to move on to.

Mother outdid herself, ordering a veritable feast of everyone's favorite seafood. I cornered her and thanked her for the new refrigerator, which was fancier than I would've picked out; I loved it. She said the old one had been beyond disgusting and smelled like someone had died inside. After a couple of phone calls, two men had showed up, put straps around it, and hauled it off to recycle the parts.

After dinner, we gravitated back inside and filled the chairs and couch in the living room.

Before Didier could call the meeting to order, Fab spoke up. "Is this going to take long?" She stuck her legs out on the couch cushions, preventing anyone else from sitting down there.

The glare Didier shot her could have singed her eyebrows off. She sat up and sat primly, hands in her lap, something she must have remembered from her convent school days.

"I was going to wait for Brad but just got a text to continue without him." Didier scowled at his phone screen, not happy that my brother had bailed.

"Where is he?" I asked. *It's so unlike him to be a no-show.*

"He's chasing down a potential property, and the seller is leaving town tomorrow. He wanted to make an offer before it got listed," Didier said. "We've got a signed contract on the apartment building at our asking price. Now we just have a punch list to finish, and once it closes, the checks will be in the mail." He made eye contact with everyone, but no one had any questions, so he went down his list. "Brad and I want to know if you're all in for the next project. Objectors, raise your hand." There were none. "We've got a line on another condo development in Miami."

* * *

After everyone left, Fab grabbed Didier's arm and took a step towards the stairs. He pulled her back into his arms. "Creole wants to talk to you and Madison." He flashed her a "behave" look.

Creole and I were on the daybed, my head in his lap. I looked up. "Are we in trouble?" I asked.

He bent over and brushed my lips with his. "Not this time."

"Make it snappy." Fab fake-yawned.

Didier pulled her down next to him, and she landed with an "oomph."

"Two things: Billy has agreed to stay here and keep an eye on the property until Carbine's murderer is in custody." Creole looked between me and Fab. "Second, I have a favor to ask."

"What you're saying, in a slow way, is that you've got some job that is a freebie. Good for you. What do we get out of it?" Fab demanded.

I looked up at Creole. "I'll do it."

Creole gave me a wolfish smile. "A fellow officer wants me to check up on his sister. He's spoken to her a couple of times since the hurricane, but the conversations were short and vague. Now he can't get ahold of her; phone's turned off. Says she's the kind who wouldn't ask if she needed help."

"Okay, so what haven't you told us about the sister? Felon? Drunk? Drug addict? You know the type." Fab curled her lip.

"Madison, I'd love to partner with you, if you'll let me," Didier offered, sliding away from Fab.

"I'll go," Fab said and flopped into Didier's lap. If he wanted to move now, he'd have to dump her on the floor. "You'd do it if she were local, so she must be out in the weeds. We drive out to nowhere, check to make sure she's okay, have her call her bro, and then leave?" She arched her brow. "You do know it's never that easy?"

"Maybe between the two of you, you can convince her to move back to civilization."

I looked up at Creole. "Or we'll strong-arm her, drop her off at her brother's place, and let him do the convincing."

"People like you. Strangers, weirdos, especially felons..." He played with the ends of my hair.

"What about me?" Fab practically yelled.

I wasn't sure why Fab had taken that comment as a compliment.

I rested my hand on Creole's chest. "Let me." I turned my head toward Fab. "You scare the hell out of people."

Creole and Didier laughed, and Fab rewarded me with a pleased smile at that explanation.

Chapter Fourteen

"Come on, let's get this done." Fab swooped into the living room, snapping her fingers for me to stand up. "I'm taking over for Didier."

I stood and allowed myself to be dragged out the front door. It had rained all night, leaving the plants and trees glowing green. A faint dampness on the concrete sparkled under the morning sunshine. "I knew you wouldn't let Didier go off and have all the fun."

"These stupid jobs always go south," Fab said, pulling out onto the Overseas. "I would never risk him getting hurt."

I made kissy noises as I stared out the window, not wanting to miss the breathtaking view of the blue-green water that ran alongside the highway. "We could pretend this is a friendly visit to someone we actually know. If she looks receptive, we offer a little friendly advice; if not, a quick reminder to call her brother, and we're out of there."

"You dispense the advice; I'll nod and pretend to listen."

I snorted.

"Do you have to make those dreadful noises?"

"Rich-girl snooty voice" was making an appearance. For Fab's entertainment, I made several of my best animal noises, not sure I got the chicken right, but I figured she wouldn't ask what the heck they were supposed to be.

"What if…" I tapped my finger against my cheek. "The house fell down, and Ms. Ramona is dead under the rubble? Or she blew down the block? Probably not, since her brother has spoken to her since the hurricane."

"I've never liked your what-ifs. They're gruesome. If we get a whiff of a body, we're driving away and not getting involved. We'll call Creole and dump it in his lap. They're all cops; they'll know what to do." Fab veered off the highway. "I'm getting good at finding these out-of-the-way places. Good thing, since I hate GPS. Almost threw it out the window when that irritating woman told me to turn around, that I had missed the turn, which was her fault, waiting until the last minute."

It didn't take long to realize that the area had been hard-hit by the hurricane. There were a few lots with hollowed out houses left standing, others only a stretch of green, with nothing remaining but a parking pad. It would have been a ghost town except for the one house and mobile home that remained. I wondered what I'd feel if mine were the only house left standing—gratitude, followed by survivor's guilt and a little creeped out.

"It probably used to be lush and woodsy out here," I said as Fab turned on a road that was once tree-lined, the storm leaving them toppled and scattered, with stumps as the only reminder in some cases. "Too desolate for me." I scooted up in my seat, looking out the window. "If it's still here, we're looking for a yellow house, turquoise hurricane shutters; I didn't see any mailboxes on the last two properties we passed."

"We're running out of paved road," Fab grouched. "What do people have against pavement?"

"Discourages unwanted visitors. Most won't go driving down unmarked streets."

"So does a gun." Fab made a U-turn at the end of the road.

"You can't shoot everything, you know." Since Fab's head was wagging side to side, I assumed she didn't agree. "Go slow." I pointed to a mailbox at the end of the road. "That's it." The last name had been carved into the post, which leaned precariously.

Fab backed up, and we sat there and stared. "Was that the house?" Fab pointed to a pile of yellow-painted wooden debris. The only structure was a shed at the back of the property. "I thought Creole said the brother had talked to his sister since the hurricane."

"Ramona apparently wasn't forthcoming with the truth."

"Who?"

"Pay attention," I snapped. "Ramona is the name of the woman we're here to check on."

"It's your job to remember the names."

"I didn't hear about this area being hard-hit." Two dogs came out of nowhere; bony and dirty, they ran barking towards the SUV. "Someone evacuated and didn't take their dogs?" I whimpered at the thought. "And worse, never came back." I'd heard that people didn't think twice about leaving animals behind but had never seen proof until now.

"No you don't." Fab jerked on my arm before I could get the door open. "If they've been out here since the hurricane, they're starving and could bite you. News flash: we don't have any food. And as much as I suck at anything animal-related, even I know snack foods aren't a good idea."

"We could start with water."

"And get your arm bitten off as thanks. I don't think so."

I pulled away from Fab. "Pull in so we can get pictures of the debris. It was obviously her house." I hadn't understood the meaning of the term "back side of the storm" until witnessing it firsthand. The devastation was far reaching, worse than the pictures on the news had shown.

I got out with a bottle of water, unsure about how I was going to share it between the dogs. They answered my dilemma by running off, tails between their legs.

Inspecting the pile that used to be an old house, judging by the shiplap siding that had once been popular for inexpensive seasonal homes, I saw that there wasn't enough left to construct a whole house, which meant that pieces had blown away.

I left the artist to work in peace, and Fab soon finished her video of the neighborhood and started snapping pictures in a frenzy. Suddenly, pounding sounds caught my attention. I turned and identified them as coming from the shed in the far corner. The racket ceased and was replaced by muffled shouts.

Fab joined me. "That can't be good," she said in a low voice and drew her gun.

"There's no chance that whoever is in there can hear us talking. Let's just go and call 911."

"What if it's Ramona, and she somehow got stuck in there?" Fab said, eyes wide.

"Mother Nature must have a sense of humor, taking the house and leaving behind a crappy shed. Since you're the *professional,* how do you get accidently locked inside when the padlock is outside?"

Whatever she had been about to say, Fab changed her mind, ordered, "Follow me," and flounced across the grass.

"Anyone out there?" a male voice yelled. "Help."

"What's the combination?" Fab shouted.

The man groaned. "My girlfriend must have

it. Please, I don't want to die in here."

Fab walked up to the door and tugged on the lock. "I'll have to shoot this off. Is there room for you to step away from the door?"

"The left side is completely clear; I cleaned it out right after the storm." The panic in his voice was evident.

I pushed Fab's arm down. "Here's the deal: start with your name, then tell us how you got yourself locked in, and we'll let you out," I said. "You better be on your best behavior, or my friend will shoot you. Got it?"

"I'll do anything you say; just let me out. Name's Petrol Handy." Petrol's rising anxiety level came through loud and clear. "I can't breathe."

Fab and I exchanged worried looks. The last thing we needed was a dead stranger.

"Stand back." Fab sent the lock flying with one shot and threw the door open, keeping her gun aimed at him.

Petrol stepped into the sun and blinked, blocking his eyes with his hand, shirtless and reeking, sweat running in rivulets down his chest. "Thanks." He stumbled and leaned against the doorframe. "What do you want to know? I'll answer your questions, and maybe you can call one of my friends, so I can get a ride back to civilization."

I handed Petrol the bottle of water I was holding.

He slid to the ground, resting his head on his knees.

"You need medical attention?" I asked.

Petrol shook his head. "Two days ago, my girlfriend and I came out here to see if there was anything left to salvage and got into a fight. I swear, I thought I'd die in there." He glanced at the shed, shuddering. "We were loading the last of the bottled water, I went in and grabbed the last case, and she slammed the door, locked it, gunned the engine, and squealed off—in my truck." He ended on a high-pitched note, his voice trailing off.

"Does the girlfriend have a name?" Fab demanded. "Maybe it would be best to call the police."

"Ramona Mears. The last thing I want is trouble with the law. I'm finally getting my act together and don't want to derail myself. I really don't want to risk getting blamed for something."

"What did you fight about?" I asked.

"This isn't pretty, but you'll still let me leave?" Desperation laced his voice.

"No matter what happened, it wouldn't be good for Ramona if you died, especially if she's the one that locked you in."

It didn't escape my notice that Fab didn't bother to reassure him that the last thing we wanted was any trouble either. I was ready to leave right then. But judging by Fab's squinty-eyed look, she wanted details. Damn her nosiness.

He threw up his hands. "Okay, I'm a jerk." He stared at the weeds and said, "We fought about my cheating with Peg at the bar. I tried to explain that it was only a hummer and everyone knows that's not cheating. How can she expect me to turn that down? I tried to reassure Ramona that I never did Peg back, not even a kiss."

"Ramona doesn't put out?" Fab demanded.

I coughed and gave her a wide-eyed stare.

"We have a pretty good sex life, except when she goes off her meds. She's been manic lately." He directed the comment to Fab.

I wondered if he thought she was the sensitive, nurturing one of the two of us. *But why spoil the surprise?* Petrol could figure it out for himself.

"Ramona caught me breaking open one of her pills and sprinkling it in her mashed potatoes. She accused me of drugging her. I just wanted the crazy mood swings to stop."

"I've heard enough. Get up." Fab motioned for him to stand and reholstered her gun.

Petrol slowly got to his feet, leaning against the door of the shed.

"Did you live here?" I asked.

He shook his head. "Not officially. We hooked up one night about six months ago, came back here, and you know… Only left when we got in a fight. I didn't even have a drawer; kept my stuff in grocery bags on the floor. I have a one-room hole above a strip mall in town. Hope that didn't get carried away, or I'm screwed."

"Any idea where Ramona went?" Fab asked.

"After the storm, we stayed with a friend of hers in Homestead. Can't believe she left me here to die. I would've once the water ran out. Only had two bottles left; didn't think about rationing it. It was hotter than stink in there; the sweat kept my clothes plastered to my body." He shuddered. "The few tools inside were worthless; didn't make a dent in getting the metal door open."

Petrol swayed, and Fab grabbed his arm before he fell sideways to the ground, her other hand in the middle of his chest. She withdrew the car keys from her pocket. "Catch," she said, tossing them at me.

It always surprised me when I caught flying objects.

"Bring the SUV closer," Fab directed. "We can't leave him here."

The fact that she was letting me drive meant she didn't think leaving Petrol alone was a good idea. He didn't look strong enough to be a threat to either of us. I assessed him as another dumb man who had let his lower friend make bad decisions and chose an unstable woman to hook up with.

I shot across the weeds in the SUV, which earned me a glare from Fab, and pulled up next to her and Petrol.

Fab helped him into the passenger seat and climbed in the back. "You make any stupid moves, and I'll shoot you." She pulled up the front of her shirt, flashing her handgun.

Petrol didn't notice; he was leaning against the window. I smiled in the rearview mirror, then asked Petrol, "Where do you want to go?"

"Home." He gave the address.

"Do you have hurricane supplies at home?" I asked. "You really should go to a clinic or something for a checkup."

"If the building is still standing, I got plenty of canned goods and water. Can I ask what you two were doing at the house…property, I guess?"

"Ramona's brother wanted us to check to make sure she was okay. He hasn't been able to get ahold of her for the last few days and was worried," Fab informed him.

"They butted heads a lot. He's overprotective, and she's not a listener; hates being told what to do. She didn't like to talk about him." Petrol sat silently, looking out the window. "I don't want any trouble, but you tell that brother of hers that she stole my truck, phone, and wallet, and if I don't get them back in the next couple of days, I am going to file a police report. I'm an asshole, but I told her that before we hooked up. Leaving me to die over a hummer is too much. You could motivate the brother by telling him that, by the time I'm done with my side of the story, it could land her in the psych ward."

Fab tugged on my hair. "Drop him off at his place. Petrol—" she turned to him. "—give us the name and address of Ramona's friend's place in Homestead. We'll get the truck back to you tomorrow if it's at that address. If not, we might need an extra day. And you keep your mouth shut. Deal? We'll supply you with a phone and some cash, and I'll give you a number you can call if you need anything. She'll call back." Fab pointed at me.

It had been Fab's idea to leave an extra phone in the glove box, which saved us a trip to civilization, and we pooled our cash, giving him a healthy sum to buy his silence until we got in touch with Creole and made Petrol *his* problem.

* * *

Arriving at the address Petrol gave us, I didn't hold out much hope for his apartment to be in any kind of livable condition. The storefront windows facing the street had been blown out, and glass lay everywhere; nobody had made an attempt at cleanup. It had been a ratty building to begin with but managed to stay standing. We drove around the back. The rentals were on the second floor. A few had boarded-up windows, but that didn't seem to bother the people hanging over the balcony or sitting in chairs they'd dragged out. With no electricity, I imagined the rooms to be insufferable little hellholes.

I questioned Petrol about the dogs and found out that they had lived next door. Ramona hated animals and didn't care what happened to them. The owners of the property had fled soon after getting the evacuation order and left the dogs behind. I thought that people who did that should be arrested. I'd bet they'd go and get another pet too, even though they were unfit.

While Fab dealt with Petrol, I called a friend at a local-ish animal rescue. I could swear the woman at the shelter groaned when I identified myself. In all fairness, I never called to say, "How are you?" But I also hit up friends for donations to keep the no-kill shelters in business.

She laughed when I told her I thought there were only two dogs and told me that she herself had patrolled the streets of the area I was talking about and that Animal Control had patrolled the streets, searching hard-hit areas for the first few days after the storm, but had stopped, since the rescue places were filled beyond capacity and they had no place to house them.

Rather than go down my list of other rescue places and listen to more heart-wrenching stories, I hit the number for Billy's friend, Nancy, who'd helped out with rescued animals in the past as a favor.

Nancy answered on the first ring, but when I told her why I was calling, she started to cry and told me her small house had suffered extensive water damage and she'd been living in her car with several animals.

"It's the only possession I have that my ex-husband couldn't get his hands on to gamble away. He was livid when he found out the title had never been transferred out of my grandmother's name." She sighed loudly.

"We can help each other," I told the sniffling woman. "I'm certain I can get you a motorhome that you can use—park it right there on your property while repairs are being made."

She started to protest that she had no money; she was still waiting on an insurance check. I cut her off and told her not worry, reminding her that we'd be helping each other.

"Billy called you a dynamo, and I can see why," Nancy said.

As if being suddenly homeless wasn't bad enough, I found out that she didn't have a job; the restaurant where she worked wouldn't be reopening any time soon due to damage. I admired her grit and that she hadn't caved under the pressure of so much loss. I ended the call, telling her I'd be calling back shortly.

Fab slid behind the wheel and quirked her brow just as Spoon answered his phone. "I've got several favors to ask," I said.

"When do I ever say no?" he growled.

"One of these times, you're going to wish you knew the favor before agreeing." I smiled at the phone. I knew he'd help with anything I asked and was careful not to take advantage or make him feel unappreciated. "Do you happen to have a motorhome sitting around that could be borrowed for a few weeks—maybe months?"

Fab rolled her eyes and laughed. She pointed to the phone, and I responded by hitting the speaker button. Eager to leave Petrol's, she had the SUV in gear before the door shut.

After a long pause, he asked, "Where am I going to get one of those?"

"You got a school bus once; a motorhome should be a piece of cake. Did I mention I need it today?" I hurriedly reminded him about Nancy and how she'd helped out on his last job and added that, in addition to being a friend of Billy's, she'd been displaced by the hurricane and needed help pronto.

He made a few undistinguishable noises. "I'm thinking… I just made an executive decision to push this off on Billy. She is, after all, his friend, so he can coordinate everything. I'm not sure what I can get over to her place today, but it will be something habitable. Anything else?"

I told him about the dogs and that the stores hadn't reopened, so he would need to send someone north to Homestead for food and asked, if the dogs couldn't be relocated, if Billy would leave kibble and water. "If Billy gets tired of helping me, let me know, and I'll put Fab on it."

Fab hit me in the arm.

"Don't you worry about Billy." He hung up, laughing.

I laid my head back against the seat and closed my eyes. "Petrol happy?"

"Not for long. He wants his truck now. Can't say that I blame him." Fab tugged on a strand of my hair. "There's aspirin in the console."

"I'd rather have a strawberry lemonade. Sometimes an injection of sugar makes it go away…at least until I come down from being high."

"Or I can take your mind off the pain by interesting you in an immediate repossession of Petrol's truck. Get it over with, and hopefully we won't run into anyone."

"There's a flaw in your plan, my friend." I reclined my seat back, thinking about putting my feet on the dashboard for the sheer enjoyment of annoying of Fab. Reconsidering, I put it on a mental list to do another time. "Petrol is going to want his keys. Getting his truck back and not being able to start it might irritate him even more; even if he knows how to hotwire it, it might motivate him to call the cops."

"Did you call Creole?"

I shook my head. "Once again, I haven't called in a timely fashion. He'll be annoyed, and I haven't come up with a good excuse—yet."

If Fab had had the room, her hands would have been on her hips; her chin did jut out. "You tell him you were helping an old lady get a home and making sure some dogs got food." She glared over at me. "You don't need to make up anything."

I took my phone from her outstretched hand, texting Creole, "Call at your convenience," and flashed Fab a lame smile. "You dealt with Petrol, and I got a pass."

"My never-ending curiosity." She shuddered. "Those so-called apartments should have blown down, but then there would be more people without a place to live. Whoever owns that is a slumlord."

My phone rang, and I held it up to look at the screen. "It's Creole." I answered and gave him the details about what went down and what we needed—and before tomorrow, but today would be better, in case Petrol changed his mind about playing nice.

"Why do I think there's more to this story?" Creole asked.

Even over the phone, he knew me so well. "Lots of devastation to take in."

"I'm going to make this up to you. Next night off, we'll get Roscoe burgers, and I'll give you a back rub."

"And french fries."

"Of course." Creole growly-laughed, knowing that it made my toes tingle. I should have kept that tidbit to myself, but it slipped out one night. "Text me the address in Homestead. I'll call you back."

"He's not happy," I told Fab. "But he's not mad at us. When I mentioned 'off her meds,' I could hear him struggling to control his temper."

My phone beeped, and a text from Billy popped up. "Taken care of. Will call when job is done."

"I knew you'd find a home for those dogs," Fab teased.

We were almost to Tarpon Cove when Creole called back. "You two can go home. Ramona wouldn't answer her phone; let it go to voicemail. I made it clear to Mike that if his sister continues to play games, she's on her own. This will be your last involvement in this drama. The truck will be delivered to Petrol in a few hours." He sighed. "I suppose I can agree to go to a black-tie dinner to make it up to your accomplice."

"Nothing so drastic."

I loved that he blew a kiss through the phone before hanging up.

"We're done for the day." It figured that Creole had told his friend, 'You take care of your sister.' I did wonder whether, if questioned, the brother would admit to the omission of a fact or two. "I'm glad we're out of it. Someone else is delivering the truck. I didn't ask for details; I wouldn't get them anyway." I grinned at her. "I didn't get to the good part: how you handled Petrol and what a star you were the whole time. But I'll be boasting later."

"Can you heap the praise on in front of Didier?" Fab asked, her tone changing to one of melancholy. "It was cold on my side of the bed last night."

"Skipping a night builds character," I managed to say with a straight face.

"Whoever said that wasn't having sex. Or not good sex, anyway."

Chapter Fifteen

Fab and I walked into the house to find Didier in a full-blown snit—directed at Brad, who wasn't there. The island was covered with a jumble of paperwork.

"Does your brother usually go out fishing with no notice?" he demanded.

Fab moved behind Didier, rubbing his shoulders.

I thought a moment, then shook my head. "What happened?"

Brad ran a highly successful commercial fishing business. He had recently turned the reigns of the day-to-day operations over to another man so that he and Didier could chase real estate deals.

"We had a meeting this morning, but Brad texted that one of his men had called in sick and he needed to fill in." Didier hit the counter with his fist. "It was unprofessional to have to make a vague excuse for my partner, but it's not like could say, 'sorry, he has more important priorities.'"

I understood Didier's frustration, but it was so

unlike my brother that it had to have been truly a last-minute emergency with no other options. "That's odd. If it were just one fisherman, he could have his pick from the ones that hang around to sign on in place of a last-minute no-show. Must have been the new captain. Did Brad say how long he'd be gone?"

Didier shook his head. "Now his phone has been shut off."

"Were you able to save the meeting?" I asked.

"Of course," he said, flashing his confident, self-assured smile, as if to say, *Did you expect anything less?*

Once Brad and Julie got serious, he didn't want to be out of town as much, hence the new guy, and before that, he'd cut his trips short so that he wasn't gone longer than a week. I was relieved to see that Didier's anger had abated. "When he gets back, kick his ass." There was no smile, no reprimand for what he constantly referred to as bad language.

Fab wrapped her arms around his neck, whispering in French. Didier stood, she grasped his hand, and they headed out of the kitchen. Didier said something, and Fab turned back to me. "We'll get our own dinner." She flashed a smirky wink, and they went upstairs.

I followed slowly, hanging out at the bottom of the steps until I heard the bedroom door close. Then I raced up the stairs and into my bedroom, changing into a two-piece turquoise tankini in record time, and grabbing a book and my beach bag to spend time by the pool.

Chapter Sixteen

The next day, Mac called to remind me that Grandmother Campion had arrived and that she had planned a "Welcome to the Neighborhood" party for the woman.

Why, when I had do-nothing plans for the day, did something always come up to derail my plans? Party time at The Cottages had me conjuring images of flashing lights, handcuffs, and the requisite drunk passed out cold by the pool. I dragged my feet into the bathroom and under the large showerhead.

Toweling off, I stared into my closet and laughed—deciding what to wear to the *party*. Hopefully, Mac had spread the word that clothing was *not* optional. I pulled a colorful full skirt off the hangar and stepped into it, followed by a sleeveless top that I could wear untucked, covering my handgun, and chose sparkly flip-flops.

It took a half-second to locate Fab, lying on the couch with Jazz at her side and Snow on her feet. Her eyes were closed, but I knew damn well that even if she'd been asleep when I got to the top of the stairs, she wasn't now that I'd hit the bottom step. The woman could hear a leaf drop to the ground. I reached for Jazz, and her arms tightened around him. "He's sleeping."

"How was your dinner with Didier?"

Fab opened her eyes. "What do you want?"

"Your tone is less than nice." I tsked. "I've been invited to a party. Do you want to be my date?"

"I got the same invitation as you and declined. Mac sent back a smiley face. There's something wrong with her."

Jazz jumped down, letting out a loud meow, and stalked off to the kitchen. It didn't take long for Snow to follow.

"There goes your fan club." I tried not to laugh and dropped down next to her in the newly vacated space.

"I suppose I'll go."

I never doubted it.

* * *

"Promise me we're not staying long." Fab slid into the driveway of The Cottages, parking in front of the office.

"If you see anyone you don't know, suggest they get the heck off the property for their own health. You know, in a nice way."

The lure of the fifty-year-old barbeque and the smoke it was emitting had several people milling around Joseph's door. One woman, who I identified as Drunken Sally, disappeared around the corner when the SUV pulled in. Reports of her demise appeared to be inaccurate. She was a longtime friend of Miss January, and if I had my way, I'd forbid them any more adventures.

"Who okayed this stupid party idea?" Fab asked in disgust.

"Mac's standing at the rear bumper; why don't you ask her?" I looked in the side mirror before getting out. I didn't say a word to Mac, glaring at her.

"This is the best I could come up with last-minute, and it's your fault," Mac snapped. "I could've hired a fake gun fight, or swords sounded fun, but you nixed that idea—'someone might get hurt.' The entertainment would've been over in five minutes." She brushed her hands together. "Everyone in bed early and satisfied."

"You know damn well that such entertainment was banned by Creole. Do you have a go-to-jail wish? That's what would have happened if someone had gotten stabbed, and the gunfight idea is an even faster way to get incarcerated." I wagged my finger at her. "I know Creole paid you a personal visit to explain the new policy. Don't deny it."

"Creole's so sweet." Mac sighed.

"You'll find out how sweet he is if he has to come back here and explain the same thing again." I renewed my glare and didn't break eye contact. "Let me make this clear: you have your own boyfriend; you make googly eyes over mine, and I'll jerk out your bouffant do."

"We broke up. If you can call it that, since we were only banging." Mac's hands shot to her hips, boobs out. Today's t-shirt proclaimed: "Surprise, I'm drunk." She'd paired it with a large, blue, above-the-knee gingham check skirt and pink-and-lime flip-flops that tied on with ribbons up her calves.

"Are you okay?" I asked.

"Billy gave me the shot of confidence that I needed. I'm on the market." She thrust her chest out even farther. "I also got the satisfaction of telling his ass to hit the road. Too much baggage for me."

"I'll let Mother know; she'll have you hooked up in no time." There wasn't anything Mother liked more than meddling in a person's love life.

"At least you showed up," Mac said. "I'm going to need help. Once the word 'party' hits the street, you know it brings out the folks."

"Listen up, you two: neither of you is to shoot anyone. Got it?" I left them at the bumper and headed to the office. I hadn't even gotten my fingers around the doorknob when a gunshot rang out from inside. In an instant, Fab was at my side. Both our guns drawn, she kicked the door open.

An older woman I'd never seen before had made herself comfortable in Mac's chair behind the desk. She was wearing an expensive designer workout outfit of black-and-purple ankle-length running pants and a lightweight black crew shirt, her lavender tennis shoes shoved up against the edge of the desk drawer. Catching sight of the two guns pointed at her, she dropped hers on the blotter.

"Don't move," I shouted. My eyes traveled to the new hole in the wall above the window. "Who are you and what the hell did you do?"

Mac, who had hung back, was the last to burst through the door. "Someone get shot?" she asked, out of breath.

"They're about to." I glared at the older woman.

"It was a big cockroach, really long." The woman feigned fright and held out her hands to indicate a medium-sized dog.

Fab climbed up on the couch, inspected the hole in the drywall, and ran her hand down the wall, then held up a big piece of black animal fur. "Is this your cockroach?"

I didn't know whether to laugh or strangle the woman and reluctantly took a more professional attitude. "We have rules in this office, one in particular being that we do not waste ammo on bugs *or* cat hair." I stared Mac down, daring her to contradict me. "Call the sheriff."

The woman's eyes narrowed on me. "I'll just call my lawyer."

Mac stepped around me. "Let me make the

introductions." She nodded in the woman's direction. "Maricruz Campion. This is the *owner,* Madison Westin."

Fab relieved the woman of her gun, swiftly emptying the bullets into her hand. "Shoot away," she said and handed it back.

"That was impressive." Maricruz appeared awe-struck. "You can call me Mrs. Campion," she said haughtily.

One more for Fab's growing group of women crushes.

Fab checked the woman out from head to toe, smiling broadly. "You weren't what we were expecting. Does Cruz know you carry?"

Cruz was apparently named after his granny, another thing he'd failed to mention, to me at any rate. Cruz had made her sound like she stepped out of a children's story, complete with sugar cookies in the pocket of a smock covering a dumpy dress. Instead, she was pretty damn well preserved, and I'd guess at a mojito in her pocket before I'd think cookies. Apparently, Grandma had a whole side that Cruz had never seen before; either that, or he'd decided to surprise me.

"It's a new hobby." She sniffed. "Another checkmark on my bucket list. A woman of my years has to live in the moment."

"Where did you get the gun?" I asked, trying to suppress the thought that I wouldn't like the answer. "And where's your carry permit? It will be the first question the sheriff asks if one of the neighbors called 911."

Maricruz didn't acknowledge that I was the one talking, instead focusing on Fab. "I was headed to a pawn shop, but then got word that a friend of a friend had this one for sale."

This was one of those moments that it surprised me I didn't have ulcers.

Fab, one step ahead of me, reconsidered her decision to give Grandma's gun back and confiscated it instead. "You're smart enough to know that if you want a gun, you buy it new from a gun store. If this was used in a crime—" she held up the baby Glock. "—you're going to need the services of your grandson, who might not be able to keep you out of jail, even with his superstar talents."

"Another rule—no firearms on the property." I returned Grandma's scowl, always pleased with myself when I made up a plausible last-minute lie. "Mac here has activities planned for you; I'm sure you won't be missing your gun." I nudged Mac's leg.

Mac, who had stood by the door the whole time, got a folding chair out of the opposite corner, snapped it open, and plopped down. "Tonight—there's a pool party and barbeque to introduce you around."

Maricruz didn't bother to hide the fact that Mac's plans didn't impress her. "Open bar? If not, where's the nearest liquor store? I'm a fan of whiskey neat. In fact, I'll have one now."

I needed to assign her a keeper. Cruz hadn't actually said anything about trouble, probably figuring I'd pick up on that red flag, but he did say that nothing better happen to his dear grandma.

Fab sat on the couch and stretched out, not bored for a change and thoroughly amused by our newest guest, judging by the huge grin on her face. "I'll drive you," she offered.

If looks could kill, the one I leveled at Fab should, at the very least, have pitched her to the floor and made her roll around.

The door flew open and came within a hair's breadth of hitting the wall. Crum filled the doorway, shirtless and sporting two pairs of boxer shorts turned backwards, with mismatched knee-high garden boots completing his ensemble, his bushy white hair standing on end.

"Ladies," he said, stepping into the already crowded office. "I need the keys to the shed. It's gardening day." He flexed his muscles.

Mac moved around the desk and asked Maricruz, "Would you move your feet?" She flicked her hand in the direction of the designer tennis shoes.

She was wearing several hundred dollars in running attire, and it made me wonder if it was all show or if she'd actually taken up the sport.

Maricruz apparently didn't hear a word; her

attention was on Crum. "We haven't been introduced." She stood and held out her hand.

Crum made a sweeping bow, taking her hand in his and running his lips across her knuckles. "Mr. Crum at your service. Anything you need during your stay, I'm in number two."

"Call me Maricruz. No need for formality." She blushed and fluttered her eyelashes.

I refrained from making the retching noise that was eager to erupt, nodding at Mac to hurry up. Mac retrieved the keys, called, "Catch," and tossed them at Crum, breaking up the uncomfortable moment. She headed in his direction, affixed her hand to the middle of Crum's back, and pushed him out the door, closing it behind him.

"He's hot," Maricruz gushed, continuing to stare at the place where Crum had stood.

I needed two aspirin…or a margarita, and I'd rather have the later. Never one to be a coward, just this once, I wanted to slip out the door and go home.

No one had said a word. Fab stood, looking at Maricruz. "Liquor store's not far; we can go get your whiskey now. We—" Fab motioned to me. "—have an appointment this afternoon."

I flashed her a limp smile. "I'll wait here. I've got some business to go over with Mac."

Mac raised her eyebrow but didn't say anything. From her commiserating glance, she knew I was looking for any excuse to stay put.

She also knew she was so efficient that when something did come up, we handled it over the phone.

Maricruz crossed to Fab, patting her on the cheek. "I liked you from the start."

Fab shepherded her outside. Mac managed to close the door without a bang. I moved to the couch and lay down, closing my eyes.

Mac rounded her desk, sitting down. "I don't have a good feeling about that woman. Can you say 'trouble'? Cruz had the nerve to pass her off as some sweet old grandma, as though she was that old woman who had kids hanging out of the windows of that shoe."

"You can't take your eyes off Mrs. Campion." This was going to be the longest week ever. "She *cannot* get into any trouble. Keep her away from Crum; he's like a dog in heat." To hell with the bet. I should call Cruz right now and demand that he pick her up. My radar had set off an annoying buzzing in my head, which didn't quiet when Mac agreed with me; *she* handled people like Maricruz every day.

"How am I supposed to do that?" Mac kicked her foot up on the desktop and then groaned because she'd hit her heel, forgetting that she'd opted out of a more substantial shoe for the day.

I winced, but she appeared to take it in stride. "Hire Liam and Shirl—between the three of you, you should be able to shadow one old woman." I closed my eyes again. "Pool party?" I shuddered.

"Where were your ideas?" She snorted, making a show of kicking at the notepad on her desk. "Last-minute plans also take time to implement, even for a friendly get together. The kook-nuts from the neighborhood expect food and punch, and I didn't plan on liquor and beer, knowing that most would show up drunk. Do I get credit for hiring a lifeguard on the likely chance that someone falls in the pool? I checked with the insurance company, and we do have liability issues if we're throwing the shindig. I passed myself off as you in the phone call; I'd appreciate you not ratting me out, since it's a crime."

"I know I don't say thank you often enough—thank you." I quirked one eye open. "Meeting called to order."

Mac laughed.

"Tell me Rocks packed his bags and left." I rolled onto my side, facing her.

"He's still here but keeping a low profile. Never around during the day, sneaks in and out late at night. Good news: the shooter hasn't been back."

"Put an eviction notice on his door."

"Can't." Mac settled back in her chair, wadding her skirt up and sticking it between her legs. "Rocks is paid up until the end of the month. I could have Billy talk to him and, as an incentive, offer a refund. I think he enjoys scaring the hell out of people."

"Under no circumstances is Rocks to turn up dead."

Mac humphed.

I jerked when my phone rang. Recognizing the ringtone, I pulled it out of my pocket.

"Maricruz gave me the slip," Fab said as soon as I answered.

It took a moment for her words to sink in. Then I yelled, "What are you talking about?"

"She picked out some cheap, rotgut whiskey, set it on the counter, and went to the bathroom. After five minutes, certain she'd died and I'd be blamed, I searched under the stall doors, only to figure out that she'd slipped out the back door and disappeared." Fab emitted a strangled noise. "No one admits to having seen anything."

"You can't keep track of one old woman?" I struggled to lower my voice. "We've got find her."

"Why?" Fab sounded as though she'd given the question some thought. "We're not her jailers. She's not senile; she can come back on her own."

"Come and get me." I sighed.

"I just pulled into the driveway. Get your butt out here." Fab honked.

Mac stood and flounced to the door. "What about the party?" She preceded me out the door and headed to the driver's side, to get an update, I presumed.

I crossed to the passenger side, got in, and

leaned across the seat. "I don't care about the party. Go ahead with the barbeque for the tenants and guests; discourage troublemakers."

"Who's going to call Cruz?" Fab asked.

Fab and I stared at Mac.

"Fine. And I get a raise. But first, I say we don't borrow trouble unless she doesn't show back up in a couple of hours."

Chapter Seventeen

Didier—in well-fitting jeans and a t-shirt that hugged his biceps, his dark hair slightly messy—handed me a mug of coffee when I walked into the kitchen. No wonder Mother snuck over to my house for her morning cup of brew. The one person missing had slipped out early, leaving me with a kiss that promised there would be more later.

I sniffed the coffee's aroma to make sure it wasn't one of his "full-bodied" blends, which smelled like tar and probably tasted the same way. It earned me a masculine growl.

"You made me a cup of my favorite." I beamed at him.

"I suggested that he encourage you to broaden your palette, try something new," Fab said arrogantly. "He ignored me."

"Mornings are not the time to try anything *new,* and I'm not sure what time of day is; same old works for me." I kissed Didier's cheek. "Thank you for not listening to your girlfriend."

Through traded texts the night before, Mac

had assured us the pool party was a tame affair. The text that had me breathing a huge sigh said, "Grandma just dragged her ass in the driveway."

I'd dreamed about my brother, and there was something elusive about it that I wanted to pull back into my consciousness so I could remember the details. The harder I tried, though, the farther away it got, dangling just out of my reach. Snippets of Fab and Didier's plans for the day invaded my thoughts; he had another meeting and was not happy that his partner would be a no-show.

"My brother's not a jerk," I said out loud, which wasn't my intention.

"Cherie," Didier said softly, stepping around the island and enveloping me in a reassuring hug. "Of course he's not. Do not think for one minute that I have a low opinion of Brad because of a last-minute fishing trip."

"Did you miss a call from him; is that why he texted you?"

"No calls, which surprised me." Didier picked up my mug. "Another?" He raised an eyebrow.

I shook my head. "Must have been one heck of an emergency. I hope no one got hurt. But surely if that had happened, we'd have heard by now. When he docks, we'll both tell him phone calls only in future so we don't worry. And for my part, I'll include a threat; I can't kick his ass, but I can whine to Mother."

Didier smiled down at me. "If I had a sister,

I'd hope we'd be as close as you two. It's nice to see."

I stretched my fingers out, reaching for my cell phone, but was a smidge short. Fab flicked it in my direction. I texted Liam, "Talk to Brad?"

It didn't take long to get back an answer. "He texted Mom—went fishing." I read it aloud. Then I called Brad, and it went straight to voicemail. "Not back yet," I told Fab and Didier.

It was then that I noticed Fab had on a black sleeveless sundress accented by a few of her favorite pieces of silver jewelry. Her hair had just the right amount of "Hey, I'm sexy" look. Since it appeared that the hot couple had plans, I could stay in my sweats and Creole's t-shirt a little longer.

Fab scrutinized me with an intensity that made me want to cross my index fingers in front of my face to ward off her snooping through my thoughts, which would leave any sane person feeling uneasy.

"You owe me," Fab announced, her eyes sparkling with amusement.

I looked over my shoulder. Didier laughed. The French doors were open, and the patio wasn't that far away. I pushed my stool back.

"You know I'm speaking to you." Fab didn't take her eyes off me. "Don't even think about running; I'll send Didier to fetch you back."

Didier held up his hands. "I'm not getting involved, except maybe to help Madison make a clean getaway."

Fab snapped a few French words at Didier, and he responded with a laugh and a look of innocence.

I took my mug to the sink, leaning over to scope out the driveway. "All clear outside, but it's early yet. Billy is the best guard; you never see him, but you know he's watching."

"I'm certain you wouldn't want me to embarrass you by producing my twenty-five-page list of favors owed. We're going to lunch—no flip-flops but casual dressy."

Just for the heck of it, I should demand said list, knowing that one doesn't exist.

"You're on." I enjoyed the surprised look on her face; she hadn't expected me to give in so easily. "See you tonight." I patted Didier's shoulder as I went by on my way upstairs.

* * *

Fab checked me over so thoroughly as I came down the stairs that I expected her to demand that I open my mouth so she could inspect my teeth.

"I was beginning to think you might need help picking something out, but you managed on your own." Fab nodded her approval.

I twirled around the living room in a spaghetti-strap sea-blue dress. I lifted my foot, sticking my low-heeled tan leather slide in Fab's direction. "Do these meet your approval?"

Fab nodded again, crossing into the entry and picking up a duffle bag that sat on the bench.

I flashed her a questioning look.

"This is a change of clothing and two pairs of shoes for those 'just in case' moments we seem to have a lot of lately."

I grabbed two pairs of plain flip-flops from the newly acquired copper boot tray. The ones in the car disappeared regularly, but my tennis shoes were left untouched. I suspected it happened on trash day when my back was turned. I followed Fab and noticed what I'd missed earlier: that the back of her dress had crisscrossed straps that showed a flash of skin.

When Fab turned north on the Overseas, leaving the city limits of Tarpon Cove behind, all hope of lunch in The Keys was dashed. "I'm afraid to ask where we're going."

"Ft. Lauderdale. Since you seem to have Brad on your mind, I thought we'd check out the docks, ask a few questions, and then you don't have to pretend that you're not worried."

I wanted to hug her, but it wasn't feasible. "And you thought this friend *thing* would never work out." I beamed. When we first met, she'd informed me that she didn't have friends and didn't want any.

My phone rang, and Fab rolled her eyes. "Hi honey," I answered, recognizing the ringtone.

"I'm sure it was an oversight that you didn't

text me where you're going," Creole growled.

I smiled stupidly at his face on my phone screen. "I don't know exactly. Fab's taking me out for a girl lunch. No business today."

"You be careful; it might be a trick." He half-laughed.

"You packing?" I asked Fab. From her look of disgust, I deduced that the answer was yes. "Two girls, two guns," I said into the phone.

"That would bother most boyfriends, but not me."

"When can I expect another late-night visit?"

"What was that noise?"

"Fab gagging." I shook my head at her, pinching my cheeks together to stop myself from laughing; Creole wouldn't appreciate knowing I found her antics funny…well, sometimes.

"Tonight. You tell her that by the time I'm done telling Didier on her, she'll be explaining her poor behavior to an irate Frenchman."

"I don't think that will turn out quite like you hope." I laughed, images of jungle sex flashed before my eyes. "Can't wait for later." I made a kissy noise.

He gave a long smoochy one in return.

Fab cruised up the highway, taking one of the exits toward Ft. Lauderdale. I continued to relax back in my seat; we were caught up in slow-moving traffic, and it didn't appear that it would let up anytime soon. Thinking back, I realized it had been a long time since I'd been down to the docks. Not telling anyone what was going on, except by text, was a huge lapse on Brad's part, and I was just happy that Mother wasn't involved. I felt a tad guilty for not keeping a better eye on my brother; I'd be informing him no more out-of-town trips without telling me first. If he complained, I'd explain about brotherly duty. Last resort was the threat of telling Mother that he must be up to something if he was being surly about my snooping. That would make him laugh; we honored the brother/sister code and never told on each other—ever. Trying to plead ignorance with Mother sometimes got us in more trouble than telling would have, but we never caved.

Fab had to circle the block a couple of times near where Brad parked his boat. Finally, the man in the parking shack removed the old chair with a "full" sign tied around it and shoved it out of the way.

I knew a shortcut that offered free on-street parking. But the path led under a freeway overpass and had an extremely creepy vibe. In the past, I'd witnessed more than one illegal transaction take place there, and I no longer minded putting out for overpriced parking.

Fab shot down the first aisle, ignoring the man, who was waving her to the last row, which had an open space in the middle. Since my brother had left early, he'd have had his pick of spaces and would have parked next to the entrance. But I didn't see his truck anywhere.

"Drive the aisles." I pulled my lockpick out of my purse. "Just in case the dock gate is locked." Fab turned back toward the front, giving me a view of the dock. "Brad's back; his boat's in its slip." I pointed, taking my phone out as Fab pulled into a newly vacated space. "Voicemail." I double-checked the screen to make sure I'd called the right number. "His phone could be dead; probably charging."

"So…he docked, but he's not here…" Fab murmured.

"I'll walk down. Someone will be able to tell me what time he docked and when he left." I kicked off my heels and slid my feet into a pair of flip-flops.

"I'm coming." Fab traded her heels for tennis shoes.

The gate was open and tied to a post, and at least one boat was making preparations to pull out. Two men hauled supplies up and down the dock to a large commercial boat parked at the very end.

I waved to the men and pointed to my brother's boat. "Do you know when they docked?"

"A few days ago. They cleaned up, and I haven't seen anyone around since," the blond one said.

"What about the owner, Brad Westin?" Fab asked.

"Since he hired the new guy, I haven't seen him around in a while," the same man answered. His friend nodded.

Fab thanked them. They reluctantly stopped checking her out and went back to work.

"What's going on?" I stood at the bow of the boat, staring, unsure what I was looking for, then walked the dock from one end to the other. All the boats parked nearby were fishing boats. It was afternoon, and they were locked up with no one in sight. I climbed aboard Brad's boat, and it was locked up too. I knew that if Brad were aboard, he wouldn't lock himself inside.

"Get back down here." Fab waved. "Brad's not here. We'll go back to the car and make a few calls. Apparently, you haven't noticed it smells."

"It's fish guts and probably more than a few dead ones." I held my breath and jumped down, landing on my feet. The image of Mother came to mind, wagging her finger and saying, "Just because she jumps off stuff—" pointing to Fab. "—doesn't mean that you have to copy her."

"Well done." Fab gave me a thumbs up. She hooked her arm in mine, and we walked back to the SUV.

"The hairs on my neck, the ones that never fail me, and the rock in my stomach are telling me I need to find my brother. Pronto. He's never been a flake; he wouldn't just lie about where he was going and disappear. He'd never worry Mother."

"I do know Brad. He wouldn't worry you

either. We'll find him," Fab reassured me. Undeterred by my desire to stand and stare at the docks, she shoved me the last few feet to the SUV, opening the passenger door and shooting me a silent dare to see what would happen next if I didn't get in.

Fab sprinted around to the driver side as soon as I'd climbed in. "I'll make a mental list of all the places he could be, starting with Alligator Alley, but I'll put that at the bottom of the list," she said as she slid behind the wheel. "You make calls. Start with the new captain."

"No one finds out that we're searching for Brad." I flashed her a squinty glare. "I don't have the new guy's number. But Brad did have Phil run a background check, called it good business; so she'll have it." I called her number and put her on speaker.

When I told her what I needed, she put me on hold. "I texted you the number," Phil said, after a long pause. "I can put the word out that I want to speak to him."

"Only if you can do it without attracting any attention."

"No worry there. I'll use my lowlife hotline," Phil said. "I hate to bother you, but your new best friend, Maricruz Campion, came in last night, demanding to have her food and liquor comped and swearing you'd pick up the tab. When I handed her the phone and told her I needed verification, she snarled at me. She wiggled herself up and down on a couple of bar rats and snagged a couple of drinks. Next time, she has to pay up front; she ordered dinner, picked at it, and then snuck out without paying. Normally, I'd have her arrested, but I figured locking up Cruz's grandmother wasn't conducive to business."

Fab laughed.

"Make sure I get the check. She'll pay, or I'll have Fab here threaten her. Anything else?" I asked in exasperation.

"It was odd to see an old gal in a white crocheted bikini, ample cleavage on display; she did have a sheer wrap skirt tied around her middle. I didn't get a peek at the shoes. She was on the prowl for someone considerably younger."

I groaned. "Did she, uh…hook up…score… I know: make a nice match?"

"Once the two at the bar realized they weren't getting any sexual favors, they left." Phil laughed. "She made a spectacle of herself on the dance floor both with and without a partner. No takers that I saw. And then she disappeared."

"I'd like to know how she's getting around. It's a long walk from The Cottages. If she shows back up, refuse service; she complains, tell her to call her lawyer." Phil was still laughing when we hung up. "Damn Cruz," I grumbled and called the boat captain.

After I identified myself as Brad Westin's

sister, the call was short. He hadn't talked to my brother and didn't seem worried. He did say that the next fishing trip was scheduled for the end of the week and they always touched base ahead of time and that he'd tell Brad to give me a call.

"It's amazing the information people will give you without asking any questions," Fab commented with disgust when I hung up. "Don't bother telling me you're the nice one; heard that before."

"Since we're this far north, I suggest we detour through Alligator Alley before heading back to the Cove and finishing up there." I leaned down and shoved my hand in my purse, fished around, and pulled out my trusty beach notepad and matching pen, which I'd bought at a tourist store while Fab stood next to me, making her annoyance felt the whole time. "Then we hit The Cottages. Mac knows everything, and I can't fault Joseph's information-gathering. It helps if he's in a cooperative mood, but that can be bought. We'll do a drive-by of the jobsite, but if Brad was there, we'd have gotten a call from Didier. Then check in with the various suspects, and by that time, we'll have found him." I leaned my head back, taking a deep breath, which did zero to calm my nerves.

"You're forgetting a stop—your mother's. We could pick the lock."

My eyebrows went to my hairline. "Mother only likes that trick when it's someone else's doorknob. If Brad were there, that would mean he was sick, and we'd know about it. And he wouldn't lie about that; he'd want a ton of sympathy."

"It surprises even me that I'm the one reminding you of the rules, but the boyfriends aren't going to like being uninformed; especially yours, since ferreting out hard-to-find individuals is his day job." Fab honked at the man in the next lane, signaling she wanted over. It surprised me that she didn't just cut him off. "If we question a lot of people, the chances are high that word will get out."

"We don't have anything to tell them." I did my best to sound optimistic. "Doesn't matter. By the end of the day, we'll have found Brad, and it will all be a big joke. And then I'll beat the hell out of him."

"Have you two ever had a physical fight?" Fab asked.

"I used to jump on his back, hook my legs around his waist, and say mean things. He'd lie on the ground and threaten to squash me if I didn't let go." I laughed at the memories. He could have dumped me in a heap, but never did; he'd had never-ending patience for my plays for attention. "There was one time..." I smiled. "He had the nerve to tell me I'd never make it as a smart-ass. I burst into tears. I boo-hooed to Mother, repeating what he'd said word for word."

"You were even weird as a child." Fab laughed at me. "I can't believe you got him in trouble."

"Mother rarely intervened in our childish squabbles. This time, she had the infinite wisdom to assure me that it was a compliment. It didn't take long before Brad agreed, probably after getting one of those looks. You know: 'you want to get out of your bedroom before age fifty, you better back me up.'"

"My sisters and I were never allowed to roughhouse; we might have gotten dirty. Yelling and fighting were not tolerated." Fab wrinkled her nose. "If you weren't a lady, you were nothing."

"Do you miss France?" I wanted to ask about her family, but she couldn't mask her sadness when the topic came up. So I waited for those rare moments when she wanted to share.

"I used to romanticize a return. All of us together, tears at the reunion, eager to catch-up." She snorted. "Waste of time. If I want mothering, I go to Madeline's house. She gave me my own key, told me I was welcome no matter the hour."

I tried to blink away my tears before Fab could see. That was what I loved about Mother—she had the biggest heart. "What if Spoon comes walking out in his, you know…nothing? Then what?"

"Your mother and I have already had a good laugh about that one. She told me, if I see his truck in the parking lot, to kick the hell out of the door." She winked. "I'm to wait until it opens on its own and I get invited in."

"Or," I said with a devilish smirk, "pick the lock, bang the door closed, and yell, 'Put your clothes on; you've got company.'"

We both giggled.

Chapter Eighteen

Fab got over in the far lane, merging onto the highway that was an almost-straight shot through the Everglades. The two lanes of the highway were separated by a large median strip that was flanked by trees and a variety of tall grasses. I'd once told my brother that the roadsides were in need of a good mow.

I looked at my bare legs and grimaced, remembering being chewed on during my last visit—a buffet for biting bugs. "We're wasting time. Why would he be out here? Something bad has happened; I can feel it." I turned from the window, bored with the view but needing to watch for landmarks.

"Stop thinking the worst; we're going to find him," Fab admonished. "Where do we turn?"

"Right after the 'Panther Crossing' sign. There's a half-standing convenience store that's been closed for years; it's set back from the highway and comes with a huge vacant lot to turn around in, so you can cut across the highway from there. There's a left turn lane, but it's damn sharp; it's not even a lane wide, which makes it dangerous unless you come to a near-stop."

Fab ignored my suggestion and took the turn lane, not paying attention to what I'd said about speed. The car fishtailed in the dirt, but to her credit, she managed to get the SUV back in the lane without a rollover.

I gripped the arm rest, refusing to let go. "Once you spot the white-and-red mile marker sign that Brad scored at a flea market, there's a dirt path a few feet beyond. This time, *slow down*. It's a deceptive road—looks like you'll be swallowed up by overgrowth—but right past the trees, the road is clear all the way to Brad's door."

"I take it he doesn't get many friends stopping by." Fab slowed at the turn-off, getting us safely off the road. Overhanging branches slapped the windshield, the foliage swallowed us up, and then it cleared to a single dirt lane. Dust flew off the back tires.

"As far as I know, the only people who want to come out here are Liam and Julie. Brad didn't want to attract the attention of passing drivers, get them thinking 'where does that road go?' Which reminds me, we don't have Julie on the list. I did an end-run around her by texting Liam." I sighed. "She'll hate that when she finds out; I would." Hitting the door locks for the third time gave me some comfort, just in case they popped up on their own, which they never did.

Fab rounded the curve. "Brad's truck isn't here."

It wasn't clear to me how Brad had found the deal of the century on a dump of a house in a secluded area surrounded by a swamp. I hadn't even known it was legal to live out here; it wasn't like there were housing developments dotting the highway, or any other residential structures, for that matter. When I asked, "How did you, hmm…find this place?" I got a vague response about a friend of a friend, twice removed. At that point, I stopped asking questions.

He'd undertaken all the renovations on his own, working on the house between fishing trips. The outside still needed a bit of work, but the inside had been completely updated. The neighborhood was, for me, the biggest drawback; a croc wasn't my idea of a great neighbor. Perhaps Brad was starting to come around to my way of thinking; since he met Julie, he'd spent most of his free time in civilization.

"Would he park it in the garage?" Fab checked out the structure. Brad had mentioned he was adding one, but failed to mention that it would be a two-story structure that could house several cars.

"Doubt it." I eyed the keypad that I guessed controlled the roll-up doors. "Who's going to hike back in here on the off chance there's a truck to jack? More than likely, the garage houses a couple of junk sports cars he owns that he insists are collector's items and worth big money once they're restored. He was so excited when he was the high bidder at the auction that I kept my doubts to myself."

"And that?" Fab pointed to a boat parked under a carport next to the garage.

"That's an air boat, and it works. Been out on one?" I asked. Fab shook her head. "Bring a good pair of noise-reducing headphones or prepare to have your ears ring for hours after the ride is over. The engine makes a ton of noise. We can get him to take us on a swamp tour at some point; the boat cuts through anything growing in the water."

The word "swamp" had Fab cringing and me laughing.

Fab turned the SUV around and parked in front of Brad's door. Suddenly, an old weathered man appeared, the shotgun in his hand already cocked and pointed at the center of the windshield.

I sobered quickly.

"Stay calm," Fab said, leaving her hands on the steering wheel. "No sudden movements, and no guns on our part."

I cracked the passenger window two inches and yelled, "We're here to see Brad Westin."

"He's not home," he hollered in a gravelly voice.

"Have you seen him?" I yelled again and whispered to Fab, "If we're going to die, I'd rather it be inside my vehicle."

"Who's asking?" His gun never wavered.

"His sister."

"Liar. He told me she'd never come out here. No appreciation for the ambiance."

"Turn on that folksy charm of yours," Fab hissed. "He gets antsy and blows the windshield to bits, I don't like our odds."

"You so owe me." I lowered the window and stuck my head out. "You couldn't convince me to step foot in this croc hole for anything but Brad. I'm worried about him. No one's seen him in a couple of days." I gripped the window ledge to hold myself steady. "You kill me, and he'll feed your scrawny ass to your neighbors one bite at a time." My gaze moved to the swampy water.

He lowered the butt of his shotgun to the ground. "You got a name?"

"Madison Westin. Any more test questions?"

"He's got a highfalutin job in the city; what is it?"

"He has a fishing business out of Lauderdale but has hung up his fishing pole—for how long remains to be seen. The apartment reno is in the Cove, which we hope will be a quick sale, so he doesn't get into the business of renting to derelicts." One of us in the family was enough.

The man spit a stream into the nearest bush. "I can see where renting to my brethren could be a pain in the backside."

The man's scrawny build was deceptive; his

dirty sleeveless wife-beater showed off well-defined biceps. He grinned liked a lunatic, his front, and only, tooth wobbling. "You got the same plain way of speaking. I can see the resemblance." He crossed to my side of the SUV, sticking his hand out. "Toady." Up close, the man had the skin texture of a reptile.

"Madison. Sorry. I don't shake hands." Even if I did, I wouldn't shake one that was covered in layers of dirt that blacked out his nails and continued up both arms. "When was the last time you saw Brad?"

In the excitement of the meet and greet, Fab had slipped out from behind the wheel unnoticed, creeping around the front of the SUV before brandishing her gun. "We're both excellent shots—we hit what we aim at the first time. You can only shoot one of us; then the other shoots you and leaves you to bleed to death. Now behave yourself." She shook the muzzle at him. "I'm Fab."

Gauging by the stupid smile on Toady's face, he'd just fallen in love or lust as his eyes devoured every inch of Fab. Another male for her fan club. He spit on his hand and slicked back his greasy hair, which had no effect, not making any effort to stop staring.

Fab flashed her deranged smile and winked at him, then walked in the direction of the house.

"Wait." Toady held out his hand. "Where's she going?"

I climbed out and stepped in front of him. "Fab's a snooper; she won't be satisfied until she gives the place the once-over. Don't worry, she's so good, you'll never know she was here." I ignored Toady's rumblings. "Brad never mentioned a Mr. Toady…so exactly where did you come from?" I looked around at the dense brush.

"Ain't no mister, just Toady. Brad and me are neighbors, amigos; my mansion is over thataway." He waved his arm behind him in a circular motion. "I look after the property when Brad's away. What's his girlfriend's name?" he asked suddenly.

"Julie, and her son is Liam."

He gave me a nod. "I like that kid."

"Liam's the star in the family." I tried to smile, thinking about how devastated he'd be if something happened to Brad. I had to stop thinking the worst. "When did you last see my brother?"

"A couple of weeks ago. He and the kid blew by, checked out the joint. We shared a beer, and then he had to get back to some shindig your ma was having at her house." Toady shifted from one foot to another, looking over my shoulder and waiting for his true love to reappear. "He said something about her cooking, then laughed. I figured she didn't know her way around a frying pan and suggested they eat ahead of time."

I knew Fab was headed in our direction when Toady stopped talking to concentrate on her every step. In her usual style, she quietly appeared at my side. "All locked up. No sign anyone's been around. Maybe him." She rewarded him with another smile and a wink.

I did my best not to gag.

A strange noise erupted from Toady's mouth, and he looked ready to faint—which I'd thought only happened to heroines in romances, which he was not. If he did, he was going down in a heap.

"If I leave you my phone number, will you call if anyone suspicious shows up? Please don't shoot anyone; just get the license number, and I'll run a check." I felt like waving my arms to get Toady's attention, but when he grunted, I knew he'd heard me.

"Brad got me one of them mobile phones. When I need to use it, I plug it into the generator, and it charges while I talk."

Fab jerked on my shirt. A not-very-subtle way of saying, "Move it." She started around to the other side of the car. Toady raced around her and opened the door, offering his hand to help her in, which she ignored.

I handed a business card to Fab. She gave it a confused once-over, then lowered the window and handed it off to Toady, who took it and rewarded her with a one-tooth smile. She gunned the engine, honked, waved, and drove rather sedately back to the main road.

I, for one, was relieved when the tires hit asphalt.

"I need a drink," Fab said.

"Make that two."

Chapter Nineteen

The drive back to the Cove was uneventful, thankfully with relatively light traffic. Fab hit the fast lane and owned the road, making record time.

As we turned the corner to The Cottages, I said, "Park in Mac's driveway; that way, we can sneak across the street, hopefully unnoticed. Pesky problems have to wait until we find Brad." My phone dinged. "Text from Phil." I glanced over at Fab, then read it. "No sign of your brother. Not in any hospital in South Florida. His truck hasn't been impounded."

"Who was the last person to actually talk to Brad?" Fab asked.

"You need to back in so we don't have to hang over the seats to enjoy the view." I twirled my finger. "The last time was the family dinner, and I don't think anyone's seen him since."

Fab hated to be told how to drive and squealed the tires into the driveway in protest. So much for a low-key arrival. A knock on the back window made me jump. Fab hit the locks, the back passenger door opened, and Mac slid into the seat.

"Happy you didn't crash into the house," Mac huffed.

Fab ignored her.

I turned in my seat. "Why aren't you in the office, doing something important?"

"Because," she sniped, "I needed a beer and a shot. But by the time I got across the street, I settled on aspirin." She hiked her ankle-length skirt above her knees, crossing her legs.

"Get your shoes off the seat," Fab ordered.

Mac screwed up her face, her tongue making a brief appearance. "They're sitting on my skirt." She toed off one ugly loafer, which hit the floor, then the other. "Happy?" she asked the glaring eyes in the rearview mirror. "Do you want the bad news first or the aggravating news? Don't ask for the good; there isn't any."

I covered my face with my hands. *One problem at a time, please.*

"This meeting is adjourned, and we're regrouping by the pool. You—" Fab pointed at Mac. "—bring the bottled water." She got out of the SUV and snapped her fingers at me through the windshield. "Hurry up" was implied. She put her arm around me, and we hustled across the street. "Sitting poolside with our feet in the water will perk us up."

I silently agreed and, when we rounded the corner, was happy that no one was currently swimming or sunning.

Fab held the gate open for Mac, who

reappeared with a small bucket of water on ice and produced our favorite snack cookies from her pocket. She removed her skirt, showing off purple bicycle shorts, and threw it over a chair.

The three of us sat on the edge of the pool, feet in the water.

Fab took charge. "There is one piece of business that takes precedence over anything else. When was the last time you saw Brad?" she asked Mac.

Mac looked between the two of us. "A few days ago, playing basketball with Liam. Julie came home, and the three of them went to dinner, dragging Kevin along. Brad stayed overnight and was gone early the next morning."

"Keep this situation to yourself; no one needs to know we're asking questions." Fab ran down what we knew.

"Not a word to Julie or Liam, and certainly not Kevin," I said. "At least, not until we have a few answers and not just a list of questions."

"Anything I can do, call, and you know that means anytime." Mac looked thoughtful. "You want me to share with Shirl? She can keep her mouth shut."

I nodded and said, "Tell her she can call me anytime, and that goes for you too."

"The bad news." Fab flicked water on Mac.

"If Maricruz Campion ever comes back, I'm going on vacation." Mac cupped water in both hands, and let it drip down the front of her shirt.

"Maricruz is not like the rest of the family—as in quiet and keeps to herself. You might as well know we had words today."

"What did she do?" Fab demanded.

"The witch started the morning by announcing to Miss January that her *f-ing* cat was dead. Miss January cried her eyes out. Whose grandmother ever uses that word? I shouldn't have taken my eyes off the woman, but I had my hands full with Miss January. Maricruz then skipped down to Joseph's. He had gone inside for a pee or a beer, probably both."

"Spit out the rest," Fab snapped.

"Her next victim was Svetlana. Granted, there was only one other chair besides Joseph's, but to throw Svet to the ground..." Mac's eyebrows rose along with her anger. "Joseph unleashed a verbal smackdown on the snotty woman, and she popped the folding chair closed and was ready to bash his head in with it. I tucked my skirt in my shorts, raced to his cottage, and jerked the chair out of her hands mid-air."

Fab laughed, and I threatened her with a handful of water.

"Is Miss January okay? Joseph?" I asked. They were major pains in the backside, but I'd come to love them both.

"The liquor delivery guy woke Miss January up; she'd fallen asleep in her chair on the porch. Before she disappeared back inside, I explained that Maricruz was a cat-hater and had made up the story because she's a mean-ass. I offered to take Miss January to breakfast; that's when she told me that food in the morning makes her barf." Mac imitated a sick cat.

"You didn't need to share the last part," Fab said.

"I know, but then I'd miss the faces you two make and my chance for a laugh at your expense." Mac smiled. "Then I told Mrs. Campion to make herself scarce before I beat the hell out of her. She pitched another bitch, reminiscent of a temper tantrum. Crum trudged out to stick his nose in stuff that's none of his business. He flashed his superior smile, whispered in her ear, and they strolled off to the beach. He lifted his skirt, flashing his ass; he's lucky I didn't put a bullet in that saggy lump."

"Svet? Did she survive?" I asked.

"Svet's made of heavy duty latex." Mac grinned. "Just a little dirt, which I was able to get right off. If she required a return trip to the doll hospital, I'd have demanded overnight service and billed Cruz."

I feared asking my next question. "Is it all quiet now?"

"Right now, it is. But I have more bad news; I wanted to save this next part for last so I could end on a high note."

"*What* already?" Fab asked in exasperation. "You're coming dangerously close to getting your bouffant drenched."

"Last night around midnight, a man came lurking around, checking out the property. He walked the perimeter and around each cottage. I called 911 from a burner phone about an attempted break-in in progress, but it was like he knew the deputies were on their way because right when the police car turned the corner, he disappeared out to the beach." Mac paused. "Wrestler build with a paunch. Bald or next to no hair. I didn't get a good look at his face; he managed to keep to the shadows."

"I'm happy you didn't confront him." I stood and got out another water, dragging a chair into the shade. "Any clue what he wanted?"

"My first thought was that he was an unfriendly associate of Rocks'. Who has disappeared, by the way. In my opinion, he's in hiding. I decided a quick peek couldn't hurt, so I opened the door and looked around; he's moved out except for a box of wine bottles and two others that were taped up. No, I didn't look inside." Mac splashed water on Fab and jumped out of the pool.

Bad idea. Fab took it gracefully, but she'd serve up payback at some point, and Mac would be drenched when she finished.

Fab motioned to me. "We've got a couple of more stops to make."

"Don't do anything dangerous," I admonished Mac.

The three of us walked down the driveway

together. Mac paused in front of the office, waved, and went inside.

"You get rid of Grandma and stop renting to the likes of Rocks, and this place will be back to being all respectable." Fab unlocked the SUV's doors.

I laughed and slid in next to her. "I'm certain I've never heard the words 'respectable' and 'The Cottages' in the same sentence."

"Once we check out the jobsite, we're out of places to go." Fab pulled out into the street.

"That's probably a waste of time. Didier goes there every day. We're doing the drive-by just to check it off the list."

Traffic was stacked up on the road through town. Fab, knowing all the shortcuts, used a couple of them, which also put a stop to her complaining about stopping at every light. It was late afternoon already, and the construction workers had packed up and gone home for the day.

Fab pulled up in front of the building, and I jumped out and ran to the front door, jiggling the knob. I sidestepped down the ramp and surveyed the underground garage—not a vehicle in sight. I walked into the middle of the street and looked up at the building; everything looked the same as the last time we were here.

"Now what?"

Chapter Twenty

"Mother's condo," I directed Fab.

Picking up my phone, I said, "Spoon." He answered in his usual friendly growl, and I alerted him not to tell Mother that I was the one calling or that we were on our way to her house. He started to grill me, and I ended the call with, "Be sure you have your pants on." Fab and I laughed.

Fearing that Mother's sixth sense regarding her children would kick in when I called and wanted to stop by unexpectedly, I'd decided the surprise option was better; that way, she wouldn't spend time worrying before I got there.

Fab watched out of the corner of her eye as I opened the ashtray and fished out a quarter. "I'll do the flipping; not just because you're driving, but because I don't trust you. No offense."

"What are you up to?"

"One of us should call Creole and Didier and have the two of them meet us at Mother's."

"You're fond of compromises; call your boyfriend and I'll do the same."

"Don't take your eyes off the road to glare at me." I flipped the coin in the air, caught it, and said, "Oh look." I held up the quarter. "You're making the phone calls."

"You cheater," she hissed. "I didn't get to call heads or tails."

"I did it for you." I smiled sweetly.

Fab pulled off the road into a drive-thru liquor store parking lot. As she pulled into a space, two scruffy men holding brown bags to their lips jumped back. She picked up her phone and clicked away; a minute later, she tossed it on the dashboard. "Happy?" she asked, nudging her way back into traffic. Her phone rang; she answered and carried on the conversation in French. "They're coming together," she told me after hanging up. "And no, I didn't give them details."

The question of where Brad was loomed large. To cut the tension, Fab and I traded juvenile jokes on the way to Mother's.

Mother had sold her house in Coral Gables and, after much drama and with Brad's help, found a top-floor three-bedroom condo in Tarpon Cove. It was shotgun style, with all of the rooms having a view of the Atlantic Ocean.

It was in a gated community, which was well maintained by an army of gardeners who came weekly, along with a muscular pool duo. We parked in visitor parking and didn't bother announcing ourselves over the intercom, opting instead to bang on the door to announce our arrival.

Spoon opened the door. "Come in." He stared down at me and then shook his head.

I slid past him, Fab behind me. Mother stood in the living room. "It can't be too bad." She hugged us both. "I'm not getting a call from the jail."

"Some children might be offended at your humor." I hugged her hard. She wiggled out of my hold. I pulled her over to the couch and sat down next to her.

Mother had sold her formal furniture and opted for a breezy beach look, fresh from the pages of a decorating magazine. The walls were painted a sea-foam green, and she'd chosen each piece of furniture with an eye towards comfort.

The doorbell rang. Spoon stood and stalked to the door. "What in the hell?" he barked. "This is a security building; two visitors within minutes of one another, and both bypass it."

"That's what you get for associating with people who carry lockpicks," I called after him.

Mother zeroed in on my tennis shoes. "You're in trouble." She pointed. She turned at the sound of voices coming from the entry and stood to hug Creole and Didier.

Creole winked at me and sat in a chair opposite the couch. Fab and Didier sat on an old wrought-iron child's bed that Mother had repainted and made pillows for, which made for a comfortable place to sit. I'd staked a claim in case she ever wanted to get rid of it.

Spoon, the consummate host, filled drink orders—beer for the guys and water for the women. I stood and motioned for Spoon to take my place on the couch next to Mother, leaning down and kissing her cheek as I moved to a seat on the other side of her.

"Mother, there's no easy way to tell you this, so I'm going to blurt it out—Brad is missing. He left bogus messages for Didier, and I believe Julie, and hasn't been seen since then."

"He's, uh…" Mother said softly.

Spoon wrapped his arm around her, pulling her against him.

"Fab and I spent the day checking out every location where he could be and have come up with nothing. We started at the docks in Lauderdale, then the Everglades, and ended up here in Tarpon. Phil checked the hospitals in South Florida; he hadn't been admitted, and no accidents were reported. He's not a guest in the Florida jail system, and his truck hasn't been impounded."

Mother's eyes filled with tears. "What do you think happened?"

I also started to cry, scooting closer and putting my head on Mother's shoulder.

Fab moved to the coffee table and sat in front of Mother. "We don't know. Freak accident, possibly. Kidnap? But he's not high-profile, and there's been no ransom demand. We're not going to stop looking for him. Tomorrow, we'll spread the word to all of our low-life connections that we're looking for information that leads to Brad being found."

"What about law enforcement?" Spoon asked.

"That's Mother's call." I looked across at Creole. "What do you think?"

"Start from the beginning, such as *when* you began to worry about your brother and *why*. Tell us who you talked to and everything about the conversations. Everyone here, look at your phone messages to see if you have any received at about the same time as Brad's last message. Try to remember the last time you actually talked to him and when the last time you laid eyes on him was." Creole made eye contact with everyone as he talked.

"I'll take notes," Didier offered. "I'd volunteer Fab, but nobody could read her writing."

Mother smiled at her, patting her hand.

Creole nodded and, grim-faced, said, "I'm thinking we report it to the chief. That way, I can ask him to put out an all-points bulletin on Brad's truck. If he takes charge, we'll be kept up to date on any new information." He pointed a finger at me to start.

"It started with a conversation with Didier about why Brad hadn't shown for a meeting. Then I dreamed last night that Brad was trying to tell me something. Fab knew I was worried, probably because I was constantly checking my phone. So she took me to look for him." I smiled at her and she returned a squinty frown. "We left early, and she drove straight to Ft. Lauderdale, so I could get some answers, and possibly a more definitive return date for the fishing trip. But no one had seen Brad in a couple of weeks. Fab suggested we check all the places he could possibly be; even if the stop turned up nothing, at least we could cross it off the list." I said to Mother, "The last thing I wanted to do was worry you over a gut feeling, and if it came down to telling you Brad's missing, I wanted to be able to tell you as much as possible."

"Nobody just ups and disappears, except those that walk away from their lives," Spoon said. "That's not Brad. He got any enemies?"

"Hardly. He's the guy everyone wants to have a beer with; will talk to anyone." I looked to Fab for confirmation.

"Sounds like his sister." She nodded.

"He's better at it than me. Case in point," I said to Mother. "We met Toady today at the end of his shotgun. Luckily for us, he fell for Fab at first glance."

Fab wrinkled her nose.

Creole's fist hit the table. "Didier?" he grouched.

Didier's hands shot in the air. "I didn't know either." He tugged on Fab's hair, and she wrestled it back.

"Toady's harmless," Mother interjected. "Interesting background—war veteran, career military. He's the caretaker when Brad isn't around. Did he have any ideas?"

I grimaced. "We got him to promise not to shoot anyone, and instead to call with a license number if anyone comes snooping around. He was a bit dodgy when it came to the actual promise, but I can hope."

At Creole's direction, we were asked to remember everything we could about the last time we saw Brad. Everyone agreed that the last time they saw him was the family dinner. The next contact from him came in the form of texts, and those went to Julie and Didier.

We agreed that someone else had to be involved, and that their first mistake was that they didn't know Brad had turned over the operation of his fishing business to another man. Whoever was behind this, and I was certain my brother had no hand in his own disappearance, wanted us to believe all was well and didn't want us looking for him.

"Tomorrow morning," Mother interrupted when everyone was talking at once, "we meet at Madison's house. The three of us—" she included Fab in her finger-waving. "—will go to The Cottages and break the news to Julie."

"We want a look at her text messages. If she's not receptive, Fab can relocate her phone long enough to get a look," I said.

"What if I get caught?"

"Oops."

Mother hugged Fab. "I'll cover for you. 'I thought that was my phone and told her to grab it.'"

Spoon groaned.

"My turn." I lightly shoved Fab out of the way and hugged Mother. "We'll find him," I whispered in her ear. "Promise."

"I know you will."

Chapter Twenty-One

"Time to wake up," Creole rumbled in my ear, nipping the lobe.

I opened one eye. "It's dark out," I whined and nestled back into his chest.

"Your mother is here. She'd make a terrible burglar; she makes too much noise, most of it coming from that heavy-footed boyfriend of hers."

"What's the plan?"

"You and I are going to work together." He rolled me over, bringing us face-to-face. "We'll share information so that we're not duplicating legwork. I'll spread the word through my associates and street snitches." He kissed me. "Text me a picture of Brad." His phone buzzed on the bedside table; picking it up, he flashed me the screen, which showed "Chief" in all caps.

Creole rolled onto his back, answered, and ran down everything that had been discussed the previous night. I nestled my head on his chest. His boss asked questions; he fired back answers. They discussed a few theories: walked away, freak accident, kidnapped, why no ransom demand? Finally, Creole thanked his boss and told him he'd keep in touch.

"Harder's question at the end was: 'Does anyone have a grudge?' I know we talked about that last night, but think about it. Unhappy business associate? Past, present?"

"The plus of keeping everything in the family, at least in this one, is that people haven't disappeared before."

Creole threw back the sheets, picked me up and heaved me over his shoulder, and headed to the bathroom.

* * *

Creole and I came downstairs hand in hand and walked into the kitchen, where Mother and Spoon sat at the island, sun shining through the garden window. On the counter sat a number of pink boxes from The Bakery Café that held enough food to feed a crowd. Next to the sink, two coffee pots sat side by side, along with bags of coffee.

I kissed Mother's cheek. "You started the coffee?" I half-laughed.

"That's the stupidest thing." Spoon rolled his eyes. "You all can't agree on one kind? How many coffee makers do you have?"

"There are a couple more in the garage that got the boot after producing an inferior taste." I hugged him. "Currently, we use those two, one for the designer brew that tastes and smells like thick swill and one for the pedestrian brand for loverboy here." I winked at Creole, who was busy filling his coffeemaker. "Happy you're here." I turned to Mother. "Why don't you go upstairs and kick Fab and Didier's door?"

"I heard that." Fab breezed into the kitchen, Didier behind her, a big smile on his face. "So mean." She wiggled her nose at me.

The six of us settled around the island.

"Talked to the chief this morning," Creole informed everyone. "He's taking jurisdiction, doesn't expect any blowback from the sheriff's department. Brad's been officially listed as missing. Harder's going to distribute Brad's pic and license plate number."

"Spoon and I went over everything again after you left," Mother said. "I'm unable to think of even a smidge of a motive of a single person harboring resentment. Brad really does get along with everyone."

Spoon cleared his throat.

I smiled at Spoon. "You'd be besties if you weren't…ah… dating his mother."

Everyone laughed, cutting the tension.

"Didier, any business deals go south; you beat anyone out of a good deal?" I asked.

"Fab and I talked about that. Nothing I could come up with. In real estate, you're not always assured of getting the deal, so if someone outbids you, you move on." Didier paused. "I can get us publicity."

Creole shook his head. "I suggest we wait a few days on that one. If someone is holding him, they might get spooked at seeing Brad's pic on the news. The text messages say he'll be back in a couple of days. Let's wait and see if there is another message."

"We've got great hacker connections. She does, anyway." I pointed to Fab. "An artiste, I heard him brag." Noticing Didier's scowl, I said, "I can ask if it's possible to pick up a signal and, hence, a location?"

"I've known Gunz a long time, and if he can't get the job done, he'll refer to us to someone who can. I'll call him today. Have you forgotten he doesn't like you?" Fab asked me.

"Feeling's mutual. Money is all he's interested in. He'll be pleased when I don't haggle."

"Try not calling him any names." Fab put her arm around Mother. "We'll drive to The Cottages first and talk to Julie."

"That won't be necessary." Spoon had taken his and mother's mugs to the sink and was staring out the garden window. "Julie and Kevin are stomping up the driveway, neither looking too happy."

Kevin cop-knocked on the front door, louder than usual, which wasn't a good sign.

"Shall we flip to see who gets to open the door?" I asked.

"Oh, Madison." Mother shook her head and turned away, but I knew she was smiling.

"I volunteer." Spoon bared his teeth, already halfway to the door.

"Find out what he wants before you let him in," Fab called.

Spoon flashed his scary smile and opened the door. After the exchange of a few words, he let them in.

Julie stalked in ahead of Kevin. "I suppose that all of you know that Brad is missing—hurt somewhere or worse?" Her blue eyes shot sparks.

I wasn't sure exactly who she was leveling her accusation at. Fab and I exchanged a look that said, "happy it's not me that has to do the explaining."

Mother crossed over to her and hugged her. "We were coming over to see you this morning."

"How did you find out?" Creole asked, his voice softer than the irritation level in his eyes.

Julie shot a question back. "Why hasn't this been reported to the police?"

"It has been," Creole informed her. "Now, can you answer my question?"

"I overheard Mac having a conversation with someone in the office earlier. 'You'll be happy to know that Brad isn't in the hospital'," Julie said angrily.

Eavesdropping. She must have learned that from Fab.

Fab must have read my mind because she glared at me.

Spoon stood and offered his stool to Julie.

Kevin, who had been silent, stepped forward. "I checked before coming over here, and no report has been filed."

"I don't want you involved," I said adamantly.

"Your entire family looks suspicious, knowing you have a missing family member, but no one calls in a report," he countered.

"You need to clean out your ears," Creole barked. "If you want in on the investigation, you call Chief Harder, but I already know he'll tell you to fuck off."

Didier laughed at his friend.

The look of outraged shock on Kevin's face amused me. "I'll take it up with the sheriff, since this is his jurisdiction, and we'll see if Harder tells him that."

"Let's all calm down," Mother said and turned to Julie. "Creole can update you. If you don't mind, we'd like to see any text messages that Brad sent you since the family dinner, and if he contacts you again, we'd like to know immediately."

Fab slipped off her chair and moved to stand between me and Didier. Creole was behind me, and I leaned against him.

Creole related what we'd talked about at Mother's. He said nothing about our future plans.

"Anything unusual happen before the family dinner?" Didier asked Julie. "Any issues with anyone?"

Julie shook her head, her anger deflated. "Nothing. We spent the day together and had a good time." She passed her phone to Creole. The one text message that she'd received was almost identical to Didier's, essentially: "gone fishing, back in a week."

"Now you know as much as we do," Mother comforted her.

"If I get a vote, I think this should be left to law enforcement," Julie said. "Unprofessional behavior could get him killed, if…"

Thankfully, she left the sentence unfinished.

After a moment's hesitation, she continued. "No one tells Liam. He'll just worry. I'll tell him when we know something for sure."

"When Liam finds out what you've kept from him… I hope it doesn't backfire on you." I didn't want to be part of any deception, but it was her place to tell him or not.

"Let's go," Kevin said to his sister. "You haven't seen the last of me. Two open cases—an unsolved murder and a missing family member that you don't seem too concerned about." He crossed to the front door, holding it open. "I'm surprised you haven't bailed out Miss January." He made eye contact with me.

"Arrested? What for? She didn't get a phone call?"

"You done with the questions?" Kevin snapped.

Three pairs of male eyes turned on him, all of them angry at his snotty tone.

"Drunk at the grocery store, riding one of those motorized carts, and knocked over a display. She got off to help, fell, and rolled around on the floor." The last part was said with disgust. "She could have called anyone she wanted, but didn't know anyone's number."

"And you," I ground out, "couldn't call for her? You certainly have my number."

Creole's arms tightened around me.

"A night in jail won't kill the old drunk." He jerked his head, motioning his sister out the door.

"You piece of—"

"Madison," Mother hissed. She walked Julie to the front door and kissed her cheek, then closed the door behind her.

"I say we double-team Julie and make friends with her, so she's not so distrustful. Your brother would want that," Fab said.

"You're right, but don't let it go to your head," I said. "I've got to get to the jail before Miss January goes into withdrawal. There's a small window in the morning when she's sober."

Creole moved to the end of the island, signaling for attention. "Everyone leave your phone on. Anything new comes in, text me. We'll meet back here at the end of the day and exchange updates. I have the day off, and I'm going to hit the streets and see what I can turn up. Didier's going to the jobsite to make it look like business as usual. Spoon, you get with your connections."

"I'll stay here," Mother said.

"Happy you're here," I whispered in Creole's ear, hugging him tight. "What do you want Fab and me to do?"

Creole hugged me tighter, nodding at Fab. "Call Phil and have her on standby to run any new info we get that might need to be checked out. Don't forget your hacker friend."

Chapter Twenty-Two

I was still on hold with the sheriff's department when Fab pulled into their parking lot. "I'll pay the bail, and hopefully, they can tell me how long it will take to get Miss January processed out. You may want to ditch me and come back when I call."

"Don't be ridiculous. I'll make phone calls. Much as I hate it here, it will give us time to brainstorm about Brad." Fab powered down the window, and a wave of fresh beach air blew in.

"Don't shoot anyone," I admonished and shut the door before she could say anything.

I knew the drill, having been here before to bail someone out. Once inside the door, I headed straight to the cashier. They made it easy to pay up—cash or credit card, the latter with a hefty fee tacked on. It didn't take long with only one person ahead of me, and she was about done. There were four other people waiting for the magic door to open, signaling a release.

I pushed my credit card under the window. It was treated the same as cash, and I'd get my money back, minus the fee, once the case was settled. The older woman didn't say anything after asking me the name of the inmate, processing the paperwork in silence.

Once completed, she said, "The inmate was transferred to Tarpon Cove hospital early this morning. I'll call over and let them know she's been released from custody."

"What happened to her?" I asked in shock.

"No idea." She waved me aside, calling for the next person in line.

I ran back to the SUV. "Miss January is in the hospital." I pulled my phone out and called Shirl.

She answered, and I explained what had happened.

"You might as well hold off. She'll be in a secure area, and it will take a while to get her moved to a public room. You're not family, so they won't let you in. It's my day off, but I can call and get an update on her condition."

"The good thing is, when she is released, she won't have to go back to jail; she can come home," I said.

After I hung up, Fab said, "I'd like to check out Brad's cottage, see if it yields any clues. I don't expect to find anything, because whatever happened, happened after he left, but you never know." She exited the parking lot, taking the back way.

"I just texted Mother that we're going to swing by The Cottages, and she messaged back that Spoon was with her and not to worry. I'm happy she has him; he's a rock for her."

"When we leave The Cottages, we can place a food order and have Phil deliver it; that way, she can update us. Who's got the better hacking skills—one of Phil's associates? Or do we use Gunz?"

"I'd thought it was settled; we're using Hair in a Can. Problems already?" Not using the man wouldn't disappointment me in the slightest, but only if we had someone else lined up.

Gunz was one of Fab's seedier longtime associates, a large bald man who, when the mood hit him, sprayed goo on his head, ran a thick comb through it, and presto: instant hairstyle. He and I had never warmed up to one another. He'd told me I was a smart-ass once; I shrugged and thanked him for calling me smart.

"Gunz is not returning my calls; it's damn annoying."

"Then let's check with Phil; her people have never let us down."

"We need to spread the word through our lowlife connections that we'll incentivize them with cash, which will yield a faster response. And do it like the cops: it has to lead to his being found." Fab slid into the parking space in front of the office. "Between the five of us—me, you, Spoon, Creole, and Phil—we'll find him. And Didier." Fab smiled. "Brad's place first," she said, slamming the door.

Mac opened the office door, waving. Shirl,

behind her, stuck her hand over Mac's shoulder and waved.

"We'll be right back," I called to the two and ran to catch up with Fab.

Fab slid her lockpick out and had the door open by the time I came up behind her, following her inside. The large open space encompassed a living room, dining room, and kitchen, with the bedroom and bathroom behind the only other door. Fab pulled out her phone and snapped pictures.

I sank into a chair, one eye on Fab, and called Phil, running down the information we needed, inviting her for an early dinner, and asking if she would please bring the food. Fab went to work searching every corner; nothing was left unchecked. The last thing she did was go through the closet and rifled through a couple of travel bags.

"Nothing." Fab held up her hands. "My guess is he left that morning with every intention of coming back."

"None of our possible options for what could've happened make sense." I stood and headed for the door. "Time to talk to Joseph, tell him about the reward. You check on Score."

"I'd sooner check on Miss January's dead cat. Her drunken boyfriend can take care of himself. He probably hasn't even noticed that Miss January hasn't been around. Didn't she drag him back from the beach? How long was he living out there? And when is his freeloader butt moving back?"

"You'd feel bad if the old guy croaked." I wagged my finger. "You can be the one to tell Miss January." I left Fab to lock up in a full-blown snit.

I knocked on Joseph's door and got no answer. Frustrated, I gave it a swift kick, and when he didn't yell back, I figured he wasn't at home and went over to the office. I planned to update Mac and leave, but Mac's ominous, "We need to talk inside," left me wondering what now.

A moment later, Fab banged the office door closed, glaring at me for taking her coveted seat on the couch. She practically sat on top of me. I pushed her away and moved to a chair next to Shirl.

"How's Miss January doing?" I asked Shirl.

"She's recovering nicely; sleeps most of the time. The doctor has her on medication to prevent rapid withdrawal. She'll be getting out soon."

"Thank you for looking out for her, keeping me informed."

"Meeting called to order." Mac kicked her boot-covered feet up on the desk, managing to snap her bubble gum at the same time.

I thought she'd given up gum chewing—guess not.

"Jump to the good stuff. I'm in a surly mood today," I said.

"Rocks is dead!" she announced. "Murdered!"

I attributed her smile to the fact that everyone's mouth dropped open, her announcement rendering us all speechless. "Inside his cottage?" I choked out, feeling faint and resting my forehead on the edge of the desk. *Not again.*

"Nope, not this time." Mac blew a bubble that covered the lower part of her face.

"You do that again," Fab growled at her, "and I'm shooting the next bubble."

Mac wadded the gum between her fingers, pitching it in the trash. "You're just grouchy you can't do it," she said and crossed her arms over her chest.

I promised myself I'd have a good laugh over that one later. "Could we get back to *Rocks*?"

"He was found slumped over in his car at the end of a one-way street down by the beach. Cause of death: not the beating he sustained or that someone had used him for target practice, but..." Mac made a simulated gun, forefinger in the middle of her head. "Bang!" She fell sideways in her chair.

"Thanks for the re-creation." Fab's words were drenched in sarcasm.

"You better tell them the other part." Shirl's eyebrow shot up.

"Yes, well..." Mac smoothed her skirt, fingering her double pack of gum; catching Fab's glare, she thought better of it, and it disappeared into her pocket. "I need an alibi. I know it's not good practice to lie to law enforcement, but it was just a little one."

"Do the cops think you killed Rocks?" I desperately needed something to drink; my mouth had gone dry. I uncapped the water bottle Mac had set out and downed it.

"I certainly hope not." Mac sniffed. "I've never even shot anyone. There were a couple of times I wanted to, but that doesn't count."

"You said alibi," I reminded her in exasperation. "If you're not under investigation, why would you need one?"

"This ought to be good," Fab mumbled.

"I got the word early from Shirl." She beamed at her friend. "Though the body was gone by the time I got down to the beach." She frowned. "Kevin came by and wanted to check out Rocks' cottage…right after I'd removed the boxes to the garden shed and called the cleaning crew. Told him he could look all he wanted but that Rocks had left a week ago. Legally, I should've waited until the end of the month to enter and move his things, but I thought, 'the hell with that.'"

I shook my head. "Since he's dead, he won't be slinking back looking for a place to hide. Any relatives show up, hand the boxes over and get a signed receipt."

"So…" Fab drawled. "You lied and now want one or all of us to cover for you. That's three favors you owe, and if we have to corroborate your story, that will be another one. Got it."

If looks could kill, one of us would be calling Dickie for a tricked-out funeral for Fab. Shirl rubbed her hands together, already contemplating how she'd use her favor.

"Fine," Mac ground out.

"Kevin find anything? Did he happen to drop any choice tidbits, such as how, why, who?" I asked.

"Kevin's always tight-lipped. I knew before letting him inside that there wasn't anything to find; I searched the place a couple of times—once after Rocks disappeared and then again this morning. Shirl and I will hit up Custer's later and get the gossip; the drunks aren't always reliable, but it's something."

Custer's was a rat-hole bar in town that did a brisk business selling beer and screw-top wine, despite the fact that the place had questionable cleanliness standards. They owed their success to the nightly impromptu entertainment supplied by the drunks. Custer's held the record for the most bar fights of any place in town.

"You make up with Billy yet?" I asked. "He won't like you cavorting at that bar."

"We went out again. I had high hopes until his phone rang and he had to run off and help another stupid woman in distress. Is it too much to ask that I be the center of attention?" Mac made an incoherent sound of disgust. "Shirl and I are branching out; we're going to be sleuths."

"Just make sure you don't get arrested." If the worst happened, hopefully I could get them out of jail in a speedy manner.

"The good news is that Rocks wasn't murdered here," Fab pointed out.

"Forgot that part," Mac said. "Rocks wasn't offed in his car or anywhere nearby. I overheard a couple of technicians grumbling about lack of evidence before I was told to beat it or risk arrest."

"Anything else?" I stood, reaching into the refrigerator behind me for another cold water. "Another murder?"

Mac's feet hit the floor; she grabbed the snack bowl off the shelf. "Oreos?" She held up a small bag.

I grabbed the bag and sat back down.

"Not yet, but it could still happen. Maricruz is supposed to be leaving tomorrow, but she's sort of disappeared," Mac announced. "She and Crum took off for parts unknown. Here." She thrust a ripped-up piece of paper at me. "Crum shoved this under the door. It's his handwriting, anyway."

It read: Gone camping.

"How in the hell did this happen?"

"If you ask me—"

I cut Mac off. "Who else would I be asking? What are you going to tell Cruz?"

Me?" Mac squealed. "He's your lawyer."

"And your lawyer, and Fab's—not Shirl's, not

yet anyway," I said to her, "and I hope you're never in need of his services."

"What the hell kind of manager are you that you can't control one old woman?" Fab asked, clearly enjoying the new turn of events.

"Maricruz needs a twenty-four-hour keeper. She acts like a teenager whose parents went out of town for the weekend. Sneaking around, causing trouble, running up tabs in your name." She glared at me. "I knew it was bad when she jumped Crum's bones like a thirsty woman in the desert; you'd think she hadn't had sex in…a long time anyway."

"Well…" Shirl snickered.

"Did you even try to warn her off? I hear there's an outbreak of crabs again; tell me that, and I wouldn't get within five feet of the person." I shivered, having heard stories about the nippy little bugs. "Anybody with a good idea might want to speak up."

Total silence.

"You listen to me, Macklin Lane: find her!" I practically yelled. "And before Cruz gets here. You can name your favor."

"What about me?" Shirl asked. "You know she'll rope me into helping."

I turned and faced her. "Done."

Chapter Twenty-Three

Fab turned the corner to the house in time for us to see Phil disappear up the driveway with shopping bags in her hands. We walked into the kitchen, where Phil was unloading the food and Spoon was in charge of the drinks.

Mother stood at the sink, waving out the garden window. "Kevin's here," she said with forced cheerfulness. "He's in uniform. And a second car just pulled up."

Fab turned to me and gave me a questioning glance. "This can't be good."

"He's probably here for me. I hope I'm not about to be charged with murder."

Fab grabbed my arm. "I'll hide you."

I threw my arms around Fab, hugging her. "If it's the worst," I whispered. "I need you to take care of Mother. I'm depending on you to find Brad."

Spoon answered the knock on the door. Kevin must have been in a good mood today; he hadn't kicked the door down. A short conversation took place; then Spoon stepped back, allowing Kevin and his partner in.

Kevin tried to control his signature smirk but

wasn't doing a very good job. "I'm here to take you in for questioning," he said to me. "It's your right to say no; then I'll just get a warrant."

"Does Cruz know about this?" I asked. Kevin shrugged. His non-answer made me ask, "Do you mind if I call him now?"

"Call him." He pointed to the cell phones on the island.

Damn! The answering service.

"Is this necessary?" Mother glared until he looked away.

Go Mother.

I lifted my skirt, took off my thigh holster, and shoved it in the back of the junk drawer. Not the best place, but it was hard to find anything in there anyway; I was happy I hadn't followed through on my threat to clean it out. I followed his orders. Might as well cooperate; if not, he'd be back.

The other deputy, who hadn't said a word, turned his attention to Fab. "You too, Miss Merceau; we're also requesting your cooperation."

"If this ends in an arrest, we'd like to request the same cell," Fab said snootily.

I bent my head and bit the inside of my cheek.

"I suppose you'd like a room service menu?" Kevin snarked.

"Wouldn't that be cell service?" Fab said sweetly. "And yes, we would."

"What is this about?" Didier demanded,

putting his arm across Fab's shoulders.

"Step back," the other deputy said.

Spoon clamped his hand down on Didier's shoulder.

Kevin led me to the door. I turned to Didier. "Call Creole. You two need to take care of the children. Don't let them run wild." I tried to smile and failed. I was disappointed when, after Kevin ushered me into the back seat of his cruiser, Fab was led to the other deputy's car.

The ride to the sheriff's department took longer than usual; somehow, Kevin got lucky and hit every red light. Fab must have been grinding her teeth. The last I saw of her was when I was led into the building and placed in a windowless interrogation room, Kevin pointing to a chair. I looked around after the door shut behind him. The walls were dingy grey and the furniture sparse: a table and a couple of chairs. I didn't bother to look around for a snack bowl. I wanted some water but figured my chance of getting any was slim if Kevin had his way.

Tired of fidgeting, I laid my forehead on the table. There was nothing comfortable about that position. Giving up, I sat up straight and closed my eyes, plotting Kevin's slow and painful demise. My rational side warned me to keep it a fantasy.

The door opened; Kevin was back. "This won't take long if you haven't committed any felonies of late." He motioned me forward.

He wrapped his hand around my arm and led me down to a door at the far end of the hall. He handed me a placard with the number two on it and ushered me into a line with four other women.

I stood next to a buxom blonde in a floor-length taffeta skirt, an ill-fitting bustier, and platinum ringlets. One bustier strap was broken, and a good sneeze would leave her topless. I suspected she'd won the bar fight. "Don't forget to smile." She winked at me.

Before I could ask any questions, Kevin yelled, "Quiet. When I open the door, you'll file in, face forward, and hold your number up at chest level."

A lineup! This was a first. Hopefully, by the time I got home, I could make an amusing story out of it.

A voice over an intercom—from behind the one-way mirror, I presumed—had us turn right, then left, then we all stood there a couple of minutes. The blonde struck a pose, hands on her hips, one hip flung out. The youngish girl on the other side of me—in a school uniform and knee-length socks that had holes in them—yawned. Her hair, with its different lengths, looked as though a drunk had cut it. She groaned loudly, hanging her head to one side. I felt bad that I couldn't offer her two aspirin and a cup of strong coffee. I wondered what kind of lineup impression I made.

Intercom voice came back on. This time, we were told to step forward, one at a time, do the turns, and then step back in line. When we were done, the brunette on the end in shorts and no shoes yelled, "Gotta pee." The door opened, and we filed out. We were led to a bench by a different deputy and told to "shut it."

I lowered my head and said quietly to the taffeta-skirted blonde, "What happens next?"

She answered with a glare.

So we're both first-timers?

A female deputy opened a door at the far end of the hall that accessed the reception area. "You're free to go," she boomed.

I waited so I could be the last to leave. I asked the deputy, "Why was I brought in?"

She shrugged. "Don't know."

I schooled my features to avoid showing her what I thought of that answer and walked to the reception desk. "I was brought in with a Fabiana Merceau; is she still here?" I did a double take at the woman sitting behind the reception desk; she'd been in the lineup.

"We don't give out that information," the woman said flatly.

"Since one of your deputies gave me a ride here, how do I get a ride home?"

"There's a pay phone outside." She motioned to the door.

"Do you have any change?" I held out my palm.

I didn't hear the phone ring, but she picked it up just then and started talking. Pay phone? That was a dead business. It would be a hike, but I could make it home; I looked down at my feet and apologized in advance for having to do it in flip-flops. Fab would complain the whole way.

As I scanned the parking lot, a disheveled man with ratty jeans hanging low on his hips, a dark t-shirt, and aviator glasses caught my eye. He was headed my way with his arms open.

I sagged at the sight of him. Creole rushed to me and pulled me tight to his chest. Holding and kissing me, he whispered words of assurance that the real murderer would be caught soon and promised there would be no more harassment from local authorities. I hugged him back.

"I'm taking you home," he said, keeping an arm around me as he guided me back to his truck.

"We have to wait for Fab."

"She can walk."

Before I could erupt into a fit, Creole said with a big smile, "Just kidding. Didier got held up by a business call and should be here any minute. I had to promise not to leave her stranded."

"How can you promise that I won't be hauled in again and questioned about Carbine's murder?" I settled back in his arms, head against his chest.

"As it turns out, this is a really big case, and it would be unprofessional of me to talk about it.

Local law enforcement knows that you had nothing to do with the deaths of Carbine and his partner, Rocks. Your only involvement is that Carbine chose your house to squat in. Kevin has now gotten the word that he's not to approach you about the case unless he has a direct order from his boss. He was also reprimanded about over-stepping his authority and trampling your rights."

"I promise I won't breathe a word of anything you share with me." I tapped a finger on his forearm. "Can you tell me why the lineup?"

"Another crazy wanting a piece of the reward money. Claims to have seen Carbine on the beach with a woman that night. Relying on information from a drunk is not the way to make a case." Creole pushed me into a sitting position. "Here comes your girl." He inclined his head. "From the swing of her hips, I'd say she weathered her time okay."

Fab's Porsche pulled in alongside us, the engine revving. Didier was barely out of the car when Fab came to a halt and recreated her sexy lineup moves: swinging her hips to the right, she twirled around; then, waving her imaginary placard above her head, she swung left.

Didier hauled her off her feet and into his arms. They exchanged some words, and he threw his head back and laughed.

"Bet you—" Creole poked me. "—Fab had to explain what happens in a lineup." He powered down the window, sticking his head out. “See you later,” he yelled.

I waved and blew kisses.

Chapter Twenty-Four

Opening my eyes, I knew, from the sun streaming in through the windows, that I'd definitely overslept. I'd slept surprisingly well, considering all the drama; it helped that Creole cocooned me with his body, tightening his hold if I tried to move away. I soon stopped struggling and went right back to sleep.

"What?" Creole whispered hoarsely.

I shifted in his arms when my phone rang. He grabbed it from the bedside table, glanced at the screen, then answered, grunting, "Morning." He held it to his ear, not saying anything, and I could hear a faint voice coming through the speaker. I wondered who it was but wasn't sure I wanted to know unless it was good news, and judging by the aggravated look on his face, along with his few terse questions, I knew it wasn't.

"You make sure no one goes near that cottage, and we'll be there in a couple of hours." He hung up and laid my phone out of reach.

"I'm tired of asking if someone died." I started to roll away, and he jerked me back to his side.

"That was Mac. No bodies, just a break-in at Rocks' cottage."

"Makes you think Rocks didn't spill his guts before the bullet to his head," I said, making a gunshot noise. It wasn't impressive, but Creole smiled slightly. "Wonder what they were looking for."

Creole turned my face to his. "How do you know about his death? That was being kept quiet."

"Mac got to the beach after the body had been hauled away and stuck around to get a firsthand look at anything else that might happen. Then hung around and eavesdropped on an *official* conversation." I cocked my head to the side. "Why are you involved? You're overqualified for a local murder, unless..." I hesitated. "Drugs! Rocks screwed someone? Aww...but when whoever it was came looking for the product or information, Rocks didn't have the right answers; hence the grisliness of the crime scene. Poor Rocks! Either way, he was a dead man."

"Are you finished, Nancy?" His voice was low and even. "Rocks was involved with some very dangerous people who don't hesitate to kill, and *you* will stay out of it. Promise me." I tried to wiggle away, and he hauled me back. "Don't think about moving until I say you can."

"Bossy much?" A muscle in his jaw tensed. "I thought Nancy Drew was a superstar when I was a kid." His scowl deepened. "I promise. You know you can trust me with information. I'm not a squealer."

He tapped the end of my nose. "How do you feel?"

Hmm…change of subject.

"Good—I slept better than ever. Now I need to get dressed. I'm guessing I need to get over to The Cottages. You told Mac 'we'; do you have the day off?"

He nodded. "I'm your backup today. Didier whisked Fab away after her lineup appearance and took her to a hotel in Miami Beach. They have a favorite hotel up there and were looking forward to an overnight getaway."

What's not to like? Five-star accommodations, oversized king bed with an ocean view, room service, and Fab had once told me they always indulged in in-room massages.

"Can I get up now?" I grumbled and then perked up. "I get to drive."

He snorted, stood and scooped me into his arms, and headed for the bathroom.

* * *

"I don't know why we couldn't go through the drive-thru," I whined. "You're slower than any girl when it comes to getting out of the house."

Creole hit his fist on the steering wheel. "Sitting down to eat like most people didn't kill you, as I'm here to attest. You've been under too much stress lately."

"You sound like Mother, but I know you're

not her; she doesn't sport morning scruff on her face." I pointed to the dash clock. "It's almost noon." He was close to strangling me, but I knew he wouldn't. He'd never be able to explain it to Mother.

"Why are you being so annoying?" Creole huffed.

"Because it's fun." I blew him a kiss. "Why don't you summarize the phone call with Mac? It's my job to come up with a plan. Then *I* can tell you what to do when we get there. Won't that be fun?" I looked out the side window and grinned.

"After talking to the chief, I had Mac call 911. The deputies have come and gone." He grunted. "The cottage Rocks occupied was broken into last night and trashed pretty thoroughly. Took the fronts off the appliances, upended the drawers in the kitchen, and the cushions and mattress were shredded. Mac assured me that Rocks didn't leave behind any personal belongings."

"Hmm...about that. Can you promise me that Mac has immunity from handcuffs?"

"What did she lie about?"

I raised my eyebrow.

"No prison time. Now tell me."

I told him about the boxes Rocks had left behind. I could tell he was disappointed that there wasn't a smoking gun.

"Now tell me about the man's stay at your property."

"Rocks made a big splash when he arrived—

contagious personality, everyone wanted to be his friend—and peddled his cheap wine. Then the night of the confrontation in the driveway happened, and since then, he's made himself scarce. Just a sighting or two of him sneaking in or out, always in the middle of the night."

"I suppose now's as good a time as any to tell you: Shirl confided to Stephan—late-night pillow talk—that she and Mac had seen a man trying to break in, and that when they called law enforcement, he got away before the cops arrived. After that, Stephan installed security cameras in all four corners of the property."

Stephan was Shirl's "insurance salesman" boyfriend, who was really an undercover cop. I rolled my eyes at the mention of his name, knowing that it was phony. Fab and I called him Help because that was the only time we called him. He came through when Creole couldn't be reached. Fab had warned him that if he hurt Shirl, he'd walk with a limp for the rest of his life. His incredulous stare at that had made me laugh.

Mulling over the pros, and the lack of any cons I could come up with at the moment, I said, "How soon can a monitor be installed in the office? Or if that's not a good location, then across the street at Mac's. She should have one anyway."

"So I guess you're not upset," he said sarcastically.

"Heck, no. In addition to catching

lawbreakers, we can find out who's screw…uhm… doing it in the pool and get rid of them."

Creole leaned back against the seat and laughed.

* * *

Creole cruised into Rocks' parking space. Thinking back, I'd only seen Rocks' car a handful of times, and that was right after he moved in.

Mac bounced out the door of the office in a colorful workout outfit: a short, full skirt and mismatched running shoes—one lime, one pink. A thick bandana was holding back her bouffant, which appeared to have been hit by a windstorm.

"When can I start the cleanup?" She marched over and put her hands on her hips.

"Once we get the okay from Creole. If it's a matter of hauling stuff to the dump," I said, "put the word out: first guy to show up with a truck gets the job. Let Creole into the shed so he can get a look at the boxes."

Mac shrieked loud enough to wake a drunk from a nap.

Creole shook his head, rubbing his ear.

"I got you up-front immunity," I reassured her.

"Give a girl a heart attack." Mac waved to Creole, disappearing inside Rocks' cottage.

I followed her in and surveyed the mess,

wondering if they'd found what they were looking for. It looked as though the cottage had been upended and set back down. The upholstered furniture was thrashed and the appliances looked iffy, but there was no structural damage. When I first inherited the property, this chaos would have freaked me out, but sadly, I'd seen worse.

Returning from the shed, Creole said, "Leave the boxes where they are and an officer will come out and collect them. They'll ask for you, Mac."

"Your professional opinion?" I asked Creole.

He shook his head, scanning the room. "Taking apart the appliances is overkill. Whatever they were looking for, they wanted it badly. Doubt Rocks was any help." Creole took one last look around. "I've got yellow 'keep the hell out' tape in my truck. I say we run it across the front door; that would deter a return visit. From most people, anyway." He winked down at me. "If they send someone to drive by to gauge your reaction, it sends the message that you called the cops, and they'll find out that everything was hauled off."

"Maybe you could accidently forget to take the roll with you," Mac said excitedly. "Next busload of Cruz relatives, I'll wrap an entire cottage, post a 'Keep Out' sign. It's better than a staged fight."

"I thought I made myself clear about scheduling activities that can bring legal charges and arrests." Creole moved in front of Mac and glared down at her. "Do we need to have another chat?"

Mac straightened to her full height, her girls shoved out, face red with irritation. "I cancelled that fight, and there hasn't been another one." She glared back. "Planning the entertainment is a thankless job."

I tried to smooth it over. "Cruz appreciates you—a lot. His rent-a-relatives never complain; they're highly complementary, mostly about you. What would I do without you? Hire Fab?" That made her laugh and eased the tension.

Creole enveloped Mac in a hug. "I'm not criticizing you. I'm looking out for you." He patted her hair, which stuck up about a half-foot above her head, giving it a closer look and wrinkling his nose. "I'll get the tape; you lock up. Most people will think 'police'; they don't know you can get a roll at the hardware store." He turned around when he got to the door. "If you make your story too outlandish, Kevin may question you. Tell him to mind his own damn business and call me if he has a problem."

"You enjoying your new partner?" Mac asked as we walked back outside.

"He likes to get his own way, but then, so does Fab, so I should be used it."

We both laughed.

Creole handed Mac the tape. "Decorate away." He grabbed my hand. "One more thing."

He motioned for Mac to follow him to the office, and ushered us in, where he told her about the security cameras.

"Can we get two monitors?" Mac asked me. "That way, Shirl and I can play cards and watch the late-night antics. Better than television. You know it's just reruns right now."

Creole's lips quirked. "Can I use your laptop? The video with the man's face on it was forwarded to me."

Mac plopped in a chair, and I took Fab's place on the couch and scoped out the street through the blinds. Creole sat behind the desk. He accessed the file and turned the laptop around for us to see. "Seen this guy before?"

I squeezed my eyes shut. "That's the guy who shot at Rocks the night of his party."

"Time to find this man, have a chat, and see what he's got to say." Creole snapped the lid shut.

"If you can print out the picture, I can get it checked out with my sources," I said.

Creole leveled a stare at me. "That's probably a law enforcement connection, and the person could lose their job. I'd like to meet these sources of yours."

"I don't want to hurt your feelings, but not going to happen."

Mac laughed.

The office door flew open, smashing into the small table that sat in the corner. Cruz, angry as a bear, yelled, "Where's my grandmother?" He zeroed in on Mac.

Oh hell, I'd forgotten about Grandma.

After a cursory check from head to toe, I refrained from giving Cruz a thumbs-up. It must be a rare day off, and he wore expensive casual as though it were designed for him. I also kept "nice legs" to myself.

"Don't make me ask a second time," he snarled and zeroed in on me. He acknowledged Creole with a nod.

"You failed to mention that we were to double as jailers or that she is…active." I refrained from saying, "annoying trouble," and pointed at Mac. "She'll know."

"Now I know how Fab feels when you throw her under the bus." Mac made a face. "Where is Fab, anyway?"

"She's off having fun with her boyfriend," I said.

The door crashed into the small table again, courtesy of Cruz's foot. He erupted in a roar, kicking it closed; it popped back open, and he gave it a second kick.

Creole stood. "Enough. You break the door, and you'll buy one ten times better."

The two men engaged in a glare-off.

Mac stood and stepped between them, although Creole was still behind the desk. "Try cottage eight. She spends a lot of time there with her vacation lay…boyfriend, or whatever you want to call it." She waved her hand in Cruz's face. "I did my best, even threatened the professor, but the man is a woman magnet in his tighty-whities and boots. One look, and Maricruz fell straight into lust."

Creole sat down, laughing.

"If he's touched my grandmother, he'll spend the rest of his life in prison." Cruz threw open the door and marched out.

I yelled after him, "It was consensual." I looked back at Mac.

"She was the pursuer; not that Crum fought her off," Mac reassured me, sticking her head out the door. "The lovebirds were supposed to show back up this morning, but I haven't seen them yet."

"Let's sneak out before Cruz gets back," Creole said.

"Oh no you don't." Mac blocked the doorway. "I'm not going to be the one to tell him that they went off for an adventurous screw someplace." She glanced over her shoulder. "Stop laughing." She pointed a finger at Creole. "Cruz is headed back, and he looks madder than before, if that's possible."

"Get *that man* on the phone." Cruz barked out the words the moment he appeared in the doorway.

"I get that you're frustrated, but don't take it out on these two," Creole said.

A coughing attack from behind Cruz made

everyone turn.

Now what?

Cruz moved aside. Joseph wiped his mouth on his shirt sleeve, Svetlana's legs wrapped around his waist. "Mr. Campion." He flashed a toothy, stained smile. "Saw you knocking on Crum's door—he went camping with his girlfriend. A little overnight on the beach. They'll be back tomorrow."

Creole lowered his head, and his shoulders shook.

I squeezed my eyes closed. Just when you thought things couldn't get worse, they did. I struggled not to laugh.

"Girlfriend? Grandmother? Where?" Cruz demanded. He eyed the rubber doll suspiciously. "What is that?"

Svetlana had on a low-cut sundress, her cleavage on display, and Joseph had chosen her blond ponytail wig.

"This is my special lady, Svetlana." Joseph held out one of her hands for Cruz to shake.

Cruz snarled.

Joseph jumped back. "Tell Shirl I need to see her," he said to Mac and flew out the door.

"Where the hell did you find him?" Cruz snapped.

"You must have forgotten that he was a client in the past," I reminded him.

Cruz snorted. "No, he wasn't. Probably turned him over to an associate."

"Before you go off on a tirade, your relatives love him and his girlfriend." It was an exaggeration about Joseph but not Svetlana, but he didn't need to know that, and I was betting that he wouldn't ask. "Svet is one of the nicest people that lives here—she's never rude," I managed to say with a straight face.

Mac snickered behind Cruz's back.

Cruz turned on her. "Get them back here. And I mean today." He reached for the door handle. "Call and update me every hour," he said in a less brusque tone. "Susie will put your calls through." The door banged behind him.

Next time I need to talk to Cruz, I'll have Mac call.

Mac threw herself back in her chair. I breathed a sigh of relief that the attorney was gone. After several minutes, he revved the engine on his sports car and squealed out of the driveway.

"Now what?" I peered out the blinds. "We've got to find Maricruz and get her back, pronto." I shook my head with a frown. "Cruz was livid, but he skipped out pretty quickly. I'd guess that his granny being a handful comes as no surprise."

"What the hell am I supposed to do when I find them? Cuff her to a chair? Tie her up? Lock her in the shed? Then the crafty old bag will sue me."

"There can't be many places where it is legal to sleep on the beach. I can help look." I ignored Creole shaking his head in a vehement *not going to happen.*

"No worries, I'll handle this," Mac said in a syrupy sweet voice. "I'll get with Joseph; he'll know the places I can check. When Shirl gets home, we'll go together. If threats won't work with Maricruz, I'll threaten Crum with pitching his ass to the curb if he doesn't get her cooperation."

"You'll call me?" I asked.

Mac nodded.

Creole stood and held out his hand to me. I took it, and he pulled me to my feet. "This has been fun." He smiled at Mac.

We walked to his truck, where he picked me up and slid me onto the passenger seat. He got behind the wheel, leaned across, and kissed me. "I'm impressed; you were calm under pressure. Makes me think this stuff goes on all the time."

"Just another day of drama."

Chapter Twenty-Five

The rain came down in sheets, battering the sides of the SUV. The windshield wipers worked overtime. The standing puddles of water that seeped to the middle of the lane forced Fab to slow down, and the traffic crawled along. The air conditioning was on low to keep the windows from fogging over from the hot, sticky, rising humidity.

Fab and Didier had gotten back to the house late the night before. Fab had informed me by text, when I didn't come downstairs for coffee early enough to suit her, that we had an appointment with Brick. I texted back, "not going." I wanted to be in the Cove in case anyone called with information on Brad. Not one to be deterred, Fab reminded me that we weren't to go on a case alone and that this would be a quick meeting.

"Do you think we could charge extra for these early morning meetings?" I bent over, fishing my flip-flops out from under the front seat and hoping not to hit my head on the dash when Fab came to a sudden stop in front of Famosa Motors.

"We show up midday, and the showroom is

full of people; how much patience do you have for 'take a number'?" Fab backed up and partially maneuvered the SUV under an awning. "Another flaw in your idea: Brick hates to pay when we get shot at—or almost shot at, in some cases—so the chances are zero he'll pay for accommodating our schedule."

"What's this case about?" I asked, smoothing down my skirt.

"I just got a text to be here and the time."

"Remember your promise to keep this short," I grumbled, slid out—only to find my feet submerged in ankle-deep water—and slammed the door.

"Try to behave yourself," Fab teased.

"I don't think these pot/kettle moments bring us closer as friends." I wrinkled my nose.

The corner of her mouth lifted in an almost-smile.

Although it was too early for the dealership to be open, the doors were unlocked. Pouring rain would not bring out masses of new car buyers. The striking fluorescent-haired woman sat behind the receptionist desk. I waved and Fab ignored her as we passed by, headed to the stairs. I'd forgotten the woman's name. Asking Fab was a waste of time; she never remembered anyone's name.

Everly, that was it.

"Stop right there." Everly stood, taking a step toward us. "There is a certain etiquette that is going to be followed from today forward. First you check in here at the desk, then I announce you to Brick, and he gives the okay for you to go upstairs. Until that time, you stay here. There's coffee and a soda machine right over there." She waved her arm toward a sitting area that was also part of her domain.

Fab yelled at the top of her lungs, "Brick, we're here."

Everly glared at Fab, not amused by her antics. "I really hate to repeat myself. But since you weren't listening or didn't understand, I'll speak slowly."

For a second, Fab's eyes narrowed, and I swore I heard a low growling noise emanate from her. "*Brick and I* have an appointment."

"That's where you're wrong; you'll be meeting with me." Everly's brown eyes shot icicles. "Mr. Famosa is sorry that he couldn't be here, but an unexpected situation occurred that needed his immediate attention."

Lightening danced in the sky and thunder roared overly long, the mood outside matching the one inside. The moment of silence was over for the noisy show, as the fast-moving storm made its presence known just to the north of us.

"Brick couldn't call?" I asked indignantly.

"You're telling me that Brick is discussing his cases with the receptionist?" Fab asked, disbelief written on her face. "Or whatever you are."

Everly wasn't the least bit intimidated by

Fab's hair-raising look, nor by the scene that was unfolding. "If you'll come over here—" She gestured toward her desk. "I'll give you your instructions, and you can leave." She flashed a tight smile.

I moved next to Fab, turning slightly, and whispered, "Don't shoot her."

"What's the job?" Fab demanded, not budging an inch.

After a brief stare-down, Everly lifted a briefcase, setting it on the countertop. "You are to deliver this to the address written on this paper." She produced a piece of Famosa Motors stationary. "You're to call immediately once you've completed the job." Another phony smile; this one had a flash of teeth. "Send me an invoice, and I'll put a check in the mail."

Invoice? Check? Both of us had gotten used to being paid in cash.

Fab retrieved the briefcase. If she hadn't had the handle in a white-knuckle clench, it would have sailed across the room. She jerked the paper from between Everly's fingers, thrusting it at me, and turned, setting the case down on the nearest table with a bang. When the locks didn't budge, she took out her lockpick, not bothering to ask for the code.

"Stop right there." Everly scurried around the desk, reaching for the briefcase at the same time Fab's forearm sent it crashing to the floor. "Your job," she yelled, "is to deliver it, and it's none of your damn business what's inside."

"That's where you're wrong," I told her, nominating myself as the calm one. "You open the case, or we're leaving." I'd had enough of the change in the way we dealt with Brick.

"You must be the pain in the ass." Everly stared at me, giving me the once-over, stopping at my feet, and turned up her nose. "I was wondering which of you it was. Brick told me it would be easy to figure out."

"There's been a change in plans. *You* deliver it, and if you get arrested, call Brick; he's good for the bail. Unless, of course, a judge denies you." I grabbed Fab's arm, silently communicating that if she didn't leave with me, I'd drag her out by the hair.

"*You* can tell Brick that when he gets back to business as agreed on, he can give me a call. Otherwise, he can find someone else." Fab marched out.

I followed, but turned back briefly to see Everly bend down to retrieve the case. Her top rode up and exposed a handgun at the small of her back.

"What the hell just happened?" Fab demanded. "She's no receptionist. Lover? I don't think he's stupid enough to mix business and sex."

"What do you suppose was in the briefcase?" The not-knowing bugged me. "I've still got the address." I pulled the paper out of my pocket, punching the address into the GPS. "Fisher Island. Millionaires and Mansions."

"Brick's up to something," Fab hissed. "Everly's in on it, and we're the odd girls out. Screw him. We need Phil to investigate Everly. I want to know *everything* that can be found on the woman."

I was supposed to order that check and had forgotten. I'd rectify that immediately.

Chapter Twenty-Six

Fab detoured to Ft. Lauderdale so that we could check on Brad's boat; nothing had changed. Driving south, the rain lessened to a heavy drizzle, and when we hit the Keys, the sun came out. The cooler weather was replaced by scorching heat.

"Mother's here," I pointed out when Fab careened around the corner. "Let's hope she brought food." Didier's Mercedes was parked across the street in the neighbor's driveway. I texted an invite to Phil before getting out.

I followed Fab inside. Mother, Spoon, and Didier were sitting around the island, eating what smelled and looked like salmon burgers.

"You two are back early." Mother glanced at the clock. "Another crappy job?"

"Once the job was outlined, Fab turned up her finely arched nose, and we left. I grinned at Fab, then sobered. "We went by Brad's boat on the way; no changes there."

Didier pulled her into his arms. Whatever he said to her in French made her beam up at him.

The roar of a motorcycle had us all staring at

one another. Spoon shoved his stool back, but before he could make it over to the garden window, Gunz smooshed his face against the glass, waving wildly. He headed to the front door, knocked, and didn't wait for an answer before bursting in, his large bulk filling the entryway.

"Nice hairdo," I greeted him. He was Fab's friend, but that didn't prevent us from sharing a mutual distrust.

Gunz ignored me, his dark eyes focused on Fab. "Hey, sugar. You called, and here I am."

"You can introduce him." I smirked. "You can skip Spoon; they're already acquainted." The two men grunted at one another in acknowledgment, each doubtless wishing they had the power to make the other disappear.

Gunz bent his head over Mother's hand. She twisted her nose and, always the polite one, said something about it being nice to meet him. I snorted, and he shot me a dirty look. He nodded to Didier. "The boyfriend," he said, unimpressed.

Another knock on the door. Spoon, as he squeezed by Gunz, said, "If you ever have occasion to come back here, wait until you're invited in." He answered and stepped back. Phil and he exchanged words, and they both laughed.

"Hey, doll." Gunz salivated. "Bartender, right? That's a waste of your talent."

I rolled my eyes, turning to Fab with an unspoken, *Get Gunz under control.*

"Did you come here with information?" Fab snapped at Gunz.

"Pinged Brad's phone." Gunz crossed his arms, proud of himself. "Nothing. Which is odd, unless he doesn't want to be located or keeps it in one of those special cases or if, for some reason, someone took the battery out."

"Stick to the facts," Spoon barked, hauling Mother to his side.

"The last of Brad's texts led us to believe he'd be back tomorrow. If I get another text, can you ping that?" Didier questioned.

"I'll have my associate regularly check the number. You get a message, call immediately." Gunz pushed himself away from the counter, waving off Mother's offer of food. "Anything else?" He winked at Fab. "You know where to find me."

Didier shot Gunz a "drop dead" look.

He laughed, stopping in front of Phil. "Can I call you?"

"I'm taken," Phil responded.

"Anything changes, Fab has my number." Gunz lumbered out the door.

"Bye, see you." I waved after the door closed.

"Really, Madison." Mother stuck out her lecture finger. "Gunz seems like a—"

"If you say 'nice man,' I'm going to cough up the two bites of food I ate right as he barged in."

Everyone laughed except Mother and Didier.

"He is helping to find Brad, and that's all that

matters, whatever his faults," Mother said.

"I tried not to be annoyed that he didn't have jack." I was on a roll with all the dirty looks today.

"Word's out on the street," Phil said. "Money in exchange for information. Doodad is helping to coordinate it so I don't have to deal with every lowlife in town."

"Doodad…" I paused. "Isn't that the civil war veteran that hangs around town, posing for pictures with tourists?" The man strutted around in an authentic uniform, regaling those that would listen with his command of history.

"He's not as old as he looks; a hard life will do that to you," Phil said. "He doesn't rip people off or steal from them; they get what they pay for and a little education, if they listen."

"Everly Lynch." Thank goodness I'd remembered this time. "She works for Brick, and we want to know everything about her as soon as possible."

"Got it." Phil saluted.

My phone rang, Mac's face popping up on the screen. "It's Miss January…" Mac said, sounding frantic, when I answered. Then the line went dead.

"Just great." I hit redial, and Mac's phone went to voicemail. "There's a problem at The Cottages." I crossed to Mother, enveloping her in a hug. "I'll be right back—hopefully."

I grabbed my bag off the bench in the entry,

fishing my keys out of the bottom. I was about to tell Fab to hurry up when I saw her back turned in conversation with Didier. I made eye contact with him and shut the door behind me.

* * *

Two police cars blocked the driveway, an ambulance in the middle of the street. Cutting it close, I maneuvered into Mac's driveway.

Miss January was being led by Kevin to one of the patrol cars. He helped her inside, and she laid her head against the backseat.

"Kevin," I yelled, throwing up my hands. "What's going on?" Struggling to control my temper, I said, "She just got out of the hospital."

"Mind your own business," he shouted back.

It surprised me to see Cruz and his grandmother; I would have thought that she'd be long gone. Mac stood behind them, waving at me, pointing at Maricruz, and frowning. Cruz, in well-fitting jeans and a white button-down shirt, appeared to be questioning the other deputy. Judging by the officer's sullen expression, he had zero interest in whatever Cruz was going on about.

It took a few short strides for Mac to reach me. "Score is dead," she informed me breathlessly. "And has been for a while."

"He is older than… He's lived a long life." Despite owning the property for a few years now, I was feeling like the new girl. "Are you trying to tell me Miss January murdered him?"

Before Mac could answer, Cruz snarled, "I want that bastard arrested." He pointed at Crum, who was slinking back toward his cottage.

Kevin strode up. "For what? Granny here having questionable taste in men? We should arrest her. You can bail her out; give you something to do, since you can't seem to control one old woman."

I clasped my hands behind my back, resisting the urge to clap.

Maricruz spun around, scowling and giving Kevin the finger. Cruz was the only person who didn't see the display.

"What is Grandma alleging?" I asked Cruz. "If we could hurry this along, you'd have time to keep Miss January from going to lockup."

"Don't count on it," Cruz said icily. He took hold of his grandmother's hand, steering her towards the pool area, followed by the cop, who whistled for Crum to go along.

Jerking on Mac's arm, I steered her off to one side. "I want to hear about Miss January first."

"Shirl was bringing Miss January home from the hospital today, so I went into her cottage to open the windows, let in a little fresh air." Mac's suntanned skin paled considerably. "The smell…hit me in the face."

"Do you need to sit down?"

Mac shook her head. "Thinking back, I haven't

seen Score in a long time. I'd asked about him a couple times, and Miss January always mumbled that he was great and gave me one of those moony smiles of hers. You know, the one where she looks demented."

"Can we get to the part about why she is in custody?"

"Unbeknownst to me, Maricruz came up behind me and got a whiff of dead body odor. I told her that I would take care of it, but she called 911 before I could stop her. That's when I called you."

"Why would she do that?"

"To get even with me because I called Cruz and told him she was back from her romp on the beach."

I squeezed my eyes closed, wishing Creole had another day off. "And Score?"

"It's unclear how long he's been dead. Miss January admitted to Kevin that she knew he was dead and didn't tell anyone. She didn't want anyone taking him away when she could take care of him." Mac shuddered.

Tired of standing in the middle of the driveway, I walked over to the barbeque area. From where I sat at one of the concrete tables, I could observe the comings and goings.

"You want some gross details?"

"Where's Fab when I need her?" I groaned. "Go ahead."

"The medics weren't here long before one ran

back out the door and got sick in the flowers. Apologized, muttering he'd never seen a body so decomposed. Score apparently died in bed, a sheet and blanket up to his neck. When the medic pulled back the covers, there was a rush of bugs skittering away from the decomposed body, which had been partially skeletonized. They're guessing he's been dead a couple of months."

I cupped my hands over my face, rubbing my eyes and hoping I didn't remember a word of this conversation. "In all of this, I haven't heard the word 'murder.' So why the arrest?"

"I'd bet on natural causes. Before he went in search of his grandmother, Cruz mentioned misdemeanor abuse of a corpse. He also ticked off state health code provisions regulating how bodies must be handled, violations of which are punishable as criminal offenses."

I groaned.

"Where's your friend—you know, the sexy one? She's going to be mad when she has to ask me for pictures of the body. I believe I'll hold out for a favor."

Kevin whistled for a medic, who came over and checked out Miss January. A moment later, he called for his partner, who rolled up a gurney.

I jumped up and ran over, stopping next to Kevin. "What's going on?"

"I'm not sure she was ready to be discharged from the hospital. She looked more like death than usual when I got here. That could be because she was upset at knowing her boyfriend was gone. I've seen dead bodies before, but I hope I never see anything like this again. I'm afraid I'll never get that image out of my head."

"You arresting her?"

"She's lucky it's almost shift change and that would delay my going home." Kevin laughed. "She's not under arrest. I put her in the back of my car so she wouldn't fall down or wander off."

Miss January was loaded into the ambulance, and it shot off to Tarpon Cove Hospital.

"I'm going to find out what's going on over there." I pointed to Cruz talking with the other officer.

"Some days, I wish I'd called in sick." Kevin's eyes glinted, and a muscle in his cheek tightened. He glared as Crum came out of his cottage.

The man carried a large ice bag. He was overdressed, in a short skirt, a button-down shirt, and brown loafers that smacked the ground when he took a step.

"Do you suppose Granny kneed the esteemed professor in the groin?" Kevin snickered.

Mac appeared at my side. "This is going to get ugly," she whispered. "Cruz walked in on his grandmother and Crum in some sort of sexual position. Considering their ages, it probably involved lying down. Now Cruz is insisting Granny didn't put out willingly."

"Maricruz can settle this issue in short order." Kevin's tone was irritated.

"That woman loves to stir trouble." Mac grimaced.

"I'll be in the office." I needed aspirin. I couldn't wait to tell Creole. He wouldn't believe me; it would take some convincing.

"*Now* you decide to mind your own business," Kevin drawled and stomped off.

"I want him arrested," Cruz yelled, pointing at Crum.

"Mari," Crum whined, "tell him we're in love."

I winced and reached for the doorknob.

"Madison, stop right there," Cruz bellowed.

Damn, I almost made it inside. I took a deep breath, turning to Cruz. "Would you like to take this into the office?"

Cruz brushed past me; one hand on Maricruz's arm, he steered her toward the couch, where they sat side by side. Accusation burned in his deep-brown eyes, as though the unfolding drama was my fault.

I cut Mac off and scooted around the desk, thinking it was a good idea to put distance between me and the lawyer. "You want Crum arrested, why? What did he do?"

Mac stuffed herself in a small space between the desk and front door. Fast escape.

"He had non-consensual sex with my grandmother. That's rape." Cruz's fury flared hotter.

For a smart man, Crum didn't have the sense

to leave; instead, he stood in the doorway, looking more unkempt than usual. He cleared his throat to speak, but I cut him off.

I zeroed in on Maricruz. "You can clear this up right now. Is what Cruz says true or not?"

The woman knew her dramatic pauses, and used this one to inch away from Cruz, who put his arm around her and anchored her to his side. She unleashed a hissing tirade in Spanish on her grandson, which clearly caught him by surprise. He dropped his arm, and she used that moment to launch herself to her feet, push Crum aside, and flounce out the door.

Cruz covered his groin with the ice bag in his hand.

Mac announced, "Maricruz is a biter."

Cruz rose to his full height; posture impeccable, he looked down his nose. "This isn't over." He glared in Crum's direction.

"Yes, it is." I jumped up. "Everything the two of them did was consensual. Don't take my word for it; go door to door. I realize that Crum doesn't present well, and he wouldn't be your first choice for Maricruz to have a holiday fling with, but if it makes you feel any better, he's a retired college professor."

He turned his full attention on me. "It does not. I expected better from you." He controlled his anger, but every syllable was spoken with knife-edged precision.

"We're not the morality police." I struggled

not to flinch under his gaze. "Your grandmother came here acting like a college student on spring break. The good news is that no one ended up in cuffs. We did everything we could to steer her into tamer activities, but she wasn't interested."

"Are you finished?" Not waiting for a response, he stalked out the door.

Crum, who wasn't so stupid after all, had already vacated the doorway, stepping out into the dirt next to a pair of palm trees. Now he shoved his head around the door frame. "Thank you for defending me."

"Just take care of yourself."

Crum nodded and limped off.

I should have known, when I saw that Crum was attracted to Maricruz, that she'd be half-crazy.

Mac patted my shoulder. "I'll test the waters when I take Granny's suitcase to his office tomorrow. Susie has a thing for iced brownie cookies; I'll take her a dozen and see if I can trade them for information."

"Tell me now—are there any more surprises?"

"They're over for today." Mac crossed her fingers in front of her chest. "But you have decisions to make."

Kevin, who had apparently been standing just outside the door listening to every word, poked his head inside. "I take it there'll be no wedding invite in the mail." When I didn't answer, he went on: "Crum pled his case to my partner, so I got a detailed explanation for why the professor is limping." He cringed and changed the subject. "Do you happen to know Score's real name? I'm thinking it's a nickname."

I struggled not to roll my eyes. "Never asked, partly because he was always drunk. I didn't object to her dragging him in off the beach because he made her happy. In the beginning, I'd hoped Miss January would drink less under his influence. I was disabused of that notion quite quickly."

"If there's no family…you going to pony up for a proper burial? He can't come back here." Kevin burst out laughing.

"You're not very funny."

"Ohh." He faked a frown.

"I'll call the guys at Tropical Slumber and alert them to an impending delivery. Dickie will be disappointed that he can't use his dressing skills."

Kevin made a puking noise.

"You promise that you aren't going to arrest or harass Miss January?" I asked. "I'll get her a lawyer." *Not Cruz,* I grimaced.

"That's up to the county attorney. As long as the old dude died of natural causes, dragging her through court would be a public relations nightmare. People around here will sympathize with her story. She warmed my cold heart when she started crying, worrying when the sheet was lowered that he would get cold and asking what about dinner."

"Pop Tarts." Mac made a face. "I need something more filling."

Kevin smiled at her. I wanted to kick him for encouraging her.

"I'm going to go door to door and make a dead-person check, and then I'm out of here." Kevin waved.

Mac checked out his butt as he walked off.

"We need to get our crime scene cleaner out here ASAP." I took my keys out of my pocket. "Suggest that he also freshen up Kitty. One of these days, we're going to inherit it, and I don't want it smelling like a dead person. The only reason I'm not going to slip into Jake's and get my drunk on is because I can't be hungover tomorrow."

Chapter Twenty-Seven

"Cherie, I'm about out of patience with you. Staring at me will not make my phone ring faster." Didier's blue eyes bore into me.

I'd already had to restrain myself from following him around the house, ultimately deciding that my best vantage point was the daybed in the living room. I propped my feet on the dark rattan headboard. Brad's boat was due in today, according to the last text message received. In actuality, I'd spoken to the new captain and knew that Brad's boat had pulled out this morning for the next scheduled trip.

"I'm reading," I said sulkily, tapping my laptop. If he thought I was going to let him out of my sight before I knew whether a new message had been received or not, he'd soon learn I had the patience to sit here all day.

The French doors to the pool were open, and crisp, salty air blew in, making me hope he'd take his laptop and go outside to get some sun. The cats had split ranks today, Jazz lying by my side and Snow in front of the patio doors, catching some fresh air. Fab, who had just finished a swim, slunk through the doors, eyebrows raised, staring between the two of us.

Saved by the doorbell. I jumped up, hoping it wasn't bad news. I opened the door to find Gunz standing there in his signature shorts and tropical shirt, his bald head glowing with sweat. Appearing impatient at the less-than-a-minute wait, he pushed past me, glanced into the kitchen, then went into the living room.

"Hey, sugar." Gunz smiled when he noticed Fab draped across a chair. He ignored Didier, which elicited a glare. "Got news for you. Phone came back on; this Brad character is here in Tarpon."

I maneuvered around a chair to confront Gunz face to face. "That character is my brother. I'd like to hear any information you have firsthand. Where in the Cove?"

"You're not my client or my friend. I'm doing this for gorgeous here." His tongue slithered out like a snake's.

Didier snapped his laptop closed, stood, and cleared the space between him and Fab in a couple of steps. He picked her up out of the chair and carried her back to the couch, where he sat down, his arm anchored around her shoulders. "Why don't you tell us what you know?" Didier's jaw tightened in irritation. "Start by answering Madison's question."

"Gunz, please," Fab tried to placate him, silently pleading with him not to make a scene.

"How close were you able to get in pinpointing his location?"

"The general area is the best I've got. It's not like you get an exact address or an intersection or whatever you were expecting. It's not bad news; the flake is back in town."

"You awful bastard—get out my house!" I shrieked out all my pent-up frustration. "My brother is not and has never been a flake." Fab jumped up, taking his arm, saying something I couldn't make out, which enraged me more. "Hustle your big ass before I get my gun and fill it with holes."

"You threaten me after I go out of my way to help you, and act like some old harpy," he yelled back.

Fab jerked on his arm, steering him to the front door, which he made difficult by dragging his feet.

"Out." I pointed.

"You'll be getting my bill. You don't pay, and I'll send a collector."

Fab got behind him and shoved him out the door. Once they were outside, it slammed shut.

Didier moved in front of me, holding me tightly with my face buried in his chest. I pushed against him. "I can't breathe." He loosened his hold. "Nice chest." I smiled faintly. "Don't worry, my gun's upstairs."

"You do know that I'm going to relate the details of this scene to Brad. He'll be as impressed as I am that you stood up to that common thug."

"Gunz's most redeeming quality is that he's loyal to Fab. I'm sure she'll smooth things over."

"My phone." It had pinged. Didier grabbed it up off the table. He held it out so that we could read the message together. "I need some time away. A few things to work out. Back soon."

"No way Brad sent that message," I said. "Someone has him, and they don't want us to worry? Probably more like they don't want the police alerted." I shook my head. "We know he's in town, or his phone is anyway. For a small town, it might as well be a big city, though, when you're trying to find someone who doesn't want to be found or who someone else doesn't want found."

The door opened again, and Mother and Spoon came in, holding pizza boxes that got dumped on the kitchen island.

"We got an update from Gunz," Mother said. "Sounded like a bunch of nothing."

"Bastard didn't look happy, which didn't bother me," Spoon said. "I didn't want to leave Fab outside with him, but she assured me that she'll be in a few minutes." He checked his watch.

Didier motioned Mother to his side and handed her his phone. "What does this mean?" she asked, handing it to Spoon.

"It means we're going to find him," I said with

a confidence that I didn't whole-heartedly feel, but I refused to entertain negativity. "The street snitches will be more important than ever. He's in town; someone will see him or, hopefully, something that will give us a clue as to where he is."

Fab strutted in, slamming the door. "Gunz got another message. Brad's phone is off again, with no ping to pick up. He suspects someone is removing the battery. The cell company might get a hit, but that would require court paperwork. That went well, don't you think?"

Chapter Twenty-Eight

Before going to Jake's, Fab and I had checked out every known haunt of Brad's and the surrounding areas. Fab thought it a colossal waste of time but didn't have a better idea. I hoped for a sighting of his truck. The local authorities had the license plate number on their radar, but that hadn't turned up anything. The only thing to do was wait and see if one of the lowlifes or the cops came up with something.

The jukebox blared a drinking song through the open doors at Jake's. Instead of sneaking in the kitchen door, Fab and I came in through the front. Every stool at the bar had been claimed, and the tables on the deck were also full. I glared in the direction of the private table, which had a sign on it—"Don't sit here."—that was regularly ignored, and recognized three local sheriff's deputies. I headed down the hall and retrieved two stools from the office, dragging them to the end of the bar and blocking the small station where drinks were picked up.

"Everly Lynch doesn't exist." Phil slapped down a printout. "At least not until a year ago. Before that, no records."

"That's ridiculous," Fab snapped.

"Why? She wouldn't be the first person we've met to reinvent herself."

I didn't bother to ask why we should care about Brick and his receptionist. Fab had had a confrontational phone call with the man about how high-handedly Everly had treated the two us and how, if we were to believe her, she was calling the shots. Brick had weaseled out of offering a straight answer, only saying that there were times when he would be busy and we'd need to take instruction from the fiery redhead.

Fab had unleashed a litany of unflattering adjectives on him that made Didier, who was listening in, raise his eyebrows, but he never said a word, although the sides of his lips quirked. It was unclear who hung up on whom, although Fab claimed victory.

"If one of you could get a copy of her personnel file, I could check that out," Phil offered.

"Brick's probably not familiar with normal business practices since he usually promotes from the stripper pool at The Gentleman's Club." The strip club out in Alligator Alley was one of his many businesses. Being out in the middle of nowhere didn't slow business one bit.

"The first thing I noticed about Everly was that she wasn't his usual type when it came to choosing a pole twirler. He likes these—" Fab put her hands out like a platter. "—unusually large, not caring that they couldn't possibly be real. They say men can tell the difference, but I wouldn't know."

"Don't look at me," I said. "Mine are real."

Phil shook her head with a smile. "This conversation would be better with a pitcher of margaritas and some chips."

Fab and I settled for water and the bowl of snack mix that sat in front of us.

"What now?" I poked Fab.

"We're going to get her life story right from her horse's lips." Fab seemed sure of herself.

"That's unkind; they're not that big." The only way Fab could pull that off was with a gun, and I didn't want to ask. This could end poorly. I had too much on my plate to be getting involved with this harebrained scheme. "Remind me: why do we care?"

"Brick is my oldest client. I feel a certain responsibility for his safety, and hiring a ghost could turn out to be bad for his health." Fab sounded so sincere, it was difficult not to laugh at her.

Phil snorted. "You're so full of it. She bested you, and you want to even the score."

"In the morning, we're going to arrive at Famosa Motors before anyone else, wait for her bright-and-early backside to arrive, and have a chat with Ms. Everly Lynch."

"I need to stay in town and you know that," I huffed.

"No more after this, I promise."

"Any word on my bro from your sources?" I asked Phil.

She frowned sympathetically. "I promise to call if I get anything."

"The more time that goes by, the less likely it seems that we'll hear anything." I laid my head on my arms.

"We're going to find him." Fab yanked on the ends of my hair.

"I hate waiting."

"When do you take the bar exam?" Fab asked Phil.

"I've got it scheduled for next month, and I need that time for studying. Overachiever that I am, I want to pass on the first go-round."

"Then what? Head to the big city?" I asked. "Work for someone like Cruz? I'd offer you a recommendation, but it's safe to say I'm his least favorite person right now. I have Grandma to thank for that."

"I've got a few ideas, and they don't include Miami." Phil grabbed Fab's empty water bottle one step ahead of it going airborne and tossed it in the trash. "Maricruz blew through here on several nights, stirring up trouble and enjoying every minute of it. The second night, I asked her what Cruz would say about her behavior. *Tell him,* she sneered. *He'll never believe your word over mine.* She flounced off and got one of the regulars at the bar to bump and grind up against her on the dance floor."

"Dance floor" was an overstatement. It was any empty space the customers could find to move around in without running into the pool players or getting in the way of a dart game, usually in front of the jukebox. Dancing was a rare occurrence and involved imbibing several beers ahead of time.

* * *

There would be hell to pay for sneaking out of my house without telling anyone. Hopefully the consensus would be that I'd gone to bed. It was hard to sit and do nothing when no one had a clue where Brad was.

Approaching The Cottages, I parked around the corner. The last thing I wanted was to get caught up in twenty questions with Mac or anyone else. Passersby trespassed on a regular basis; surely I could sneak around unseen. Thanks to runners from the law, I knew all the unmarked exits. Shimmying around a palm tree, squeezing through a fence opening, and reaching the open beach was a ticket to a quick getaway.

I cut down the side street; the keys in my pocket meant I didn't have to scale the fence that ran along the pool area. I listened before shoving the gate open; all was quiet for a change. The water glistened with multi-colored floating lights.

"What are you up to?" a male voice whispered hoarsely.

I clapped my hand over my mouth to cover the scream that threatened to erupt. "What the devil?"

Liam looked around me. "No backup. I'm in." The gate that normally slammed shut was closed quietly. He hugged me. "You're the last person I expected to find lurking around."

I knew I had that deer-in-the-headlights look. I wasn't sure what to say; Julie wanted to be the one to tell him about Brad. "Since I'm the landlord, I thought an unscheduled visit would show me to be conscientious."

Liam put his arm around my shoulders and led me down a side path. "Brad's not here and hasn't been. Nothing inside his cottage has moved for days." He answered my unspoken question with, "I have a key and check every morning."

We stopped in front of Brad's door.

"You want to go in?" He took out his key.

I nodded and followed him inside. Liam was right; nothing had changed since I'd been here last. Going back outside, I sat in one of the deck chairs. The cool ocean air brushed my cheeks. "How did you find out?"

"Eavesdropping, tricking info out of a drunk; probably should feel bad about that, but it was kinda fun." He settled in the chair next to me. "The downside was that I got a bunch of really personal information that no one should ever have to hear."

"Your mom will flip."

"She doesn't want me to worry. She thinks there is some reasonable explanation; she's hoping Brad will walk in the door at any moment, and it will be something everyone will laugh over." Liam didn't look convinced that that would be the outcome. "Why are you skulking around by yourself?"

I told him about sneaking out, not being able to stand one more minute of doing nothing, even if I was wasting time.

"You're going to be in so much trouble. Glad I'm not you." Liam's laugh rolled out into the night.

"I'm a grown woman and can do—"

Liam waved his hand, cutting me off. "Wrong attitude. You walk back in, all sad-faced, which won't be hard, and you say something short and heartfelt. Make Brad proud. Just like you taught him, or so he told me...unless he wasn't telling me the truth?" He arched his brow.

"We were such emotional scammers. Hats off to Mother; we didn't get away with it every time." I didn't want to dwell on memories. I needed to keep focus; Brad and I would be making new ones soon. "I shouldn't be asking you this, but anything else going on around here that I haven't heard about yet?"

"Decorating Rocks' cottage in police tape was

a good idea. Some junky lowrider car cruised by the first night, pulled around the block, and came back for a second pass with a flashlight. Haven't seen the car again." Liam flashed a lopsided grin. "Don't worry, I stayed out of sight."

I rose to my feet and enveloped him in a hug. "Don't do anything to put yourself in danger." I grasped his shoulders, giving him a slight shake. "Do you understand?"

"Promise. If someone comes snooping around, my first call is 911."

"Think I'll go back to my car via the beach." I hugged him again, kicked off my shoes, waved, and took off down the sand.

Following the same route that I recently took with Fab, my last stop was the apartment building under renovation. This time, I parked on the opposite side of the street and checked each floor for a stray light. We hadn't checked the building floor by floor, but Didier assured us that the construction crew had searched every corner. He'd reminded us that the building had security and there had been no breaches.

My luck was sure to run out soon, and I wanted to get home before my phone started blowing up with calls. I turned off the air conditioner and rolled down both windows. Warm and humid, the night air blew through, smelling of salt and sand. With no traffic, and not having to worry about blaring horns, I poked along, scanning each side of the street as I made my way home.

I turned off my headlights before turning into the driveway. On the off-chance that no one had noticed my absence, I decided to sneak back in like a teenager. Back in the day, Brad and I had crawled out our bedroom window after Mother had gone to bed and gone off on a planned adventure with our friends, then snuck back in the same way. That was the disadvantage of having my bedroom on the second floor. I crept down the secret path, and found Fab standing at the end, arms crossed, clearly irritated.

"Where the hell have you been?" she hissed.

"Went for a walk on the beach." I did walk a few feet in the sand, so that was a stretch, but close enough.

"I don't believe that excuse for a minute; it would be far more believable if you'd shown up with a bucket of shells."

"I'm going to bed." I turned on my heel and headed back to the driveway.

"You're going the wrong way."

I paused, turning. "I'm going in the front door since it's closer to the stairs."

Turning the corner, I heard a car door slam. Glancing out to the street, I waited to see if we had a late-night visitor, breathing a sigh when no one strolled up the driveway. Reaching for the door knob, I took a deep breath and pasted a pleasant smile on my face; without a mirror to check myself out, I hoped I didn't look deranged.

I walked in, passing the kitchen and living room, where a few heads turned my way. "Sorry if I worried you."

"Fab told us you went for a walk," Mother said. "No news."

One hand on the banister, I backed into something hard. "A walk, my ass," the wall said.

Damn, the man was so quiet, sneaking around.

I turned and looked up into his devilish blue eyes.

Creole's index finger touched my cheek and trailed its way down my face to my jaw, his eyes following its movement.

"I, uh…" His touch affected my thoughts. I no longer wanted to run and hide in my room but wanted instead to go back out the door and down to his beach house.

"That's exactly what I thought." His hand on the small of my back pushed me up the stairs as he said to the others, "We'll see you in the morning."

So embarrassing. My cheeks turned bright red. Facing forward, I didn't have the nerve to even glance over my shoulder.

Creole closed the door, turned the lock, and flipped on a sound machine that emitted ocean noises and claimed to drown out sounds. It had been a gift from Fab, who'd smirked when I pulled it out of the shopping bag. Despite my extreme embarrassment, I'd plugged in that night.

"You know what I like about your clothes?" Creole pulled my skirt off. "A couple of yanks, and you're naked." He winked, and my top sailed across the room. "You can skip the walk story. When Madeline called, I tracked you on that app I installed on your phone. It squeezed my heart, knowing that you felt helpless doing nothing and ended up driving the streets." He kissed the end of my nose. "You spent a lot longer at The Cottages than I expected. Anything I need to know?"

I leaned my head against his chest and related what Liam had seen. I shut my eyes, pushing the tears back, which didn't work; they spilled down my cheeks without any regard for what I wanted, which was to not cry in front of him. He held me away from him and caught my tears with his thumb, wiping them away, then kissing me lightly. After I sniffed a couple of times, a Kleenex appeared under my nose.

He tossed the extra pillows to the floor, followed by the comforter, and pulled back the sheet. "Get in." He pointed. When I hesitated too long, he scooped me up, put me in the bed, and covered me up. He twirled around, singing off-key, a tune that I didn't recognize; he swiveled his hips and treated me to a striptease. He finished with a complete turn and a bow.

I pulled the sheet up, covering my nose, and giggled.

He slid in next to me, pulling me into his arms.

Chapter Twenty-Nine

"You're lucky Creole had to leave early, or I wouldn't be on this ridealong to watch you try to ferret out who Everly Lynch is from the woman herself. I'd be off with him, searching for Brad. He promised to stay in touch, even if he has no news." I warned as she weaved in and out of traffic as she sped towards South Miami: "You will not maim or kill the woman."

"Drama Queen!" Fab sniffed. "I want to make sure she's not going to hurt Brick and that he knows what he's dealing with."

I made a gagging noise.

"You'd feel bad if you had to attend his funeral. The guilt."

"I have a long-standing rule of which you are well aware; I don't go to the funerals of strangers and certainly not to those of people I couldn't stand when they sucked air. Unless it's a job for our favorite gravediggers." I caught Fab's glare and waved my hand in frustration. "You seem to have a short memory. Brick's lied to us, over and over, sent us into dangerous situations with no heads up, and I've lost count of the times we've been shot at."

"We survived all those hiccups, and look at us." Fab flexed her muscles. "Badass PIs."

I squinted at her, shaking my head. "You're nuts."

Fab had her private investigator's license; I had what could laughingly be called a backup card. I'd technically been working under Brick's license for the necessary hours to get my own. I'd thought several times about asking when I'd be completing my servitude but figured I'd have a long wait for him to stop laughing.

"We're here. I'll do the dirty work. No need for both of us to get into trouble with Brick," Fab said, as though she had a plan.

"If law enforcement somehow gets invited to this party, we'll both end up in ugly orange." I pointed to Everly's Porsche. "We're late." She was parked in one of the three reserved VIP spaces. "How does a receptionist afford a 100K sports car? Unless she gets the freebie rate, like you."

Fab's face tightened; she didn't like that idea. "That would mean… I don't want to think about it." She slid out from behind the wheel and stalked to the side door.

Following her, I guessed that, if Everly and her job survived this day, she'd never leave the door unlocked again.

Fab walked in and looked up at the darkened window of Brick's office.

Everly stopped in mid-stride, turning. "Was

Mr. Famosa expecting you? I don't have you on the calendar." She made a dismissive sniff and moved toward the coffee maker.

Quick as lightening, Fab tripped her, sending her to the floor, relieved her of her gun, and kicked it across the floor.

I stared, open-mouthed, surprised that Fab had caught Everly by surprise. After a short tussle, she even made getting her into cuffs look relatively easy. Fab retrieved the woman's gun and shoved it inside her waistband.

Then she nudged Everly with her foot and rolled her over. "Who the hell are you? I'll save you a few lies. We already know Everly Lynch has only existed for a year."

"You're a dead bitch," Everly spit through her teeth.

Fab stepped out of range. "Not if you're dead first," she said sweetly.

"Brick will never let you get away with treating me like this."

"Banging the boss?" Fab sneered.

I stepped forward. "You should call Brick. If he's not available, then call Casio; no one *screws* with his family." Brick's brother was a highly decorated Miami detective; if the stories were true, he'd take her into custody and lose her in the system.

"You two are frighteningly stupid. You shouldn't be allowed outside without a leash."

I knew a couple of people who thought I

needed a keeper but had never heard it said about Fab. Probably because they were afraid of her and knew she'd kick the hell out of them.

The decision was taken out of our hands. Just then, Brick's Escalade pulled in next to Everly's car. He strode through the door and did a double take. He rushed to Everly, helping her to her feet. "What the hell is going on?" he yelled at me.

I shook my head, pointing the finger at Fab.

"Uncuff her." He lowered his voice, but not by much.

"I don't think so." Fab stiffened her stance and stood her ground. "You need to know a few facts about your employee here. Starting with who the hell is she?" she yelled, her anger rising to match his.

Brick hooked his arm around Everly, whispering in her ear. Whatever he said, her anger hadn't lessened, but she jerked her head in a nod. "Give me the key to the cuffs. Now!" he barked and thrust out his hand. "Or I swear I'll take the keys off you and do it myself."

I moved next to Fab, nudging her, not wanting Brick to hurt her, which considering that his eyes were filled with anger, he might. My girl would never admit defeat.

Fab and Brick engaged in a stare-down. Finally, she took the key from her back pocket and moved behind Everly, who winced when she unlocked the cuffs.

Brick scanned the empty showroom. "We're

not having this conversation down here." Neither Fab nor I were offered an elevator ride, so we took the steps.

The door dinged on the second floor but didn't open for the longest time. When it did, Brick stalked past us, his hand possessively on Everly. He came to a halt just inside his office. "Have a seat. Everyone behaves themselves."

Fab glared and headed straight to her usual seat, the ledge that overlooked the showroom. "You might change your mind once you see this." Before sitting, she pulled a copy of the background check from the back of her jeans and tossed it on his desk.

I sat in a chair against the wall, close to the door.

Brick jerked the paperwork up and gave it a cursory glance. "How stupid do you think I am? I know all of this already." He swiveled in his chair and opened the refrigerator, holding up a water bottle; only Everly nodded. "The receptionist job is a cover. Everly is my bodyguard." He turned his attention to her. "I'm sorry you had to go through this."

"You're a bastard," I said. "Fab was worried about your worthless life. After everything she's done, you allow this woman—" I pointed to Everly. "—to demean her. I know telling the truth never occurs to you, but you owed Fab."

"I'll talk to you later." He stood and came around his desk, crossing to Everly, who hadn't bothered to sit and was standing in front of the open door.

He said something to her that I couldn't hear, even though I was closest. Then, louder: "Anyone calls, I'm not in." She left without a word. He pointed his finger at me and then the door. "Get out. Close the door behind you."

I waited for the signal from Fab to stay or leave. She nodded at the door, and I left quietly, not slamming the door, which I itched to do.

Everly waited at the top of the stairs.

"Just remember this little scene, Ms. Lynch," I told her. "Don't be surprised when it happens to you. Fab and Brick have done business for a long time, and all it would have taken was one word from him to avoid this whole drama. He owed it to her, and he didn't bother."

"I hope he severs his relationship with her. She's unstable."

"What she *is* is fiercely loyal. Brick, not so much, unless it's in his best interests. His vague relationship with the truth and habit of not disclosing all the pertinent facts have, in the past, gotten people shot, which is, I suspect, the reason he can't keep good help." The woman didn't show a flicker of emotion. "Except Fab, who has some misguided need to never say no to Brick because of their longstanding relationship."

After a long pause, during which neither of us said a word and it became clear she had no comment, I brushed past her and hustled down the stairs. I forced myself to walk and not run back to the SUV.

Chapter Thirty

It surprised me that, when Fab slid into the driver's seat, she was fully composed. She checked the rearview mirror and backed out. The only sign that her anger hadn't dissipated was her white-knuckled grip on the steering wheel.

"You're not going to talk to me. Your best friend in the whole wide world." I sighed dramatically. "It is the world, isn't it, and not just Florida?"

"You don't have to know everything." She headed out into traffic rather sedately, another sign she wasn't herself.

The smirk was quick, and had I taken my eyes off her for a second, I would've missed it. "That's a good one. I hope you don't have a hissy fit when I use it on you. In the meantime, I sit here, all ladylike, waiting patiently to hear every last word that you and that bastard exchanged."

"They're not sleeping together."

"Just damn ick. I hope you've got something better than that."

"It was Everly's idea to test my loyalty. The last time he got shot, it was after a case the two of us worked on. Everly discounted you as being too dumb." Fab grinned at me.

"So you're both the hot one *and* the smart one?"

Fab didn't bother to hide her smile. "Brick explained away her bogus identity as her needing a fresh start."

"That doesn't pass the smell test. It's damn difficult to get a new identity. Besides being illegal, it takes someone with computer skills and cash to pay for the transaction. I'll bet Ms. Lynch has something big to hide."

"Brick did half-ass apologize, which surprised me—probably him too—said he should have handled the situation better. He explained he tended to act on his brilliant ideas before thinking them through."

What a jerk! "Did you sweep everything under his desk, pretend it never happened?"

"Anyone watching the two of us would think so. I would've welcomed that until he let it slip that he'll be using Everly on the kinds of cases I turn my nose up at. He made it clear that the extra charges for shots fired aggravated him and—though he didn't outright say so, he might as well have—that he felt my claims were made up."

Thinking back, I felt bad; it was my idea to charge more. However, the boyfriends would be ecstatic that we wouldn't be working for him as much.

"How did you leave it?"

"Now that I know the truth of Everly's hiring and extended duties, it made it easier to tell him that Didier had gotten an offer too good to turn down—being the face of a European clothing line—which will require him to relocate to Italy for four to six months, and that I'd be going with him. I no longer have to feel a twinge of guilt at leaving him in the lurch. Brick didn't hide that he was stunned, which made me feel as though I might be missed after all. He did wish me well."

The air was sucked out of my lungs in a short whoosh. *Italy? Four to six months?* "When were you going to tell me?"

"I just told you everything."

A scream erupted from my lips. "You tell Brick that you're leaving town before *me*? No heads up, from you or Didier, that you were thinking of such a move?"

Fab rubbed her ear. "That wasn't as much fun as I thought it would be. I made it all up. Not all of it. I did tell Brick that story because I didn't want to be pressured to work for him anytime soon. If he finds out, I'll just make something else up; not sure what, but something."

"So you're not leaving?"

Fab shook her head, and I slugged her in the arm as hard as I could.

"Ouch, dammit."

"You're not funny." I glared.

"Oh well." Fab flashed a sly smile. "Let's stop at Jake's and get a drink."

"I'm not drinking until Brad comes home. I need to be sober and ready to go. You drink, I'll drive."

"We're going to find him."

My phone rang. "It's Shirl." I answered and said, "You're on speaker." I clicked the button.

"Miss January is getting released tomorrow and going to a rehab facility for a week to get back on her feet, since she can't be released unless she has someone at home to care for her. It's illegal to discharge a patient when we know they need care and have no one. Luckily, she has insurance."

"I appreciate you coordinating all of this. A week will give us time to get her cottage disinfected."

Fab made an unidentifiable noise.

"Miss J asked to see you; she's worried about Score," Shirl said.

"Does she know he's dead?" Fab asked.

"I think she knows. She's more worried about where he'll end up. It did finally sink in that she doesn't get to keep him."

"Once the coroner releases Score's body, it is going to the guys at Tropical Slumber. Which reminds me, I need to call them and give them a heads up." I disconnected and leaned my head against the window.

Chapter Thirty-One

Fab drove into the driveway of the Crab Shack at the same time as Mother. The restaurant wasn't far off the main highway and looked out over the cool waters of the Atlantic. Phil had texted that one of her snitches wanted to hook up, so I invited her to join us. At Fab's suggestion, I'd called Mother after we'd gotten home and suggested we meet for a late lunch with a water view.

"Let Mother do her diva act so we get a table with an eye-popping view," I told Fab. "The last time we were here, you annoyed one of the shift managers; if she's here today, we'll get seated by the kitchen."

"I admit that telling the woman my fish tasted like shoe leather went a little far."

Mother knocked on the hood, and we got out.

Fab and Mother hugged and walked inside. I hung back and waited for Phil, who had just rolled in.

The restaurant had a low-key atmosphere and was decorated with fake palm trees scattered around, dead fish mounted on the walls, and rope lights strung across the ceiling.

Mother snagged us a corner table at the window that afforded a wide view of the blue ocean water, which wasn't diminished by the dark thunderclouds that could be heard rumbling in the distance. In addition to an appetizer, she also ordered drinks for everyone. Fab and I were used to such high-handedness, but I hoped it wouldn't annoy Phil.

"I ordered everyone's favorites." Mother beamed. "Fab just gave me the highlights of your trip to Brick's. Damn, I wish I could've gone." She pouted. "He's a feckless prick."

"Madeline Westin," I gasped, my cheeks turning pink.

"Sometimes, you can be such a priss." She smiled fondly. "At my age, I can say what I damn well want." She looked toward the front door. "And Spoonie's nowhere around."

"I thought you were forbidden from using his bedroom name in public." Fab grinned.

Phil's eyes sparkled with amusement.

"I need a drink." I felt my resolve to restrict myself to only one slipping away. In an attempt to keep the conversation out of the bedroom, I asked Phil, "What do you think your snitch wants and when's he calling back?"

"Doodad doesn't have a phone. He ventures to town about once a week and always stops by to catch up on the latest gossip. Not sure how the old hermit manages to stay up on the latest, but he does. He's proven to be more reliable than most," Phil told us.

"Doodad? What kind of name is that?" Mother asked.

My first guess would be progeny of stoners.

"His real name is Charles Wingate III, but he thinks Doodad is more fitting for a retired sea captain."

Fab beat her fist on the table. "Drink," she moaned, a little loudly.

"Fabiana, wait until Didier hears about your antics; you don't even have the excuse of being drunk." I shook my finger at her, using my best "Mother" voice.

"He's not here." Fab winked at Mother. "And you better not tell him."

Just then, the server interrupted with the delivery of Mother's Jack Daniels on the rocks, Fab's martini, and a pitcher of margaritas with two glasses dipped in salt with a lime garnish. It was well timed to steer the conversation in a different direction.

"To Brad," Mother toasted. "He'll be home soon."

After taking a long drink, I asked Phil, "Why can't we pay a visit to Doodad?"

"Don't know where he lives. Says he likes a solitary lifestyle and doesn't want anyone intruding on him unless it's an animal. Has a big heart for strays." Phil downed her glass. "Rumor has it that when he comes to town, he also gets laid."

"That's nice. He can get all his errands done in one day." I held out my glass for a refill.

Mother waved her hand at the bar, refilling our order in the hand signals that bartenders understood.

Before I got too sloshed, I needed to a make a call, so I fished my phone out of my purse. "Got a job for you," I said when Mac answered. "Pays good. Well, maybe not, since Fab is paying." I laughed at Fab's look of disgust.

"Speaker," Fab whispered, loud enough to be heard at the front door.

"Yeah," Mother toasted.

"Mac's on the phone." I told them, then told Mac, "Mother, Fab, and Phil are eavesdroppers."

"Hi, everyone," Mac yelled through the phone.

"I need this info ASAP. Get me the address of and a map to the mansion of a character named Doodad. Don't mention my name. How you get the info, I don't care. If you have to pay, you'll get reimbursed. Right, Fab?"

Fab growled at me.

"Hopefully, I can get lucky with Joseph," Mac said. "If not, I'll head down to Custer's and hit up the owner, Huff; he knows everyone. Once I get the information, I'll get it to you." I heard a door slam before she disconnected.

"Now that's the attitude I like to see." I held out my lime to Fab, who smacked it away.

"Don't pick on Fabiana. That's not nice."

Mother beamed at her, patting her shoulder.

I shook my head. "Mother really does love you better."

Fab flashed me an arrogant smile.

The server rearranged the few things on the table, making room for a large platter of assorted appetizers. By the time we'd eaten one or two of each, we'd be stuffed.

The conversation turned to a serious discussion about where to find designer shoes at a discount. The stores Fab and I frequented in the past had gone out of business. It disappointed me that Phil turned out to be a lover of stilettos; even Mother wore a higher heel than me.

My phone vibrated on the table, and all eyes flew to it; I flipped it over.

"Oh no, you don't. No business at the table unless it's about Brad," Mother said in a huff. "Who is it?"

"Do you have to know everything?" I asked her.

We all dissolved in laughter. Thank goodness the bar had filled up and all the tables were full; the four of us being noisy went unnoticed. I needed to slow my drinking, or I'd be contributing to the noise factor.

Fab slid my phone out from under my fingers and read the screen. "Creole wants to know where you are," she said, punctuated with loud smoochy noises. "Let's vote on a response." She raised her hand. "Mine is: 'none of your business.'" She pointed to Mother. "Next."

"What are you wearing?" Mother said.

Everyone erupted in laughter. I wanted to bang my head on the table, but I still had my plate in front of me and didn't want food on my forehead.

"Phil's turn," Fab said.

"Come and find me, big boy." Phil swiveled her hips in her chair.

I stood and leaned over the table to grab my phone but came up empty-handed. I glared at Fab. "If you message anything back, end of friendship."

"I sent one of those creepy smiley faces." Fab handed it back.

My phone rang. I stared at it and waited for it to stop. Not to be denied, it rang again. Finally, I answered.

"You okay?" Creole asked.

"I…uh… this was Fab's idea, and then…you know how Mother is, and Phil's here, and I'm the innocent party."

He snorted. "Where are you?"

"Putting you on speaker phone."

"Don't you dare," Creole roared.

"Too late," I said over the shouts of hello.

The server came over to find out what else we wanted. I asked for a to-go container. He scanned the table. "There's nothing to pack up, except that little bit of shrimp in front of you. Refills, anyone?"

"No," Creole shouted over the phone. "What's the name of your restaurant?"

We let out a chorus of "Sshs," fingers across our lips.

"Do you ladies have a ride home?" Creole asked.

"Mother, call Spoonly and tell him we need a flatbed with room for three autos."

"It's Spoonie, but you know that's his bedroom name," Fab whispered hoarsely.

"They're making fun of me," Mother said into her phone. "They think we're old people that don't know how to…" She cupped her hand around the phone, said something no one could hear, and giggled. Then said, starting louder and ending in a whisper again, "When people tell me I should find someone my own age, I answer: look at him."

"You women are too much," Phil said.

"Says the woman who's banging the Chief of Police. Oops." I looked down at the phone. "Damn, still connected." I tossed the phone to Fab.

"We're friends who enjoy a good dinner and sex. Both of us are busy, with no time for anything serious, at least right now," Phil said.

Fab handed the phone back. "Creole hung up."

"Liar," I said when my phone rang again. I downed the last of my margarita and answered. "Mother just said Spoonerly is picking us up and transporting the cars."

We all dissolved into a fit of giggles.

"Wait until I get my hands on you. You're in big trouble—drunk as a skunk."

Creole's growls didn't have the effect on me that he wanted them to when behaving was the last thing I wanted to do.

"I don't smell like one," I said cheerfully. "Later, will you sling me over your shoulder and carry me off, caveman style?"

* * *

Mother squealed at the top of her lungs, launching herself out of her chair into the arms of Spoon, who caught her easily.

Creole and Didier loomed over the table, arms crossed, the muscles in their jaws tensed, their eyes nothing but pissed as they made contact with each of us.

"Aren't you the one who's supposed to be setting a good example?" Spoon looked down at Mother. "We could hear you carousing the second we stepped in the door."

"I called you, didn't I?" Mother cooed and rubbed against him like a cat.

That brought giggles from the rest of us. Creole and Didier shook their heads.

"Come on, ladies," Creole said. "Your rides are here." He pulled my chair back.

Didier stood behind Fab, hands on her

shoulders; she leaned back and smiled up at him.

"We haven't paid the bill," Mother said.

"Spoon took care of it on the way in," Creole told us.

We chorused, "So sweet. Thank you."

The big man's cheeks took on a little color.

"Wait." Phil pushed her chair back. "I don't have an escort." She made a sad face.

Didier held out his hand to Phil. "If you allow Creole and me to, we'll see you home."

Phil took his hand and beamed at him. "I'd like that."

Fab stuck her finger in her mouth.

Creole caught Fab's antics, arched his brow, and wagged his finger at her.

I stood and pressed my face to Creole's chest. "Happy you showed up. Riding with you is way better than in the cab of a flatbed."

His laugh sent shivers down my spine.

Chapter Thirty-Two

Didier put a glass of some green concoction down in front of me. "You'll feel better," he said.

I squeezed my eyes shut. Yes, I had a bit of a headache, but I'd done nothing to deserve this. I opened one eye. The Frenchman glared down at me, arms crossed. I ignored him, got a water out of the refrigerator, and slid onto a stool.

Creole came down the stairs and into the kitchen.

"I want him arrested—" I jabbed my finger at Didier. "—for attempted murder."

Creole's eyes landed on the glass; he took a sip, downed it, and licked his lips. "You owe me, buddy; I just drank the evidence."

"Fab drank hers," Didier said.

"Sure she did," I said with all the sarcasm I could muster. "Did you actually see her? Or did you leave the room, and when you came back, there sat the empty glass?"

Didier scowled at Fab as she glided into the kitchen. You'd never know the woman had tossed back a couple of martinis the night before, encouraging Mother to be her most outrageous. As she slid onto a stool, her phone vibrated, dancing on the island countertop. She eyed the screen and ignored it. I grabbed it out from under her hand.

"Oh look, her other boyfriend: Toady." I held the phone next to my cheek and stroked the side. "Bon juree, ma petito," I said into the phone, hitting the speaker button.

Fab thrust her hand out. "Give me that damn thing," she whispered. I ignored her.

"Morning, Fabanna," his grizzled voice came through loudly. Fab winced at the mangling of her name. "Haven't been able to get you off my mind, hon. It's Toady."

"Of course. I know who this is, *hon*," I purred.

Creole stepped in front of Fab, preventing her from kicking my butt and possibly saving my life.

"Thinking about you and me and how good we'd be together." Toady punctuated his comment with an engine rev. "You come to my house, I'll barbeque up some fresh alligator, and we can sit under the stars. What say you?"

"Oh, Toady," I cooed, "I felt the connection when we met. I did. But, and it's a big one, I have a boyfriend and we've been together for a while. Now that he's trained to my liking, I can't just kick him to the curb."

"Trained?" Didier huffed, and Fab laughed at him. He wrapped his hand in her hair, pulling her into his chest and searing her lips with a kiss.

Creole shook his finger at me, struggling not

to laugh. He moved behind me and wrapped his arms around me.

A long, loud sigh blew through the line. "Not like I didn't expect it, but damn, I did hope. You don't seem like a cheater to me, but if you should consider taking me for a test drive, so you know you're making the right decision, I'm available."

"Oh Toady, if only the timing were better."

"Will you give me first crack if the two of you blow up?" Toady didn't bother to hide a robust burp.

"You'll be the first call I make."

"If you ever need anything, Toady's your man."

"Hors d'oeuvres, ami."

"I love that frenchy talk." He half-laughed and hung up.

"I hate you," Fab exploded, taking a step in my direction. Didier held her back.

"I did you a favor," I said in the patronizing tone I knew she hated. "You would have said something mean and hung up on dear Toady. Now you have another fan club member."

"You're out. I'm getting a new best friend."

"Calm yourself. You can't get everything you want in one friend. Pluses and minuses. Take you. You're high maintenance; your motto is shoot first and then ask questions. Me…" I poofed my hair. "You know what you're getting. Besides, who would you find to annoy you as much as I do?"

Creole and Didier laughed.

"If he calls me again, I'll shoot you. What's his name again?" Fab asked.

"That right there is a good reason to keep me around; you can never remember anyone's name."

"We'll be back." Fab scooped up her phone, and Didier put his arm around her shoulders and walked her into the entry, where she grabbed her purse.

French again – so annoying. "Be back in time to take me to lunch," I half-yelled before the door closed.

Creole surrounded me with his arms. "I want a promise from you that, when you hear back from Mac, you won't go off by yourself."

I'd told him that Mac had texted last night that it was Huff's night off at Custer's. She planned to be at the bar this morning when he unlocked the back door. "Fab will back me up."

He raised his eyebrows. "You sure about that?"

"Do you know how many times she's said she's getting another friend? And here I stand." I put my hand over my heart. "There isn't anything I wouldn't do for her, and she always has my back, and we've proven that more than once."

His face was set in a stern expression. Eyes boring into mine, he traced my lips with his finger, kissing me. "Anything at all, call me."

"Have a good day at the office."

I hung over the kitchen sink and watched out the garden window as he walked to his truck. When he got to the street, he turned and waved. A minute later, he rolled by the driveway, honked, and roared away.

I cut across the living room to the daybed, scooping up Jazz, and the two of us lay down and closed our eyes.

* * *

I woke to the phone ringing; thankfully, I'd left it in reach. "Got you a map," Mac screeched. "Just faxed you a copy."

I held the phone away from my ear, shaking myself awake. A large cabinet stood against the far wall, one shelf of which held the office equipment, which consisted solely of a printer and all the connections it took to make it work. The shelf underneath held a handful of office supplies that didn't see much use. I favored decorated note pads and cute pens, which I had to keep out of Fab's reach or they disappeared.

I heard the printer making a whirring noise, got up, and opened the cupboard doors in time to see a letter-size page hit the tray. I grabbed it up.

"This looks to be out in the wilderness," I grumbled, turning the crude drawing around. "Did Huff know if Doodad is still in residence?

The hurricane ravaged some of those areas."

"Doodad has been in for a beer since the hurricane and didn't mention any damage. Huff doesn't socialize outside the bar. Says he needs time to rest up from being reasonably pleasant."

"I can see where that would be tiring."

"Huff said that Doodad likes his solitude and has no appreciation for uninvited guests. Also, he didn't think Doodad would shoot you."

"That's why I'm taking Fab. She can sweet-talk the old hermit."

"You need anything else, I'm your girl. Be careful. Don't take any chances."

"We'd never do that." Anyone who knew Fab and I would know that was a false assurance.

I text Fab, "Get your ass back here—pronto," and ran upstairs to get changed. This trip required sturdy shoes and long pants. Weeds bred bugs, and I wasn't eager to come home covered in bites.

Hearing the door slam, I holstered my gun inside my waistband, rolled up the legs of my pants to my knees, and squished my feet into laced-up tennis shoes. I paused at the top of the stairs. Didier was at the bottom, and the intensity in his eyes brooked no argument. The Frenchman could do fierce. I took a breath, mostly certain he wouldn't strangle me, if only as a courtesy to my family.

"Thank you for not dawdling." I breezed by the man. "Got an address on Doodad that I want to check out."

"Where is it?" Fab held out her hand.

I was ready for her tricks. She wasn't going anywhere without me. I'd stuffed the map down the front of my pants, figuring no one would look there. I jabbed at my temple. "It's all up here. Ready?" I grabbed my tote and, without waiting, headed to the SUV and climbed into the passenger seat.

Hearing the back door shut, I didn't have to turn around to know that Didier was seated behind me. "Pretty boy is coming?" I said to Fab. Looking over the seat, I added, "In linen shorts?"

"This was all Creole's idea." She beamed.

"Head south on the Overseas. There's bug spray in my tote," I said over my shoulder. "It's not one hundred percent, but at least they won't make an entire meal out of you. You happen to have a gun?" I flipped down the visor and saw that Didier had moved to the center.

He lifted his designer short-sleeve shirt and showed off the handle of a handgun sticking out of the top of his shorts.

"You know how to use that?" I asked.

"Pay attention to the road," he barked. "Where are we going, anyway?"

I pulled the directions out of my pants and handed them to him. "It's the first exit after the state park. Not as out of the way as it appears." I nudged Fab. "I need you to work your magic—he's older, a hermit, you know the type."

"You say that, but who worms the information out of them? You."

"Pave the way. Once I get him talking, you stalk the property and do whatever it is you do, in addition to taking pictures." I nodded at Didier. "What about him? We tie him up, leave him in the car?"

Fab looked at him in the rearview mirror. "It's better if Madison and I make the initial contact. He sees you, and he might not be so friendly. If something goes awry, you'll have to save us both."

"And how would I accomplish that," Didier snapped, "from inside the car?"

"I'm not expecting any trouble," I said. "I just want to ask him a couple of questions. That's it. This is *my* brother." I was annoyed at having to explain why this was so important. "You both stay in the car, and I'll do it myself."

Didier patted my shoulder. "This is the only time you'll get this offer. You tell me what to do, and I'll do it."

Fab and I turned to each other. She winked, and we both burst out laughing.

"Don't think I won't get back at you if you use this as an opportunity to prank me," Didier grouched.

"Next turn to the right. I think." I waved my hand at Didier. "Can I have the so-called map back?"

"That would helpful," Fab said sarcastically.

"If I'm wrong, you'll turn around." I studied the map and the landmarks Huff had drawn in, starting with an abandoned house, the yard filled with junk, a mailbox with a dog's head, and an old rowboat. The house was all that remained.

Fab veered off at the exit at the last minute. I was used to her driving and grabbed the sissy bar. Didier rocked back and forth and muttered something in French.

The sides of Fab's mouth quirked up, but she pretended to concentrate on the road.

At the stop sign, the trees that were shown on the map as flanking the gravel road were now missing. Nothing but a healthy growth of weeds and a cement pad where a structure once stood. The hurricane winds had done some field-clearing.

Fab turned onto the bumpy road, driving slowly to the end, then making a U-turn and heading back to a single-lane driveway that we'd passed about a half-block back. A small structure at the back of the property could be seen from the road.

"At this point, there is no element of surprise." I scooted up on my seat, peering out the windshield. "Head up the driveway and we'll check it out. We meet up with a human, turn on the charm."

The building at the back was nothing more than a storage shed. It wasn't new but had escaped the ravages of the storm. As we started up the drive, the door flew open. A goliath filled the opening—a good six foot five, with shoulders as wide as a football field and a full beard—leaning on the butt of a rifle.

Fab took a coin from the ashtray. "We'll flip."

I ignored her and opened the door as soon as the SUV came to a stop. "I've got this." I kicked the door shut, drowning out whatever Fab was yelling.

"Doodad!" I waved and pasted a smile on my face as though we were old friends; it would work for a few minutes anyway.

I breathed a sigh of relief when he shoved the rifle back inside the shed and met me halfway, checking me out from head to toe.

"How have you been?" I continued my bluff.

"Just so you know, I never forget a face, and I've never laid eyes on you before. But I'll play along." He pointed to a beach chair. "Have a seat and get to the point. First, you got a name?"

"Madison… Madison Westin."

"Before you get started, who's in the SUV? Don't say no one; you jumped out of the passenger side. Couldn't believe you kicked a dent in that fine automobile."

"The driver is my best friend, or was, and it was supposed to be her job to make the initial contact and have you thinking with your second brain, and I'd come in with the point of the visit. In the back is her boyfriend; he invited himself along as our bodyguard, in case you turned out to be a whack job."

"From the backseat." He snorted. "You could be dead by now, with me long gone. I know every acre of this weedy jungle."

"We have friends in common. Huff gave me directions, or gave my friend directions anyway; I don't know the man." I handed over the map.

He barked a laugh. "This stinks. I'm surprised you found the place based on this." He handed back the map.

"My brother's missing, and I'm desperate to find him." I went on to tell him that I owned Jake's and was also Phil's boss and that she'd put out the call for information from her snitches at my request when I'd run into nothing but dead ends. And finally that he'd scored high on the list.

Fab honked, and I waved without turning around.

"Your friend apparently found your response unsatisfying; she just got out of the car, along with the bodyguard." Doodad snickered.

"Fab and her boyfriend, Didier. She has a short attention span, won't hang around long, and would rather snoop around your property. You'd make her day if she stumbled over a dead body."

"That's a perk of hurricane season; the big ones roll through and clear out the bodies." Doodad waved his hand around. "Heard about the reward, stopped by Jake's to get a look at the picture, but it was Phil's day off."

As I reached into my pocket, Doodad's brow went up. I held up one hand. "Just getting my phone." His mouth softened a little from its serious expression.

Doodad looked over his shoulder. "Your friends are fighting."

"They're French. They'd probably disagree, but I think they fight so they can make up…you know, in a loud way."

He laughed. "I get the picture."

"This is my brother, Brad." I handed him my phone, telling him what we knew about Brad's disappearance.

"I wish for your sake that my answer could be different, but I've never seen him before." He flicked to the next picture. "Who's this?"

"My mother, Madeline, the general in our family."

"I trust a woman who smokes a cigar." He continued to scroll. "Nice family."

"I got really lucky there."

He held up the phone. "Can you make this one bigger?" He showed me a picture of Brad standing next to his truck.

I reached across and showed him how to do it.

"This I've seen, and the reason I remember is that the couple in the truck were arguing while the man helped the woman into the passenger seat. Then he went around to the driver's side, and after he got in, she leaned across and hit him." Doodad demonstrated a downward fist blow. "The man hunched over. I couldn't see what she did next. There was a bunch of moving around; then she climbed over him, got behind the wheel, and drove off. Figured I'd hear something about that story, like that she got arrested, but nothing, not even an unidentified body showing up somewhere."

"Do you remember where you saw this happen?"

"You're right about your friend being nosey." He stared over my shoulder. "I'm surprised she hasn't gone inside my shed; she's circled it twice. The boyfriend just shrugged, guess he just admitted she wears the pants."

I stared at the ground and laughed.

"Where were we?" Doodad flashed me a stern stare. "Oh yeah. Down by the docks," he went on, looking back at the picture. "I was looking to apply for a job on the apartment construction. Figured they had everyone they needed, but what the hell. Know where I'm talking about? The small area that's been hyped for revitalization."

"I can get you a job." The lump in my throat threatened to choke me. Noting his look of skepticism, I added, "I'm not blowing smoke."

"Sissy over there is now spraying himself with something." He chuckled.

"It's bug spray. He's about to be one of your new bosses, so you might not want to call him a sissy. He and my brother own that building. At least until the sale goes through. When they go on to the next project, they use the same guys, if you're not a slacker."

"Right. Keep the name-calling to myself." He mock-saluted. "Bugs aren't bothering you."

"Spray before you leave the house—" I shook my index finger. "—as my mother would say. Can you give me a description of the woman?"

"Slim build, no curves on her frame, dark hair; she wouldn't have stood out if it weren't for the scene the two of them were making. Never saw his face—just a side glimpse—and then, when he faced me head-on, the tinted passenger window didn't give me a clear view." Doodad leaned back in his chair, looked up at the sky, and closed his eyes, lost in thought.

"Did it seem like they knew one another?"

"I thought it was his wife or girlfriend. And the shit I witnessed made me happy I'm single."

"His girlfriend is a blond, and they don't fight—at least not in public."

Fab and Didier must have gone back to the SUV, because Fab was blowing the horn again. I was certain it wasn't Didier and also sure they were exchanging angry words.

"She just gave you the all-clear," I said. "No dead bodies and she's ready to go." I stood and motioned for him to follow. "I want to introduce you to Didier; get his card, and I'll give you mine. Sending a message through Phil also works. If you remember anything—I don't care how meaningless you think it might be—please get in touch. Tell Phil you qualify for the Madison discount—free food."

"I'm happy now that I didn't shoot you." He stood and followed me. "What are your friends going to think about you helping me out?"

"That won't be a problem." I half-laughed. "Didier and Brad are friends as well as partners. Didier is eager for news."

Didier leaned against the SUV, not having gotten back in when Fab did. Before making introductions, I asked about job openings. Caught off guard, Didier hesitated, pulling out his wallet, handing over his business card. "Call me tomorrow."

I retrieved my purse and handed Doodad my own card and some cash.

Doodad shook his head. "This is too much."

"No, it isn't," I told him sternly. "Besides, once I drag my brother's behind home, I'll be billing him."

"He's a lucky man, having a sister that loves him. I'll get a picture from Phil and ask around town, and I'll work on remembering everything I can about the mystery woman."

"Maybe next time, you'll tell me how Charles Wingate III became Doodad."

His eyes narrowed. "Some folks don't know how to keep their traps shut."

* * *

"You two acted like children. I'm not blaming him either." I tossed my head in Didier's direction. "*You* probably provoked him."

Fab raced down the highway toward home, and with practically no traffic, she had the road almost to herself.

"Merci, cherie."

"It was a dreadful place." Fab sniffed. "You must have found out something, since it took you long enough. Just once, could you skip the person's life story and get to the point?"

"Mr. Doodad had some helpful information that I'm not in the mood to share right now." I turned to the window and smiled.

"I'm going to pull this car over, drag you out, and dump you on the side of the road."

Didier leaned over the seat and roared in French.

"I'm putting you on speaker, so behave." I took my phone out and called Creole. "Meeting with Doodad wasn't a waste," I said when he picked up, and went on to relate the conversation, not skimping on the details. Too wordy, but Creole would cut through all the minutia.

"Dark-haired female, same age." Creole paused. "They had some association; otherwise, why let her into his truck? Did Brad have any intense hangers-on?"

"No one hung around the job site," Didier said. "And yet, it seems he was attacked right in front of the building."

"He never mentioned another woman," I said. "He's happy with Julie and Liam, and he's not the type to cheat. He'd break off the relationship and move on."

"What about his past? Anyone unstable stand out?" Creole asked.

"Years back, mental stability wasn't a quality that was high on his list. In most of his relationships, the women were more involved than he was. All that changed when he met Julie."

"Check with Madeline," Creole suggested. "Maybe she'll have some insight into his relationships. This is good news; odds are, Brad's still alive. Whatever the woman wanted, she knew she'd get resistance and brought something she could use to overwhelm him."

"We know he's being held against his will. How long until whoever she is gets frustrated and does something drastic? More drastic than what she's already done?" I asked.

"Your brother is smarter than he looks," Fab said. "He's probably doing his best to placate her, talk her down; he'll offer the moon until he can get away."

Didier pulled Fab's hair.

"Oww," Fab yelped. "I was nice."

"The new guy worked out okay," I told

Creole. I turned and winked at Didier. "But I suspect he'll quit soon."

"I'll see you at the house in a couple of hours." Creole ended the call.

A hottie in a silver Porsche pulled up alongside Fab at the signal and honked, lowering his window and waving at her.

Fab waved and, when the light turned green, shot ahead of him.

"Happens all the time." I answered Didier's frown with a smile.

Chapter Thirty-Three

Miss January's cottage was only feet away, but I couldn't force myself to move in that direction. Instead, I paced the driveway. I needed fresh air to make some decisions, and despite having just been cleaned, the interior still held a faint odor. My nose had picked it up immediately, and gagging, or worse, in front of anyone wasn't high on my list today.

"Rip out the carpeting and window coverings and get rid of the furniture," I directed Mac, relieved that everything could be replaced at minimal cost.

"The cleaner figured that would be your decision." Mac pointed to the pickup truck that had just pulled into the driveway. "That's his cousin; he's here to haul everything to the dump. Then I'll leave the windows open."

"If an industrial fan would help, there's one in the shed."

"Snagged that already. I wore a gas mask and cleaned out her belongings." Mac choked out a noise. "Did you know that in the state of Florida, you can bury a body out in the yard?"

"I'm happy to point out the obvious fact that

no one I know has a *yard.* If Miss January gets that ridiculous idea in her head, I'll know how she heard about it, and although I hate to threaten violence, I will kill you." I headed to the office in search of a cold drink.

"You could be more appreciative," Mac said, following.

I flashed an evil stare over my shoulder. "Would you mind?" I pointed to the doorknob and stepped aside.

"Someone forgot her lockpick, I see." She held the door open, and I headed straight to the refrigerator, snatched up one of her sugary sodas, and popped the top, settling on the couch.

Mac settled behind the desk, adjusting her "You're the stupid one" t-shirt. Satisfied, she said, "Score's real name was Theodore Dixon. Located his daughter in Alaska. Her first question was about the health of his bank account, and upon finding out that he died with a dollar forty-two in his pocket, she didn't care what happened to his remains."

"What you're telling me is that they weren't close?"

Mac snorted. "Never even asked how he died."

"Now what?" I didn't bother to hide my disgust. *What the hell was wrong with people?* "We can't let him go unclaimed. I'm not telling Miss January that when she gets released from the hospital. So, as I see it, another dirty job for you."

"Figured as much. I'm one step ahead of you." Mac patted herself on the shoulder.

I wanted to laugh, but why encourage her?

"Took care of it already. I got a power of attorney out of the daughter in exchange for sending a notarized statement that we wouldn't try to squeeze money out of her in the future. That gives me final say." Mac thrust out her chest. "I'm thinking you don't want Score moving back into the bedroom, even if we could perfume him up."

I groaned. "Let the guys at Tropical Slumber handle the pickup, details, and whatever it is they do."

"Done." Mac banged her fist on the desk.

"And Kitty?"

"Cleaner dude thought his chemicals might evaporate her. She passed his smell test. That was good enough for me." Mac beamed.

* * *

The next morning, with Fab and Didier still asleep, I went to the Bakery Café to bring back a box of danishes. Arriving home, I saw Fab sitting at the island, a smirk on her face. "How was your day?"

Before I could retort with something appropriately sarcastic, my phone rang. Glancing at the screen, I shoved it across the countertop to Fab. "It's for you."

"Phone calls for me come on my phone, not yours," Fab said snootily. The ringing stopped.

"Missed call." I pouted. Fab's phone started ringing. "Guess it was for you after all." I smirked. "Hurry up and answer, or they'll have to call again."

I grabbed a cup of coffee and walked outside, sitting by the pool.

Fab came to the doorway. "Miss January is at the funeral home and has decided she wants Score delivered to The Cottages and placed in a standing coffin outside the front door."

"What the…?" I had a few more questions, starting with why she wasn't in the hospital and then how she got to the funeral home. "Who are you talking to and where's Mac?"

Fab mouthed "Raul" and relayed the question. "She's not answering."

"Tell Raul I'm on my way. I've come to accept that I have to go by myself, but don't blame me if another dead person wakes up mysteriously and you're not there to see it."

"At least they don't smell."

"Raul can explain to Miss January about burial laws and that her latest harebrained idea could land her in jail."

"Raul said he'd handle it." Fab shoved her phone in her pocket, came over, and offered me a hand up. "For a change, I've got a better story for you. Tell Miss January that if she leaves him outside, another woman will probably come along and steal him."

I was shocked speechless, but only momentarily. "That's a great idea."

Fab tugged me through the house, grabbed both our purses, and escorted me to the SUV. She got behind the wheel, powering the passenger window down. "You know I don't usually allow this, but today, you can hang your head out the window. Suck up the fresh air; you'll feel better, put color back in your cheeks." She patted my shoulder.

My phone rang, and Mac's face smiled back at me from the screen. "Bad news," she groaned.

"How in the hell did Miss January get released from the hospital without me knowing?" I screeched.

Fab glared and rubbed her ear.

"That's the news. I don't suppose you know this next part yet. She's missing again."

"Miss January is at the funeral home, wanting Score back," I said in disgust.

"Good news," she said cheerfully. When she got dead silence from me, she continued. "She found out that she was being released to another care facility and pitched a fit. Instead of going back to her room, she walked out the front door, her hospital gown exposing her backside, and got into a cab that had just pulled up and let someone else out. Apparently, the driver didn't recognize her patient attire and brought her home."

"And how did she get to the funeral home?"

"That's unclear." Mac promised to call with any updates, and we ended the call.

The drive over to Main Street was shorter than usual, thanks to Fab gunning through every yellow light.

As we pulled into the driveway, the question of who drove Miss January there was answered by the run-down multi-colored Cadillac parked on the red carpet. Crum's newest acquisition. He'd recently boasted about a new business enterprise flipping crappy cars: buying an old wreck and selling it for profit. I'd responded with something short and insincere and walked away from him. He'd shouted after me, "Wait, you'll see."

"I'm putting a stop to all this nonsense," I said, shutting the car door and cutting across the driveway. "Keep up." I motioned to Fab. "If I start to go soft, you poke me in the back, but not too hard."

Crum stood in the doorway of the funeral home in ill-fitting, knee-length athletic shorts and a dress shirt that had once been white but had greyed considerably.

I came to a halt in front of Crum. "If you traded the ride for sex with Miss January, you can forget it. You won't have time to consummate the transaction because you'll be too busy moving out."

Crum's face flushed with anger, and he

stepped around me. "I'm not an old whore," he ground out.

"Happy you cleared that up."

He stalked to his car and, after a couple of cranks of the engine, squealed out of the driveway, the muffler scraped the ground.

"Did you tell Miss January?" I demanded the moment I saw Raul.

He shook his head. "I tried, and she started to cry. She's sitting in the viewing room, up at the front."

I stopped to greet Astro and Necco, scratching them under the chin. Not bothering with subtlety, I tossed them two sandwiches each from the leftovers from the previous sendoff.

I tried to blow off my frustration before I got to the front and sat down next to Miss January, putting my arm around her. "I've got good news for you," I said and proceeded to lie through my teeth. "Score had a daughter, who wants her father cremated, but she's allowing you to keep the ashes until you pass on. We'll have a beautiful memorial and invite all his friends; everyone can say nice things about him."

"Can we have food?" she asked. "Score would like that. How nice he has a daughter. I never knew."

"I'll take care of all the details. You ready to go home? You're riding with Fab and me."

I steered Miss January to a seat in the entryway and crossed the room to talk to Dickie and Raul. "Can we do a memorial service, preferably on the patio? Midday would be best. Miss January will be partly sloshed and happy with whatever happens. If not enough people can be found to say something nice on Score's behalf, you'll have to hire seat-fillers. Food, but absolutely no liquor. Doable?"

"I'm impressed." Raul smiled.

"You know how I feel about cremation." Dickie grimaced. "But in this case, it's for the best. The condition of the body was the worst I've seen, and this way, it won't show up somewhere unexpected that will necessitate a trip to the police station."

Dickie prided himself on his dressing skills, so I knew if he was suggesting a cremation, then the body was gruesome.

I turned to Fab, who had checked out all the viewing rooms and looked disappointed. "I don't feel like dragging Miss January across the parking lot; can you get the SUV as close as possible and we'll put her in the back? Unless you'd like a little one-on-one time up front."

If looks could kill…

Chapter Thirty-Four

Creole left right after dinner for a "business meeting," which I took to mean the bad guys were going to jail. He left with admonitions not to worry, that every contingency had been planned for. I made him promise not to get hurt or I'd kick his butt, which made him laugh. "I'm sure I'd enjoy that." He kissed me hard and left. Great, so now I could obsess about both Brad's and Creole's safety.

I'd finished swimming and, my feet up on a lounger, was staring at the stars in the almost-darkened sky. Didier and Fab had left to go for a walk on the beach.

My phone beeped. The text from Phil read, "Doodad's here and wants to talk to you." I messaged back that I was on my way.

I scribbled a note that I'd be back soon and pulled a sundress on over my bathing suit, slipping into a pair of sandals. Grabbing my purse and keys, I ran out the door.

Hoping Doodad's appearance was good news, I tried to stay calm on the short drive to Jake's. Maybe his photographic memory had unearthed another clue. I had talked with Mother about Brad's love life and the women he'd dated in the past. We'd shared a few giggles, but nothing stuck out.

Ignoring a shoving match in the parking lot, I pulled around to the side and parked in front of the kitchen door. I'd send Phil out to break up the drunks; the sound of the Mossberg rifle that was kept behind the bar being cocked was enough to stop any fight.

I entered through the back door, waved to Cook, and headed for the bar. Doodad, who sat at the end of the bar, waved as soon as he saw me. "Fight outside you need to break up," I told Phil.

"Why not you?" She reached for the rifle and came out from behind the bar.

"I'd shoot them just for being a nuisance." I took Phil's place. "What are you drinking?" I asked Doodad.

"I'm good." He put one hand over the top of his longneck and motioned me over with the other. "I saw the woman again—last night at the grocery store."

"Was my brother with her?"

He shook his head. "I do my shopping late. Parked only a few cars from her. Took me by surprise when I caught sight of her loading a couple of bags into the trunk of an old blue Mazda. Never forget that car; the passenger side, which was visible when she opened the door, appeared to be gutted by a fire. Got the first three letters of the license plate: W-K-T. The last three, she had covered up. Surprised me she hadn't gotten pulled over for that trick. By the time I got back to my truck, she was on her way out the driveway. Tried to catch up, but once she hit the highway, she disappeared."

Phil came back with a smirk on her face. "I should charge extra for breaking up fights."

"Not when you didn't get a shot off." I traded places with her and slipped onto a stool next to Doodad. "Now what?"

"People usually go to the same grocery store: habit, closest, whatever," Phil mused. Doodad must have told her his story while they waited for me. "If she's using the Food Barn for proximity, then she's nearby. Night shopping… She doesn't want to be recognized?"

"What about the license number?"

"I already gave it to my guy." Phil smiled confidently. "In the meantime, hire someone to stake out the parking lot every night. If the woman shows up again, give strict orders to follow at a discreet distance to see where she goes, and under no circumstances approach her. You don't want to give her an excuse to do something stupid. Even if it only yields a street name, I've got several boxes of useless advertisements in my garage that you can litter people's doors with while you canvass the neighborhood, and we'll find her."

"I've got experience doing that." I grimaced.

"You may need to keep a low profile. I don't mean absent yourself entirely, but this may be someone from Brad's past that would recognize you. And that goes for your mother too. An easy disguise would be a hat and sunglasses."

My phone rang. I recognized the familiar ringtone and pushed it over to Doodad. "You can answer."

"Your mother or something?" He glanced down at the screen. "That's the screaming shrew you brought to my house that day. What's she want?"

"I snuck out of the house without leaving a note. 'Back later' is not enough info for her."

"Now I remember, nosey too." He answered the phone. "What's up, sister?"

"Who the hell are you?" Fab screeched through the phone.

"You call back when you get a few manners," he said stonily and hung up on her, rubbing his ear. He turned off the phone.

Phil and I laughed.

"Would be nice if Didier happened to catch her reaction to the phone call on camera, but he probably didn't." Phil continued to laugh. "Maybe he can recreate it for us."

I opened my purse, withdrew the cash I had ready in a side pocket, and passed it to Doodad. "Don't argue with me; you're not going to win. When do you start work?"

"Monday." He pushed it back. "Really, a job is enough."

"Don't make me shoot you." I mimicked Fab's fierce stare. "You've come through, and your latest sighting might be the break we need. Lunch, dinner, come in anytime you want."

"Does that look usually get you what you want?"

Oops, maybe I'd mixed up fierce with unhinged. "So what you're saying is I need more practice?"

Phil held up her phone, Fab's face on the screen.

"Wait until she calls back and tell her I'm on my way home." I picked up the money, shoved it in Doodad's shirt pocket, and waved to them as I left.

* * *

Driving back home, I felt the need to hoard the latest information, detouring by the Food Barn, cruising the parking lot, scoping out the exits and which parking space had the best vantage point for a stakeout. If anyone was watching the security cameras, they might think I had a felonious plan in mind—grand theft grocery store. Not a common target, though occasionally a random story would make the local throwaway: "woman hides ham between her thighs and goes on the run."

Turning the corner to my house, the first thing I noticed was that Billy's RV was no longer partially blocking the driveway and Creole's truck was parked across the street. With Billy gone, that meant the case was over and the bad guys, I hoped, were all in jail. Hopefully Creole's "business" had picked up everyone and not just the low-hanging fruit.

All my worries about what to do next evaporated; Creole would know. I slid in next to Fab's sports car. Was that dust on it? I jumped out and ran my finger across the hood, smiling, and scribbled "Wash Me" in big print.

Creole stood at the bottom of the stairs, arms crossed, as I came inside and dumped my bag and keys on the bench. "Where have you been, young lady?" he growled.

Before I could turn away, he saw the tears running down my face. I'd tried to keep them under control on the drive home. He closed the space between us and scooped me off my feet.

"We'll be back in the morning for breakfast. It would be nice, Fab, if you'd cook it and have it ready." He laughed all the way out the door. He slid me onto the seat of his truck and wiped my eyes with his t-shirt. "I don't like it when you cry. Bad news?"

I shook my head, sniffing, not wanting to cry in front of him.

He pulled his shirt over his head and handed it to me. "You can use this to blow your nose."

"I love you."

"You know the feeling's mutual. I wouldn't offer up my shirt to just anyone for bodily fluids." He shut the door and went around to the driver's side. "Ready?" He brushed at my fallen tears, wiping them away with his thumbs.

He pulled through Roscoe's, our favorite drive-thru, for hamburgers, then tore down the Overseas to his beach house. "Fab said you disappeared. Didier said you left a note. Fab thought you were at Jake's, but everyone there always covers for you. Which she hates, by the way," he said with a big grin.

I told him about the conversation with Doodad.

"That's good news. The first big break. Two of them, actually. Put the word out about the car; an eyesore like that, people will remember, even drunks. We'll start staking out the grocery store tomorrow night, and every night after that. Tonight, you and I need to get some sleep."

"Just sleep?" I stuck out my lower lip.

"More good news. I'm on vacation for the next couple of weeks. I've got time saved up that I need to use. We'll find Brad together."

Chapter Thirty-Five

"Get up right now." Creole tugged my leg over the side of the bed.

"No," I moaned and fought against going anywhere.

"We already blew off breakfast." He wrapped his fingers around the other ankle before I could get away. "My phone has been blowing up with texts. Fab and Didier both know I have an update on the Carbine Wills case. I'd planned to relate the details last night, but something more important came up—you."

I looked over my shoulder. "Everyone in jail?"

"Those that aren't dead."

"That's all Fab needs to know." I smiled up at him. "Text: 'Case over. Jail for everyone.' and come back to bed."

He stood me on my feet. Laughing into my neck, he wrapped his arms around me and walked me into the shower. "You tell her that."

* * *

Creole parked in front of my house and came

around the truck to open the door. "You are to behave yourself."

"Me?" I said in shock, leaning forward and wrapping my legs around his waist.

He hauled me out of the truck, kicking the door closed, and kissed me all the way to the front door, where he set me on my feet and ran his hands over the sides of my hair.

"You covering up the evidence of your manhandling?"

He grinned down at me and opened the door, pushing me inside.

"We're back!" I shouted.

"Is that what you call behaving?" Creole chuckled.

"It gives them time to pretend they weren't doing anything either."

"The whole neighborhood could hear you," Fab grouched as we walked into the living room. She motioned for us to come out on the patio. Knowing we'd be spending the afternoon by the pool, Creole and I had come dressed to swim.

Fab and Didier were seated at the table under the umbrella with a cart next to them holding a pitcher of iced tea and a white, oval enamelware bucket filled with ice and an assortment of beers and bottled water.

"This look great." I leaned down and kissed Didier's cheek, then slid into a chair opposite him. Creole grabbed a beer and sat next to me.

"What about me?" Fab huffed.

"You want a kiss too?" I bit my lip, trying not to laugh.

"A 'thank you' for my contribution." Fab preened.

"I'm going to instead apologize for all the bossing around of Didier that you must have done." This time, I couldn't stop the laughter.

Creole and Didier clinked bottles.

Creole took a drink and started: "You've both probably noticed that Billy is gone. The case of Carbine Wills and his friend Rocks is now closed."

I had asked him ahead of time to not let on that I knew a few things I hadn't shared. Fab would understand keeping my promise to Creole, but not without a few fireworks.

"Carbine Wills and his pal never had jack to do with Madison. He and his pal Rocks were growing high-quality weed out in a remote section of The Keys and had cornered the local market. That didn't sit well with a cartel out of Miami that had moved in and wanted to control the drug distribution from Homestead to Key West. Some of the smaller operations had been given get-out-of-town orders, along with a few bucks and threats about what would happen if they came back." He downed the rest of his beer.

Creole continued, "Carbine and Rocks weren't as easy to get rid of; they got greedy and intercepted a shipment of weed and cash. Not taking kindly to that, Oscar Santos decided the way to weed out the culprits was to kill his way through the rival organization."

"Didn't he just die in a shootout?" I asked, having seen the headlines that morning when I flipped on my laptop to peruse the local news.

"Oscar took exception to being taken into custody. Thankfully, none of our guys got hurt or worse."

"I saw that story and thought it was a fit ending," Didier said.

Creole nodded. "Oscar got wind of you suing Carbine, which is what led him to your door. A break for him; his usual motivational style of shooting people in various body parts and ultimately in the head clearly wasn't working for him, since the body count continued to climb." He reached for a bottled water, uncapping and downing half of it. "Carbine's murder was the break in the case we needed. Turned out he owned land south of here, where we found a six-trailer drug operation, all the trailers sprayed with bullets and all the workers shot in the head. Which apparently was the only thing the assailants were interested in, as they left behind grow tables ready to turn over six figures in product."

"Glad you were able to take Oscar out before an innocent party got hurt," Didier said. "I assume you put Billy on guard duty because you were worried about us?"

"When Billy spotted the same car driving by

the house a few times, there was no damn way I was leaving this property unprotected. Ran the plate, lucked out with an outstanding warrant, and that guy's in jail."

"No more lineups?" Fab held a napkin in front of her chest as though it were a placard.

"That's her." I pointed. "Number one. She did it." I laughed at Fab's scowl.

"You don't know how much I wanted to kick Kevin's ass for that," Creole growled. "He claimed not to know that you'd been cleared. Not sure I believe him, but I can't prove it."

"I'm happy it's over and you're in one piece." I laid my head on his chest.

"Now our focus can be on Brad," Didier said.

"About that," I said, remembering that I hadn't updated them on the latest. "I met with Doodad again last night; that's where I was." I told them about the woman he saw at the grocery store.

"It's hard to be in on this together when we're just now hearing about this," Fab said.

"As you know, I was upset when I got home last night. If it makes you feel any better, you're the first to hear the update," I said.

"Who grocery shops late at night?" Fab asked.

"I drove through the parking lot last night and quite a few people do. Surprised me," I said.

"You can count on our help." Didier stood.

"You're about to get a taste of the exciting world of stakeouts. Unless there's a shootout.

Right, Fab?" Creole winked.

Didier nodded to Creole. "I'm ready to kick your butt in a game of water basketball."

"I need a break and a swim, and then it's time to come up with some new ideas," I said.

"Me and Didier against you and Creole in a little water fun," Fab said, a sneaky look on her face.

"No thanks." I turned up my nose. "You know that's not fair, sticking Creole with the weakest player."

Creole picked me up out of the chair and walked to the edge of the pool.

"You better not!" I screeched.

He jumped in.

Chapter Thirty-Six

The four of us were once again staking out the parking lot of the Food Barn, which we'd done for the last three nights, awaiting a sighting of the crappy Mazda. The only other market in town was an upscale healthy foods variety, and we agreed that she probably wouldn't frequent that one.

We'd parked the SUV in the back of the lot in the only aisle that faced the front of the store. Fab and Didier had offered to trade off nights, but I wanted to see the woman and not have any more delays in finding Brad. It was my hope that we'd be able to follow her and rescue my brother. If the guys had their way, Fab and I would be sitting at home.

"I say we up the stakes of the next poker game and make it strip." Fab yawned.

"How do I explain to the sheriff about the two naked people in the back seat?" I winked at Creole.

"You're sure of yourself." Fab sniffed. "Tell them the truth: Didier and I won and made you two get in the back." She yawned again, this time with sound effects. "I'm bored."

I glared over the seat, shaking my head. "You of all people know that stake-outs aren't exciting, even on television. And count yourself lucky: law enforcement officers huddle in way crappier cars than this one and eat junk food."

"That's the truth," Creole said. "Try making yourself inconspicuous while hiding behind a tree or in the bushes."

"I hid in the bushes once and almost got peed on by a cat," I said.

Didier patted me on the head. "Something Fab got you into, I'm sure."

Fab was right—it did get boring. It had been her idea to play cards, so she should be the one to come up with some new entertainment. I realized suddenly that I was resting my head against the back of the seat; my eyes popped open and I felt a surge of guilt. It had been the plan to arrive before dusk and hold vigil until midnight.

Mother and I had talked after my initial conversation with Doodad, and we couldn't come up with anyone from Brad's past who could have come back into his life. We agreed that he hadn't recently mentioned another woman, only talking about Julie and how happy he was in the relationship.

Didier stiffened, leaning forward, and pointed. "There's the car. Fits the description. Surely there can't be two."

The female at the wheel drove past us and slowed, pulling into a space an aisle over. It took several minutes for her to get out.

"What took her so long?" Fab peered over my shoulder.

I stared hard, wishing I could jerk off the woman's ugly bucket hat. The small brim was covering her brow.

She didn't head into the store; instead she stood on the ledge on the driver's side and peered over the roof…right at us.

"I think we've been made." Creole groaned. "Everyone duck. Madison get on the floor; no way she'll be able to see you there." He started the engine and drove another aisle over in the opposite direction, stopping next to a man pushing a shopping cart with several bags and rolling down his window. "Sorry to bother you. It's me and the wife's first time here in The Keys; any restaurants that stay open late?"

I didn't hear the man's response. Creole thumped the outside of the driver's side door in acknowledgment. "Thanks, pal. Appreciate it." He waved and headed for the exit. "Well?"

"That was odd," Fab said. "She didn't move from her car, eyes glued to the SUV while you talked to the man. As soon as you were in gear, she got back in her car and beat it for the back exit."

"Two things: she knows you, Madison. Or she recognizes your car." Creole turned to me. "We'll find that woman. I'll bet she's got the answers to our questions."

"It was too dark for me to get any kind of a look at her," Fab said. "It did appear that she recognized the SUV, so we can't use it to follow her; she'll be more paranoid the next time she comes out."

"Tomorrow, I'll get us another car." Disappointed didn't cover what I was feeling. The woman was so close, but still out of our grasp.

"Both my and Fab's cars are available to you anytime," Didier offered.

"Merci buckets." I watched as Didier grimaced. "Not to be rude, but I think we'll fit in better with a beater car. I'll arm-twist an ugly ride for our use."

"It's still grand theft auto, even if the car is only worth ten bucks," Creole said.

"I'm hardly going to jack a car. Besides, much to Mother's and my disgust, Fab hasn't held the hotwiring seminar…yet."

Fab squealed from the back seat.

Creole chuckled. "Didier, we'll need you and Fab in one of your cars so that we have both exits covered."

"When she goes into the store," Fab said, "I could wait for her in the back seat of her car. Scare the…you know…out of her, in a friendly way."

I turned in my seat. "Thanks for the laugh. Felt good."

"That trick works on some people, so I've

heard," Creole said. "We don't know how crazy she is, though; she might have nothing to lose, and people could get hurt if, say, she decided to ram her car through the store window."

"We got a plan?" Didier asked.

"You guys go for a run in the morning, and the girls will take care of the details," Fab answered. "First stop, The Cottages. Am I right?" She kicked the back of the passenger seat.

"Isn't the old dude's funeral tomorrow?" Creole asked.

A snort came from the back seat.

"Really, Didier," I admonished.

"Excuse my manners," Didier responded. At the same time, Fab yelped.

"Since I'm sure you guys would do anything for the benefit of this team, there is one more thing," Fab said. "You attend the funeral in our place and be sure to go shirtless. It's a Keys funeral; you'll fit right in. Miss January thinks you're both hot; she'll never notice that Madison and I aren't there."

Creole choked. "Ain't gonna happen."

"Thank goodness," Didier mumbled.

"None of us need to go. Mac's got it under control." Creole shirtless made me smile, but it wasn't for other women to look at. "It violates my policy of going to funerals of people I don't know." A handful of conversations that didn't last longer than a sentence or two didn't qualify as knowing someone. "Fab, you didn't know

Score, but did you ever threaten him?"

Fab grumbled under her breath.

Creole pulled halfway into the driveway. "You two in the back—out."

"You're so rude." Fab sniffed.

"You must be used to it by this time." Creole grinned.

Didier cut off whatever Fab was about to retort by pulling her across the seat and out the door. Her feet barely touched the ground, as he immediately scooped her into his arms and carried her into the house.

Creole turned the SUV around and headed back to the highway.

Chapter Thirty-Seven

The next morning, Creole and Didier hit the beach early for a run that I would have needed a nap for first. He pulled into our driveway and jumped out of the SUV, and before he could grab his bag, Fab slid behind the wheel. He scowled at her through the windshield. Going around to the passenger window, he stuck his head inside and claimed my lips. "Any trouble, I'm your first call, not your lawyer."

Once the window was rolled up and Fab had pulled out, I said, "Didn't think now was the time to mention I'm not sure we have a lawyer anymore. A new one needs to be a priority. Not having anyone we trust to call is a bad idea."

Halfway down the block, Fab rolled her window down, yelling, "Stay out of the street, old man." She waved.

I flinched, even though the man waved back with a smile on his face. "Fabiana."

"Stop mimicking your mother. That's Hank—lives one block over. Sad day when I know more neighbors than you do."

"He's an old man and doesn't count. You're a babe magnet for the over-eighty crowd."

Fab rocketed out into a break in traffic. "We'll never get the lawyer deal we have now."

I blew out a breath of frustration. "There is that. Hopefully Mac can smooth the waters. On the plus side, the relatives love coming to visit. Cruz will have a hard time telling them the free entertainment's over."

"Drive-thru?" Fab raised her brows.

"Oh yes." I licked my lips. "I need a caramel extra whipped intravenous caffeine drip. And a pastry. I graciously let Creole have the last donut, insisting I wasn't hungry."

Fab made a retching noise.

I shrugged. "Get me my usual in large and two pecan rolls." By the time I got half the coffee drunk, I'd be ready to fly.

When she returned, Fab handed me the drinks, followed by a pink bakery box. "You do know that, this early, your tenants will still be asleep."

"Perfect timing. It's a big day, so everyone should be around. Mac posted a signup sheet on the office door, asking for volunteers to speak at the funeral and be brief—said word got out and it filled up in an hour. Never underestimate the power of free food."

Fab pulled into The Cottages, and into the space next to the barbeque area. An out-of-state vehicle had the office one. Mac must have had her head hanging out the window; we barely shut the car doors before she came running across the street from her house.

"Crum home?" I asked.

"Just got back from his morning run—that's code for digging in the trash. It was a light day for him; he came back with one plastic grocery bag, and it didn't look to have much in it." Mac pulled her knee-length skirt out of the waistband of her shorts.

"Are you coming?" I motioned to Fab.

"It's too early for Crum. Have fun." She waved me off and sat in the barbeque area across from Mac at a cement table, where they could watch the driveway.

I cop-knocked on his door and smiled at the thought of shouting, "Warrant." Real cops probably didn't do that, but the idea of scaring him amused me.

"That knock of yours makes me want to wet myself." Crum filled the doorway in only tighty-whities.

This was one of those times I wished I could enforce an indoor dress code. The law said he was "dressed." I disagreed. "Would you mind putting on one of your skirts? I need to talk to you."

He swept out his hand, opening the door wider. "Come into my humble abode."

I entered, looking around. It never failed to amaze me that his cottage was clean, even though the junk stacked up in neat little piles was overwhelming. "Hi, Harlot." I sat down next to the cream-colored cat and scratched her head and ears. "Happy to see she's healthy and appears content. I forgot to ask what became of her children." I checked the corners. At least the place didn't reek of cat box smell.

"I placed my grandchildren in good homes. Women that I had relationships with who would enjoy a reminder of our time together."

"Have you checked to see that they're still alive?" I said, thinking both the cats and the women needed a welfare check.

Crum stiffened. "This isn't the right attitude for someone who clearly wants something."

"Today's Score's funeral, and I'm hoping that you'll escort Miss January and keep an eye out for fights or other unsuitable behavior before it erupts."

"Don't you worry; I talked this over with Mac and volunteered to make sure Miss January gets there, and I'll keep an eye on her. I'm going to liquor her up a little so she'll stay calm. She can't really do anything sober."

"Please tell me you're wearing something appropriate," I blurted.

"I went out and got a real nice outfit," he said, clearly proud of himself.

I glanced down, squeezing my eyes closed and taking a breath before meeting his gaze. I didn't have to wonder long. He held up a pair of knee-length bathing trunks.

"They're black." I pasted a smile on my face.

He held up a white dress shirt that was actually white and not yellowed or grey. "This I had in my wardrobe." He presented a multicolored tie that hung off the tip of his finger.

"You're wearing a tie?"

"I'm wrapping it around my neck and letting it hang loose. Same thing, don't you think? It's too hot for a coat, but I'm taking my green wool smoking jacket with the black elbow patches." He preened and pointed to the door of the bedroom, where it hung.

"You'll look nice," I lied. "Thank you for helping. Fab owes you another favor." She'd kill me, but I knew he'd prefer one from her than me. I stood and scratched Harlot one last time. Before closing the door, I said, "*Any* problems, call me."

Coming down the driveway, I yelled, "Fab," pointing to the SUV. "You need anything, call," I told Mac. As we pulled out, I told Fab, "Next stop, JS Auto Body. Mother says Spoon is in the office today." I also relayed my conversation with Crum, leaving out the part about the favor; that could wait until he went to redeem it, then I'd fess up.

Chapter Thirty-Eight

"Someone actually rented you this car?" Creole looked over the rusted-out, beige Dodge Dart. He pulled me out of the way and opened the passenger door, sticking his leg in and kicking the floorboards several times. "Just wanted to make sure it won't drop out from under us." He held my arm while I got awkwardly into the seat. The two front seats were small and had a foot of space between them. I was certain they weren't factory issued, but they were better than the non-existent back seat.

"Free." I flashed a gloating smile. "Step-daddy dearest came through." Good thing Brad couldn't hear me call him that. He liked the man but wanted his mother with a *nice* retired gentleman who would bore her to tears. One major stride, though: he'd stopped suggesting she date other men.

Creole snorted. "I'm going to ask him; see if you just made the story up."

"I would never…" I sniffed. "Well, maybe, but not this time."

He checked the eyesore's interior over once

again and rocked against the driver seat in an effort to squeeze out more legroom.

I went on, "Just because JS Auto sits behinds barbed-wire fencing and the sign boasts that he specializes in high-end vehicles doesn't mean he doesn't have a 'little gem,' as he called it, hanging around that he's saved from the crusher."

"Coming from Spoon, that gives me confidence that it won't break down just around the corner."

"Spoon promised it was in good running order." I sighed. "It was awkward to ask him not to tell Mother about the latest developments. I didn't want her to get her hopes up, in case it turns out to be a dead end. He agreed, but only after I assured him I'd keep him up to date."

We parked a couple of spaces over from where we were the night before. Fab's Porsche went by; they waved and continued to the far side of the lot. This time, we had both exits covered.

"What are you doing?" Creole asked.

I finished twisting my hair into a clip, then put on a baseball cap and reached for a pair of glasses, tying a hoodie around my neck. "My disguise. For when I go into the grocery store and get an up-close look at this woman."

"Hear me out." He sighed. "I knew this would come up, and I should've said something sooner. You know that there's a chance that this person may recognize you. Tweak this plan a little: send

Fab in, and she'll get pictures. While she's dogging the woman, I'll go over the car."

"What about me and Didier? We're talking about *my* brother."

"It's your decision. But think about the best option before deciding."

He did have a good plan, but I felt petulant at having been left out of the planning. I wanted to snap, "Fine, do it your way," but that would be a fight-starter. "Your plan is the better one," I said with lukewarm enthusiasm, ignoring the sudden tick in his jaw. "Let's hope our mystery woman comes back tonight."

Creole reached for his phone and tapped out a text. A response came back quickly.

My phone beeped. "I know you're annoyed; I can feel it over here. I won't let you down." And Fab thought she couldn't do sensitive. I smiled at the screen.

"What's next?" I asked Creole.

"This is the sexy part—we wait."

* * *

The mystery woman showed up right before dusk, earlier than she had the night before. She cruised up and down every lane before deciding on a parking space, the closest one she could find to the entrance that had the option to either drive straight out or back out. Getting out, she scanned the lot again, grabbed a cart, and went inside the store.

"So much for hoping she'd chose a space farther away from the front." Creole leaned over and kissed me, handing me his binoculars.

Watching through the windshield was not where I wanted to be, but if the woman did recognize me, we might not get another chance. I'd never forgive myself if I roused her suspicions and never saw her again.

Fab cut across the parking lot and was already on her way inside the store as Creole halted behind the Mazda. He snapped pics of the rear license plate, then moved along the side, snapping more of the interior. Finally, he flashed a penlight on the dashboard and snapped another, which was most likely of the VIN number. To my surprise, instead of coming back to the car, he followed her into the store.

I was positive Fab would have a dozen pictures already, and if the woman paused to blow her nose, that would be included in the pictorial array. She had her picture-taking abilities honed to an art; very few ever knew that they were the object of her attention. However, I did have to admit that a lot of her talents were focused on dead bodies.

Creole exited first and, taking almost the same path as Fab had, only in reverse, headed to the Mercedes. Fab sauntered out a minute later, paused to pull out her phone, then changed direction and headed towards the Dodge.

I gave her a dirty look when she finally slid behind the wheel of the car.

"We're tag teaming her back to where she came from," Fab said. "Creole gets to lord it over Didier that he's the better driver, and you already know I am. It will give us time to bond."

Even when Fab annoyed me, she could make me smile. "Do we at least get to go first?"

"That depends on which way she leaves." Fab pointed. "Here comes Miss Junk Food Shopper." She shuddered. "The worst food choices ever, if you can call it that. She filled the basket with those cheap TV dinners times two. Spent too much time in the cut-rate treats aisle."

It would be worth the waste of money to bring home that kind of food, or whatever it was called, and unload the grocery bag in front of Didier. The imagined outrage on the health food nut's face made me bite my lip.

"Give me your phone." I held out my hand.

"Hang on." Fab flipped it across the seat. She had the Mazda under her personal microscope.

"Don't lose her," I said, more to annoy than remind. I flicked through the pictures. "Nice job, as always." A close-up of the woman's face came into view; of course she knew me and Mother. What was her name? "Psycho Patty," I whispered.

The woman left the parking lot and headed south on the Overseas, our Dodge and the

Mercedes following.

"Heads up, she's turning," Fab said as we breezed by her. "The guys will take over. I'll make a U-turn and fall in behind. Call Didier; we need to stay in touch," she ordered. It didn't take her long to catch back up and pull up behind the Mercedes. Patty turned left into a housing tract.

"Since it's late and there aren't many cars on the road, we'll swap positions every time she turns," Fab said, which happened at the next street.

Eventually, Patty turned into a driveway and pulled into a garage with an open door. The Mercedes pulled into a driveway just ahead of where she'd turned off. Fab and I passed the house, a one-story block-style white structure that showed signs of neglect, making another turn and parking at the corner. The neighborhood was made up of old beach houses; some had been renovated, others torn down and overbuilt for the neighborhood.

The phone rang, and instead of handing it to Fab, which earned me a scowl, I answered and asked if it was all right to put it on speaker phone.

"You could use your own phone to talk to your boyfriend," Fab hissed.

"Didier, would you have a few words with your girlfriend in French? She's being mean to me."

When Creole and Didier stopped laughing, I said, "Her name is Patty, an old girlfriend of Brad's from years ago. Last name eludes me, if I ever knew it. Mother may remember. They met in South Carolina." I paused to remember how much havoc she wreaked back then. "They dated, and possessive doesn't being to describe her attitude. She hated me and Mother. Patty became increasingly erratic, and Brad eventually had enough and broke off the relationship." I suspected Brad had been slow to come around because his lower friend didn't want to give her up, or more accurately, didn't want to give the sex up, but I kept that to myself. "She flipped out, to put it mildly, retreated into some make-believe world. I'd wondered at the time if it was a con, but the judge must have thought it was real; he ordered her to the nut house." Where I'd thought she still was. Which was probably why neither Mother nor I had thought of her when we tried to figure out which of Brad's crazy exes might be responsible.

Now she's out! Normal for half a second, and someone thought unleashing her on the public was a good idea.

Creole pulled back out of the driveway, parking behind us. With the house not close enough to have a view of the corner, both cars would go unnoticed. "Didier is going to go knock on the door."

"Oh no, he's not," Fab came close to

screeching. "That bitch is crazy."

"Didier came up with his own plan." Creole half-laughed. "Sort of. He boosted it off someone else."

Didier's voice came over the phone next. "It's not so late that she won't answer the door. Send me a picture of Jazz. I'll show it to her and share with her how heartbroken my daughter is that her cat has disappeared. Flirt subtly, try to get a peek inside, then leave.

"That stupid animal trick of Madison's." Fab hit her head on the steering wheel.

"One little tweak," I said. "Sending a picture of Snow."

"Didier's going to take his phone, so we can listen in on the speaker. Hit your mute button before he goes in, so there's no noise slip-ups," Creole said.

"So she won't get suspicious, after I leave the house, I'm going to make my way down the street, house to house." Didier sounded pleased with his plan. "If I get the 'Where do you live?' question, I'll give her the name of the street around the corner."

"If that psycho invites you inside, the answer is, 'I have to get home to the wife and kids,'" Fab said.

"Yes, wife." Didier sent a kiss through the phone line. "Creole will wait until I get to the end of the block and pick me up." The car door slammed.

"Don't worry so much." I tugged a strand of Fab's hair. "Just because he doesn't do this all the time doesn't mean he's in danger. He's in great shape and can handle himself, and Patty has no reason to be suspicious."

"I'd tear down this eyesore. There's a lot of yard here that's wasted," Didier said as he crossed the weed-filled dirt to the front door. "The garage looks bigger than the house."

Didier knocked, and seconds later, Patty answered. "Hello," she practically purred.

"Eww," I said, "she thinks he's cute."

Fab wrinkled her nose.

Didier used his sexy voice, launching into his story about the missing "Fluffy." Instead of an address, she asked for his phone number, which he didn't hesitate to give her. She promised to call if Fluffy turned up and wished him luck.

"Thanks." Didier waved, quietly reciting the house number as he walked away.

Patty stood in the doorway and watched him walk to the neighboring house before shutting the door.

From halfway up the next driveway, Didier scanned the house. "It's all closed up. No one home here. Any reason I can't go straight to the corner now that I'm out of sight of the house?" Without waiting for an answer, he started down the street. "The inside of the house has been gutted back to the studs, at least in the large room I could see, which probably used to be the living room/dining room."

"Wonder if she's squatting," I said, thinking about Carbine.

"Patty's clever. She opened the door just enough to thrust her head out. After I showed her the picture of 'Fluffy,' she opened it farther and stood in the doorway. Not sure that was her original plan, but if she hadn't made the move, I don't think I would've seen much."

"We need another plan," Creole said. "Let's go to Jake's and convene a meeting on the deck." He hung up.

"Drive by the house slowly so I can get a good look." I shifted in my seat, looking out the driver's side window.

The house was in need of attention. Mold grew up the walls from the ground to about two feet up, and the windows were completely covered by brown hurricane shutters, one held in place by a couple of 2x4's. The front door was a new addition and seemed out of place. The oversized garage didn't sit level to the ground and had, at one time, suffered severe water damage.

* * *

Fab and I weaved through the busy bar, where all the seats were filled, moving past a raucous game of pool to the best table, which was tucked into the corner of the deck and reserved for family and friends. I removed the "do not sit here" sign and cleaned off the table. Fab hit the switch for the overhead ceiling fans, and the white Christmas lights wrapped around the railing and across the overhang set the mood.

Didier appeared with a tray of beer and bottled water. Creole, following him with two baskets of chips, kicked the door closed behind him.

I waited until we were seated and everyone had a chance to take a long swallow of their drink of choice. "Isn't this where we call the cops and have them kick the door down for a look around?" I directed my question to Creole but wanted everyone's input. "Did you just roll your eyes at me?" I scowled at Creole.

Fab leaned back, arms crossed, and grinned at Creole.

"Enjoying yourself?" Creole's blue eyes darkened, narrowing on Fab.

I scooted away, mildly annoyed with the man. I didn't get very far; he reached out and tugged me to his side, clamping his arm across my shoulders.

"We have zilch for a search warrant," Creole said. "Doodad fingering her is sketchy at best because he couldn't identify Brad as the man behind the wheel. However, considering their history, we definitely need to get in for a look around."

"So we get to do the illegal dirty work, so you

can swoop in and make it look all legal-like," Fab said.

Didier arched his brow at Fab. "Why not stake the house out, wait for her to leave, and go in?"

"I know." I slammed my water bottle down on the table so hard it sprang a leak. My voice rising, I said, "I'll knock on the door and, when she answers, stick my Glock in her face." I couldn't tell from the look on Creole's face whether he was annoyed or amused.

Fab raised her hand. "You've got my vote and backup, of course."

Didier pushed her hand down. "That's not going to happen…at least not like that. Patty could have her own firearm, and you two could get hurt or worse."

"We smoke her out on some pretense. You, my dear, are good with the stories." Creole laid his arm across my shoulders. "That's a one-shot deal, though, as she'll probably get suspicious. Or we grow some patience and wait for her to make another food run."

"While you're flipping on option A or B, I'll go back to the property and check it out." Fab stood, and Didier jerked her back down. "Patty won't expect someone to be lurking around in the middle of the night."

I returned Fab's sly smile, knowing that was exactly what she would do.

"Everyone at this table knows you'll do what you want, regardless of what the rest of us agree on." Creole pinned Fab with a stare. "I'll be your backup."

"That's not a good idea." I put my hand over Creole's. "You could get in big trouble—your job could be on the line."

Creole leaned down until we were nose to nose. "You're not going, even if I have to tie you up to prevent it."

"I'll go," Didier offered. "How hard can be it to peek in a few windows? As small as that house is, there won't be many." He shook his finger at Fab. "Don't think about sneaking out; I'll tie you to the same piece of furniture as her." He tossed his head in my direction.

"That's settled?" I glanced at Fab, who nodded slightly. "What if Brad is inside? You walk away?"

"That's exactly what they'll do." Creole slapped the table. "Chief Harder will issue a search warrant. You want this to go down legally, with no chance that you end up in jail with Patty as a roommate."

"What do we tell Mother?" I asked.

"Nothing," Creole said adamantly. "Not until we have something definitive. Why get her hopes up, when it might turn out that Brad's not inside?"

"Mother isn't going to like it when she finds out we weren't forthcoming." I pressed my body against Creole's.

"Got that covered. We'll finger Fab, say it was her idea," Creole said. He and Didier laughed.

Chapter Thirty-Nine

Creole sat in a chair out by the pool with his feet up to make a few phone calls. I watched him from the French doors, making plans for my getaway. Out of ideas for how to get around the watchful man, I had bided my time, and now I would sneak away right under his nose, or rather, behind his back, since he was turned away from me. Not being at Patty's house with Fab and Didier and watching everything go down firsthand was killing me. I grabbed my bag, snuck out onto the patio, slipped quietly around the side of the house, and tiptoed down the path, which I illuminated with my phone. A good getaway didn't include falling down. When I reached the driveway, I breathed a huge sigh, inserting my key into the lock of the Dodge. It didn't open because a paw-like hand held it closed.

Creole's face was set in a stern expression, his mouth firm and unsmiling; his eyes bore into me and with one look reduced me to a naughty child. Hands on my shoulders, he turned me around and walked me back inside, the front door closing with a resounding bang. Before he could unleash the lecture that clearly sat on the tip of his tongue, his phone rang. He answered with a grunt.

"Who is it?" I asked and got a growl for an answer.

"Don't let Fab do anything illegal," he said. "Park where we did the other night and keep an eye on the house in case Patty decides to leave. I'm on it from my end." He hung up. "Brad's inside. Fab spotted him."

I grabbed my bag. Creole grabbed my other arm and hauled me back until I stood in front of him. "You better not be about to suggest I sit at home and wait for what…the cops to show up?"

"That depends on you. My first choice is to handcuff you to the bed. Can you promise to follow orders?"

"Yes, I promise."

"You're lucky I believe you, or you'd be headed upstairs." His phone resting under his chin, Creole opened the door for me, one hand at the small of my back, and led me towards his truck. He gunned it out of the driveway, stopped at the corner, and made another call.

I guessed it to be Harder as he updated the chief. "They found one hurricane shutter half open, the rest nailed closed. Television screen glare illuminated the room, and Fab saw Brad lying on a mattress, one arm secured to a wall stud, Patty asleep next to him." Creole shook his head. "Thanks, Chief." He ended the call. Turning onto the main highway, he glanced over at me. "Harder's sending agents to serve the warrant, and it will go down right around sunrise." He held up his hand. "Trust me: I know what I'm doing, and I'm not going to put Brad in any jeopardy."

I powered the window down and hung my head out. It had sprinkled earlier, and the cool wind whipped at my hair. I let the sea air blow in my face, carrying the faint smell of the Gulf waters. It had always had a calming effect on me in the past, and I hoped it wouldn't let me down now.

Turning onto Patty's street, I spotted the Mercedes parked farther up, at the corner. Creole pulled in behind the twosome, who were hunched down in the front, heads barely visible over the dashboard.

"We'd look less like hoodlums if we crowded into the Mercedes." When Creole's eyebrows shot up, I added, "Or not." I slid out of the truck and into the backseat of the Mercedes. "Anyone bring cards?"

* * *

Two hours later, Creole's phone rang. He glanced at the screen and got out of the car. I pasted my face to the window, and he scowled and turned his back, but not before I saw a quick smile.

"I've been informed that under no circumstances am I to set foot outside this car," Fab snapped, banging her head against the back of the seat. "Unless it catches fire."

"Stop that." Didier slipped his hand behind her head and rubbed. "This is going to be over soon; the psychotic one will be off to jail, and you'll be going home with me. The last thing Brad wants is to have his first hours of freedom marred by his sister and her friend getting locked up."

Two unmarked cars turned the corner at the opposite end of the street, leading the parade, followed by three boasting that they represented Miami-Dade County and a lone local sheriff's department car.

"Harder sent a lot of manpower for one lone woman," I said, impressed by the turnout.

"They have to be prepared for any scenario once they get the door open." Fab made shooting noises and didn't stop until Didier glared at her. "Brad and Patty are over on that side." She pointed toward the far corner of the house. "I ran the options; I'd have someone at the window, and if she pulls a gun, shoot her."

"Just as long as Brad doesn't get shot in the process," I said.

The officers congregated behind one of the cars, all outfitted in bulletproof vests. One popped the trunk and got out a battering ram.

"Should we offer our lock-picking services?" I asked, and Fab laughed.

The officers walked up the driveway and readied themselves at the front door. The lead cop held the battering ram, the four behind him armed with impressive rifles with scopes.

"Warrant," echoed in the early morning stillness. "Open up." One swift jab, and the door flew in, the four with the rifles moving into the interior.

I opened the car door and moved down the sidewalk to stand opposite the house, Fab by my side. From the corner of my eye, I saw Creole tug on Didier's arm, shaking his head at the two of us.

All was quiet inside, and I took that as a good sign. I held my breath, not moving an inch. The waiting seemed interminable.

Fab elbowed me. An ambulance rounded the corner. "Breathe." She slapped me on the back. "It's probably routine."

Patty was led out first, hands cuffed behind her back. She made eye contact with everyone in the street and did a double take when we locked eyes. Fab saluted her. Fury filled Patty's face. She was lucky I had a handle on my mental health, no matter what other people thought; at that moment, I wanted to dispatch her to hell. The officer led her to his vehicle, squashed her head forward, and guided her into the back seat.

I made my way across the street, coming to a stop next to the officer who appeared to be the man in charge.

"You should go back across the street, Madison. Let us do our job."

"Have we met?" I squinted at him.

He smiled and stuck out his hand. "Varner. Hard-hearted Harder is apparently a fan. Sent me a picture of you and your cohort, as he called her; asked me to make sure you two didn't get arrested." He handed me his handkerchief. "You better not be crying."

I forced a smile. "Just tell me my brother is okay and you didn't call for the coroner."

"He's fine. My guys say that Ms. Shanks took good care of him; he doesn't appear to have suffered at her hands. He might have enjoyed the attention under different circumstances, such as not being restrained and wondering if he'd ever have a normal life again."

"So the medics being here is precautionary?" Fab said as she came up beside me; I was surprised she'd waited this long.

Varner nodded and looked her over as though he'd seen her on a wanted poster and was trying to remember the charges.

"This is cohort," I introduced her. "Most people call her Fab." I mouthed to her, "Be nice."

"Your brother will be taken to Tarpon Cove Hospital to be checked out," Varner said.

"Can I ride with him?" I asked.

"Go stand next to the ambulance and tell the driver I said it was okay for you to ride along. I'll be having a short conversation with Brad before he leaves and arranging a time for a longer talk."

I sidestepped in front of Fab and lifted the back of my shirt slightly. She withdrew my gun and made it disappear, I guessed down the front of her pants.

"I saw that." Varner winked. "Good idea, firearms are frowned upon in hospitals."

"Any time you're down this way, stop in at Jake's, shoot some pool. You get the cop discount—free—and can use my private table." The first medic appeared in the doorway. "Thank you." I waved to Varner and crossed to the ambulance.

Brad came out lying on a gurney, one knee bent. He said something to one of the medics, who laughed. Joking was the best sign of all.

They rolled him up to the open doors and lifted him in.

"Hey, sis. I never doubted you'd find me." He looked exhausted but managed a smile.

"You're in so much trouble." I stepped up and sat down, and the doors slammed shut. "If you think you'll know a moment's peace… I'm having a GPS tracker attached to your ankle."

"Mother?" Brad asked.

"You know Mother never caves in a crisis. She's had Spoon as a cheerleader, holding her hand the entire time."

"You know, I do like the guy." He made a face.

"You have to accept that they're…" I scissored my fingers. "It's not like we have to call him 'daddy.'"

Brad groaned and covered his face.

The medic laughed. "Spoon? Is that… hmm…?"

I nodded, and he laughed again.

Chapter Forty

"Get me out here," Brad whispered.

Brad had been staying at Mother's since his release from the hospital two days ago, and she was driving him crazy, trying to anticipate his every need.

Mother flew into the hospital not five minutes behind the ambulance. Creole had called from the scene, breaking the news to Mother and Spoon. Brad and I were in an exam room, waiting for the doctor. We heard her before she swept through the door, steam coming out her ears, Spoon behind her, irritated that he couldn't get control of his woman. I'd have to have a talk with the man and tell him it was best to wait until she wound down before attempting a rational conversation.

"Why am I the last to know?" Mother demanded. "I'm his mother." She bent over Brad, brushing his hair off his forehead and kissing him.

"Mother, he just got here five minutes ago," I said.

The glare she shot me would have made a lesser person fall over. She put the back of her hand to his cheek.

Brad caught her hand in his and kissed it. "I don't have a fever. I'm tired is all. I'd like to be sitting on the back of my boat, sucking in the salty air; I missed fresh air, being cooped up inside."

"I never liked that Patty girl," Mother hissed.

"Mother." Brad sighed. "I don't want to talk about her. Not ever."

The door opened, and Shirl entered. "Everyone out." She smiled at Brad. "The doctor is ready for you."

"I'm not going anywhere," Mother said and flounced down into a chair.

I raised my eyebrows at Spoon, signaling, *She's your girlfriend.*

Spoon moved around the bed and hauled her out of the chair and onto her feet. "He's a grown man," he growled. "We'll be in the waiting room." He grabbed my arm and pulled me out the door along with Mother. Before it closed, I winked at Brad.

He was released an hour later with a clean bill of health.

"You're on your own, bro." I sat down next to him on the couch, sipping my favorite morning brew. Anticipating Mother's eagle eye, I had shown up early, hoping for a private conversation. I'd surprised Creole when I left the house at the same time he did, when daylight was just making its appearance. "Before you tell

Mother that she's smothering you and you're ready to run away, where are you going exactly? Isn't Julie still here?"

"Do I need to remind you that we always stick together?" Brad wrapped his arm around my shoulders, giving me a hard hug. "After dinner and my edited version of events, Julie aired her grievances. Starting with 'why couldn't this investigation involve law enforcement?' Then she went home."

"I did involve law enforcement. She means pain-in-the-rear Kevin. I don't know if she knows he wanted to arrest the whole family, starting with me and Fab. Creole's boss made this case a priority."

"Julie just wanted more input. She felt compelled to remind Mother more than a couple of times that she loved me and wanted timely information."

"I should've stayed in touch. I'll talk to her. Truthfully, I was obsessed with finding you. Driving around in circles at night, hoping to spot your truck. That activity would normally earn me a lecture about personal safety from Creole; instead, he hugged me and promised we'd find you." I laid my head on his chest.

"I counted on you to notice I was missing. I hung onto that thought, talked to you every day inside my head, wondering if I could get messages to you telepathically. Did you have any strange feelings? Woo-woo moments?"

"You appeared in a dream that was upsetting, and I'm not sure why because when I woke up, it faded and all I could remember was that it had been unsettling. The next day, Fab and I stalked all your haunts in South Florida."

I told him about how it had started with a conversation with Didier about his not showing for a meeting. "I couldn't get it out of my head that you'd never do that. When we got back home, out of options, we put the word out to our street snitches. It came down to a man named Doodad with a photographic memory. Which reminds me: about your hellhole in the Alley…" I poked him in the side. "Met Toady. Miss him?"

Brad shook his finger at me, mock sternness on his face. "Toady is devastated." His lips quirked. "He finally found the love of his life, and the woman in question is hot for a furr-a-nor. Heard you'd been out there, so I called to tell him I was alive. He could not have cared less; whined through the short phone call about Her Frenchness. Some drivel about her breaking his heart gently." He shook his head. "Knowing Fabiana like I do, she'd either not take his call or hang up on him. *You,*" he stressed, "were the one on the phone, running a con on the old guy."

"It was one of my better performances. I threw in a few French mutterings and butchered the language so badly, it made Didier flinch. I didn't want to break his heart, but I also wanted to leave the door open for another smokin' hot woman who's looking for a man who doesn't bathe."

Brad chuckled.

We sat in silence, finishing our coffee.

Brad scooted forward on the couch to look down the hall, then settled back. "I can trust you with something big, can't I? Ouch." He rubbed his ribs where I'd elbowed him.

"That's insulting. If not me, then who? We've been keeping each other's secrets since we found out it sometimes takes a united pair to stay out of trouble."

"I…uh…" Brad squirmed, reaching into his pocket. "How do you like hearing really weird news: the hedge method or spit it out?"

Knowing my brother wasn't given to melodrama, this new turn worried me. "The latter, please."

He took his hand out of his pocket and opened it. Lying in the middle of his palm was a plain silver band. "I'm married."

"You and Julie snuck off? When? Mother is going to kill you."

"Patty."

He clapped his hand over my mouth before my screech could be heard down the block.

I slapped it away. "Nooo… You married that woman?"

"Not willingly." He groaned. "There's more to my captivity than anyone knows about, and I'd like to keep it that way. But damn, I need someone to talk to." He leaned his head against the back of the couch and stared a hole in the ceiling.

"You can trust me." I took his hand in mine and squeezed.

"I fed into her delusions that we could have a real relationship that included a happy family life and children. Anything that didn't include me being chained up for the rest of my life. Not my finest moment, but I'd have done anything to get out of that house. I wondered why Patty put on a dress and fixed her hair one afternoon. And then a preacher came a knockin'; he wasn't completely sloshed, but he'd been drinking."

I shuddered at the images flashing through my mind.

"I should've known something was up when she let me put my pants back on," he said in disgust. "I wasn't allowed a shirt. Once I realized the drill, I told her I wouldn't say yes unless she released me and we could do it the right way. She laughed." He stared out the window. "Didn't matter. Preacher gave us the shortened version. When he got to the vows, Patty spoke for both of us and signed our names on the marriage certificate. Favor?"

"Anything."

"Several, actually." He half-laughed. "Having a sister who is a professional sneak is about to come in handy."

"Stop with the compliments and spill."

"I need you to go back to that house and retrieve a file of papers she kept in one of the couch cushions. Don't think the cops found it, and I didn't say a word, not wanting it to end up who knows where. Not sure what all she kept in it, but I do know she stuffed the marriage certificate inside. I'm hoping, if I can track that man down, to find out if he filed it. And if he did, I'll kick the crap out of him."

"Don't you worry your pretty head; I've got this covered. The paperwork and the preacher." I cracked my knuckles.

"Man hands," he mimicked Mother, and we laughed.

"Next favor."

"Get me out of this house. About the only thing I can do in private is pee. I'm fine." He flexed his muscles. "For all her delusions, Patty took good care of me." He grimaced. "And did I mention, please do it without Mother making me feel guilty with those doe-eyed hurt looks of hers."

"Why didn't you call instead of waiting for me to stop by?"

"With what?" He held out his hands. "My old phone is who knows where; Patty used it a few times and dismantled it after each call. Spoon came up with a phone the first day—I didn't ask where it came from; didn't give a damn—but it disappeared five minutes later. Mother blew it off and said cheerfully, 'Use the house phone.'

I'm a grown man, and I've got my mother listening in on my calls. Would've left a note and snuck out in the middle of the night, but oh yeah, no ride."

"Truck's not in the garage; any idea where Patty hid it?"

"A few days after she nabbed me, she picked up the keys to the truck and disappeared, and when she came back, she threw a completely different set down on the table. Patty ignored my questions, and from that, plus the fact that her purse was stuffed with cash, I figured she sold it. I wouldn't put anything past her."

"I'll put that on my to-do list. Girl Wonder and I have experience legally jacking cars and returning them to their rightful owners, and yours would qualify." I stood up and put my hands on my brother's shoulders. "I'll get you out of here. If things look like they're going south, don't give up hope and blow my plan. What is it, you ask? Work in progress." I crossed to a chair and retrieved my phone out of my purse. "What are you doing?" I asked Fab when she picked up the phone.

"Ogling Didier's backside while he pours me another cup of coffee."

"Okay, a moment of silence for that amazing sight; now focus. Can you shake him and sneak away, meet me at Jake's? Bring my Glock; I need backup. Sooner is better."

"One hour."

"Perfect." I shoved my phone in my pocket.

Mother eyed me and Brad as she came into the living room, hands on her hips. "What are you two up to? And don't say 'nothing.' I'm experienced with your tricks."

I grabbed our coffee mugs and walked to the kitchen sink. "I'm taking Brad to breakfast. We need some brother/sister bonding time. Well, he probably doesn't, but I do."

Mother followed on my heels. "Nonsense. I can make breakfast here." She opened the refrigerator, taking out a couple of bakery boxes.

Behind her back, Brad made a gagging motion.

"Mother." I wrapped my arms around her, kissing her cheek. "Is Brad grounded?"

"Of course not." She sniffed. "I just don't want you to get him in trouble."

"Really." My brows shot up. "I had nothing to do with this whole incident, except in the finding; Patty was never a friend of mine."

"I didn't mean it like that. I'd just like to keep him in sight for the next few years."

I didn't have to look at my brother to know he was ready to bolt out the door and hike to Alligator Alley, where no one would find him.

"It's only for a couple of hours. We'll be back," I said, feeling slightly guilty, not knowing if, once Brad escaped, his need to feel normal would trump Mother's pouty looks.

"Just give me a few minutes, and I'll go with

you two," Mother said.

Brad stomped out to the balcony, scraped a chair across the concrete, and threw himself down in it.

"Listen to me: stop smothering Brad. He wants his life back, and it's natural that he wants to go out and claim it. I'm guessing he's craving a normal day: business decisions to make, time with his girlfriend, and probably a hot, sweaty run on the beach. You keep trying to restrict his movements and he'll walk out, and it will be uncomfortable and weird and he won't want to come back—for a while, anyway."

Spoon came into the kitchen. "What's going on?"

It would have been hard not to notice that Mother and I were engaged in a stare-down.

"I'm taking Brad to breakfast. We'll see you later." I arched my brow at Mother. "Okay?"

"You both better come back in one piece."

I kissed her cheek and yelled, "Hey, bro." He turned, and I motioned for him to get moving. I picked up my purse and moved in behind him, pushing him to the door. "I notice you don't have a wallet. I suppose you're going to mooch off me and make me pay the bill."

"That bitch Patty had it—who knows where it is now. I'd like to drive, but no license."

I laughed, and he glared back.

"I'm happy you think this is amusing."

"You think you're irritated now; just wait until

you're a passenger in my slow-mobile."

He grinned at that. "I'll chalk it up to penance for all the times I flew over the speed limit. At least I know we'll get where we're going in one piece."

Chapter Forty-One

It was a short drive to Jake's. We pulled into the parking lot alongside Fab's Porsche. Motioning for Brad to follow, I slid out of the driver's seat, opened the back door, and slid in, Brad behind me.

"You couldn't ditch him?" I smiled at Didier when he climbed in, shutting the door. I shoved my hand over the front seat. "My Glock."

Fab withdrew it from the waistband of her jeans. "I'm not willing to go without sex until Didier stops being irritated."

Brad threw his head back and laughed. "Feels good to laugh."

"Where are we going?" Fab asked, as she pulled out on the main highway.

"Why?" Didier grunted.

Brad gave them a watered-down version of the "life with Patty" story he had disclosed to me previously. He focused on his truck and kept quiet about the marriage.

"I'm afraid to ask, but what do you think you and Fab are going to accomplish? I vote we run this by Creole and see if it's legal," Didier suggested.

"Of course it's not legal. And if you need a house ransacked, it's stupid not to use the best." I tugged on Fab's hair, which she jerked out of my grasp. "Fab can toss the place, and I'll be backup. If this is a job that you can't abide—" I turned to Didier. "I'll go myself. I've watched the master often enough; maybe it's time for the student to graduate."

The last comment didn't sit well with Didier. His head snapped around, his expression angry.

"I didn't think I would be starting a fight," Brad said. "Turn around, Fab. It's not worth it if no one is speaking to anyone else at the end of the day."

"I can't believe I'm going to be the calm one." Fab banged the steering wheel. "The house is empty. It's an in-and-out job."

Time to text Creole. *"Back at the scene of the crime. Brad forgot something."* I'd wait until we got out of the car to push send.

Fab circled the block twice. Not a single neighbor was milling around. It was early; we had that going for us. She chose the same parking place close to the corner.

I had slipped into tennis shoes on the ride over. Not knowing when I left the house that I'd be searching a house, I wasn't as prepared, in my skirt and t-shirt, as I'd like to have been, but it would have to do. Before I got out, I handed my phone to Brad after pushing send. Coward that I was, I figured he could talk to Creole when he called demanding answers.

"Let's take the direct approach." Fab withdrew her lockpick and a pair of latex gloves. "Do not look around; pretend we have the right to be here. Patty's not getting out anytime soon, is she?"

"I hope not." I shuddered and pulled on a pair of gloves. "If she does, I may have to use one of those connections I loosely brag about to have her fed to the alligators."

I'd found out that the house had been a foreclosure that was owned by the bank. Someone had come by and padlocked the door, which Fab had open in a flash.

Didier had been right about the interior condition of the house. The previous owner had apparently run out of money after gutting it, and now only an investor would want it, and then for dirt cheap.

"You guard the door. This won't take long." Fab looked at the makeshift bed slapped down on the floor, two sagging upholstered chairs, equally shabby couch with suspicious stains, and marred wooden coffee table.

"Brad says there's no bug issues."

"That's the only good thing about this place." Fab pulled out a knife and headed to the couch, examining all four sides and patting down both cushions. She slit one side of the cushion open, removed the folder Brad had said would be inside, and tossed it on the coffee table. The second cushion got the same treatment, as well as both chairs.

"It stinks in here." I wrinkled my nose.

"Get a whiff over here." She left the couch and moved to the bed, flipping up the sheets and inspecting the mattress. "This is interesting." Her hand disappeared out of sight and came back with a laptop. She made a few strategic knife cuts to the mattress and, then ripped it open and, with a little digging, held up Brad's wallet, keys, phone, and watch. Satisfied that there was nothing left to find, she headed to the kitchen and searched the cupboards. They were all empty.

Fab disappeared down the hall and, within minutes, returned with a small plastic box containing a couple of USB drives and some cash. In her other hand was a camera. "There are a few personal items in the bathroom that belonged to a female, but nothing important."

"Let's get out of here while it's still quiet," I said.

Fab scanned the interior one last time, pushed me out the door, and replaced the padlock.

"Thank you for doing this. I know Didier isn't happy."

"Don't you *ever* go sneaking off without me."

I walked to the passenger side, Brad opened the door, and I handed him his personal belongings. I kept the file.

"Thanks," he said, pulling me into a hug by

my hair. "Creole's not happy," he whispered in my ear. "Wants to talk to Fab."

Didier moved across the seat to behind Fab, and I climbed in beside him.

"Take us back to Jake's," I said to Fab. "Brad needs a phone—his current one is missing the SIM card—and then our curfew is about up." When Fab had handed me the pieces of the phone, the battery and card were both gone.

"I took care of that," Didier said. "Called Madeline and told her we ran into the two of you and I insisted that Brad come back to the house and go for a run and a swim. Barbeque later, and of course, I expected to see her and Spoon. She wasn't happy, but she agreed."

Brad turned to me. "Now that I've got my license back, can I borrow your car to go surprise Julie at The Cottages?"

"Be sure to invite her and Liam for dinner."

Chapter Forty-Two

Alone for a moment in the kitchen, I filled my mug with coffee and took it poolside. The previous night, I had gone through the manila file and found Brad's marriage license, a copy of the title to his truck, and a bill of sale. I made copies before stashing the file in a locked desk drawer. It wouldn't keep Fab out, but it would most people. During dinner, I drew Brad aside, telling him where I'd hidden it and that I'd flipped through the contents and had everything I needed to piece together what Patty had done and hopefully undo everything as quickly as possible. I'd hugged him hard. "Don't worry about any of this." I promised to sort out this mess as soon as possible.

Now that I had the contents spread out on the patio dining table, the file held several surprises. Patty had assumed Brad's identity and taken control of his life, thanks to a forged power of attorney. I fished my phone out of my pocket and left a message for Phil, asking her to find Marvin Pink, the preacher, and Violet Tipp, the notary who signed the power of attorney, and saying that the job was a rush.

I'd loaned my SUV to Brad and told him no hurry to return it, knowing he need time with Julie, which left me without a ride. I texted Fab: "Can I borrow your car?" and when I didn't hear back, gave her the benefit of the doubt; she probably thought I was kidding.

It wasn't often that I had the house to myself, but I had no time to enjoy it. I ran upstairs and changed into a pair of black running shorts and a hot-pink skirt, sports bra, and short-sleeve top. Emptying out my purse on the bed, I transferred what I needed to a small backpack.

Pulling my hair into a ponytail and grabbing a baseball cap, I went back downstairs and out to the garage. I waved to my beach bicycle, propped up in the corner. "I know. Long time, no ride." I checked the tires, wondering if talking to my bike was worse than talking to myself.

Even though there was a bicycle lane alongside the road, I cut down to the beach and took that path most of the way to Jake's before I had to brave the busy tourist traffic blowing through town.

Drenched in sweat, thanks to off-the-charts humidity, I rolled my bike in through the kitchen door and parked it out of the way, waved to Cook, and made my way to the bar. Jake's wasn't officially open yet. The first to arrive, I flipped on the lights and ceiling fans and helped myself to a cold bottle of water, spilling some on my chest before taking a long drink and settling on a stool.

The front door opened, and Phil waved from the threshold.

"You're late, Phyllis." I imitated Fab's snooty tone.

"It's Philipa." She returned my condescending stare and checked her watch. "I have at least a minute, and I intend to walk very slowly."

"What have you got for me?"

"You just texted the request," she grouched. "I planned to do it myself, since it's fairly easy."

"Good thing I have that 'if it needs to be done, I'll do it' spirit. I'll set up the bar while you tap away on that laptop of yours."

"Gee thanks, boss, but no thanks." She rolled her eyes. "Lucky you, I can do two things at once. I'll set up the bar, so I can find things when I need them, and walk you through which websites to check out."

Phil gave rapid-fire instructions, starting with the notary, which led me easily to her contact information. She wasn't local, but close enough—Marathon Key. The only thing stopping me from making an appointment was that I didn't have a car. I also ran a check for Preacher Pink.

"I need a ride; my brother has my car."

"Call your mother's lover; he delivers." Phil smirked.

Wincing at hearing their status put so bluntly, I pulled out my phone and called the man in question. When Spoon answered, I said, "I need a favor."

"Done."

"I've got six dead men in the back of my SUV. Can you make them and the car disappear?"

The silence went on for so long, it was uncomfortable. "What do you really want?"

"Brad's using my SUV, and I need a ride, preferably something a little sexy. But I'll take what I can get. And I need it delivered."

"How about my convertible Mercedes?"

"Nice." I'd ridden in that car once, and frankly, his driving scared me.

Spoon promised to deliver it to the house within a couple of hours. I told him to park it on my side of the driveway.

Resuming my search for the preacher, I noticed first off that there wasn't one easy step, like with the notary. Pink was listed on a classified ad site, but it didn't include contact information. I passed a note to Phil, asking her to track that one down.

Finally, all that was left was the truck. "How do I find the buyer?" I stared down at a copy of Brad's truck title, having already filled Phil in on what my brother had told me.

"I've got a connection for that information. I'm warning you upfront, though, that it might be messy if the buyer figured the deal was on the up and up. And why not, when the sale included a title? Not like some, who don't find it necessary to have the legal paperwork. Your brother will have to prove the fraud."

The first customer of the day came through the door on unsteady legs, moaning; for him, it had been a long night. "I'll take a cup of coffee and a beer. Horrible hangover. Aspirin, if you've got it," he said and slid onto a stool at the opposite end of the bar.

I shuddered, happy it wasn't my job to think of something sympathetic to say. Phil made that part of the job look easy; she clucked over him, and he smiled back at her in adoration.

"Call me, no matter the time." I repacked my backpack, pushing a copy of the paperwork at Phil.

"I can get you a ride home."

"No thanks." Mr. Hangover was the only one in the bar, and Mother had always told me not to accept rides from strangers. Seemed like a good excuse.

I helped myself to another bottle of cold water and waved as I left.

Chapter Forty-Three

When I came through the door, dripping with sweat after ditching my bike, Fab had her legs draped over the back of the couch, Jazz asleep next to her and Snow right below her hand, which hung over the cushion, petting her intermittently. She gave me a thorough once-over, her nose wrinkling in distaste.

Hand on the stair railing, I asked, "Where are the keys to Spoon's Mercedes?"

She flashed me an innocent look and shrugged.

"Put them on the island." I went up the stairs to my bedroom. All I'd thought about the last mile home was how good a shower was going to feel.

* * *

I changed into a hot-pink slip dress, attaching my thigh holster and trading my flip-flops for a pair of leather slip-on sandals. Cleaning out my backpack, I shoved the paperwork into a tote bag. Grabbing my phone, I noticed a text from

Phil. I went downstairs and settled on the daybed, ignoring Fab.

Phil had come through with an address for Marvin Pink that I recognized as a pay-by-the-hour flop motel. I called Violet and arranged to meet her at a local coffee shop. Interestingly enough, she didn't ask what kind of document she'd be notarizing, only saying that she'd be the one with the large red briefcase.

"Where are we going?" Fab asked when the call ended. "Didier had a meeting, so we can go blow things up."

"We've never done that—sounds fun. As long as we don't get hurt. Or you'll have a lot of explaining to do." I sat up and dropped my phone into my bag. "Thanks, but I've got this covered." I crossed to the kitchen and collected the keys to the Mercedes.

Fab blocked the front door. "I'm going." She tried to grab the keys, but I managed to put them in my pocket.

"So sweet of you." I ignored her eye-roll and continued, "I'm driving. At least part of the way."

I unlocked the passenger door for Fab, went around to the driver's side, and slid in behind the wheel of Spoon's pristine silver Mercedes. "I'm thinking we shouldn't eat in here."

Fab laughed. "Spoon would kill us."

On the drive down the Overseas, I tossed Fab my scribbled directions for the appointment with

Violet and updated her on the information we were after.

"Since I'm just sitting over here—" Fab sniffed. "—I've come up with a plan: you do the talking, and if she doesn't cooperate, I'll threaten her." She put her feet on the dashboard and looked out the window. "Oh yeah, next exit."

The drive had, thus far, gone smoothly, and I hadn't embarrassed myself with any sudden stops or starts. But with barely enough room to make the turn, I hit the brakes and managed to get over, despite the barrage of horn-honking from the irate driver behind me.

"I would appreciate more notice," I snapped.

"You made it, didn't you?" Fab turned the paper around a couple of times. "Up here, turn right."

"Could you be more vague?"

"Your directions, let me say this nicely, stink."

I grabbed them out of her fingers and pulled over. "Not one word." I shook my finger at her. "The street name is right here." I pointed and screeched away from the curb.

The coffee house was an easy find after that. Since nature had delivered another steamy, scorching day, the outdoor seating area was empty. I grabbed my bag, checking to make sure the title paperwork was on top, and headed for the entrance.

Violet wasn't hard to spot, as she'd set her red briefcase in the middle of the small table. She wasn't quite what I'd expected, a curvy woman with blond ringlets in a black dress with white polka dots and red accessories. She reminded me of the fifties, though she herself was a thirty-something.

"I'm your next appointment," I said, not bothering with introductions. I pulled out a chair and sat down, Fab sitting next to me. I pulled out the title and set it down in front of her.

"This has already been notarized." She scanned the document. "And by me," she chirped. "What's this all about?"

The fact that her eyes had hardened to pinpoint dots didn't escape my notice. "This is the title to my brother's truck, which you illegally notarized. I know because he's never set eyes on you. And I'd like to know why you'd do something so boldly illegal. What's in it for you?"

"I don't know what you're talking about. If I could charge you for wasting my time, believe me, I would." Violet stood and shoved a smaller bag into her briefcase.

"Sit down," Fab ordered, producing her fake police badge.

Violet sneered. "I have one of those."

"You leave, I'll file a complaint against you with the state. Proving you didn't commit an illegal act can be costly and put a damper on your business," I said.

Violet glared, but whatever she saw in my face

caused her to back down, setting her briefcase on the floor and retrieving her journal. "Normally, I wouldn't do this, but I want to prove that I have nothing to hide." She perused the title and flipped through the pages. "I did everything required of me by law." She pushed it across the table, pointing to Brad's name.

My heart sank as I looked at the signature line. It looked just like Brad's signature. Even I couldn't tell the difference. She could claim up and down that it was genuine, and it would require an expert to prove otherwise.

"As you can see, I have—" Violet turned the book towards her, then back to us. "—Brad Westin's current address, driver's license information, and the signer matched the ID because I always check."

"Why no fingerprint?" Fab asked.

"It's optional." She flashed a weaselly smile. "Not required by law."

"How convenient," I murmured.

"You're lucky you're dealing with her," Fab said. "You helped a psycho defraud her brother. And for what? A few bucks. I voted for shooting you, but she won't let me."

Without a word, Violet grabbed her book and briefcase and practically ran out the door.

"This isn't going to be easy to unravel." I found it interesting that, despite the fact that she'd committed a felony that could land her in jail, Violet had held her ground and never showed the slightest crack.

* * *

I happily relinquished the drive back to Tarpon to Fab, although I'd never admit it to her. I kept our next stop vague.

"You've got the wrong address." Fab peered out the window, having turned into the driveway at my direction before realizing we'd arrived at the rundown Bluebird Motel.

The cream-colored building sat back off the highway just outside the Cove next to a liquor store and the Pole Lounge, a stripper joint under new ownership. It was rumored that they had pay-by-the-hour rooms; the others, they rented to anyone who checked in with a fistful of cash.

Fab's eyes narrowed at my insincere smile. "This was all a trick," she said in a snit.

"Stop your whining. You'd never let me come here by myself, even though you'd want to. How would you explain it to Mother and everyone else if something dreadful happened?" I fake-swooned against the back of the seat.

"I'm waiting in the car."

"I will *so* tell on you." I pointed to a parking space. "Marvin's room is across from the pool." All the rooms were situated around a U-shaped patio area.

"We'll both need to be disinfected." Fab grunted. "If the supposed pool doesn't have water in it, it's nothing more than a hole in the ground."

"It was probably hard to keep it clean."

Fab made a face and slammed the car door. I looped my arm through hers so she couldn't stay behind and tugged on her until she started moving.

Standing in front of the door, we found that the window was ajar, and the sound of snoring drifted out loud and clear. I stared at Fab, and she stared back with little empathy. I cop-knocked and noticed there wasn't even a break in the racket coming out of the man's nostrils. I tried again, and Fab kicked the door. The door to the room next door opened, and a woman in a ratty muumuu stuck her head out.

"Marvin sleeps like the dead. Only you know he ain't for all that racket. Door's unlocked, help yourself." She waved. "How did he afford you two?"

Fab flashed her badge.

The woman caught her breath. "I don't know nuttin'." She slammed the door.

Fab used her top to cover the door knob and open it, giving the bottom a shove with her foot at the same time. The room was a roach's delight, as they raced across the countertop and over the microwave. The bed was against the far wall, and I assumed the closed door in the corner was to the bathroom.

"Got an idea for how to wake him?" An

unidentifiable odor assailed my nose, which I quickly covered with my hand.

Fab kicked the bottom of his foot, which hung over the edge of the bed.

"Huh," Marvin mumbled, coming awake. His eyes bugged at the sight of Fab's weapon pointed at him.

"Don't worry about her unless you don't answer my questions," I said. "If you cooperate, you'll have enough money to buy a bottle of your choice."

"Gotta pee." His hand disappeared under the sheet.

"No climbing out the window," I warned. "That will only get you a bullet in your backside."

He stumbled out of bed, one foot caught in the sheet, then righted himself and raced across the room in dingy boxers.

Fab cased the room, not touching a single thing, although she toed a couple of items left on the floor. She put a finger to her lips and threw the curtain back. The woman we'd met earlier had her ear on the screen. Fab slammed the window shut.

Marvin opened the door on a loud belch. He grabbed a pair of pants from the chair, stepping into them, and wiped his hands on an already stained undershirt, which he pulled over his head.

"How can I help you ladies?" He crossed to

the small refrigerator, removing a beer. "I'd offer you one, but I only have one." He kicked a chair around and sat at the small round table.

"I want straight answers, not excuses," I said, dropping the marriage certificate in front of him. "You married my brother. I'm sure you'll remember him." I scrolled through my phone for Brad's picture and held it out.

Marvin squinted at the phone like it might bite him and gave it a cursory glance. "My eyesight's not as good as it used to be."

"Your signature is at the bottom of the certificate. Maybe this will jog your memory: he was chained to a stud inside a mostly empty house. And that part where you ask the groom do you even want to marry this wackjob? He answered no; several times, in fact."

"The woman told me he was delusional and his family wanted to commit him. They needed to get married to stop them."

"How did she find you?" Fab asked.

"I heard her asking at the convenience store, and I stepped up. Good pay, and she let me know I'd be doing a good deed."

"Where did you file it?" I asked. "I haven't been able to find a recorded copy."

"Well… I…uh…" He took a long swig of his beer. "I haven't."

"That means what?" I snapped.

"I didn't file nothing. No good anyway, not licensed anymore. People got mad. I couldn't remember the vows, and the time I showed up drunk, a complaint was filed. A disciplinary hearing was set, I was a no-show, and my license got revoked. Kept calling myself a preacher because it sounded classy."

"So Brad and Patty aren't really married?" I didn't realize I was holding my breath until he nodded and it came rushing out. Thank goodness for that. "If I ever hear of you performing another phony marriage ceremony, I'll make sure you go to jail. Or she will." I snapped my fingers at Fab, who produced her badge. Marvin paled. I pulled more cash than he deserved out my pocket and tossed it on the table. "There's enough here to buy your silence in this matter."

Fab practically pushed me out the door. "We didn't sit down, so we won't have to burn our clothes."

Chapter Forty-Four

Fab had picked the wrong time to start an argument with Creole, who was shooting daggers at the fiery woman. Didier and I stood in the living room watching the fireworks.

Creole slapped his hand on the island. "Get in the car. Let's get this surprise on the road." He whisked the keys out from under Fab's hand by a hair's breadth.

Fab crossed her arms, in a full-blown pout. "I want to drive."

I almost applauded the stamp of her foot.

"Well, you are not. What you are going to do is get in the backseat with your boyfriend and try your hardest to behave. Besides, you don't know where we're going." He mimicked her body language. "If you get behind the wheel, I'll drag your butt out and leave you in the driveway while the rest of us drive off and have fun without you."

Fab and Creole looked at Didier.

He waved his arms. "Oh no, you two can work this out." He turned to me and rolled his eyes.

"The bright side is that I'm not driving." I smiled at Fab, which earned me a fierce "you're not helping" frown. I reached for her arm, and she twisted away. "Creole promised that we're going to love this road trip, even you, so that means we'll be camping somewhere with room service."

Fab sulked in silence. She timed the venting of her outrage to when the SUV reached the Overseas Highway, where south- and north-bound traffic split, separated by water in the middle.

"The seat's uncomfortable. There's a spring in my butt." Fab jumped around; getting no response, she kicked the back of the driver's seat. Creole let out a low growl.

I lowered my head and laughed silently. I should have sat behind him and insisted that Didier sit in the front.

"I'm hungry and I've got to pee," Fab complained, along with another kick.

Didier turned to look out the window; his shoulders shook a little.

Pee? I raised my eyebrows.

Fab kicked her feet on the floor. Didier attempted to throw his leg over hers and was unsuccessful. She launched into non-stop kicking of Creole's seat.

"Enough," Creole bellowed. "Can't you control your girlfriend?"

Didier shrugged. "Go ahead; you do it." He smirked.

Creole came to a screeching halt in the emergency lane. Adjusting the rearview mirror, he glared at Fab. "Two choices. Behave, and not another kick or outburst the rest of the way, or you can get out here and a ride will be along shortly. Your ass can sit at home."

"She'll behave," I answered for her, glaring at her over the seat, knowing she'd push it until he was forced to make good on his threat.

"Yes, she will." Didier tugged her closer to him and put her in a headlock. The two whispered back and forth until finally, Didier unbuckled his seatbelt and scooted over next to Fab.

Thank goodness. What if her foot slipped again?

* * *

The rest of the ride was uneventful; quiet, in fact. The guys talked, and Fab closed her eyes and pretended to sleep, a self-satisfied smile on her face. When Creole veered off at Little Torch Key, I got excited, knowing that there wasn't much out there except a resort that was accessible only by boat.

Our bags were loaded onto the boat in short order, and we left the SUV parked in the lot; no cars allowed on the island. Fab wrapped herself around Didier for the ride over. Creole and I claimed the far corner. Sitting in his lap, I wrapped my arms around his neck.

The private beach of the resort was like a slice of heaven, the white sand sifting through my toes. I was the first one to take my shoes off. The hotel was built on its own private beach, within several hundred feet of the blue-green water surrounding the entire property. It didn't take long before we were checked in and a golf cart took us to our cottage. Two bedrooms, one on each side, totally private, and bathrooms with waterfall showers and sunken marble tubs. We had our own patio area nestled under palm trees on the sand, complete with a fire pit and choice of loungers and hammocks.

Trying to decide what to do first, we voted on waverunners, spending the rest of the day cruising around the open waters, exploring the smaller nearby Keys.

* * *

In order to guarantee a dining table on the beach in front of the resort restaurant, we had to make an early reservation, which suited me fine. Both Fab and I had on sleeveless, black mid-calf dresses and sandals.

On our way to dinner, I curled into Creole. "Can we go to bed early?"

"You tired?"

"A little."

"Come to think of it, me too." We stopped to kiss until Fab whistled loudly, a reminder to hurry up.

Once we were seated, Didier ordered a bottle of white wine and offered up the first toast. "To good friends." We clinked glasses.

Surprisingly, there wasn't a single contentious word between Fab and Creole. Didier had already banned work talk. He took on the role of entertainer and kept us laughing.

Once dinner was over, we split up, going our separate ways. Fab and Didier left to go for a walk on the beach, while Creole and I walked along the shoreline back to the cottage. Lanterns had been lit along the sand, and as we got closer, we saw that the outside deck was awash in hanging down-drop lights. We lost none of the view, as the French doors to the bedroom opened onto the private patio overlooking the same stretch of beach.

* * *

The next morning, Fab and I sat out on the deck, enjoying the view and drinking coffee, and the guys went for a mini-run down the beach to get more information about a dive trip.

"You must have morphed into Mother," I said to Fab. "There's enough food here to feed us for a week." Fab had surprised everyone by calling room service and ordering breakfast.

"Creole doesn't look happy." Fab inclined her head at the two men walking up the beach. "Neither does Didier."

"Spoon called," Creole said, climbing the steps and sitting in a chair next to me. "Not a happy man. I think he expected me to know what he was talking about, and I didn't."

I shook my head. "Don't know what you're talking about."

"No," Creole said. "Some surprise get together at Madeline's starting in the morning. Supposedly, you two promised you'd be there, and 'Why aren't you home when she needs your help?'"

"I don't know what Spoon's talking about either," I said in exasperation. "Mother has these impromptu family events all the time. We can miss one. She probably wants my help in corralling Brad into living at her house. Which my brother vehemently denies he's going to do." I stood and stomped into the cottage.

Out of patience, I slammed the bedroom door with a resounding bang. I dumped the contents of my purse on the floor, fishing out my phone. I took a couple of deep breaths, trying to get the petulant child who'd invaded my body under control.

Then I flounced on the bed, calling Mother. If only I had a bit of blackmail material to hang over Fab's head to get her to make this call, but I didn't have anything good.

"Mother," I said when she answered. "Thank you for the invitation, but the four of us are out of town for some much-needed relaxation. We can get together when we return to Tarpon."

"Honey," she started.

"I know you understand."

There was a long silence. "Of course," she said and hung up without a good-bye.

I lay for a long moment staring at the ceiling. "Damn." I threw my phone across the room, knowing damn well that Mother had been crying when she hung up. I'd never come close to the "worst daughter of the year" award, but today, it felt like I'd won it with no close competition.

Creole stuck his head in the door, shaking his head at seeing my phone on the floor. "Is it safe to come in?"

"I made Mother cry."

He pushed me onto my side and wrapped me in his arms. "I'll call and tell her we're on our way back."

A loud banging on the bedroom door made Creole growl.

"You decent?" Fab yelled.

"Good thing I locked the door, or she'd already be in here." He crossed the room and opened it. "Would you like to come in?"

"Hardly. Didier's got an update you'll want to hear." Fab hobbled off, one foot bare, the other in a tennis shoe.

I slid off the bed and linked my hand with

Creole's; we kissed briefly and followed.

Fab threw out her arm in a sweeping motion, pointing to the loveseat. "Make yourselves comfortable. This one's a doozy."

Didier tossed his phone on the table. "Spoon called, shouting; about put my ear out. Fab told me to bill you if I need to go to the doctor." He smirked at me.

"Could you speed it along?" Creole snapped.

"Let me see if I can remember the man's exact words." He paused, enjoying his friends' rising irritation level a little too much. "Oh yes. 'Get your asses back here; you're not ruining our wedding.'"

That's a good one. Then I realized Didier wasn't kidding.

Fab raised her hand. "I heard him. For once, Didier let me listen in."

Chapter Forty-Five

"We are gathered together to celebrate the love between Madeline and James by joining them in marriage."

Fab and I had sat in the back of the SUV on the way home, lamenting over what to wear when we had not one detail about the pending nuptials. Didier had flipped a coin to decide who was going to call Mother and ask questions, since neither of us trusted the other not to cheat. I didn't gloat, except for the fist pump when I won. Fab refused to put the call on speaker, so I did the next best thing and practically sat on her to listen in.

Mother laughed after talking to Fab, informing us that the dresses and accessories were already hanging in our bedrooms and no shoes were required and confiding that the wedding would be beachfront at a local resort that specialized in them. As expected, she'd chosen beautiful dresses. Fab's and mine were pale pink, strapless, and ankle length. Mother also apologized and admitted that after she hung up, she realized that in the excitement of planning the wedding, she'd forgotten to ask us to save the date.

"Is this the first time you've worn a color other than black?" I asked Fab.

She wrinkled her nose at me. "Of course not."

"I must have missed that one time."

"Pay attention." She tossed her head to where a woman was motioning for us to get in line.

We walked down a wooden deck that had been laid out in the sand, ending at a deck platform with a pergola, the columns covered in gauze and the top decorated in flowers that matched our anklets and the flowers in our hair. Ending several feet from where the waves rolled on shore, the deck itself was lined in lanterns of various sizes.

Spoon and his two attendants, who I didn't recognize, were in black tuxedos, the bottoms of their pants rolled up, the white roses pinned to their lapels matching the bouquet that Mother carried.

Mother came up the aisle, all smiles for her groom, in an elegant ankle-length, rose-colored A-line dress, low-cut, with lacey straps. She kissed us before turning to the minister.

The ceremony was short and sweet, and I teared up at the I-do's. Spoon swooped her into a kiss that had the guests clapping.

Round tables had been set up under another pergola strung with rows of lights across the top and down the columns. The guests gravitated to the bar, and since most knew one another, there was no one left off to one side by themselves or running for the exit. Except for my brother.

Weaving through the tables, I ended up next to him. "You okay?"

"Have I told you that you're my favorite sister?"

"I'm happy that I've retained my 'number one' status." That earned me a smile. "You worried about Mother?"

"Not so much," he said on a resigned sigh. "If she's happy, then I'm happy. I corralled Spoon yesterday and told him that if he hurt her, I'd kill him and there would be nothing left to bury."

"What did he say?" I'd never thought anyone would have the nerve to threaten the man.

"Oh, he had something choice to say, but he bit it back, nodded, and left." He hugged me hard. "I consulted a lawyer about my truck, and I'm letting it go. It could end up costing me as much as the truck is worth in legal fees and wouldn't be settled overnight. I'm spending the money on a new ride." He sighed. "There's talk of a plea bargain for Patty. She goes back to the nuthouse until she's declared competent, at which point, she'll be tried."

"You okay with that?"

"I just want to forget any of this happened."

I linked my arm in his. "We should get back."

The reception flew by. The guests ate and drank; great stories were told about meeting Mother or Spoon, all ending in laughs; the happy couple shared their first dance; and everyone made toasts, all with the backdrop of the water gently lapping the white sand.

Mother, in a flashy show, dragged Fab, Julie,

and me to the front, producing three garters and throwing them at us.

I hooked mine over my finger, sought out Creole, and twirled it around, laughing.

"Which of you will be first?" Mother asked wistfully.

"I have some news." Julie beckoned to Brad and Liam.

Creole wrapped his arms around me from behind and whispered in my ear, "Is the preacher waiting in the wings to perform a group ceremony?"

I turned in his arms. "Don't suggest that. Even if he's left already, Mother would get him back."

"I've been offered the leading role in an Indie film." Julie beamed, clutching Brad's hand. "I'm leaving for Los Angeles in a couple of days and will be back in about two months."

There was a round of congratulations and clapping.

Brad looked like he'd reconciled himself to it, but Liam was harder to read. I congratulated Julie, knowing she was talented and how much her big break would mean to her.

Mother and Spoon then made their escape into a waiting limo, which was taking them to a private island off the coast of Key West for their honeymoon.

Creole whirled me around on the dance floor.

I pulled one side of my dress up over my wrist, and he lifted me onto his feet. I'm a really bad dancer. Unless I'm a bit tipsy. I refrained for Mother's sake, not wanting to turn the wedding into Madison behaving badly.

Fab and Didier walked up arm in arm.

"Ready to sneak out? That way we don't get delayed by all the goodbyes," Fab said. "We found a path that goes straight to the parking lot."

"We?" Didier arched his brow.

"You were with me in spirit." Fab smiled up at him.

"That's a good one," I said. "I'll have to remember that."

Creole laughed and shook his head.

"The newlyweds are gone; no need for us hang around. I've had enough of pink," Fab said, looking down at her dress.

"You both look great," Creole said.

Didier nodded in agreement.

"We can't all leave together; it will draw attention. Go left—" she pointed. "—and around that post, and it's a straight shot to the parking lot." She linked her arm through Didier's. "Any reason we need to wait for you two?"

Creole squeezed me to his side and shook his head. "Got this covered. We'll see you in a couple of days." He kissed me. "Let's go to the beach house."

~*~

PARADISE SERIES NOVELS

Crazy in Paradise
Deception in Paradise
Trouble in Paradise
Murder in Paradise
Greed in Paradise
Revenge in Paradise
Kidnapped in Paradise
Swindled in Paradise
Executed in Paradise
Hurricane in Paradise
Lottery in Paradise
Ambushed in Paradise
Christmas in Paradise
Blownup in Paradise
Psycho in Paradise
Overdose in Paradise
Initiation in Paradise
Jealous in Paradise
Wronged in Paradise
Vanished in Paradise
Fraud in Paradise
Naïve in Paradise

Deborah's books are available on Amazon
amazon.com/Deborah-Brown/e/B0059MAIKQ

About the Author

Deborah Brown is an Amazon bestselling author of the Paradise series. She lives on the Gulf of Mexico, with her ungrateful animals, where Mother Nature takes out her bad attitude in the form of hurricanes.

Sign up for my newsletter and get the latest on new book releases. Contests and special promotion information. And special offers that are only available to subscribers.

www.deborahbrownbooks.com

Follow on FaceBook:
facebook.com/DeborahBrownAuthor

You can contact her at Wildcurls@hotmail.com

Deborah's books are available on Amazon
amazon.com/Deborah-Brown/e/B0059MAIKQ

Made in the USA
Las Vegas, NV
24 June 2024